Kate Carlo

Kate Carlo

Dennis Schreiner

To order additional copies of this book, contact:
Xlibris Corporation
1-888-795-4274
www.Xlibris.com
Orders@Xlibris.com
29135

Chapter 1

We're in bed when Kate tells me that we're going to take it upon ourselves to solve yesterday's murder in the park. This is the fourth such murder of the year and a feeling of tense uneasiness is really beginning to swell. It's the talk of the city, everywhere you go. Myself, I guess I'm one of the few who doesn't really bring it up, what with my problems with Wanda, my uncle and all. I'm preoccupied, you might say. And then there is also Kate, sweet pretty Kate, lying right here beside me, having not more than fifteen minutes earlier turned down my latest marriage proposal. It is indeed a frustrating time. And now this. This talk of solving some murders.

I feel bewildered by such talk, feel myself grasping to string together some kind of mental coherency about it all. But then something happens to shred my collecting thoughts completely, something worse: Wanda appears. From out of the blue. Wanda! Right at the foot of the bed, here and now. The wild open fling of the door throwing me and Kate into a momentary state of immovable shock, Wanda in the midst of another big freak out.

"A-ha!" she declares, twirling an accusatory index finger in the air with great authority. "I knew it!" she bellers.

Kate yanks a sheet up over her nudity. "How did you get in here? Keep your voice down, people are trying to sleep. What's wrong with you? Who do you think you are? Get out of here!" she orders, questions and statements flying from her mouth with great pointed validity.

Wanda stomps about, pacing back and forth at the foot of the bed, her hands now in a behind-the-back clasp, her curvy posture stooped, her mind brooding, her manner belligerent. She starts lecturing. "The two of you. You two. Both. Pah! Who do you think you are? You think you can just flutter around, flaunting your sinfulness in front of everyone with eyes. And with so much business unfinished and unattended to. The bloody nerve!"

She stops pacing, turns her hard green eyes to us and smacks a left fist into a right palm: a rigid, dry sounding crack if ever I heard one. I feel cold and sense goosebumps working their way along my arms.

Kate is less easily put on the defensive. Sitting bolt upright now, sheet in a mysteriously professional tuck around her breasts and all things private, she begins to let Wanda have it. "You are a real demented creep, do you know that? And not only that, but by busting in here you have just broken the law. Now get out or your next dinner will be behind bars."

"A likely tale. Though you two would get big laughs out of hearing I was raped, wouldn't you?"

"What are you talking about? You're as paranoid as ever. Now, for the last time, get out!"

"No! Things must be taken care of," Wanda says, walking past the bed and over towards my dresser. "This!" she says, picking up the ashtray she made for me in a pottery class. Her face grimacing with bitter thought, she takes to examining it, a thumb running along the edge and over the indented grooves where the cigarettes rest. Without warning she throws it at me and hits me in the left temple. My mind scatters, emptying like a punctured inner tube. I struggle about on the floor where I've collapsed, having fallen out of the bed.

"Ohh!" I hear myself moan. My left eye is clouded. I wipe at it. Other fingers wipe at it. Kate's. I can feel her breath against my face, hot and sweet, full of concern.

"Blood," she says quietly, her voice soothing, keeping me calm.

"Serves you right," Wanda says to me, her voice dripping with satisfaction, her shadow tall and looming, her figure framing the door.

Kate turns to her, standing up, her right hand gripped around the sheet tuck at her chest.

I crush my left eye shut, to block out the blood, my right eye owlish, big and white with fright, taking the confrontation in.

"I've just about had enough of you," Kate says, her voice even, her words underlined with ultimatum.

Wanda sees it. Sees the steel in Kate's gaze. She backs up. "He had it coming. By God, you know he did." Her voice stumbles with hesitancy.

"Silly woman. Get out! I will say it no more." Kate steps forward.

Wanda steps back. And then lunges to her left and disappears around the corner, catching us both by surprise with this leggy gambit. Kate steps quietly to the door and peers around it cautiously.

"Watch it!" I cry, worried about Kate getting bashed in the skull with a lamp or some such thing.

She too disappears out of sight.

I stand up, groggy and discombobulated, but ready to throw myself into the fray to try and fend off Wanda's tricks if need be, ready to defend my Kate. I stumble out. I hear voices.

"Don't come near me!" Wanda screeches. She's standing at the entrance door, waving a knife. She has our toaster tucked bulkily under her arm. "I'm taking this and that's all there is to it. I'm owed it and you know it. You both know it!" Her last is statement directed at me, whom she has just noticed. I stumble up close beside Kate, who slips her left arm around my waist, pulling me close, making sure I don't drop to the floor in a woozy collapse.

"Don't you dare take that appliance. Give it here," Kate says to Wanda, her voice unwaveringly calm.

"Never!" Wanda shouts. She then inexplicably turns her voice down to near inaudibility. "You'll never take this toaster from me. Never," she says, looking down at it emotionally, almost motherly. She then chucks the knife at our feet. I back up in a hop of deep worry. Kate doesn't move. The knife twangs into a wooden floorboard, a mere half inch from her beautiful big toe, vibrating like a guitar string. Which reminds me: I can hear the music playing. The music that's still going, oblivious to the bust-in that has ensued. We all hear it, as we engage in stares. "You, you're not that pretty," Wanda snarls insultingly at Kate, her words obviously unconvincing. Then she backs up, slams the door and I can hear her feet shuffling away down the carpeted hallway, her deep throaty laughter of victory bending its way back, through the cracks at the door, and winding its way to our ears.

"She's not getting away with this," Kate says hotly. She pulls the knife from the floorboard, smoothing over the splintered cut with a finger. She sets the knife on a cabinet, really irritated. She suddenly turns to me, her attention shifting. "How are you?"

"I guess it hurts," I say. I think about it. I have a headache. My neck is kinked from the whip-back of my head after the ashtray's impact. I touch my wound and wince. I pull away my hand.

"Come here," she says, clasping me by the hand and leading me into the bathroom. I sit down on the toilet cover as she wets a washcloth and dabs the sticky blood stuck to my eyebrow and all around my eye. Then she gently works the cloth around the broken skin at my temple. There's a bump there already. But the worst is over. Her fingers on my forehead work wonders. She puts a band-aid over the broken skin. "It's stopped bleeding. It's not that bad."

"Do I look tough with this band-aid on?" I ask, as I give her a kiss on the lips.

"You don't look too bad," she says agreeably, a smile coming over her. But then her face goes cloudy just as quick. Her attention shifts again. She becomes rather enraged, justifiably so of course. "That . . . that . . . that Wanda! Oooh! She makes me so darn mad. Come on, let's get dressed."

"What for?"

"What for?! To get our toaster back, of course. That's a four slicer and I'm not letting her have it. I let things slide with the juicer incident, for your sake, but enough is enough. We have to nip this in the bud right now," she says, bolting out of the bathroom. "We've let this thing fester long enough," I hear her say.

I stand up and wobble my way back to the bedroom. "I think my balance is out of whack," I say, trying to change the subject, but also out of a momentary concern for myself.

"You'll be fine," she says, rather dismissively I think, though I suddenly begin to wonder if I'm starting to try and milk this for more sympathy than I deserve. If I am, it's not working. I straighten up and lean against the bedroom doorframe, my eyes taking in Kate, who has discarded the sheet and is now in the act of getting dressed. Her pure and wondrous nudity is all too brief a sight for my eyes as she pulls her clothes on with expert quickness.

I decide to try and talk her out of going, try and talk her back out of her clothes. "Come on, leave it be. At least till tomorrow. After all, it's . . . Say, what time is it anyway?" I ask, clasping my wrist, realizing I'm not wearing my watch. I'm not wearing anything save for a pair of underwear. I start to feel chilled. "God, it's cold in here," I say, changing the subject and going over to the bed and wrapping the warm sheet that had been around Kate around myself.

"It's a quarter after midnight," she says, now fully dressed, her attention reverting back to me. "Are you coming or not?"

"Surely you're not going to go by yourself if I don't go."

"Surely I am."

"But you don't even know where Wanda lives."

"I thought you said she was staying with her sister."

"Did I say that?"

"You did."

"You know, I told myself that I wasn't going to tell you where Wanda was staying because I knew that something like this was going to happen. In fact, I was just thinking about it in bed tonight, coincidentally, just before this whole crazy scene went down. When did I tell you where she lived, just out of curiosity?"

"Last week, when I asked you. You had been drinking."

"Ahh, that explains a great deal. I can't keep anything from you, can I?"

"You keep enough."

"What's that supposed to mean?"

"Quit trying to distract me. Are you coming or not?"

"Okay, okay," I say, tossing aside the sheet and beginning to search about for my clothes. They are scattered all over the place. I find one of my socks hanging on a lampshade. I am a very wild and passionate disrober. I collect all my clothes and begin to put them on. Kate is sitting patiently on the end of the bed. "Is it still raining out?" I ask, as I begin to button my shirt. I see the ashtray lying by my feet. I pick it up and gently set it back on my dresser.

"Yes. That's why it's so cold in here tonight. I'll bet it's close to minus five outside, colder with the wind."

"We should be in bed, listening to Kris Kristofferson and having all sorts of fun."

"We *are* listening to Kris Kristofferson."

"But we're not in bed."

"Oh quit complaining. I'll bet she could take the Galaxie and you'd let it slide. Come on, hurry up. Why on earth are you wearing that shirt? It's taking forever for you to button it up," she says impatiently, getting up and coming over to me. She hastily brushes my fumbling fingers away. "Here, let me do it," she says, buttoning it up for me.

"It's the one I was wearing earlier. I just wanted to look nice for our dinner tonight."

"Well, I must say that you did. You looked very dapper. It was a very nice dinner, wasn't it?"

"Yes it was," I say. "Another memorable night under our belts," I add.

She finishes with the last button and pats it, the flat of her hand coming to rest against my chest. "Are you ready now?" she says, smiling sweetly at me.

I shake my head. "Absolutely not."

"Good. Let's go," she says, grabbing me by the hand and leading me out of the bedroom. She grabs our coats and has me out the door before I know what's what. I slip my coat on as we make our way down the stairwell.

"We forgot to shut the music off," I say.

"Oh, let it play. Let the neighbours learn what real music sounds like," she says, zipping up her coat.

"You're sounding awfully snappy."

"I'll be more mellow once we get that toaster back. Say, did I tell you that Hav came by the other day?"

"Yeah, you mentioned that. It's not like him to leave the house," I say, as I pull open the lobby door and allow her to step out before me. It is indeed cold and windy, the rain drops cutting into our faces. We hurry to the Galaxie—a red 1965 500 XL that Kate's grandfather gave to her in celebration of her first win back in 1989—and I unlock it quickly and we both hop in. I start it up and crank up the heater.

"He brought a few jars of jelly by," she says of Uncle Hav.

"Yeah, you mentioned that too. What kind of jelly?"

"Apricot."

"I don't like apricot."

"Oh? I do. Anyway, I was thinking at work today that tomorrow morning I would like some nice toast and apricot jelly for breakfast. It would go nice with the chamomile tea that I planned on having you make for me. In fact, you were going to do the whole schmooze. I want breakfast in bed tomorrow."

"Oh you do, do you?" I say, amused and distracted at the same time, a twinge of worriment about Uncle Hav beginning to nag at me. Whenever he starts into canning or making preserves his troubles are acting up and his personality becomes impossible—more so than usual.

"Yes, I do," she replies oblivious to my meagre thoughts. "And if it's going to happen, we have to get that toaster back, *tout de suite*, as Juliette Binoche might say. So hurry up, start this thing and let's go."

"Alright, but remember, this was your idea," I say, washing my hands of all responsibility for what might happen. I start the car and we are soon on our way.

Chapter 2

"The rain is really coming down, isn't it?" Kate says, the first real bit of conversation we've had since I pulled out of our parking space and began driving. "I *said*, the rain is really coming down, isn't it?" she repeats.

"Yeah, I heard you."

"Well, then you should have said something."

"I was just thinking."

"Look, I know you hate confrontations, so I'll try to be on my best behaviour. Though that won't be easy. You know how she is better than I. Tell me again what it was you saw in her."

"She looks good in sweaters."

"Ahh yes, the physical aspect. You always say that."

"And I always mean it."

"But there must have been more to it than that."

"She liked me. She was there and you weren't."

"So, it's my fault?"

"Of course not. Though if you *had* been there, well, who can say? Though I'm pretty sure that if you hadn't taken off halfway through Grade 10 I never would've hooked up with her."

"I'm not so sure about that. If there's one thing you aren't it's expedient. You would have dragged it out until it got to the point where it was too late to ask me out anyway and I still would have ended up gone from your life. You know that to be true, don't you?"

"I suppose. But look, I'm now trying to make up for all those past mistakes. Marry me."

"You're overcompensating. Besides, how do I know you don't see in me what you saw in Wanda?"

"You're nothing like Wanda," I say, immediately aware of a possible, hanging insinuation that she isn't as appealing to me physically as Wanda was. But Kate seems to understand my meaning.

"I darn well hope so. And I didn't really mean it. I'm sorry to have said it. I know our relationship is a lot different."

"Good. And, just for the record, my attraction for Wanda wasn't as superficial as I tend to make it out to be either. I just want you to know that too," I say, trying to straighten a few things out.

"Okay. Though I know it couldn't have been anyway. I know you're not superficial."

"Thanks. You know," I say, changing the subject somewhat, "I was thinking about what you said earlier. You implied that I keep things from you."

"Well, you *are* a pretty closed up person."

"Is that why you won't marry me?"

"Can't we talk about this later?"

"I guess so." I sigh, wearied about hashing it all out again, even though I'm the one who brought it up.

"Say, that sister of hers lives by the park, doesn't she? That just occurred to me. Take a little drive around it before we go over to her place."

"You want to go to the park?" I say, perplexed. We should be in bed.

"Yes. Maybe we'll catch him in the act."

"I doubt it. That's the first body to be found in the park. And that's another thing I want to talk about," I say, not really wanting to bring anything up anymore tonight but there's just too much going on to keep quiet about. "What was all that lunacy you were spouting earlier about solving these murders? You sounded absolutely serious. But I can't for the life of me believe that you were."

"Well, believe it. Think of it. If we catch the killer we'll be preventing untold future murders. We'll be saving lives. Don't you want to save lives? Don't you want to be a hero?"

"Well, of course. It all sounds nice and right, full of benevolence and great self-satisfaction, but I hardly think we're equipped to do such a thing."

"You underestimate the both of us."

"It just seems farfetched is all," I say abstractedly, annoyed with her conviction on the matter. I'm sure nothing will come of it, but why she insists on pretending something will is beyond me at the moment. I pull into the parking lot and park close to the edge of the greenery. The vertically stacked dual headlights of the Galaxie cast a deep fan of light out into the freezing rain. I listen to the motor hum and feel sleepy. Kate peers out the windows with great watchful intensity. I turn on the radio. I begin to watch her. The downward glow of one of the parking lot lamps outlines her face in an ethereal glow. I look at her ear, at the lustrous light brown hair that she has pinned behind that ear. I reach out and touch her earlobe, gently picking at the little hole where an earring would otherwise be. She hardly ever wears earrings though.

"What are you doing?" she asks me, turning her gaze away from the window and directly upon me, her soft brown eyes enveloping me. Her gaze then turns down to the car stereo. "Hey, that's Modern English on the radio," she says, full of quiet excitement about this fact.

I nod. "Yes," I say, as though I knew it all along, but was in fact so preoccupied with the sight of her that I have only just realized myself that it's them.

She puts a hand to my cheek and caresses it. We listen to the song. When it ends she exhales and opens the glove compartment. There is box of sugar cubes in there. She removes two and pops them into her mouth and then shuts the glove compartment back up. "Well, I guess there's nothing doing tonight. Though of course we're hardly getting a good look at the whole park. And this weather! Who can see anything? Anyway, let's go and have that hash out with Wanda."

"What?" I say, for some reason continually expecting this visit not to transpire. I look at the clock in the stereo face. "It's almost one for pete's sake," I say. "She'll be in bed."

"So much the better. After all, we were in bed when she ambushed us. We'll catch her off guard the way she did us, and then let her have it. Kaboom!" she says, smacking a fist into the palm of her hand with gleeful resonance.

"That's true," I say, the thought of Wanda's interruption starting to fill me with ire too. If it wasn't for her we'd be in bed right now. "She ruined our night," I say, backing the car up and then pulling out of the parking lot, now heading to Wendy's with sudden determination.

Determination that dissipates the moment I pull into the driveway. I once more feel meek and hesitant about the whole thing. The driveway is full of dead leaves. The birch trees in the yard look barren and dead.

"Nice place," Kate says, taking in what she can via the car headlights, the streetlight and outside porch light.

I nod.

"So this is where the now famous Wendy lives."

Again I nod. "Her dad helped her pay for it. Though of course that was back before she had her own tv show," I say, offering a bit of history on Wendy. My throat feels constricted, a cold sweat working its way through me. Kate says nothing, just looks out at the house, an older house, something from the forties or something. Lots of character to it too, lots of peaks and windows and wood. It's sort of like Uncle Hav's house in a way, though not as large.

"How many times have you been here?" she asks.

"Twice," I say.

This time it's her turn to nod. "How much do you think she makes, this Wendy? I saw her show once. I wasn't that impressed."

"That doesn't mean anything. She makes quite a bit, I think. I heard her show might be going into syndication."

"Ugh. That would figure, wouldn't it? It's probably true. Come on, let's get that toaster back," she says, full of resolve, opening the door and hopping out of the car.

I shut off the engine, take the key out of the ignition and follow suit. We make our way up the wooden porch steps and walk to the door. I ring the bell, deciding such an action will be my first step in taking charge of this situation. But that's as far as it goes.

The door flings back and through the screen door we see Wendy.

"Hello, hello!" is the greeting we get. But then come knitted eyebrows of perplexity. "Hey! You're not Babs! And you, you're not Hillary! You're Dean! Hiya, Dean! And you, you I don't know," she says, pointing a wagging finger—her little finger strangely enough—at Kate. She's in shorts, despite it being late October, bra-less, a tight t-shirt covering what it can barely cover, her breasts even more cartoonish than Wanda's. My eyes magnetize themselves to her chest.

Kate notices my near drooling leer and punches me in the arm. Really hard. "Ouch!" I holler, my left hand immediately beginning to massage my right shoulder.

"Ha! That'll teach you," Wendy says knowingly, as exuberant as ever.

"Yes, get a grip. This is business," Kate says to me. "I'm Kate," she then says to Wendy.

"Oh! You. I know you. At least by name. Face too, actually, now that I think about it. Funny, you don't look like a cunt."

"Nor am I," Kate says matter-of-factly, completely unfazed by Wendy's vulgar turn of words. "We have business with your sister. May we come in?"

"By all means. You must come in from the cold, spies or not. It's nasty out there, isn't it? Maybe it's the weather keeping everyone away. You two are my first guests of the night," Wendy says, seemingly oblivious to the late hour, pushing open the screen door and stepping aside to allow us to enter.

"We won't inconvenience you for long. Or so we hope," Kate says, slipping out of her shoes and following Wendy down the short hallway and into the kitchen off to the right. I follow Kate. There is a lit cigarette sitting in the ashtray on the kitchen table, which Wendy picks up. She begins to smoke. The air is thick with it. "May I get either of you anything? A cola? Would you like a cigarette? I think I have some mescaline around here somewhere too. Or did I leave it at the studio? How about a cigar? I've got those."

"What kind?" Kate asks, intrigued.

"Pre-cut rum soaked Cubans. The only kind me and my other half smoke. At least he used to be my other half. That cunt hound," she says, another thought seeming to pass through her, but one that has no effect on her mood. She smiles, tosses back her head as she puffs again on her cigarette, her medium length, dark brown hair in a playful bounce. She always used to have it cut shorter, I remember, thinking about the few old times we spent together. She butts out her cigarette.

Kate turns to me. "When one quits smoking, do cigars count?"

I shrug. "I'm not sure of the rules," I say, another thought suddenly hitting me. Kate has seemed preoccupied with a number of things of late. She is always full of great buzz and energy, her attention on several things at once, more so than usual it seems to me. She is trying to keep busy so that she won't think of smoking. That's it! I conclude deductively. She has to keep her mind busy or else she's afraid she'll fall with a great big thunk into a nicotine dream, a reverie if you will, that will last and build and accentuate itself until finally she has no choice but to give into this desire of hers and have a cigarette.

"Hmm," Kate says, really tossing the idea of a cigar over in her mind. "I haven't smoked for three weeks," she says to Wendy. "I guess I'd better not start. Cheating is cheating no matter how you justify it. Do you have a beer?" she asks, a statement which soothes and upsets me both: soothes me because I could use a beer myself, to ease my anxieties, yet upsets me because a beer indicates a stay of indeterminate length. I was hoping we'd only be here a minute or two.

"Of course, a beer. How silly of me not to have offered one right off. Do sit down," Wendy says, motioning to the chairs at the kitchen table. We comply as she goes over and magically pulls two bottles of Corona out of a very heaping full fridge—carrot tops and lettuce leaves sticking out everywhere—and sets them on the counter. She digs around for a bottle opener. Finding the opener she opens the bottles. Then she opens the fridge again and hunts around for a lime. "I know there's one around here somewhere," she says. Suddenly she stands up. "Goshdarnit to hell," she says, stretching and wincing, her lower back a seeming sore point. "I overdid it in my Winsor Pilates class last night. But my, how you two must be bored. Some party this is."

"That's okay, for as I said, we came here on business," Kate says, but Wendy is not in the room anymore and fails to hear her words. Kate looks at me. "Busy, isn't she?"

"Imagine how she'd be if she quit smoking," I say, getting a dig in, an allusive one, but not an elusive one. Just as I'd hoped, Kate picks up on it.

"There's no merit to that comment whatsoever," she says, trying to look offended but I know that she isn't. Not at all. It would take more than that to get to her.

Wendy's absence seems to drag on forever. I breathe deeply, looking yearningly at the Coronas on the counter, beads of condensation glittering on the bottles. I'm suddenly in a real drinking mood. It's all this stress.

"I must say that so far I'm finding I like much her more in person than I do on her show. She's much less didactic," Kate says.

"Yeah, I like her too. I always did. She's very personable."

"It looks like you married the wrong sister."

I shrug, mulling this possibility over. Wendy darts back in, music from the stereo in the living room signalling her entrance. The Monkees are playing.

"There. Now your wait won't be so interminable," she says, in reference to the music.

"Wait?" I question.

"Oh, yes, it occurred to me as I was looking for the limes that Wanda's not here," Wendy says, rifling through the lettuce crisper in search of those ever elusive limes.

"It's alright if you have no limes," Kate says.

"A-ha!" Wendy says, standing up and holding one up for us. "I knew there was one of the little buggers in there." We nod as she turns and begins to cut it up on a cutting board near where the beers are sitting. She cuts off two big wedges and sticks one in each neck of the Coronas. But the wedges are too big and won't go down. "Goshdarnit. You'd think that just once something would go as smooth as peanut butter. But oh no, not in this lifetime little sister." She grabs one of the bottles with her left hand and begins to pound on the lime with her right hand, trying to get the lime to drop down the neck and into the bottle. But all she does is turn the lime into a messy pulp. Not learning from the futility of this experience she then does the same thing with the other bottle.

"So, Wanda's not here. Where is she?" Kate asks.

"Off shagging would be my guess," Wendy says, now engaged in a clattering search through the cutlery drawer. "Where in heck is that goshdarn butter knife. We're always losing them around here. That damn Wanda. I know there was one around here yesterday though. I just saw it. Yesterday I saw it. Damned if I'm not sure I did. Hmm." She stands up straight, looking out the kitchen window in a silent pose, pondering away. "I know! I used it to fix that loose screw in the back of the stereo. It's in the living room!" she says excitedly. She skips out of the room and is back in a flash.

"When do you expect Wanda back?" Kate asks upon Wendy's re-entrance, trying to pinpoint things.

"Poste haste. I expect her anytime. Wanda likes to fuck, but never for very long. But look who I'm talking to," she says, pointing the knife gregariously at me. "You would know better than I, Dean. And were likely very frustrated by it. Were you? I'll bet you were." She looks at me, awaiting an answer. Kate looks at me too, curious for one as well.

I shrug. "Yeah, I guess. She did like to keep it brief," I say, keeping things brief myself.

"No doubt. Her other husband—remember that loser?—he said the same thing. You must've been frustrated all to hell. And for such a long time too," she says.

"We were only married for two years," I say.

"Two years! God. I don't know how you managed it. That's a horribly long time to be married," she says. Using the knife she manages to push the limes down into the bottles. Both bottles overflow with foamy beer but she seems unaffected by the dripping mess they create. She hands us each one. I take a big quick gulp. "Thirsty, huh?" she says, pulling a frosty bottle of vodka out of the freezer, grabbing a shot glass off the counter and coming over to the table. She pours herself a shot and downs it. Then she pours another and begins to sip. She lights up another cigarette, takes a puff and looks at it. "These things just went up again today. Another fifty-five cents. Did you know that? No, of course you wouldn't. For you said you've quit, didn't you?" she says to Kate.

"No, I didn't know that. And yes, I did say I quit."

"Are you enjoying your life of tobacco sobriety?"

"You start to get used to it."

"I'll bet," Wendy says, sucking back a deep pull. "Me, I've thought about quitting too but, when you boil it right down to the hard egg, I find that I just don't want to. I just don't. The things I have to put up with, well, it all makes me glad that I gave up not smoking," she says, nodding stiff and authoritatively. "Besides, I haven't been smoking all that long, so my lungs can hack it. So, Dean, Kate, what brings you two here? Why the urgent need to see Wanda? I can't imagine it being a social call."

"She stole our toaster tonight. Busted right in out of the blue and took it. She hit Dean in the head with an ashtray too."

"The hell you say! I can't believe it. I simply cannot." Wendy stands up, offended and mortified by her sister's actions. "That's bloody nerve for you. Bloody nerve!" she says, sitting back down. "I was going to ask you about your head when you first came in, but in all the commotion of getting you a beer I guess I forgot. How callous of me. Does it hurt?"

"It throbs a bit. It was the shock of it more than anything."

"I'll bet. I'll just damn well bet."

"And it was a four slicer too," Kate says, as though finding this to be the biggest affront of all.

"A four slicer!" Wendy slams a fist onto the table. "Leave it to her to take the best. That volatile little piker! I'll give her a piece of my noodle when she comes home, you can be sure of that."

"Thanks. We appreciate your concern, we really do. But there is also the matter of her constantly harassing us," Kate says, letting it all out, having found a soul sister in Wendy. "She can't seem to get it through her head that she and Dean are divorced and that Dean owes her nothing."

"That Wanda, she's, well, she likes to play roles. She is very uninteresting to talk to otherwise—it's like talking to a stuffed fish, it really is. So in your case, Dean, she is obviously taking on the role of a scorned wife, scorned ex-wife in this case. I did a whole show on it last month. Did you see it?"

"No," Kate and I both say, almost simultaneously.

"I'm afraid we missed it," I say. "We're both usually still at work when your show's on."

"Tough nuts. I can get you tickets if you want though. They're not easy to come by anymore, you know. If you want some, just say the word. It's weird, the first shows we couldn't pay people to put their asses in the seats, and now they pay us. And you should see those asses! What a bunch of lazies. Still, all in all it's a grand deal."

"Yes, we've heard you're doing well," Kate says. "Dean told me you might even be going into syndication."

"Indeed. There's a snafu over the title though. They want to change the title to *The Wendy Michigan Show.* But I prefer to stick with *Afternoons With Wendy.* It's much more informal, more cozy sounding, don't you think?"

"Yeah, it sounds good," I say.

"I'll reserve you some tickets. I won't take no for an answer. In fact I was going to call you, Dean. Your uncle's going to be a guest on my show and I wanted to ask you some questions about him for my background research."

"My uncle?" I say, positively stymied. Kate looks just as shocked as I do.

"Yes, Havilah Pilbeam. At least he told me he was your uncle. Normally, I don't take any calls from people off the streets—too looney. But when he dropped your name, the screener asked me about it and so I decided to give him a hear. I know he's your uncle but I must say that he sounds a bit strange. I hope I don't offend you with such an observation."

"No, he is strange," I say, mystified by this horrifying development.

"Yes. Just as I thought. Is he harmless though? I mean, how likely is he to fly off the handle if my questions sharpen into needles?"

"He'll likely get upset. He shouts a lot. But that's as far as I've ever seen it go with him."

"Perfect. A shouter, that's usually good for ratings, isn't it?"

"I guess. You're the celebrity, so you should know," I say.

"Celebrity, pshaw. Listen to you. You're stroking my ego. I like it. Even though I don't buy it. Still, a syndication deal would be nice. Big money in it you know. And that's what it's all about."

"Yes," I say. I watch Kate, sipping away on her beer. I expected to see her looking disinterested in all this small talk, but instead she seems content, humming silently to the Monkees song playing on the stereo. "Anyway," I say, trying to steer the conversation back on track, "do you know where Wanda would have our toaster? She also took our juicer and a book of mine."

"They're in her room, no doubt. But she keeps it locked up tight. Say, I hope you didn't come back to pick up your book tonight."

"Oh? How come?"

"That Wanda, she was really viciously happy about having it. Says it's your favorite."

"It is," I say.

"That's what she said."

"Why shouldn't I pick it up tonight? I like that particular copy and really want it back. A lot of memories go with it." I pause, feeling thoughtful. "I like the way it smells," I say after a bit.

Wendy nods. "Yeah, it does smell nice, doesn't it? I know, because I'm reading it. That paper pulpy smell, it's great. It was just sitting there and I needed something to read in the can so I grabbed it. I got hooked. I hope you'll let me finish it. I'm good with books. I never bend the spine."

"Okay, you can finish reading it. It's no big deal I guess," I say, still somewhat apprehensive, my experiences in lending out books having always usually been bad.

Kate continues to drink and begins to thumb through a stack of piled papers on the table, quiet now that she knows we won't be confronting Wanda. She's tired out, I can tell. But not for long. Her interest begins to perk up as she examines the papers. She pulls them close and begins to look at them more fully. I glance at them to see what it is she has become immersed in and feel a frown coming on. All the papers and clippings have to do with the murders.

I look at Wendy, who is looking at me. She sips on her vodka and arches her eyebrows, innocently flirtatious.

"Where'd you get all this stuff?" Kate asks.

"I'm what you might call a murder buff. I've been collecting info on this case ever since it began. I'm thinking of doing a show on it. Who knows, maybe I can bust the case wide open, what with the influence I'm starting to have in this town. As a talk show host I have gained the public's trust."

"Really?" Kate asks. I can see the wheels begin to turn. I suddenly realize that we'll be back here again, and not just for a showdown with Wanda.

"Yeah, but first I'm trying to get a better grip on it. I go over it again and again, trying to figure out motivation, you know? I'm like an amateur profiler, I guess you'd say."

"And have you any ideas as to the motivation yet?"

"Sex would seem to be the likely choice. It always is."

"But there's never been any evidence of rape in any of the cases."

"Maybe he shoots off in his pants, while he's strangling them. Oh, and for what it's worth, they're strangled from behind, did you know that? He's a sneaker upper."

"No, I didn't know that. How do you know?"

"Well, the police don't release everything to the public, they never do. I mean, can you two keep a secret?"

"No," I say, hoping to discourage Wendy from confiding in us.

"Good," Wendy says, oblivious to my comments. She leans forward. So does Kate. So do I. Our heads are close together for this moment of clandestine revelation. "I happen to know the lead investigator," Wendy says, her voice resonating with deep import. "Trish Mindy. She's an old gadabout chum of my mom's. You remember Mom, don't you, Dean?"

I nod, memories of her mom swirling about my head. Tuppy Alabaster: a real loose cannon. "How is she?" I ask.

Wendy shrugs, her expression disgruntled. "You know her. She's cooking in the nude again. At her age! She even cooks bacon that way. Can you believe it? I think she does it to show off her new tattoo. The silly old bitch."

"Oh," I say, hoping a dinner invitation isn't going to come about. Once was enough.

Kate looks at me with astonished eyes. I never told her about Tuppy. She's right, I do keep things from her. I just shrug. I'll tell her later. Kate turns her attention back to Wendy. "Anyway, this Trish Mindy. You're really good friends with her?"

"Oh mercy heck, yes. We chat all the time. Trish hasn't told me everything though. I know she's holding back. But tomorrow's my sprout night and, as Trish is a sprout person too, we often get together, you know, to meet up for some talk and chewables and to hash over this town's seamy side. It's quite a big side, you know, lots of whacked out questionables roam these streets, you'd be surprised. Or maybe not, you might not be as naive as I tend to be. Anyway, Trish has to be on the q.t. about this case, and I can understand that, but I'm not going to take no for an answer. I'm going to get the rest of the scoop from her tomorrow night and that's all there is to it. Be sure of that. And when I do, look out. Rather, Mr. Sick Killer should look out. I'll use all the means at my disposal to cast a noose over that murderous piece of vermin, mark my words."

"We're taking up the case too," Kate announces.

"Good. This town needs more citizens like us, it really does."

"So, will you tell me what you get from Trish?" Kate says, sounding bold and intrusive.

"Oh sure. I can trust you. I like your face. I always did. I remember you when I was fifteen. Your picture was in all the papers. I remember you on the tv too. I wanted to look just like you. I don't suppose I do, but I'm okay with how I turned out."

"Thank you for the compliment," Kate says, always appreciative of them. She finishes her beer. Mine is already long gone. She stands up. "Well, it doesn't look like Wanda's going to show."

"She'll be back here sometime."

"I'm sure. But I'm getting tired right now. We really should go. We don't want to keep you from your plans."

"That's sweet."

"But we'll be back. For Wanda and so that the three of us can go over the case."

"I had a feeling this was going to be a fortuitous visit, from the moment I opened the door. I thought to myself that finally, here are some good sensible friends for me. It will nice to be friends with you, Dean. I never saw much of you when you were married to Wanda. But those were during the feud years, so it's understandable."

I stand up and nod, not knowing what to say. "Enjoy the book," I finally manage to sputter out as I am putting my shoes on at the door, feeling exceedingly stupid with such a comment. But Wendy receives it airily.

"I most certainly will. I most certainly will."

"Good luck with your profiling. And with your show," Kate says.

"Thanks. Oh, and remember. I'll reserve a couple of tickets for you when your uncle is on the show, Dean. It should be real soon, though I'm not sure yet of the exact date. We haven't dotted all the i's with the upcoming schedule yet. I'm sure you'll want to try and get a day off to see your uncle though, won't you?"

"That should be interesting," I say, trying to be noncommittal.

Kate nods agreeably at my comment. "Good night and thanks for the beer," she says to Wendy.

"Yes, thanks," I say too, and we leave. Wendy watches us get into the car and then shuts the door.

Kate opens the glove compartment and grabs a couple of sugar cubes. She pops them into her mouth. She looks at me as I start the car. "You've known some interesting people in your day," she says.

"I thought I'd seen the last of them," I say ruefully.

"I just wonder what we're going to have for breakfast tomorrow," she says, mercifully changing the subject.

"Oh, we'll think of something," I say, unperturbed.

"Yes, I suppose so. We always do, don't we? We always do."

Chapter 3

Kate wakes me up, poking me. I shake my head and look at her. She is at my side of the bed, standing over me, wearing her flannel pajamas, the ones decorated with the Looney Tunes characters.

"What is it?" I say, casting a glance at the alarm clock. It's barely past nine. "It's Saturday. Why the pokes?" I say, sitting up.

"I made you some breakfast," she says, skipping out of the room with sinewy deftness. She comes back in with a breakfast tray which she places over my lap.

"I thought I was supposed to make it for you."

"That was before the toaster was stolen," she says, turning back towards the kitchen, her voice still sore on that point. She comes back into the bedroom with a tray of her own and sits down on the bed beside me. I look at what she has made. Scrambled eggs and bacon, toast and apple juice.

"Hey, how'd you make the toast?" I ask, as she grabs the remote control and clicks on the tv.

"In the oven. But I burnt them a little bit," she says, flipping through the stations. "But hopefully the jelly will neutralize the taste of the burnt crumbs."

I notice the jelly spread on her toast. Apricot. My toast is bare, save for melted butter. I begin to spread some egg onto a slice. "I hope you weren't cooking this bacon in the nude," I say, memories of last night still fresh in my mind.

"Good God, no. Does Wendy's mom really do that? Cook in the nude?"

"Yes. At least she did the one and only time I was there."

"See, this is what I mean," she says, turning to me. "There's so much you don't tell me. Why on earth wouldn't you tell me that? It sounds like a heck of a tale."

"It was mostly nauseating. She has the whitest breasts I've ever seen."

"What does that mean?"

"Exactly what I've said. They looked so cold. And they were veinous. Blue wormy veins all over the place. She didn't even dress when sitting at the dinner table. And Wanda never even warned me to expect anything like that. In fact, she seemed entirely oblivious to the fact that her mother was naked."

"What were her nipples like?" Kate asks, intrigued, though her expression conveys that she feels she should be disgusted with herself for asking such a question.

"They were colourless for the most part. Only the vaguest tinge of pink."

"Were her breasts big?"

"No, hers are nothing like her daughters. But they didn't sag at least. I was glad for that."

"What did you have for supper?"

"Ribs. Wanda told her they were my favourite. They were very good," I say, taking to munching on a piece of bacon. "It was actually a very congenial night for the most part, believe it or not. Once one got past the initial shock, that is. She played the guitar too."

"Is she any good?"

"Not bad. She played mostly folk songs," I say, the evening suddenly seeming less horrifying in my mind. Kate seems satisfied and lets the subject drop. We start watching *The Flintstones.*

"When did they start showing this again?" I ask, pleased that they have.

"I don't know," Kate says, quickly absorbed with the show. We watch it for a bit, silent. "You know, they never did give enough screen time to Joe Rockhead. They should have, don't you think? I mean, everyone knows a Joe Rockhead."

"That's true," I say.

"Anyway, eat up," she says, already having wolfed down her food. "We've got a busy day today."

"Why, what's going on?"

"Well, first we have to go to Hav's. See if he's okay. And get the hard scoop on his going on Wendy's show."

"That sure came as a surprise, didn't it?" I say, shaking my head at this seemingly new bit of stupidity that Uncle Hav is about to engage in. "It's all so bizarre."

"He's off his chair if he goes on that show and starts caterwauling."

"I just hope he doesn't mention us."

"Good grief, I never thought about that. Anyway, up up," she orders, standing up with her tray and taking it into the kitchen. She comes back in. "Done yet?"

I nod, swallowing the last of my juice. "It was good. Thanks."

She nods, grabs the tray and takes it into the kitchen. Then she once more returns. She starts to stretch and begins to run a hand through her hair. "I'm thinking of letting it grow longer again."

"I noticed that last night. I noticed how it's already grown to the point where you can pin it behind your ears."

"You noticed that, did you?"

"I notice everything about you."

She jumps playfully onto the bed and sits on my stomach. She pins my arms down, her hands on my wrists, and begins to bounce up and down on me. "This is nice, isn't it?"

"This? Yes. All of it."

She cranes her head downward and kisses me on the lips. Then she hops off beside me, sitting cross-legged, her hand beginning to rub through her hair again.

"Itchy?" I ask.

"I just need a good shower. It's from going to sleep with damp hair. That rain last night was horrid."

"What's it like out today, or do I even need to ask?"

"The same. Yuck!" she says, sticking out her tongue. She begins to examine her toes. "Do you think I need a pedicure?"

"No."

"I don't mean putting nail polish on them."

"I still don't think you need one."

"Ahh well, perhaps I don't. How come you don't like nail polish?"

"It's not that I have anything against it, I just don't think it does anything for you. You don't need anything to enhance you."

"You've got the right words down pat, I'll give you that much," she says, uncrossing her legs and stretching up close to me. She runs a thumb along beneath my left eye and then moves it gently up towards the bandage on my temple. "How's the head?"

"It still stings a little bit. It feels tight."

"It's still swollen a bit. A little goose's egg. We really should charge her with assault."

"Nothing would happen to her."

"Just our luck," she says resignedly, sitting up. She grabs a sugar cube from the plate sitting on her nighttable and pops it into her mouth. She slurps away on it.

I sit up and swing my legs over the side of the bed. Kate comes up behind me on her knees and slides her arms around me, pulling me against her. She begins kissing my neck with wet sugared lips. "You seem to be feeling amorous," I say. "Are you sure you want to go to Uncle Hav's?"

"I just like our Saturday mornings together. No kids to try and discipline, no having to correct their grammar, no anything. Just the two of us."

"The way it was always meant to be," I say, turning my head and kissing her cheek.

"Remember when we first met?"

"Yes."

"You were such a little punk," she says lovingly.

"I was only five."

"But already getting in trouble. Dean Dorian, the bad seed. What is it with little boys and urination?"

"I didn't start it."

"Oh no, of course not."

"Don't you believe me?"

"Nope."

"It wasn't me, honest. It was Pete and Kyle, those little instigators. They started it. I just returned the favour."

"And you all came out of the bathroom, looking guilty and full of mischief. And there I was, sweet little me, holding onto my mother's hand as she was about to turn me over to the principal. I was scared stiff about going into that kindergarten class in mid-year, absolutely frightened."

"I don't know why that business wasn't conducted in the principal's office, instead of the hall, it sure should have been," I say, still sour about such a fact after all these years.

"But then I wouldn't have gotten to see you, in all your pee-stained glory, all three of you—and laughing away about it on top of it all! I was completely horrified. I could smell it too. It was awful. I hid behind my mom's leg. What did you think of me when you saw me? That I was a little fraidy cat?"

"I don't know. You were wearing a red coat and shoes. I remember you were shaking. I could see your legs shaking in those red shoes. Your shoes were too big for you, weren't they?"

"Yes. See? You never remembered that last time. Another new detail to flesh out the memory. Go on. What else?"

I close my eyes, trying to visualize it. Without even looking at Kate I know hers are closed too and that she's doing the same thing. "I just remember that you were a little girl. And that you seemed stricken."

"How did that make you feel?"

"Like I just knew that I wouldn't tease you or anything."

"And then you got the harsh end of the stick from the principal."

"I think it was hickory. Actually, it was just lines, lots and lots of lines. Our parents were told too."

"I tried not to look at you after that first day I saw you. I thought you were bad. Simply bad."

"That was a long time ago," I say, beginning to reflect upon it somewhat wistfully, a mood which Kate picks up on immediately.

"Feeling nostalgic?"

"Yes. It doesn't take much though."

"They say it gets worse the older you get."

"I guess we'll find out," I say.

"Yes. Anyway, time's a-wasting," she says, pulling away and giving me a friendly slap on the back. "We have things to do and people to see. I'm going to shower now," she says, hopping off the bed and disappearing from the bedroom. I soon hear the noise of the shower. I think about when we first met some more. Kate always likes to bring it up, likes to try and get us to revisit and relive it. She remembers things about it that I don't. But she'll never tell me what. She wants me to remember them for myself. And I always get the feeling that the one big thing about that day is the one thing that I cannot remember. The one detail that is most important to her. Whatever it is.

Chapter 4

Uncle Hav calls just as we are about to leave. Kate answers it. I know it's him right away. She says hello and then nothing more for about two minutes. He never even comes up for air anymore. Finally she cuts him off to say that we're coming over. "Bye," she then says and abruptly hangs up the phone.

"I'm just surprised it took him this long to call today. What's eating him now?" I ask as we leave the apartment.

"Oh, I don't know. He was mostly griping about us. When are we coming over? Why aren't we here yet? That type of malarkey."

"I should buy him a blowup doll. It would serve all his purposes. He could talk to it too. What does it matter who his sounding board is? Nobody gets a word in anyway."

"True. But he's still part of your family. We have to be there for him, through the tough times and the good."

"Yes, but when are the good? There are never any good times. It's all gloom with him," I say, in a funk at the thought of being stickpinned with all his problems yet one more time. I get into the Galaxie after Kate unlocks the passenger side door. She's going to do all the driving today. She puts her Bangles cd on after starting the car up.

It doesn't take long to get to Uncle Hav's. About ten minutes. He lives in a house by the river. I like where he lives. All the houses are old and haphazardly built in relation to one another. Plus, the river seems to somehow enclose them all, which I find inviting. We get out of the car and look out across the street, at the river. It's really rushing today; a foggy mist is saturating the air and the dark trees on the far shore look cold and implacable.

We walk up the driveway and through the gate. The gate squeaks horribly. "Listen to that," Kate says, oddly offended by the noise.

"Bit of a sticky wicket," I say, liking the phrase.

"Yes. Sticky indeed," she says, shutting it behind us as we proceed along the cement slab pathway. Uncle Hav's house is on an incline at the end of the street and has a great view of the neighbourhood. Plus, it's high enough that he never has to worry about being flooded out.

He's standing on the porch already, in a moth-eaten burgundy bathrobe, awaiting us, one hand on the porch swing, the other gripping a can of cold looking beer. "It's about time," he grumbles. He kicks an empty that's by his slippered feet right at us just as we're climbing the stairs and it just about wings me in the head.

"Hey, fuck off," I say, surprising myself with such early morning profanity, already peeved with him as we step onto the porch. "You just about hit me and I don't need that. I'm already wounded," I say, forcibly pointing to the band-aid on my forehead and grimacing disapprovingly at him. He looks at me and shrugs unconcernedly. He opens the screen door and proceeds inside. We follow.

"You sure have a noisy wicket," Kate says as we all step into the living room.

Uncle Hav takes a swig of beer and then crumples up the can in his fist. He tosses it at an overflowing wastebasket beside the mouldy old couch but it misses and lands in an aluminum clang on a pile of other similarly discarded beer cans. "That's to alert me if intruders are about to enter the premises," he says to Kate.

"I don't like it. It makes the place seem run down."

"It is run down."

"Well, it doesn't have to be. Where's the WD-40?"

"Why? Are you going to fix it?" Uncle Hav asks skeptically.

"Yes, I am," Kate says sturdily, up to the challenge.

Uncle Hav shrugs, in his usual pose of indifference. "Try the garage. Or maybe the laundry room. No, it's in the hall closet, I think." Kate nods, pats me on the shoulder and leaves.

"That stuff's supposed to be good for bad backs," I say, sitting down in a chair. The lampshade tassels of the lamp standing beside the chair jingle from the breeze I create in doing so. The room is dim.

"What? WD-40? They just say that to stimulate sales. I know how it all works." He sits down and sifts through numerous crumpled cigarette packets on the coffee table until he finds one that isn't empty. He extracts one and lights it up. "Dot left me. She broke it off last night," he says miserably, exhaling deeply and then letting out a defeated groan.

"Who the hell is Dot?" I ask, the name new to me.

"Dot Tureen, the girl I've been seeing. I met her last weekend at the Truck Show."

"Man, another new one already? I thought we were coming over here to council you about Olive and here you are off on some new sex jag with a chick named Dot."

"Quit criticizing your uncle. Do you know how lonely it is out there? Do you have any idea how lonely it is in *here*? Any idea at all? Not likely. You're off in Wonderland with Miss Golden Leaf," he says bitterly.

"Do I hear myself being alluded to?" Kate says enthusiastically, already back in the room. She sets the can of WD-40 on the coffee table and then sits down on the arm of the chair I am sitting in. She puts a slapping hand to my knee and grips it massagingly.

"Yes, yes, of course you. You know I'm always talking about you. Both of you. You're my idols, the two of you, I'll be damned if you're not."

"Listen, Uncle Hav—"

"For the last goddamn time, Dean, quit calling me Uncle Hav! I'm three years younger than you and I'll be damned if I'll let you age me by calling me 'uncle'."

"But you *are* my uncle."

"I don't care. It doesn't seem right. And it's not just the age thing. I'm too naive to be anybody's uncle. If I were your true uncle I would be dispensing advice to *you* and not keep calling you over in the hopes that you'll give *me* some."

"He's upset," I say, turning to Kate. "He broke up with some girl named Dot."

"What happened to Olive?" Kate says disconcertedly. "I liked her."

"I thought she was the one," Uncle Hav cries, oblivious to Kate's wonderment about Olive, ready instead to pour out his grief about Dot, and in his typical manner: looking away from us and up at the ceiling, off at the great invisible metaphysical strains that he feels are always above him and jerking him around like a puppet, always pondering to them, always wondering why he has such a rough go and no one else does.

"She was a lot like Belinda," he says, now introducing his second wife into his talkative stew. "She listened. Dot was always willing to listen. To anything and everything. She found me charming, she did. That's what she said." He turns his attention to us again. "She said I was interesting. She really did. So why? Why then the big brush off last night? That bitch," he says, his emotions on the gamut roll now, right down animosity alley. "She's a total bitch to treat me like that, don't you think? To lead me on like that. She's a lot like June," he says, now bringing his first wife into the loop. He begins pulling at his hair. "Oh, the cunts. The cunts, the cunts! They're all dirty cunts!" He stands up and begins to pound a fist into the side of his head. He then plunks down onto the sinking couch, quickly worn out. "I'm sorry Kate. I really shouldn't talk like this around you. I'm glad you came. I really am. I love looking at you. You know I've always had this crush on you."

"So you've said," Kate says sprightly.

"But I'd never act on it. I would never hurt Dean."

"So you say," I say dubiously, even though I am sure that he never would.

"It's just—Do you ever look at yourself in pants, Kate? You're so—Ohhh! It's too much. Too damn much. Why can't I have a woman like you? Why?"

"Give it time," I say, even-toned, ready to try and cheer him up. "You can't force these things. They have a way of happening in a manner that you can't predict."

"That's easy for you to say."

"It is now, I suppose, yes," I say, full of gratitude at the world, pulling Kate down onto my knee and wrapping my arms around her neck.

"Why did this Dot break up with you?" Kate asks, her hands pliantly around my neck as well.

"Oh, who the hell knows? it had something to do with—Well, let me see," he says, sitting up and butting out his cigarette into an overflowing ashtray. He begins to ponder some more, looking distant and zoned out.

"We should stop at a bookstore and get that book today," Kate says to me in a quiet aside as Uncle Hav ponders on. "And maybe go see Kim."

"Kim?" I frown, not liking the sound of this at all, even though I like Kim. It's beginning to sound like a real busy day.

Uncle Hav's ponderings end, for the moment. "I guess I told her that I wanted us to come to the understanding that we are both free people and, as such, free people are free in all the ways that freedom allows. You can understand where I'm coming from with such an ideology, can't you? Either of you? Because it's very important to me, this way of life. It's the only way." He begins to furiously rub his temples, his hands going through his wild shock of wiry reddish-brown hair, which is sticking every which way.

"You could use a haircut," I say.

"Quit riding me!" he blurts out unpredictably, jumping up, a clenched fist in the air, looking ready to attack me, but then just as quickly going off on another tangent. "It's this damn society! I wasn't made to function in it," he says wrathfully, going over to the window and pulling back a curtain. He looks outside. "This damn rain. I wonder if the suicide rate is up this fall."

"What's that rattling noise?" I ask, aware of it the instant we came in, but only now conscious enough of it to comment on it.

"I'm canning fish. It's the canner. Letting off steam. That canner is my saviour, as well as the great metaphor for my life," he laments, letting go of the curtain and clasping his hands behind his back. He begins to walk about, looking pensive and intense. Then he disappears into the kitchen, only to return moments later. "They're done," he says to us, only to disappear back into the kitchen again.

"Look what I found," Kate says, pulling a pair of plastic safety glasses from her back pocket.

"Where'd you get those?" I ask, as she puts them on.

"In the closet, where the WD-40 was. Do I look sexy?" she asks as she sits on my lap, her right hand behind her head, her body twisted in an upwards slant, in a modelling pose.

"Industrially so," I say.

"Industrially so," she repeats laughingly. "Would you kill me with these on?"

"What kind of a question is that?" I say, put off by the morbidity of it.

"The case."

"What?"

"The murders, silly. Every girl found was wearing a pair of these things," she says, taking them off now and waving them before me. I take them from her and look at them.

"I guess I haven't been paying much attention." I examine them more closely. "That's bizarre. It must be a calling card."

"Some kind of clue, most definitely. I should have asked Wendy to ask Trish about them. It's important somehow, I'll bet. It's a great symbol."

Uncle Hav comes back into the room. "I took all the cans out. If you hear popping sounds it's just the cans sealing themselves," he says informatively.

"Where'd you get the fish?" I ask, handing the glasses back to Kate.

"On one of the reservations. They let me have some real swell salmon. Cheap too. I sure love canned fish," he says, momentarily brightening. But the pall comes back in an instant. He refuses to let himself feel upbeat. He's always been resistant to it. I don't know why. "They make me gaseous though. There's always a downside." He frowns. "What's wrong with freedom?" he says, reverting to that old point of contention, posing the question to us as he goes over to his old record player and puts on a scratchy record of Janis Joplin's version of "Me and Bobby McGee." He plays it often, which makes me glad that I like this song.

"I think this song answers your question," Kate says, looking about the room and coffee table. The fingers of her right hand are tapping against her leg with fidgety musicality. I can tell she wants a cigarette.

"Explain," Uncle Hav says, sitting down, intrigued.

"Well, absolute freedom entails zero in the way of attachments. And that is what you say you want. And that is why you keep losing your Bobby McGee."

"Sounds simple enough. Oh—I suppose it's true too!" he vigorously mourns. "Is there any halfway point? Can I have a woman and can she have me and yet the two of us remain separate but united entities at the same time?"

"You're afraid of commitment. That's your big problem, it always has been and it still is," I say, my words distilled, his problems so simple to me.

"I know it!" he whistles deeply, wiping tears of regret and self-recrimination from his eyes with the sleeve of his bathrobe. "It's just that none of them ever seem quite right. I always think that. Think about where my Miss Golden Leaf is.

Where my perfect pretty one is. Where is she? You have yours, Dean. How did you get her? Tell me, Kate, how did he get you?"

"With great difficulty," Kate laughs.

"I knew it!" he hollers, accusatorily its seems to me, finding no humour at all in Kate's comment. "It's no fair, no fair I tell you. Mom sure did a number on me."

"What are you talking about?" I say, sitting up, Kate hopping back up onto the arm of the chair, this blame being thrown at his mom a new development in his endless titanic battles with remorse and reproachfulness.

"Can I tell you two something? Can you keep a secret?"

"Probably not," I say.

"I have contacted Wendy Michigan's people, and even got to chat with Wendy herself. Do you know who Wendy Michigan is?"

"Sure, we had drinks with her last night," I say.

"I'm serious."

"So am I. And besides, nitwit, I was married to her sister."

Uncle Hav's eyes light up. "Holy crap, you're right. I knew that too. I mentioned it when I called about going on her show. How could I have forgotten so quickly?"

I shrug. "Too self-absorbed?" I offer up as an amusing yet pointed possibility.

He fails to hear me. "I hope I don't have syphilis," he says, momentarily aghast. But then he snaps out of it, looking at us. "Did you really have dinner with her?" he asks, sounding awestruck.

"It was just drinks," Kate says correctingly and then, turning to me, "Say, do you think she's had that hash out with Trish Mindy yet?"

"I think it's supposed to be for tonight."

"We'll have to call. And we must remember to ask about the glasses. And inquire about our toaster too. That Wanda. Oohh! Hav, I need a drink," Kate says, still fuming about Wanda, and in need of something to replace her desire for a cigarette. I'm surprised she's lasted this long without a crutch.

"Get me one too," I say, never one to say no to a crutch.

"There's beer in the cooler out on the porch," Uncle Hav says. "What does Wendy eat? I'll bet she likes her meat," he says after Kate leaves the room, his eyebrows arched suggestively, becoming real lewd in his demeanour.

"For the last time, it was just drinks. Anyway, we already know you're going on her show. What's this all about anyway?"

"It's that girl at the gas station. The one I buy my lottery tickets from. She's why Dot left me. I wanted to keep myself open for the both of them. You'd think . . ." His face turns bitter. "Some women are so closed-minded. The worst kind of whore is a whore who won't admit she's a whore," he says vaguely. He looks at me, bleary and red-eyed. I wonder if he slept at all last night. "What are your thoughts on pubic wigs?" he asks out of the blue, dead serious.

I snap my fingers, trying to get him to focus. "Are you drunk? You keep going way off topic."

"I am not drunk at all," he says, taking offense. He catches the can of beer Kate tosses at him upon re-entering the room. She sits back down on the chair arm beside me, the remaining five beer of the six pack dangling from her finger. She hands me one. I pop it open and take a drink.

Uncle Hav shotguns his, tosses it aside and then holds open his hands, awaiting Kate to toss him another. She takes one herself and then tosses him the remaining three. He opens one and begins to sip on it. "Do you like my mother?" he asks me.

"I love her. She's my grandmother, after all."

"You don't have to suck up. She's not here you know. Though she might as well be."

"What does that mean?"

Uncle Hav leans forward. He's in deep confessional mode now. "I had a great childhood. Absolute perfection. But it was too good. I never wanted to grow up as a result. I never wanted it to end. I wanted everything to stay that way. That's why I can't cope. My mom was too good to me and her niceness in no way prepared me for the nastiness of the real world. My life failed as a result and it's her fault. Her great big fault. She's given me the mental gout. I can't think in the real world. Every time I try my mind flames up in a welter of confusion. This is what I hope Wendy can fix when I go on her show."

"THIS?! . . . This is what you're going to bellyache about when you're on her show? You are a twit," I exclaim. "A supreme twit."

"Don't talk to your uncle like that," he says, belching between his words, waving his half-empty beer can at me in a vaguely menacing manner.

"I'll talk to anyone like that when they start spouting off the inanities you are."

"Scoff if you must, but it's true. If there's anything I hate it's a non-believer. Nuts to you."

"Is your mom going to be on the show too?" Kate asks, quite horrified by Uncle Hav's new strain of lunacy. "I can't imagine Fiona consenting to something like this."

"Well of course she's not going on. Are you kidding? She doesn't even know *I'm* going on. She would kill me if she knew. That's why you've got to keep this a secret."

"But it'll be on tv! Everyone in this town watches Wendy's show. You can't keep this from her," I say, shaking my head in disbelief.

"Don't exaggerate. Besides, Mom lives like a shut-in these days. There's no one to tell her I'm going on. She's afraid of anthrax. She's turning into Howard Hughes, if you ask me. She'll never find out."

"I wouldn't be too sure," Kate cautions. "After all, she has a tv. What's to stop her from watching it?"

"I appreciate your concern, Kate, I really do, but she never watches those shows. She says they're for incontinent idgets. Still, you're a good friend to be so concerned about me, you really are."

"What about me?" I say, pretending to be offended by his exclusionary comments.

"You? You're a snot," he says.

I glower at him but it doesn't last. Both of us half-laugh.

"What happened to your head anyway?" he asks, finally throwing some interest at me.

"Wanda hit me in the head with an ashtray last night," I say. I look at Kate and see her stiffen at the mention of Wanda.

"The first time I saw you two together I knew it was going to end up in disaster," he says sagely.

"You should have said something."

"Would it have mattered?"

"Probably not," I say, rueful about this fact. "She had me all wrapped up. I was smitten." I hear a couple of jars pop in the kitchen.

"Just like me and Belinda. That bitch," he says, turning against Belinda again, his teeth gritting as bad memories begin to overtake him. "Why did we ever marry, Dean? Why?" he bemoans.

"Yes, why?" Kate says, turning to me attentively. "Was it love?"

"I thought I loved her," I say, feeling myself beginning to straddle a dangerous zone.

"I think you did love her," Kate says.

"I know I loved June," Uncle Hav says, always full of emotional contradictions when talking about his ex-wives. "I loved her most of all."

"I guess I did," I say, in response to Kate. "I was turning thirty too. And then there were all the friends and relatives, of which there were two camps: those who thought I would never get married and those still holding out hope. I try to go my own way but what people are thinking about you really does sometimes plague you."

"You married her because you thought it was the thing to do?" Kate asks, always probing me about this part of my life whenever the opportunity arises, never happy with my explanations about it thus far.

"Well, that hastened it anyway," I say, never too sure myself as to all the reasons why I married Wanda.

"Ahh, yes," Kate says contemplatively.

"All I know is that I'll never make that mistake again," Uncle Hav says. "Twice bitten, thrice shy, that's my motto. Learn it, live by it. Be happy," he says, spouting off epigrams with great haste now.

Kate stands up. "Anyway, we should be going, Hav. We have a busy day. We just came to touch base," she says.

Uncle Hav stands up and stretches, then finishes off his beer. "I appreciate the visit," he says. "Are you two coming to Wendy's show when I'm on? Just knowing you're both in the audience will give me all the strength and support I'll need."

"Wendy said she'd reserve us a couple of seats but we'll have to see. We're usually at work when she's on," Kate says, not really warming up to the idea of going to see Wendy's show. Myself, I'm already beginning to see no way out of it.

"Ahh, take a sick day. You're a teacher after all. Most of them never make it through the week without calling in and saying they've got a runny nose or cough, some damn thing," he says to Kate, his thoughts on teachers mostly always negative.

"We'll see. We'll see," Kate says, noncommittal. She twirls the plastic safety glasses before her. "Say, Hav, where did you get these?" she asks inquisitively, her mind turning over the facts of the case, looking for a lead.

"Those? Weren't they in the closet?" he says, looking distracted. "I use those for weedeating. At least I did back when I gave a damn," he says, full of exhausted disillusion.

"Yes, but where did you buy them?"

"Oh, damned if I know. The hardware store I guess."

"Yes, the hardware store," Kate frowns. "You can buy them anywhere, I suppose," she says, her hoped for lead stopped by the commonplace banality of the glasses. A dead end. "Do you mind if I borrow these for awhile, Hav?" she asks, not content to forget about them.

"Sure, I don't care. Why do you want them?"

"I just want to look at them and muse. Those murdered girls were all found wearing them. I find that intriguing, don't you?"

"Oh, those murders. That's all anyone ever talks about. I'm sick of the whole thing. It's really getting old," he says with callous dismissiveness. "I should have a shower," he says to himself, scratching at his scalp.

"Yes, alright. We should be going anyway. Dean, let's go," Kate says, taking charge.

"Alright, we'll see you around," I say to him.

"Next weekend for sure," he says, already setting up the date. "And make sure you both come to the show. I need you there."

"We'll try," Kate says, still noncommittal but offering him some hope with this statement.

"Alright, see you," he says to the two of us, suddenly distracted again and looking like he wants us out right now.

We leave. "Check out the wicket," Kate says, swinging it back and forth.

"You removed the sticky from it," I say.

"I know what I'm doing," she says, full of abundant good humour, as she always is on the weekends.

We get into the car and she starts it up. We have the rest of the day before us.

Chapter 5

We go straight from Uncle Hav's to the bookstore. Kate, ever direct and efficient, finds what she's looking for immediately. "This is the one Kim recommended," she says, handing it to me.

"Oh," I mutter somewhat gloomily as I examine the book.

"What's the matter? You liked the last one she recommended."

"That's true," I say, still not convinced I'm going to like reading it, even though I probably will. I hand it back to her.

"It's good to come to a bookstore," she says, looking around at the numerous people perusing the shelves, feeling very comfortable in this milieu, "if only for the commonality. We're not the only ones taken with the written word. And that reminds me, I should soon get back to work on that short story of mine, don't you think? I've really been neglecting it."

"I thought you were suffering from writer's block."

"Yes, that's true. But after awhile that just becomes a convenient excuse not to write more than anything else, don't you think?"

"I suppose," I say, looking at a number of books on the shelf before us. "I never know what to buy," I say, always somewhat disconsolate over this undramatic fact.

"You don't need to buy anything. Read this one," she says, waving the book in her hand before my eyes. "You can tell me if it's any good and worth my while."

"But I thought you *were* going to read it. Because of Kim's recommendation."

"No. I'm buying it on Kim's recommendation, but I'll only read it on *yours*." She smiles at me. "Come on, let's have lunch and see if we can outlast this rain." We can hear it beating down, in a pulsing pound. We look out the windows. It's coming down in sheeted blasts. I sure don't want to make a run for the car so I nod, agreeable to lunch. Kate goes and pays for the book and then we proceed over to the bookstore's cafe. We are fortunate to get the last remaining table.

"Everybody's got the same idea about outlasting the rain, it looks like," I say.

"Nonsense. They all stole our idea is what it is. Remember, we set the trends in this town," she laughs. So do I. She's in a fanciful mood today. "What would like for lunch? I'm paying. It's my turn after all, isn't it?"

"I'm not going to argue," I say. We take off our coats and hang them on the chairs. She sets the book she just bought on the table. Then we go and stand in line to order our food.

"What would you like?"

"I think just a piece of lemon pie and a glass of milk," I say, breakfast still holding off my appetite for the most part.

"Such an order has a ring of innocence to it."

"I've never admitted to worldliness."

"Or a lot of other things. But that doesn't mean they don't apply to you."

"What does that mean?" I ask. Kate's being esoteric with me. I don't know why. It's our turn to order and my question goes unanswered. I get just what I said I was going to get and Kate orders the quiche lorraine.

"They make the best quiche lorraine in town," she says as we return to our seats. She patiently awaits for her order as I delve into my pie and milk.

I swallow a mouthful. "I'll take your word for it. I never was much into that kind of food."

"What kind of food?"

"Atypical food. Food one doesn't eat everyday."

"You need to be more gastronomically adventurous. There's more to life than ribs and porkchops."

"Maybe. But why change a good thing?"

She reaches over and finishes off my milk. I'm done with my pie so she knows such an action won't annoy me too terribly much. She licks the liquid mustache from her upper lip that the milk leaves. "Because change is a good thing," she says at last.

"Then marry me," I say, ambushing her out of the blue, surprising even myself with the statement, for I hadn't even been thinking about marriage at all mere seconds ago.

"Why do you continually want to put us through this unpleasantness?"

"Because I expect that at some point it will be pleasant. What's your answer?"

"My answer is no," she says, just as her food arrives. The girl who took her order brings it to her and sets it down before her and this conveniently brings the marriage issue to a close for now. "Thank you," Kate says.

"You're most welcome," the girl says cheerily and leaves.

Kate leans forward, over the steaming quiche, working a fork down into the cheese, and whispers to me. "What do you think of that girl? The one who just brought us the quiche?"

I shrug. "Why are you whispering?" I ask, refusing to engage in such subterfuge when I see no reason to. I answer her question in my normal tone of voice. "I've always thought her to be quite appealing."

Kate continues to whisper. "She's constantly changing her hairstyle. Did you ever notice that? It's different just about every time we come in here."

I glance at the girl, buzzing about behind the counter. I turn back to Kate and lean forward, now feeling the need to whisper myself. "I guess I never paid that much attention to her. But, now that you mention it, yes, I guess she does."

"To me that suggests she is unhappy with herself, or at least dissatisfied. She's searching for a certain look that she has yet to find, that has yet to satisfy her."

"You read an awful lot into an awful little sometimes."

"Not at all. Here, try the quiche," she says, her voice raising to its normal tones. She sticks a heaping fork in my face. I take a bite. "Well?"

"It's good," I say, surprised that I like it.

She nods, as though to say that she knew I would all along. Then she begins to eat. "I should call Kim," she says, after she is about half done with her meal. "I told her, on Wednesday I guess it was, that I would. I told her we would come over. She has a bottle of absinthe for us to try."

I frown.

"How come you're always frowning?"

"It's just my nature. I'm appalled at the idea of everything, but usually just the idea. The thing itself usually turns out not to be so bad."

"That *is* an interesting character trait of yours, one that hasn't gone by unnoticed I'll have you know," she says amusedly, pointing her fork at me.

"Is it one of my quirks that irritates you?"

"Now and again."

"I'll work on it," I say, meaning it, wondering why it is that any little thing out of the ordinary puts me off. "But absinthe," I say, feeling the need to somewhat defend myself in this instance, "that is some rough stuff. Where'd she get it?"

"A friend of hers got it from a friend of hers. Something like that. If you drip it down onto sugar cubes it's good though."

"Oh," I say, watching her as she finishes off her meal.

"In fact, I think I'll call her up right now." She gets up and goes over towards the back entrance, where the payphone is. I watch her, lean and lithe, her brown eyes glittering, her comportment anxious—a foot tapping the floor, a finger drumming the top of the phone, awaiting for Kim to answer. I see her lips move and strain to hear her. Her voice comes through to me, though her words are unintelligible from where I am sitting.

She comes back and sits down beside me. "I left a message on the machine. There's no answer."

"Well, that's no surprise. She's never home. Neither one of them are."

"True, but she said she was going to make a point of staying home today. To hear from me and to catch up on her work. She's behind. Sam's behind in his work too."

"They're always behind," I say. "They never want to go out and just have fun anymore."

"Not everyone has your immature leanings, although I do agree with you somewhat."

"Then you yourself must have the same such leanings."

"Nonsense. They've just been really busy as of late. We should just learn to cut them some slack. Look the rain has slowed down a little. Should we go?"

"Yeah, let's get out of here," I say, standing up. We put on our coats and I grab her by the hand. We walk outside and stroll to the car, the drizzle that is now occurring not of enough force to make us run. We get into the car.

"Well, where to now?" I ask.

"I don't know. I really did want to go to Kim's," she says disappointedly, thinking our options over. She picks up the plastic safety glasses from the backseat and becomes distracted with them. "What do these mean?" she says wonderingly to herself, seemingly oblivious to my presence. She sets the glasses on the dashboard and examines them. "I just don't get it . . . yet." She looks at me, her mood turning to one of light perplexity. "What movie was it where there were glasses sitting on the dashboard like this?" she says, her hand waving at the pair before us.

"Well, in the first part of *Kill Bill,* with the sheriff—"

"No, I know that. I mean the other one."

"If you would've let me finish—"

"I'm sorry. I shouldn't cut you off. That's one of *my* irritating quirks, isn't it?"

"I suppose," I say casually. "Anyway, it was in *Gone in 60 Seconds,* the original version."

"That's right. That's what it was!" she says, looking oddly relieved and excited to have recovered this knowledge. "Anyway," she says, quickly changing the topic, "I have nothing more on the burner. I'm ready for home. Unless you have something you want to do?"

"Do we have wine at home?"

"Yes. Are we ever out of your precious zinfandel?" she says, starting up the car and pulling out onto the street.

"You make it sound like I can't get by without it."

"I didn't mean to imply that you were anything other than a weekend lush."

"Alright then," I say.

She drives us home. "I thought for sure the glasses would fall off the dashboard," she says upon pulling into our parking space and shutting off the ignition.

"Especially the way you drive."

She glowers at me with falsely sinister eyes. We get out of the car and enter our apartment building, Kate carrying the glasses and the book she bought. She sets them both down on the counter by the sink right after we enter our apartment. I slip out of my shoes and coat and go lay down on the couch, ready to relax. I reach down under the couch and pull out my baseball. I begin to toss it gently up into the air and catch it.

Kate comes in. "Are you going to watch tv?"

"No," I say, becoming fully enamoured in catching the ball.

She goes over to the stereo and puts on some music. She begins singing "Fernando" before it even comes out over the speakers. "I've been in the mood for this song all week," she says.

"I thought you said you never wanted to hear it again," I say, intrigued and sitting up, still tossing the ball up into the air and catching it on its way down. I look at her and lose sight of the ball. It hits the edge of my hand, bounces onto my knee and then onto the carpet. It rolls towards her.

"I'm feeling better about it. I think Wendy had something to do with it." She kicks the ball towards me.

"And Uncle Hav mentioned it this morning too. See? You're still a celebrity," I say admiringly, picking up with the ball where I left off.

"I must admit that still receiving a little bit of recognition is nice," she says, picking up her flute and pretending it's a microphone. She starts into singing "Fernando" again. "And, after all, this was the song that clinched it for me back in 1989. Never underestimate the talent contest," she says.

"I always did until I saw you singing on tv, though I knew your looks alone were enough to carry you through to victory."

"There were prettier girls than me there."

"No there weren't."

"You sound so definitive," she says.

"I am, when it comes to you."

She sets the flute down and comes and sits beside me on the couch. She snatches the ball away from me and sets it aside. "It seems like such a long time ago," she says, as wistfully nostalgic now as I was this morning. "It was so many years ago already," she says, her voice simultaneously full of disbelief and acceptance. I put my arm around her and we lean into each other until our heads are touching.

"This getting old, it's not for the weak of mind," I say, feeling quotable.

"And we're not even old yet. Not really. But there're already so many years to look back on, aren't there?"

"Yeah," I say, suddenly beginning to lament the passage of time myself.

"This is silly," she says, snapping out of her little moment of yearning for lost time. "That's why I don't listen to this song." Even though it's already over she goes and shuts off the stereo.

"It should recall to you your moment of triumph and nothing else."

"It should, but it doesn't," she says, a little irritable now, picking up a couple of sugar cubes from the dish by the lamp on the endtable.

I get up. "How about a glass of wine?"

She's at the computer now. "Okay," she says, trying to get her mind off her worries over her age.

I go into the kitchen and pour some zinfandel into two long-stemmed wine glasses. I come back into the living room and set Kate's glass down on the desk by the mouse of the computer. I see she is trying to start up on her short story again. I stand behind her and look at the screen, waiting for the fireworks I know are about to ensue.

"Quit it!" she says in no time flat, defensive and self-conscious, her arms coming up to block the screen. "I don't want you to read it until it's done."

"Sorry," I say, feigning regret for my actions, retreating back to the couch and collapsing onto it. I grab the remote control and turn on the tv. I begin to flip through the channels. There's nothing on.

"No, I'm sorry. I'm too touchy about it is all. You can't be a writer and not let anyone read what you write. Let me read you the first sentence. Are you ready?" she asks, looking at me nervously.

I shut off the tv. "Okay, I'm listening," I say, sitting up straight, intent on hearing her words.

"Alright," she says, clearing her throat, a note of trepidation in her voice. "Here goes: 'Jean-Paul always combed his hair with a fork.' . . . Well, what do you think?"

"It's bizarre. But it makes me want to read more."

"I knew it!" she hollers delightedly. "I knew it was a killer first sentence, I really did. It just grabs you because it's so peculiar. Doesn't it?"

"It does. It really does. After all, who combs their hair with a fork?"

"Right. Exactly. Unfortunately, I can't come up with anything that's on par with that first line," she says, her voice quickly draining into inconsolable notes.

"Do you know where you're going with the story though?" I ask, trying to spur her on.

"Sort of. He's going to be combing his hair and one day there'll be this seismic quake and it'll jerk him around and he'll accidentally jam the fork in his eye and have to wear an eyepatch after that. And then the local kids will tease him and call him 'Pirate' and he'll get so enraged by this that he starts to kill them off, one by one. As well, he'll be a real neat freak and kind of anal and it will bother him to only have one eye, so much so that he eventually pokes out the other one to create the aesthetic symmetry that he feels is necessary in life. I think it will end there, with him poking out his other eye. But I have to connect it all, not to mention explain just why it is he combs his hair with a fork to begin with. It's all such a mishmash."

"Wow. I never knew you had such a warped mind."

"But do you think it's a good idea?"

"I love it. It's very creative."

"Hmm. I wonder . . . Even if I do complete it exactly the way I want it, what will *The Atlantic Monthly* think of it? I'm sending it to them first. Aim high I always say. You never hit anything shooting low."

"Don't worry about them. If you start thinking about what they might like or dislike you'll compromise in order to try and please them and then you'll end up writing junk and please no one, especially yourself. Write it your way, the way you want. Be true to yourself."

"Yes, that's good advice. You're right. But good gosh, I can just tell I'm going to have to scrap it all after the first sentence and start again."

"Nobody said it would be easy."

"But nobody said it would be this hard either." She turns away from the computer and takes a sip of wine, her first. I'm already done my mine. I get up and go into the kitchen and pour myself another glass. I then set it aside and turn my attention to the refrigerator. I'm hungry now.

"What are you doing?" she calls out and soon she is in the kitchen too, watching me rustle through the contents in the fridge.

"I'm already hungry," I say. "I guess I should have had more than just that pie." I stand up. "Want some goat cheese?" I ask, holding out my hand and showing her what my exploratory search in the fridge has come up with.

"Is it from Quebec?"

"I don't know. You bought it."

"Then it's most definitely from Quebec. Are there tomatoes in there?" she asks, pointing at the fridge.

"Yeah, I guess."

"Good. Here's what we'll do. I'll make white wine cream sauce, with the tomatoes and cheese, and we'll dump it all on some black linguini. How does that sound?"

"Enticing. You've been watching Christine Cushing again, haven't you?" I say.

"I don't know where I picked up this recipe. But speaking of Christine Cushing, I did tape her show yesterday. Why don't you put it on? It'll spur on your appetite even more and plus I know how much you have a crush on her."

"She is very nice," I say, taking my glass of wine and exiting the kitchen to allow Kate room to demonstrate her culinary expertise. I rewind the tape in the vcr and sit back, ready to watch Christine Cushing.

"What's she cooking?" Kate asks, popping into the living room every now and again to catch a glimpse of the show.

"Floating islands, whatever those are," I say.

"They're good is what they are," Kate says knowledgably. "Don't you hate her guest chefs on these shows though," she adds testily.

"Why? What's wrong with them?"

"They lack passion. They make her do all the talking and just sort of nod."

"It reminds me of my Victorian literature class," I say. "The one I took in my fourth year. The teacher was just so passionate about the Brontes and Thomas Hardy and she always tried to instigate these great discussions. But no one would engage her. I tried to, you know, I would say this or that about Bathsheba

Everdene or whatever literary character it was we were discussing, you know, try and say something that was perceptive and not just obvious and old hat. I didn't say much but she really seemed to appreciate what I did say. Near the end of the semester she would basically just talk to me and let the others listen in, very much aware that she was lucky if she was even getting that much attention out of them."

"Why did they even bother taking the class?"

"English majors are a shy bunch. Though only when they're sober."

"I wouldn't know. I've never met one who was."

"Yeah, we are a rather celebratory bunch, aren't we?" I say, taking a sip of my wine, her sarcasm about us suddenly seeming to ring with a certain degree of truth.

"So I guess it's hard for people very passionate about something, be it cooking or reading or whatever, to come across people they feel to be equally committed to said passion."

"I guess that's what I was saying. Was it?" I ask, suddenly not sure, returning to the kitchen to be near her, liking the congestion that the warm oven burners are filling the room with.

"Sure," she replies. "But I still wish they had better guests on that show. A real talker, you know? Someone who could take the reins away from Christine for five or six minutes every now and again and give her a chance to relax."

"She's having fun, don't worry," I say, leaving the room in a moment of inspiration and turning the tv on mute. I feel in the mood for music.

"Don't put on any ABBA," she says. I turn to see that she is watching me.

"Don't worry. No music to remind you of past beauty pageants," I say.

"Put on the Bangles."

"The cd's in the car," I say. I can't decide what to put on. So, when in doubt . . . I put on Dean Martin. She seems pleased with my choice.

The dinner seems to evolve in no time. Soon we are eating it.

"Slow down. Dinner is supposed to be a civilized activity."

"I can't help it," I say, gorging everything down faster than I ought to be. "I know I'm not providing you with visual pleasure, eating this way, like a pig, but I'm just so hungry." Still, I try to slow down, taking numerous sips of wine between each mouthful to help me in my quest.

"Better be careful. You might get drunk," she cautions as I pour myself another glass.

"Don't worry, it's almost gone. You better take the rest," I say, sliding the bottle her way. She finishes off what she has in her glass and then pours the rest in. She stands up, glass in hand, her other hand clapping her thigh, to the strains of "Little Ole Wine Drinker Me." She goes over to the counter, to where the book she bought is resting. She picks up the glasses sitting on top of them. She puts them on again. "What does it mean?" she asks, speaking to herself it seems to me.

I notice her plate is empty. And she even had seconds. "How did you do it?" I ask.

"What?"

"Here I am, eating like I'm at a trough and you pick away like a dainty bird and still finish before me. It's amazing."

"There's an art to everything," she laughs.

"Yeah, well, you'd think that, after thirty-four years, eating would be one of the ones I'd have picked up somewhere along the way."

"I have confidence that you some day will, I really do," she says, looking at me through the scratchy lenses of the glasses.

"Why don't you take those off? If you want to put something on, put on your bowler."

"I guess that means you're in a mood."

"*The* mood. The one and only. You cook for me, you read me your story, you sing—you can't expect me to sit still through all that and not become enthralled."

"You're a-tingle, is that it?"

"To put it mildly."

"Hmm," she says, her face one of delicate contemplation as she takes off the glasses and sets them back on top of her book. She disappears from the kitchen, going into the bedroom. She reappears wearing the bowler.

Kate's favorite literary character is Sabina from *The Unbearable Lightness of Being* (it's one of her favourite movies too) and the bowler is her one small yet trenchant way of invoking the spirit of that character. I often have her wear it as a prelude to sex because if there's one thing that thrills me it's a great woman in a great hat.

But then the phone rings. It never rings. But of course it is ringing now. Kate rolls her eyes and sighs. She goes over to the phone. "Don't worry, I'll get rid of them post haste," she says.

I nod, momentarily appeased by this assurance. But then I realize it's Wendy on the other end. Wendy who never called once when I was married to Wanda but who is calling right now.

I listen to Kate's end of the conversation, her interest perking and peaking with every comment and question:

"What did you find out?"

—?

"I meant to call and tell you about the plastic glasses. Did you ask Trish about them?"

—?

"Yes, I agree. It is awkward talking about this over the phone."

—?

"Yes, we are in the mood for a drink as a matter of fact. That would be just great. Where do you want to meet?"

—?

"No, I've never been there. But I know where it is. And say, is Wanda there by any chance? We really do want that toaster back."

—?

"Well, I guess we'll just have to play it cool until she decides to make an appearance. Anyway, we'll meet you there in a half an hour. Alright?"

—?

"Okay, goodbye Wendy." Kate hangs up the phone. I down the rest of my wine.

"I can't believe she called," I say, not liking my luck at all the last day or so.

"She just finished having her sprout night with Trish. It ended early because Trish was called away on some sort of business. But she did find out a few things and she said she thought of me right away. Isn't that nice?"

"More annoying than nice," I say sullenly.

"Oh, quit sulking. I'm wearing the hat, aren't I?" she says, posing before me.

"Yeah, I guess that's something," I say, my spirits lifting with each silly yet alluring pose she offers me. "So, where are we going?"

"Are you in the mood for a beer?" she says, her eyes sparkling gleefully, her hands coming together in a loud reverberative clap.

I nod. Maybe my luck isn't that bad after all.

"Good. We're to meet her at The Hob-and-Nob in half an hour. We were just talking about going there the other week, remember? And now we can. It'll be good to get out on a Saturday night for once."

"Yeah, I guess," I say, standing up.

"You still seem disappointed. What's the matter? Can't delay it?"

"Can. Just don't want to," I say, aware of my childish sounding mood.

"Alright then," she says, looking at her wristwatch. "I suppose there's always time for a quick little dalliance. Let's go." She grabs me by the hand and dances me into the bedroom.

Chapter 6

I can hear the pitter-patter of rain bouncing off Kate's bowler. She doesn't wear it out much but tonight is different. I don't know why tonight is different, it just is. It feels different. I don't wear anything on my head, hoping the drops of rain will cool me off. I feel scorched.

"We were really good tonight, weren't we?" she says, just as we enter The Hob-and-Nob.

"You never let me down," I say, feeling depleted but content.

"Drained you dry, huh?" she says proudly, sucking on a sugar cube.

"Yes," I say, digging into her coat pocket, taking out a sugar cube and popping it into my mouth, hoping for replenishment.

"Well, you did ask for it," she says. We look around the pub. It has an upstairs, which I like right off the bat. We see Wendy sitting up there, at a table in the corner by the railing, the one with probably the best view to the whole place. She sees us and waves. We wave back and make our way upstairs, over to where she is sitting.

"Hiya," she says, a bottle of Corona sitting on the table before her, a big mounted moose head above her on the wall, making the place look regal. We take off our coats and drape them over the backs of the chairs we sit down on, across from Wendy. We barely make contact with our seats when a waitress is hovering before us, waving some menus about as though fanning herself.

"No need for a menu," Wendy says, taking charge. "Just bring us the biggest plate of nachos you have." She turns to us. "I love nachos. One of my weaknesses. Along with sex, pills and handguns." She reaches across the table and slugs me in the shoulder, laughing boisterously.

The waitress asks us what we want to drink.

"I'm feeling kind of European tonight," Kate says. "I'll have a Heineken."

"Make it two," I say and at that the waitress smiles and takes off to fill our orders.

Wendy is still cackling away. "Man, what a day. What a crazy day!" she exclaims. "Let me tell you what happened." She takes a drink of beer and tosses her head back. "Do you ever have raw nipples?" she asks Kate.

"What? No," Kate says, taken aback by such a question, looking at Wendy quizzically.

"Me, I do. Wanda says it's a hallucinatory ailment, a side effect if you will, from the pills I take. But if it feels real it is real, right? That's what I always say."

"You do have a point," Kate says.

"Exactly. Anyway—oh, about Wanda. I didn't mention this over the phone but she came back a few hours after you two left last night and I told her that you'd both shown up in search of your toaster. I told her she can't be doing things like that and that she'd better give it back. But of course she blew a gasket and called me a dirty cuntbucket, said that the toaster was rightfully hers, a deserved piece of the alimony that the courts denied her. She's right over the cuckoo's nest. I don't know what we're going to do about her."

"We'll figure something out," Kate says confidently, though all that Wendy's told us has only made me feel even more uneasy about the whole situation. And what court? It was never a court case. I begin to feel a heavy plague of unpleasantness gnaw away in my brain.

"Yes, it always works out in the end," Wendy says, generally optimistic. "Anyway, she came home just as I was rubbing my nipples in Vaseline. To get rid of that rawness that had been irritating them so."

I can't help but look down at her chest. Her big heaving chest beneath a t-shirt with a caricature of a chain-smoking Jack Kerouac on it.

"Anyway, I applied a rather excessive amount and then fell asleep on the couch, watching a classic old western, *Johnny Guitar*. I love the Dancin' Kid. Anyway, I awoke the next morning, which would be today, and I was a total frightened mess. It turned out that I was out of pills. I need my pills, right? This job of mine, it has pressures you cannot comprehend. So I ran around in a big tizzy, slipped on a t-shirt and jeans, very casual Saturday wear and, tossing on my sneakers and coat after a quick comb of the hair, I rushed out to the car and drove over to The Lily Pad. Have you ever been there?"

Kate shakes her head. Wendy looks at me. I nod. "A few times," I say, refusing to feel guilty about it.

"Yes," Wendy says, giving me a sly dog look, as though she knew what my answer would be all along. Our beers come and Kate and I take near simultaneous drinks of them. The nachos are also here. The waitress sets them down before us, a real mountainous platter. I take a nacho and munch on it. Wendy continues on. "Anyway, The Lily Pad is open early now, about seven a.m. You can buy an early bird breakfast there too, for Christ's sake. Have a ham and egger and at the same time watch some chickie strip right on down to her shaved pussy and whistling asshole. God, what a world we live in. Anyway, I've for a long time thought about doing a show on the girls of The Lily Pad. One of my friends works there. Fluff Chang. Do you know her?"

"I don't think so," I say, Wendy's questions about the strip club now being directed to me and me only.

"She's Asian. Real supple. Nice looking tits too. A nice evenness to them. She sells me my pills. It's what she does on the side to supplement her income. She does alright as a stripper, don't get me wrong, lots of money gets tossed her way, especially since she was given the prime working hours, the six to nine grind time slot, right when all the sweaty blue collars get off work and are looking for a little entertainment to appease their weathered souls. They appreciate a good stripper. And Fluff doesn't disappoint. She can gyrate like no one I've ever seen—Holy cow, you mustn't have seen her there, Dean. If you had you would've remembered her. She's unforgettable, as far as strippers go. She should be in Vegas. She's a born entertainer. My only concern—I'm talking about *my* show now—is how to broach this subject in an audience friendly way, in a sanitized manner that doesn't get us in the hot soup with the censors. That's why the whole scene is causing me such a headache. How does one do a clean show on this without skirting the main points?

"But like I say, Fluff sells me my pills. But she only sells them in the club. She hardly ever leaves the club. Off stage she's a real agoraphobe. I know, it's strange, but *c'est la vie*. Anyway, in deep need of my medicine, I rushed over to The Lily Pad in a mad dash. Fluff was sitting by the bar when I arrived, reading a paper and eating a bowl of Fruit Loops. She saw me enter and I motioned to her and she followed me into the bathroom, which is where she does all her business. As well, the john is the only place in the whole darn establishment where one is allowed to smoke. I just don't get it—a strip club with a No Smoking rule. It just runs contrary to the natural order of things, don't you think?" Wendy says, suddenly extracting a cigarette from the pocket of the coat that is draped over the back of the chair she is sitting in. She lights one up.

Kate bites her lip, watching Wendy smoke. "Are you allowed to smoke in here?"

"Oh yes, so long as you're upstairs."

We look around and do indeed see a few people smoking. I guess we had noticed it without really thinking about it.

"That's the big reason why I invested in this place. If there had been no smoking at all, forget it. Wendy Michigan will have no part of a fascist state. None of it. But I checked the by-laws. We can get away with this. And that'll have to do for now."

"You own this place?" Kate asks, surprised and impressed.

"Thirty percent of it. But when my show goes into syndication, and here's hoping it does"—Wendy holds up her hands, fingers crossed—"I plan to make a power move and squeeze out one of the other investors. A real pasty eunuch with a head full of not one single vision. You need vision to open a bar and keep it going. It was me who made them put the moose head in here. My old boyfriend shot it and had it mounted for me as gratitude for me mounting him. You know what his name is? The moose, I mean."

"No," I say.

"Chuck. After Charlton Heston. He was in here, you know, that time he came out to give a speech to the gun association. I was there too. He told stories about Kirk Douglas and Burt Lancaster and about the making of *Ben-Hur*. He's great, a real legend. He had a beer here afterwards. I met him and told him that my favorite movie of his was *Major Dundee*. He seemed impressed. No one ever mentions that movie to him he told me. They always want to talk about *Planet of the Apes*."

"Wow," Kate says, about all either of us can say, getting a word in edgewise with Wendy having always been a difficult thing to do once she starts to roll, as she is doing now.

"Anyway, like I've been saying, what a crazy day! I do my business with Fluff in the bathroom and we have a smoke or two and toss back a few war stories about our respective jobs and I'm feeling good again, a pill in my stomach and some nicotine in my lungs—I know, it doesn't sound healthy but who's to say I won't outlive all the naysayers and tisk-tiskers?—and Fluff mentions how worried she is about the sadist running loose. The first girl who was killed used to work at The Lily Pad and that connection has Fluff on edge. But I told her not to worry so, that I was going to bring this whole ugly situation to an end with my investigative forays. Anyway, as we're gabbing away it occurs to us that there's someone in one of the stalls. Not just one person, but two. There's some real juice fucking going on in there. They'd tried to keep quiet, off our radars, but we were in there for so long that they couldn't do it any longer. They gave themselves away, what with the shakes of the stall and the primal moan of a ripping hard on. It was Grundy, the bouncer slash bartender, and he's got some stripper in there. One of the perks, I guess. But you'd think they could have found a better place, though some people like it sleazy I'm told, but, even so, I would've at least flushed the toilet, my God! You could see the dirty water and a floating log in there when they came out—blecch!

"Anyway, after they did their deed, she rushed out of the bathroom with her arms wrapped around her head, embarrassed to the hilt. But him, he came out and tried to shuffle it all off like an aww shucks country boy who shouldn't have such unsavoriness held against him, hemming and hawwing and kicking the scuffed floor like a poor innocent rube. But then he looks at me and asks me if I would consider going on. 'Not on your life, prick,' I said. That's what I said, 'cause he is a prick, thinking of me that way, the mutant jackanape. My God, what nerve. And so he kind of clams up, all miffed at me for calling him a prick and then he says, 'Well then, you shouldn't come in here dressed like a greasy slut,' and I say, 'Just what in the name of sweet Lee Marvin are you talking about?' and he casts an accusatory finger my way and begins pointing at my mammaries. Upon which point I turn to the mirror and look at myself and there's my t-shirt, glued right to my nipples, which you could see in a very accented manner. It was the Vaseline. I forgot to wipe it off when I slipped on my t-shirt. You could really notice my nips, in pretty much all of their ruby redness. Is that crazy or what?"

"It must have been embarrassing," Kate says, really enjoying this extraordinary story. I'm not too put off by it either. Wendy's never been shy about telling anyone anything.

"Was it ever!" Wendy hollers, finishing off her beer. She bangs it on the table. The waitress appears eagerly. "Another round for me and my friends. Thank you, Gwendolyne," she then says to the waitress before returning her conversation back to us. "Let me tell you, I buttoned my coat up right quick and hauled ass out of there. Right home and into the shower I went. Whew! Rough day all over. And then, to top it off, I just get out of the shower and the phone rings. And who is but that uncle of yours, Dean. What's his name?—wait! Havilah Pilbeam. He called. He wouldn't tell me how he got my unlisted number either. Did you give it to him?"

"No."

"And I started thinking—say, are you by any chance related to Nova Pilbeam?"

"I don't think so. Who's Nova Pilbeam?"

"Well, as you know, I used to be a co-host of the movie nights that used to be on ArtVision, which is of course where I got my start. I'm a real buff. Movies will always be my one true love. And Nova Pilbeam is the actress who starred in Alfred Hitchcock's undeservedly obscure 1937 British film classic, *Young and Innocent*. She was quite fetching. But the name is so unusual that I thought maybe you were somehow related to her."

"No. At least no one's ever said anything to me about it."

"*Young and Innocent*," Kate says, remembering the name, always on the lookout for a decent movie. "It's good, is it?"

"Very fine. Good luck finding it in this era of the Blockbuster Video monopoly though. The whole wondrous era of movie renting is coming to an end I fear," Wendy laments.

"Still, we'll keep an eye out for it."

"What did Uncle Hav want?" I ask.

"Just to whine, it seemed to me. My God, I don't want to offend you with a critique of a family member, but how do you put up with him? Bitch and moan, piss and groan. I had enough after five minutes and told him to contact Gay Linus. Let him try and appease him."

"Who's Gay Linus?" Kate asks.

"He's my personal assistant. Wanda suggested I steal him away from my former boss, T. Dooley Bilge, the president and founder of ArtVision. He used to be T. Dooley's personal assistant but, like me, became disillusioned with the whole scene when T. Dooley turned to showing porno flicks to boost ratings. The slob. Anyway, I don't want any assistant to fall in love with me and become jealous and bitter at seeing me date whoever it is I choose to date because when that happens it usually means that they turn to the media and spill one's secrets. I don't have to worry about Gay Linus getting jealous though and that's why I hired him. I trust him. It's not a new thing though. It's an old trick that many celebrities employ."

We both nod, satisfied with this explanation.

"That Wanda, that's the only bright idea she ever had. That and marrying you, Dean. I'm just sorry it didn't work out. Though I can plainly see you are better off with Kate. So I guess I should be happy it didn't work out."

"Thanks," I say.

"Yes, thanks," Kate says, now beginning to assert herself. "Now, I understand you have some things to tell us about your meeting with Trish Mindy."

"Trish—oh yes. But can we put that subject on hold for a sec or two?" Wendy says distractedly, her attention diverted by the claps and whistles that are occurring down below. "The band is just coming out. The house band. I hired them on the spot when they played a wicked version of "Last Train to Clarksville" at one of my house parties. Listen. They're about to start," she says excitedly, leaning over the railing, looking down at the band on the stage below. We lean over and look down as well.

The gaunt hippie of a lead singer looks up at Wendy and acknowledges her presence with an upthrust—and heavily tattooed—arm, his index finger pointing right at her. "That's Rennie," she says, turning to us. "A real old burn-out. Did time in Hackensack for carjacking. But a real cat when it comes to singing. Come on," she says, standing up and grabbing me by the wrist. "It's dance time," she says. "You too, Kate. Let's make Dean the envy of every man here."

"How's my hat?" Kate says, adjusting it level on her head.

"You look snappy," Wendy says. "But you always do."

We get up and are halfway down the stairs when the band begins their first song, "I'm Movin' On."

"I requested this to them in the dressing room earlier! Hank Snow's one of my favorite singers!" Wendy screams to Kate as we conglomerate onto the dance floor, her voice amplifying so as not to be drowned out by the band. "In fact, this is the song me'n Dean danced to on his wedding night! Remember, Dean?!"

"Yeah," I say. "It pissed Wanda off!" I holler, adjusting my voice upwards, after my 'yeah' withered sickly away into the pounding sound waves around us.

"How come?!" Kate yells.

"Wanda didn't think it was appropriate wedding music!" I yell, the band really roaring through this song, re-inventing it with furious, driving guitars.

"Anything that is good music is appropriate wedding music! Don't you think?!" Wendy yells, her hips swivelling madly, breasts bouncing, shoulders reverberating, arms flapping, her whole body a shaking dervish—and a hypnotically enticing one at that.

Kate puts both hands to my cheeks and diverts my eyes to her. "I can keep up with her, in case you're wondering!" she yells merrily. She points a finger at me and pokes me in the nose playfully, her eyes gleaming, the beer and music putting her into a great dancing mood. She imitates Wendy and then winds up the pace even more, her sinuous body one crackling pulse of bursting energy. I cannot take my eyes off her.

The band doesn't fade out with the song but rolls right into "Quarter to Three" and we keep going, the pace now set by Kate, accelerating her joy of the moment even more and, in doing so, goading Wendy and myself to increase our own rhythmic motions. The dance floor is crowded now, bodies banging against each other and Kate is so involved with the nature of her dance that it spreads out and envelops me, making me forget all about my usual self-consciousness when it comes to doing this sort of thing. I just keep going, keep pace, my breath threatening to fade but always managing to come up with an extra gulp to propel me along, coasting along on Kate's kinetic potency.

We keep on going as the band cuts into another song, this one "Twist and Shout," all of their song choices odd in sequence and segue but every one seeming to be the perfect choice right now, Kate's body in a near busting thrust, the sight of her filling me with a surreal delirium, my senses smote by her physical voltage.

But then the immediacy fades rapidly. Fulfilled and complete, she stops, turning her dancing self off as quickly as she had turned it on. The band takes a breather, says hello to the crowd and introduces themselves. Kate uses her t-shirt to wipe her brow, momentarily taking her hat off. I look at her exposed stomach, flat and supple. Her t-shirt then drops back down to cover it and I look her in the face. Strands of hair are stuck sweatily together to her forehead. She is smiling and pert, breathing heavily and in a momentary need of a break.

Wendy slaps me on the back, breaking the spell. "Boy, wasn't that a blast?"

"It was great!" I say, still yelling, giving my excitement for Kate away, to Kate at least. Her smile enlarges, her dimples show. She plops the hat back onto her head and adjusts it until it is comfortable. She touches the end of my nose with her index finger. I laugh. This is what it's all about.

We all leave the dance floor. "I insist the band plays older music. You know, the good stuff. I fought my partners over this hand and tooth. But I know my onions. I know what people like, what gets their asses out of the seats and onto the floor. That's the key. Get 'em to dance and they get joyous and thirsty and then they buy more booze. And that's what it's all about, believe me," Wendy says, telling us about the bar business and convincing us that she does indeed know what she's talking about. We make our way past the crowds shuffling up and down the stairs and return to our seats. Wendy takes a handful of nachos strung together with melted cheese and begins to munch on them. I take a big gulp of my beer, my eyes still on Kate.

"This is a very nice place," Kate says to Wendy. "I know we'll be coming back again. It's got atmosphere. The *right* atmosphere."

"Exactly," Wendy says. "Everyone's always so worried about getting the drink specials advertised when all they need to really care about is just getting people in here to begin with. Once they're in here they'll drink. That's not the problem. Just get 'em in, I say. And what better way than to have a happening place, cozy. Look at the wood on the walls, the open rafters, just look," she says, her arm spreading across the scene before her. We look around. "It's like a ski lodge in here. A fireplace and everything. Two of them! One up here and one downstairs. And real wood burners too. None of that gas shit. It makes the whole scene, like I said, cozy. And then the good music—my God man, who wouldn't come to this haven?! I wanted a place like from the movies, like something, for example, from the Howard Hawks racing movie, *Red Line 7000*. Have either of you ever seen it?"

"No," we say, shaking our heads.

"Not many have. But don't let the fact that it's a racing movie deter you. I know, I hate them too for the most part—cars doing laps, how boring is that?— but this one treats the races almost as an afterthought. The racers all hang out in this really hip bar and talk and drink, hot women everywhere, and that's what I remember most from that movie, that bar. I want people to think of this bar the way I thought of the one in that movie. Something pure cool. Pure cool."

Kate takes a sugar cube out of her coat and pops it into her mouth. Wendy watches her and says nothing, just smiles, always knowingly. Kate then takes out a little notepad and a little nub of a pencil. She flips the notepad open to a blank page. I watch her write. She writes down *Young and Innocent* and then *Red Line 7000.* "I don't want to forget those movies," she says. She takes a drink of her beer, her second bottle already gone, mine down to the dregs too.

"This place is most definitely conducive to drinking," I say to Wendy, who accepts the comment heartily.

"Atmosphere is what it's all about," she reiterates and than motions to Gwendolyne, who hurries over to our table. Wendy then orders us each another beer and also tells Gwendoylne to bring us some brandied cherries. "Wait till you taste them," she says gleefully, barely able to contain her desire for them. "Anyway, we should get down to silver tacks here. Time to talk Trish."

"Yes," Kate says, very much intrigued now, leaning forward to hear all that Wendy has to impart.

"There's not much to say, I'm afraid," Wendy says, deflating Kate's expectations somewhat. "Though there are a few oddities to impart." Just then our drinks arrive.

"You're sure fast," I say to Gwendolyne, as she sets our drinks down before us.

"That's another thing necessary to having a hot joint. Service. I hate those places where you order a drink and by the time it comes you're ready for bed." The brandied cherries arrive in a transparent vase sitting on a silver platter. There are three tongs on the platter. Wendy grabs one and extracts a cherry from the vase. She pops the cherry into her mouth and I see it bulge from one cheek to the other in slow savory enjoyment. Then the pit emerges, glistening, between her wet lips. She spits it onto the platter and it dings like a bullet ricochet. Kate takes her turn with a pair of tongs and I watch her eat a cherry. Watching them eat cherries is like watching the art of seduction, the pits dinging and zinging onto the platter, brandied cherry juice saturating their lips, the band playing "Party Doll," my arousal level off the charts. I eat a few cherries myself.

"They're good, aren't they?" Kate says to me, wolfing them down like peanuts.

"You don't know the half of it," I say, flush for breath.

Kate turns to Wendy. "When Gwendolyne set it down I thought there was no way we could eat so many. That's a pretty big vase. But it doesn't take long with stuff this good. Where did you come up with the idea of serving them in a vase, by the way?"

"I just think about what tickles me and if the notion has a certain degree of panache, I go with it. It just seemed the right way to go. They're a very popular order here."

"I like your ideas, I really do," Kate says, her opinion of Wendy growing by the second. "But what about Trish? I don't mean to harp, but I really am curious."

"Right, Trish. Well, she's menopausal right now and really bitchy. It's hard to push for details but she did say that all of them were found in the same positions. Lying on their backs, straight as an arrow, hands in a clasp over the stomach. All four of them were found wearing those plastic glasses and—oh! Here's something that hasn't been released to the general public and media. All the people who found the bodies were sworn to secrecy about this, but you know people, so God only knows how long before the papers get wind of this, but all the glasses were gone over with a big black felt marker."

"What? What do you mean?"

"Whoever put the glasses on them darked out the lenses with a black felt pen."

"Why?"

Wendy shrugs and removes a pit slowly from her mouth, a little bubble of saliva between the part in her lips, which she sucks back in. I reach out under the table and grab Kate's leg. She lurches upright in surprise and smacks me in the hip. "Later," she says, turning to me, a sweet look nevertheless upon her face. "This is business."

Feeling scolded, I take a drink, casting furtive glances at these two great women I am sitting with.

"Who knows why?" Wendy says at last. "This case is a real headscratcher. Oh, and here's something else. The last victim was missing a lateral incisor and her second molar. They had been pulled out. Her mouth was bloody and her gums were ragged from the extraction."

"Really?" Kate says, her mind lost in a maze of perplexity. "What do you make of it?"

"Maybe he's taking keepsakes from them now."

"Were any of the other girls missing teeth?"

"As far as I know this is the first. He's upping the ante, at least to his way of thinking. At least that's *my* way of thinking," Wendy says, taking a drink of beer. "And that's all I got out of Trish. But it's enough to keep my noodle puzzling away."

"Do you think she's holding anything back?"

"Hard to say with Trish, but probably. You know menopausal cops."

"This is all so ghoulishly fascinating," Kate says, writing down a few facts in her notepad.

"It most certainly is and on that note, I really must go. I'm meeting an acquaintance of mine soon." Wendy stands up, putting on her jacket. She finishes off her drink. "Don't worry about paying, it's all taken care of, though you can leave Gwendolyne a tip if you like."

"Are you sure we can't pay you something?" I say.

"Hey, what's the point of owning a bar if you can't have your friends drink for free?"

I shrug agreeably. There's a lot in what she says.

"Say, what are you two doing tomorrow, around six-ish?"

"We have no plans," Kate says.

"My mom is having a dinner tomorrow. Why don't you two come?"

"No—no, really," I say immediately, stammering for an excuse. "We have that thing," I say, turning to Kate. "Remember, that *thing*?"

"What thing?" Kate says, deliberately obtuse.

"Well, you have to mark papers for one thing," I say, switching gears and throwing out a more definite excuse instead.

"Oh nonsense. I'm the teacher. The boss. I can mark them whenever I want."

"Good deal. You set the rules. I like that. Are you two coming then?" Wendy asks.

"We'll be there," Kate says affirmatively and determinedly, looking at me with a defiant smile as she does so.

"Alright. Oh, before I forget, here's my number," Wendy says, handing Kate her business card. "Now, I must bid you both adieu and go see my friend.

Maybe get another moose head out of him, who knows, huh?" she says, winking. We watch her go.

I turn to Kate. "Don't look so sour," she says, smiling.

"You don't know what you're in for. Tuppy is insane. Wanda and Wendy are straitlaced and inhibited compared to her."

"You're exaggerating."

"I wish I was."

"Still, it's no need to be so gloomy. It'll be interesting. I'll get to learn more about your secret past."

"It's not secret."

Kate looks at me doubtfully. "Besides, it'll give us a good chance to toss out some more theories on the case."

"I'm sick of this case."

"So am I. That's why we need to solve it."

"You're crazy," I say, putting my arm around her and pulling her close. "Do you know that?"

"More nonsense," she says dismissively, putting a cherry to her mouth and working it from one cheek to another before sticking out her tongue, the pit sitting on it in a coat of saliva. She spits it at me and hits me in the cheek, just below my left eye. I flinch and laugh. "I saw how turned on you were by the way Wendy was eating these things."

"By both of you. I'm all randy again."

Kate smiles and flicks at the underside of the bowler rim with her index finger. The front of the hat rises about half an inch on her head, her eyes appearing out of the shadows of the rim, sparkling and insightful. "Seriously, why did you grab me like that, when you grabbed my knee? After all, it was Wendy who was turning you on."

"Lots of women turn me on but when they do I think only of you. I think of how what they're doing to me you do so much better."

"Want to go home?"

"Yes."

"Will you slow dance with me first?"

"They haven't played a slow song yet. Who knows when they will."

"It doesn't matter. Will you?"

"Yes," I say, grabbing her by the hand.

Chapter 7

When we got home last night from The Hob-and-Nob the answering machine was blinking. There were two messages. I knew who one of the callers was before even listening to them. Just as I know that it is that same caller on the other end of the phone when it starts ringing this morning: Uncle Hav. Kate crawls out of bed and goes out to answer the phone. I can hear her talking, full of explanations as to where we were and why we haven't called back. Then she returns.

"It's Hav," she says, standing in the doorwell.

"I know. It's always him. Always always," I say, emphasizing my weariness over this fact.

"He wants to talk to you."

"About what?"

"I don't know. I think he's going to want us to come over this morning. Tell him we can't. We have to see Kim today." It was Kim who left the other message last night.

I sit up and take the glass of water from the bedside table. I take a drink. "Dry mouth," I say, standing up and slipping into my jeans.

"I think it was the brandied cherries," Kate says, suggesting that she is feeling the same way.

"Maybe we'll have to give them up."

"Nonsense. These wan feelings will pass soon enough."

"Yeah," I say, not really taking to my suggestion either. I never like to give up things I like, no matter how negative their aftereffects may be. I pass Kate, who is on her way back to bed it looks like, and leave the room. I grab the phone and sit down on the couch.

"Hello," I say.

"Dean, where were you two last night? I called at least six times. I even left a message for you to call. I hate those damn machines. So where were you?" Uncle Hav asks, demanding an explanation, even though Kate no doubt already told him the whole story.

"We were out at The Hob-and-Nob last night. We had a few drinks with Wendy. When we got back it was late and we thought you'd probably be asleep. So we thought we'd return your call today," I say, laying it all out in straight facts, even though the last two are made up. I had no intention of calling him last night no matter what and I wasn't planning on it this morning either.

"Hmmph," he grunts, full of disbelief and scorn. "You might have let me known you were going out. I wouldn't have minded a drink or two last night. I wouldn't have minded at all."

"It was kind of a last minute thing."

"It would've taken less than that to call me and let me in on it."

"It never occurred to me," I say, in an honest dance around the subject.

"It's so easy for you. So damn easy. When you've got a girl like Kate on your arm the world opens up for you. You just hatch into a social butterfly without even trying. Is it asking too much of you to let me join in on your fun once in awhile? Is it? Answer me, goddammit!"

"Don't snap at me like that. I don't owe you anything," I say, starting to lose my cool. "You're awfully clingy lately," I say, turning pointed.

"A hell of a thing to say to your uncle, a hell of a thing. If you weren't so self-absorbed and had any kind of consideration for me and my solitude it would have occurred to you to invite me and maybe set me up with Wendy. That Wendy, she's a hell of a woman. A real looker. A guy could fall hard for her. Yes sir," he says and I groan, knowing that he's now turned his passions onto Wendy. I try to douse them right away.

"She's already got a guy, so put her out of your mind."

"What?! Who?! Who is her guy?"

"I don't know. But she left us last night to go and see him. It sounded like she was off to get laid."

"What?! Did she say that?"

"Not in so many words. But the inference was hanging there plain as day."

"Damn," he says through bated breath. "I thought she might be the one." He turns rueful. "It would have been a hell of a thing if me and her had started dating, wouldn't it have? The two of us—you and me—dating celebrities. It would have been so fine."

"Kate's retired. She's not a celebrity anymore."

"I heard that," Kate calls out from the bedroom, having overheard me.

"Once a celebrity always a celebrity. Ahh well—Say, did Wendy mention me at all last night?" he asks hopefully.

"She said you'd called."

"That's it?"

"Wendy doesn't like to talk business when she's not working," I say tactfully, happy with the way I'm managing to obscure the truth of the matter.

"That's understandable," he says acceptingly, exhaling. I can tell he's smoking. "Well, why don't you and Kate come over? Try out some of that canned fish."

"I don't think we can make it. We have a packed day. Besides, we have to go and see Kim."

"Kim? Who the hell is Kim?"

"Kim Rist. She's one of Kate's best friends. One of mine too. You know her. You've met her several times."

"You don't say."

"I thought I just did."

"Hmm? Oh, yes. I don't recall her. What's she like, this Kim? A real looker, is she? She must be, if she's Kate's friend. Kate would never hang out with a dog," he says, his mind already turning over new possibilities.

"That's a dumb thing to say. Kate would resent it."

"I'm sorry. But what's she like?" he asks, his love for Wendy already fading.

"She has dark hair—she's slim and good looking and really nice, if that's what you're getting at. But she's also taken."

"Goddammit! Will this poor string of luck ever end?" he laments.

"She lives with Sam Dart. You know Sam. Remember? We all went to The Lily Pad together a few times last year, back when we did that sort of thing."

"Me, I still go there, on occasion. But you, you had to go and get domesticated," he says accusatorily, as though I have abandoned him by doing the worst thing possible.

"We can go again, if you want," I say genially, trying to appease him, in no way adverse to going to The Lily Pad with him should he want to go.

"You're just saying that," he says in an abandoned voice.

"Well then, forget it," I say irritably.

"No, no, don't be so hasty. If you really mean it, maybe we could work something out. Maybe we could go tonight."

"Tonight's no good. We're supposed to go to my ex-mother-in-law's for supper," I say, just remembering this fact, the reacquired knowledge of it filling me with extreme trepidation and a great feeling of ominousness.

"Well that's just sweet, isn't it? Rub my nose in your goddamn full life once more, why don't you?" he says acridly. "Well, maybe I should just hang up and let you call me when you can find some precious time for me, huh? What do you say? Maybe I should do that."

"Okay," I say, about to hang up, something which he seems to sense, by the finality in my voice.

"No, hold on!" he cries out. "This conversation has turned into a big holy mess. I apologize," he says.

"No, that's alright," I say, always too ready to give into his innumerable apologies.

"I guess I just need something to eat. That's what I need," he says affirmatively, deciding that a lack of food is what is currently ailing him and causing him to fly off the handle. "I'll let you go. But I'm holding you to this Lily Pad excursion. Call me about it, okay? Okay?"

"Yeah, I will," I say, sensing the conversation about to come to an end and feeling relief.

"Alright then, bye," he says and hangs up before I can even say goodbye to him. I set the phone down. I go into the bedroom but Kate isn't there. She's in the kitchen, dressed and drinking a glass of orange juice.

"How was it?" she asks.

"Excruciating. I promised him we'd go to The Lily Pad together sometime soon, just like old times."

"Tough punishment," she says sarcastically and then continues on in the same vein. "I bet he really had to twist your arm into that."

"Actually, I guess I was the one who suggested it."

"Visions of Fluff Chang dancing in your head, are they?"

"Don't be ridiculous," I say, offended by the notion. "Well, are we going to see Kim and Sam or what?" I ask, changing the subject as Kate hands me the remainder of her juice. I drink it down.

"I have to call her," she says distractedly, looking as though her mind is mulling over a hundred different things at once, all of them of equal importance to her. "I'll call," she then says and disappears around the corner to where the phone is. I hear her on it. Kim is obviously home. They don't talk long. Kate comes back to where I am. I haven't moved an inch, the glass still in my hand. I set it down, alert to Kate's presence now. "Let's go," she says, grabbing the car keys off the counter and going over to the coat rack for her coat.

"Alright," I say, rushing into the bedroom to slip on some socks and a t-shirt. Then I go into the bathroom and brush my teeth, comb my hair and wash my face. Kate is waiting by the door in her coat and shoes, her little purse strung over her shoulder. "And they say women take forever to get ready," she kids.

I grimace. "Uncle Hav set me back some," I say, spreading the blame.

"Sure. Sure. That's who it was," she says cuttingly, in a needling mood. I put on my coat and shoes and we head out.

"Your turn to drive," she says, handing me the keys as we reach the Galaxie. I unlock the doors and we get in. She immediately begins to fiddle with the stereo, putting on this cd and that, changing them every few seconds, unable to decide on her musical mood.

"Just stay with the Bangles," I say, attempting to make her ultimate decision for her.

"Yes, I think so. I think so," she says, following my advice. "But they're not really a rainy day group. Or are they?"

"They're an any day group," I say, my defense of them growing more and more over the years.

"That's true," she says, the music issue now settled. "Are we going to see Hav today at all? Did you give in to him?"

"No. We don't have the time. Did you forget that you accepted that invitation to Tuppy's tonight? God," I say, my more or less decent mood momentarily eroding because of this fact.

"I guess it was the brandied cherries," she says by way of an excuse, opening the glove compartment and taking out a few sugar cubes. She pops them into her mouth. "I was a bit tipsy by the time we left. Everything seemed like a good idea."

"Yeah, those damn cherries," I say, diverting the blame away from her. I think of the fun we had after we got home last night. And all those good ideas. "Those damn cherries," I say again, my voice far from bitter. "We'll have to go there again soon," I add, changing my tune.

"I was thinking the same thing," she says.

It doesn't take long to get to Kim and Sam's. We park on the street and make our way up the steps of their place. There are a couple of dead plants sitting on the stoop. Kate eyes them. "We have to get some plants for *our* place," she says thoughtfully, always looking for ways to cozy up our apartment. I nod.

I ring the doorbell. "I need a drink of water," I say as we wait for Kim to answer the door, once more as much as confessing the mist of a hangover that is coating me.

"I'm sure Kim can provide that."

I feel myself sneer.

"Why did you do that?" Kate asks, always noticing my facial expressions.

"I don't know."

"Are you still upset that she didn't like the book?"

"You know, I think I am," I say, the idea becoming epiphanously concrete and accurate to me.

"She's liked every other one you recommended she read."

"Yes, but this one was special—" I say, my voice cut off by the opening of the door.

"Didn't you hear me? I called out for you to come in," Kim says wonderingly.

"We're hungover," Kate says, explaining away our poor ears with this single admission.

"Goodness," Kim says concernedly, allowing us in. We trudge upstairs after kicking off our shoes. Kim and Sam live in the upstairs flat. I notice he is not around. I peer into all the rooms as I make my way into the kitchen and sit down at the table.

"Where's Sam?" I ask.

"Gone," Kim says. "He flew home. He has a bad tooth."

"And—?" I say, needing more information.

"He only goes to the dentist he had when he was growing up."

"You mean whenever he has a tooth problem he flies home to where he used to live to get it checked out?"

"Yes."

"That is the dumbest thing I've ever heard," I say.

"Goodness, you sure sound surly," Kim says. "Should I chalk it up to your hangover?"

"He's still a little miffed that you didn't like that book," Kate interjects, opening up a minor can of worms right off the bat. I feel myself rolling my eyes. I notice Kim is drinking.

"What are you drinking?" I ask, trying to change the subject.

"Wiser's," she says, picking up the glass—a big tumbler—and swirling the smoky golden contents before taking a little sip. "What book?" she asks, not allowing me to change the subject.

"*The Sound and the Fury*," I say, replying before Kate can, feeling I might as well own up to it myself.

"Oh that," Kim says. "It's not that I didn't like it. I just couldn't get into it like I could some of the others you recommended to me."

"There. Right there!" I say, leaping out of my seat, pointing at her. "How could you not? It was riveting. I ripped through it," I say righteously.

"Calm down," Kate says. I look at her moodily.

I sit back down. "Ahh well," I say, turning suddenly reflective. "I guess most women don't like Faulkner," I say, throwing out a sweeping generalization that contradicts Kate's own opinion of the book and, as of Friday night, Wendy's thus far too.

"I can only speak for myself," Kim says. "Say, would you like a drink?" she asks, trying to appease me.

But I determine not to let her weaken my belligerence. I watch her take a drink. "Well, maybe a small one," I say, already weakening. Kim sets down her drink and pulls two similar tumblers from a cupboard. She pours a splash of Wiser's into each, handing one to Kate and one to myself. I take a sip.

"Nice, isn't it?" Kim says, momentarily disappearing from the kitchen. I lean forward in my chair. I can see down the hall. I see her in the living room, at the stereo. She comes back, just as the music begins to play. She has put on "Whiskey on a Sunday," an old Irish Rovers song.

I nod approvingly and take another drink. Kate takes one too. So does Kim. We drink away. "What were we talking about?" I ask after a bit, distracted by the warm and friendly state of the flat.

"You're mad at me because I don't like *The Sound and the Fury*," Kim says, willing to meet me head on and not dodge the issue. Kate is sitting back in her chair, watching me, happy to just let us fling out our disagreements. But my animosity is completely diluted by the whiskey, the music and my simple inability to hold a grudge against someone as nice as Kim.

"Why don't you like it? Is it because many of the women he writes about are screaming, castrating harridans?" I ask, throwing out a common yet erroneous complaint that many naysayers of Faulkner have, now much more interested in *why* she is not excited by Faulkner rather than I am in condemning her for it.

"No. I guess I just thought it was turgid. His style, I mean."

"I see," I say slowly, full of a deep hyperbolic contempt for such an opinion. I pound back my whiskey, get up and pour myself another. The kitchen floor is made up of boards. But the finish is wearing on them. A sliver jams itself in my foot. Startled, I grimace and hop back to my chair.

"We have to do something about this floor," Kim says, as though she has been expecting what has happened to me to happen for quite some time now.

"Do you have a pair of tweezers?" I ask wincingly.

Kim disappears down the hall and into the bathroom. She comes back with a pair of tweezers. I pull off my sock and begin to devote medical attention to my wounded foot.

"You say Sam went to the dentist," Kate says, standing up and approaching Kim, as though miles behind the conversation that has been ensuing.

"Yes. He'll be back on Wednesday."

"Tell him to call me," I say, trying to get a hold of the sliver in my foot. "We're going to The Lily Pad, me and my Uncle Hav. Do you think he'd want to go?"

"I'll tell him to call you," Kim says, not offering an opinion as to Sam's possible intentions.

Kate pulls the plastic safety glasses of Uncle Hav's from her coat pocket.

"What do you think of these?" she asks Kim, handing them to her.

"You're much too obsessed with those things," I say, pulling the sliver out of my foot and breathing a sigh of relief. Kate gives me a hard stare, unappreciative of my opinion. "Well, you are. All you do is cart them around and study them," I say defensively. "It's true, you know. That's what you do."

Kim looks at the glasses and then hands them back to Kate. "I don't know. They look like simple ordinary safety glasses to me."

"Exactly. Those four murdered girls were found wearing them."

"Oh. I guess they were. That is strange, isn't it? You should see Sam, he's paranoid about this whole case. Whenever we're out of bagels or cheese and I tell him that I'm just going to dash down to the store for some he comes with me. He never wants me to be alone. Even during the day he thinks there's a threat."

"That's sweet. How come you're not like that with me?" Kate says, turning to me with accusatory eyes and poking me in the nose.

"Because I know you can take care of yourself," I say, swatting at her poking finger as though it were a fly. "Besides, when are we ever not together?"

"That's true," she says, the issue dying with her response.

"I can take care of myself too," Kim says to me forcefully.

"I didn't mean to imply that you didn't," I say. The whiskey is going down good, which is my only compensation for being in the company of two girls—best friends—who are likely to gang up on me at any moment for any old thing.

"You said Sam went to the dentist," Kate says again, sounding like a real old broken record, the whiskey in my empty stomach fogging my ability to realize that she is getting at something.

"Yes," Kim says.

"These are the types of things that they make you wear at the dentist, aren't they? So pulp and filling don't spit into your eyes, right?" She hands the glasses back to Kim.

"These look like the type, I guess," Kim says.

Kate turns to me. "Remember what Wendy said last night? That the last girl found was missing her lateral incisor and a second molar."

I shrug, somewhat sure of where Kate is going with this now but refusing to acknowledge that anything she submits to us is nothing less than dismissive lunacy.

"He's a dentist. The killer's a dentist! Those girls are wearing protective dental glasses. And the missing teeth—it's all there, don't you see?!" she exclaims elatedly.

"Sounds farfetched," I say.

"Truth is stranger than fiction," Kate says, tossing out that hoary old epigram. "I'm sure of it. I'll bet those girls were all patients of the same dentist and he's deranged. He has a thing for his patients and kills them. That's what it is. I'll bet you a dollar and a donut."

"She's insane," I say to Kim, shaking my head.

"It *could* be a dentist," Kim says musingly, sitting down, refusing to go against her friend's opinion.

"This is nuts," I say disparagingly.

"When did you become such an Old Mr. Negatory?" Kate says chidingly.

"I don't even know what that means. My foot hurts," I say, starting to whine in hopes that some sort of sympathy will be offered to me.

"I can't wait to tell Wendy," Kate says, ignoring my rather baseless whimpers.

"Who's Wendy?" Kim asks as Kate heads down the hall and into the living room to use the telephone.

"Wendy Michigan. The one with the tv show," I say.

"Oh. Her? Isn't she—I mean, wasn't she your sister-in-law at one time?" Kim asks me.

I nod. "The one and only," I say disgustedly but then decide I am acting wrongly towards Wendy. "Actually, Wendy's really nice. At least compared to Wanda."

"How's that going?" Kim asks, in the loop as to my problems with Wanda.

I point to the band-aid on my forehead. "Wanda hit me in the head with an ashtray late Friday night and then stole our toaster."

"You're kidding?"

"Not at all."

"How did she get into your place?"

"You know, I don't know. That's a very good question. One that has to be answered." After all, when she took my book I had invited her up to try and straighten things out and she took our juicer from the moving van when we were unloading our stuff into the apartment we now live in. I mull it all over. "Say," I say, once again changing the subject, hating to talk about Wanda for very long. "Is there anything around here to eat? I haven't had anything yet today."

Kim gets up and goes over to the fridge and begins to dig through it. "Do you like cantaloupes?"

"I doubt it," I say. Nonetheless, Kim takes out a half a cantaloupe and begins to slice it up on a cutting board. She begins to chew on one of the slices.

"I'm all out of porkchops," she says airily.

I shake my head. "You and Kate talk too much about me, you must."

"You're a rather interesting specimen. A real character."

"Thanks. I think," I say, just as Kate comes back into the room.

"I got a hold of Wendy. She's in worse shape than us. She drank a bottle of tequila last night after she left us."

"So the dinner's off?" I ask hopefully.

"Of course not," Kate says tersely, as though I've just offered up the dumbest comment imaginable. She turns to Kim. "What are your plans tonight, Kim?"

"I have none."

"Come with us. I asked Wendy if you could come and she said the more the merrier. What do you say?"

Kim looks at me. I shrug. "Don't ask me. They're all crazy, that's all I'm saying. But that's enough, as far as I'm concerned. So don't say I didn't warn you."

"I guess—"

"Good," Kate says, cutting off Kim's somewhat hesitant remark and going over to the counter where the cantaloupe slices are lying. She picks one up and bites into it. I watch her chew and swallow it. "This is good," she says.

"Dean doesn't like it," Kim says, her voice exaggeratedly critical and offended.

I yawn. I'm tired, too tired to offer up witticisms in my defense. "This whiskey is wearying me," I say, explaining my condition. I look at Kate. "What are we doing today? When's that dinner?"

"We're to come over at any time after five. We have lots of time. Why, what do you want to do? Go home?"

"I'm tired," I say, all of a sudden flat out of steam.

"Poor Dean Dorian, can't cut it anymore," Kim pesters. Kate laughs and eats another slice of cantaloupe.

"I know I should be annoyed with you and I will be yet. I'm just postponing it," I say to Kim, my snarls muted and weak. "What are you two going to do? Just yack all day? Talk about work?" They always talk about work.

"We do whatever we feel like doing," Kate says, her voice ringing with independence.

"Go up in the loft and have a snooze," Kim suggests.

I clap my hands and stand up, very taken with this suggestion. "Yes! That is what I will do. I will go and have a nap." I stagger my way into the living room. Kate and Kim follow me. They sit down on the couch and begin to talk, already having forgotten about me. I climb the rungs of the sturdy but creaking ladder leading up to the loft, the effort agonizing to me. I crawl over to the mattress and stretch out on it, my head on the pillow. I stare up at the pitch of the roof, my eyes following the lines as they converge. I shut my eyes and let the familiar soothe of Kate and Kim's voices overtake me. They are indeed talking about work.

"I was helping one of the students with a perspective problem on Friday and he kept calling me 'Ma'am'. 'Yes, Ma'am' and 'No Ma'am' and 'Thank you, Ma'am.' It made me feel strange. Not old exactly, but like I was in the military or some such thing," Kim says, a little bemused and disconcerted it seems to me. I try and picture her as a 'ma'am' but cannot. But neither can I picture myself as a 'sir', yet have been called one already in a variety of places, with ever increasing regularity. I try and shut my mind to it, for it is a thought that leads to the notion of getting older and I am not ready for that right now. My weary condition has done enough to serve notice to me that I am older than I used to be. My eyes grow heavy and soon are lidded shut. I see nothing but dark. I can hear the mellifluousness of Kate's voice but the words are vague and distant. Something to do with absinthe.

Absinthe, yes. That's why we came here, it occurs to me in my stupor. My mind floats along the inchoate strains of Kate's voice. I feel content. Kate's sweet voice. Sweet Kate. I turn onto my side, my mind turning over at the same time, turning back, back to when we met, trying to tease out the completeness of the memory of when we first met. I think about it and think with so much more concentration than I'd anticipated that I am threatening to think myself awake. It occurs to me that I'm a bit chilly. I reach out for a folded up blanket beside the mattress. I notice, in the wan and shadowy light—notice perhaps because of feeling more than of actual sight—that I have goosebumps on my arm. I grab the blanket and flap it out of its folded up state and pull it messily over myself. Then it hits me—the goosebumps! A new development:

I was wearing my gym clothes when I first met Kate that day. The principal had caught us (how he knew what we were up to I'll never know. It was that little bastard from Grade 1 I'll bet, he was always a snitch) and after giving us the riot act he told us to change into our gym clothes. Which we did. And when we came out he was talking with Kate's mom and Kate was there, looking at me, holding her mom's hand, and then she moved behind her mom and grabbed her mom's leg and I looked into her face and her face looked, as I always say—stricken, and I passed her, carrying my wet and stained folded up pants and it was a cold and rainy day, it was almost snowing out and it was cold in the entranceway and I had goosebumps on my bare legs, just my gym shorts and t-shirt on, yes . . . and that was it. Or at least that's all I can remember at the moment. But it's quite a bit, in my mind.

I sit up, eager to tell Kate about this newly recovered piece of memory of our first meeting but I can hear that she and Kim are still talking away nonstop. Kim is in a good mood, not drunk, but whiskey loosened enough that the conversation is flowing easily from her. I lay back on the mattress and listen to the Irish Rovers music that continues to play away, floating about cheerily and leaving me feeling free of any and all that might otherwise be plugging up my mind with worry and dread.

The next thing I know Kate is poking me. I can hardly breathe. She is sitting on my chest, poking it, poking my face, gently but with enough force to fully wake me, my mood turning into quick playful annoyance. "Cut it out," I say.

"Come on, Mr. Van Winkle, it's time to go."

"What time is it?" I say. I look at my watch before she can answer. It's about a quarter to five. "Good grief, I must have really zonked out."

"You were talking in your sleep too."

"Really? What did I say? Was it interesting?"

"It was gibberish. It was just like you were wide awake."

I sneer at her. "Oh!" I say suddenly. "Guess what? I remember something. I wasn't wearing my pants the day I met you. I was wearing my gym clothes. I was carrying my pants and I was cold and had goosebumps on my legs when I passed you—when I passed poor forlorn little Kate," I say, pulling at her, getting my arms around her and starting to wrestle with her. We roll over and I get on top of her and pin her to the mattress with unusual easiness. She is giggling away like a lunatic. I look at her curiously. "Are you drunk?" I ask.

"Certainly not!" she declares. "I am just, I am just—" She belches. "Horrors. How unladylike. I am merely . . ." She pauses. "Yes. I am a little cut," she admits at last and then emits a satisfied gulping laugh. "Your memory is getting better. I remember your bare little five year old legs well. And now, from the vantage point of twenty-nine years later, I can confidently say that even then I knew. I knew it would be me and you and nobody but. I knew that one day it would be, be just like this, me and you, my little buddy you," she says, her voice vigorously playful. I get off of her.

"Are you okay? Can you get down the ladder?" I ask.

"I got up it alright, didn't I? I am fine," she says, drunkenly assured.

"Hey, Dorian! Hurry up!" Kim calls out to me. She too sounds a bit boisterous. Whenever Kim calls me by my last name I know that her mood has picked up.

I climb down the ladder and stand at the bottom, spotting Kate, braced to catch her should she fall down. But she makes it down alright. "I told you I am fine," she says, aware of the doubts I had. I look at her and Kim.

"What a fine pair I am staring at here. Sam would be abhorred and disgusted."

"Well, Sam's not here. Let's forget about that bum. Here, have a sugar cube," Kate says, picking one off the coffee table and tossing it my way. I catch it awkwardly and pop it into my mouth, noticing the brown-stained colour of it as I do. A bitterness wells up before the sweetness of the sugar overrides it. I cough, the taste unexpected to me. "What's with this sugar cube?" I ask suspiciously.

"They're laced. Laced to the grains with absinthe. Gives them a bit of a kick. Puts them over the top and into the joy that you see before you now," Kate says wobbily, her arms stretched out, as though she's about to embrace me. "Have another," she then says, picking one up. She tosses it at me. And then another and another. Soon I am dodging them.

"Cut it out you wacko!" I holler good-naturedly, my arms coming up to block the cubes flying at my head. I find a few lying on the floor. I pick them up and pop them into my mouth. "This absinthe, it's harsh."

"You should try drinking it," Kim says, collapsed in a wicker chair. She turns to Kate. "I can't believe you let him call you a wacko," she says, trying to stir something up.

"I can't believe I did either," Kate says, yawning, seeming to calm down somewhat. "We're in bad shape, Kim," she says, suddenly self-critical, in examination of the facts. She looks at me. "Come, let's go. You've got to take us to get some coffee. We'll be okay after a coffee or two," she says, turning to Kim, in a voice of steady assurance.

Kim stands up. "What do you suppose Wendy will be making for supper?"

Kate shrugs and looks at me.

"Don't ask me. Tuppy's doing the cooking, or so I gather," I say, suddenly unsure myself.

"You were there once before. What did they have? Oh wait, it was ribs, wasn't it?"

"Yes."

"She'll probably cook them again then," Kate says decidedly.

"Maybe I should bring something," Kim says, sounding concerned, fearing the possibility of a lack of the weird food she likes to eat. She looks at me. "We have to stop at a grocery store," she decides. "I'll buy a cantaloupe to bring along."

"And booze too," Kate interjects. "We must bring something."

"The liquor stores are closed today," I say.

"Right. Fudge," she says disappointedly.

"We have a little mickey of Wiser's here. Sam bought it in case of emergency. This would qualify as such I'd say, wouldn't you?" Kim says.

"Yes. We'll take that. We need something more though."

"There's a bottle of muscatel under the driver's seat," I say. "Never been opened."

"Muscatel? Ooh, I like the sound of that. Where did you pick that up?" Kate asks.

"A guy at work gave it to me, just last week," I say, having forgotten about it until now.

"Okay then, let's go," Kate says, everything settled to our satisfactions.

We shut off the lights and stereo, grab the Wiser's, put on our coats and follow Kate downstairs. We slip on our shoes. Kim is wearing her blue and white bowling shoes. I don't know if they actually are bowling shoes, but they look like they could be. "They're comfortable," she says in defense of them, seeing me eye them curiously for the umpteenth time.

We leave Kim's and she locks the door. I am already down the steps and on the sidewalk, ready to get on with this thing. She and Kate are standing about, talking about one of the plants sitting on the stoop. I am growing impatient with them. I go over to the Galaxie and unlock it. I look about. I stare at Kim's car. The license plate says 'Basil'. "Hey, come on!" I finally yell, impatient with their slack movements, the wind picking up and starting to cut into me with a a heavy chill.

They heed my call and come down the steps and we all get into the Galaxie. I start it up and we take off. "There's a Starbucks somewhere around here, isn't there?" I ask, wanting to get the purchases they think we need out of the way right now.

"Oh, don't go there. Go to Angie's," Kate says.

"Alright," I say, agreeable to this since it is on our way to where Tuppy lives anyway. We stop at a grocery store on the way and Kim picks up what she says is a dandy of a cantaloupe. Then we go to Angie's. And then we get involved with the Coffee Cup Bandit.

Chapter 8

It's not really what I expect to be doing when we get here—chasing after someone stealing a coffee cup, but that's what happens. We enter the coffee shop, await our turn in the seemingly perpetual lineup and when we finally get down to ordering, Kim orders a vanilla bean latte and Kate orders three lattes, two for herself and one for me, everything to go.

"Hello, Angie. How are you?" Kate asks, now in a state of self-enforced sobriety. I feel uneasy. Though Kate frequents this place on a steady basis and gives Angie all her caffeine business, and though they have had many conversations at the till, they are not what I would in any way call friends. Acquaintances I guess is the best way to put it. To my knowledge Kate knows nothing of Angie's history with Wendy—a rather volatile history—and, as such, it leaves me wondering how Angie will react should Kate bring up the fact that we've been seeing Wendy as of late. Angie knows Wendy was my sister-in-law but never held it against me, in part because Wendy and I weren't talking at all during those years, the 'feud years' as Wendy termed them the other night.

"Hello Kate. Hello Dean. Hello Kim," Angie says. I don't know why I am surprised that she knows Kim but for some reason I am. She continues, answering Kate's question as she takes our orders and one of her employees takes to filling them. Angie owns this place, having bought it out a little while back in a move that surprised me, since she often told me (and still tells me) how much she hated working here and how she was going to pack it in, pack up and go to greener pastures. I listen to her now. "I'm doing about how you'd expect, Kate. I need some time off. Look at it rain. Day after day I look across this counter and out the windows and see nothing but that rain," she says, dour and depressed.

"Business seems to be doing alright though," Kate says encouragingly. Kim studiously looks at muffins in the glass display case at the counter. I stare off blankly at nothing in particular, watching Kate and Angie talk, still uneasy that the topic of Wendy might come up.

"Aggh, it's about average, Kate. The big crowds are forever gone though. My dad told me that in the seventies it was all crowds. You could make money hand over fist without even trying, no matter what you did. That's what my dad said. It's Trudeau's fault, you know, that this country's economy is still toilet bound. But that's the way it is. We missed out and there's not a damn thing we can do about it," she says, her words a familiar refrain to me. She always speaks as though in the throes of deep ill-humour, even though she's very easy to talk to. She puts too much stock in her dad's negativity it seems to me. She always mentions him. And Trudeau. "And those murders, they're not helping. Lots of people are staying away. Just what we needed, another damn Jack the Ripper running around, offing us girls. Just great," she says, the needle on her asperity metre rising.

We slide past the till and over to the end counter, where we will receive our orders. Angie moves over with us and continues to talk, letting another girl take orders.

She takes off her glasses and rubs her eyes, feels along her scalp and adjusts a safety pin, one of the many stuck about her oddly appealing, stylishly unkempt hair, which is auburn and spiky, not quite punkish but most certainly not innocuous.

"Angie, there he is!" the girl who is making our orders exclaims to Angie all of a sudden, hastening over to her and tugging at her apron with great emphasis.

"What? Where?" Angie says, her voice immediately rancorous, pushing her glasses up tight against the bridge of her nose, her eyes squinting into focus.

"There!" the girl exclaims, pointing. We all turn our heads to see who's being talked about and what's going on.

We see a stringy, whiskery guy in a dirty light brown coat and black toque scoop up a cup off one of the outside tables and slip it into his coat.

"There! He did it! Did you see?!" the girl who is pointing squeals, her voice threatening hysterics.

"I did!" Angie erupts, teeth gritted. She looks at Kate, at all of us. "He's not getting away with it, not ever. Not anymore! Angie Villandry wasn't born to take this kind of witlessness!" She grabs a sawed-off broom handle from behind the counter, holding it as though she's a saloon keeper who's just brought out a shotgun to restore peace, and tramps past us.

"What's this all about?" Kate asks the girl who has finished making our orders.

"It's the Coffee Cup Bandit. He steals all our cups. But we've only seen him do it three or four times, counting now. We've already had to buy I don't know how many to replace them. He's killing our overhead. Killing it!" she says breathlessly, trying to bring home to us what she feels is a very alarming fact.

"Does she know what she's doing? It could be dangerous," Kim says, full of deep concern, as we watch Angie disappear out the door, broom handle firmly entrenched in the grip of her hands.

"Maybe I should go out and make sure she doesn't get hurt," I say apprehensively.

Kate looks at me, full of dismay herself. She nods. "Yes," she agrees. "We must be good samaritans, we must. Otherwise what will happen to us?"

I look at her, her assertions seeming to me to reek of hyperbole while simultaneously inundating me with the ring of truth. I look at Kim, who's eating a muffin, her eyes nevertheless expressing concern. I look at Kate, still hesitant.

I turn and take a step, about to follow Angie out, my heart pounding, never ready for a confrontation. Kate grabs me by the wrist and pulls at me. I swing around and look into her eyes at close distance.

"You'd better hurry. I don't know if it's ever occurred to Angie that she's not that tough. She probably doesn't know what she's doing. But for God's sake, you be careful. Play it cool. And don't worry, we're coming right behind you," she says, touching my nose with her index finger. I feel brave now, the kind of forced bravery one is always able to come up with wanting to impress a woman and look good in front of her.

I rush out the door and scan the scene. I see Angie hurtling across the parking lot as fast as her little legs will carry her, broomstick raised and ready to rain down blows, her voice screaming threats and epithets, profanities and ultimatums. I run after her, dodging moving cars and weaving through those already parked. I see the Coffee Cup Bandit at the edge of the parking lot, making his way up a steep, littered incline, Angie close behind him. I run towards them. Angie falls. I see her trip while trying to hike up after him. The broomstick escapes her grip when she lurches forth onto her hands and knees. I catch up to her, my eyes on her the whole time. I grab her by the shoulder. She jerks free of my grasp.

"Let go!" she growls. Turning her head to face me head on, she sees that it's me. "Oh. Dean," she says, extending her arm, grateful for help now that she knows it's me. I pull her up onto her feet. She wipes at the grass and dirt that has stained the knees of her pants. "These darn little legs of mine," she bemoans. "I tripped," she says.

"I saw. Are you okay?"

"That bastard," she mutters. We look up at the top of the incline and see him, looking down on us, his body still, his lips smirking relief and victory at the same time. Angie turns about and looks for her broomstick. The thief disappears. "This isn't over, you dirty rotten wretch!" she calls out after him, shaking a fist in the air, her voice in a churning choleric seethe. She finds the broomstick after a brief search and picks it up. She hands it to me. "Can you get him?"

"What? I don't know. I mean—he's got a quite a headstart on me," I say, having thought the incident to be over.

"I can't have him pilfering my cups, I just can't," she says, looking utterly victimized, her little five foot frame seeming to gather all of its weight into her imploring eyes, forcing their gaze up at me.

I look at the broomstick and then back at her. "I'll give it a shot," I say, smacking one end of it into my hand. I begin to climb the incline. Soon I am on the edge of the busy avenue, looking across to where I suspect the bandit might have gone. I think I see him, far gone from us in his mind, and hence his slowed pace. I turn and look back and see Kate and Kim drinking their orders and getting the story from Angie. Kate looks in my direction and raises a hand of acknowledgment. I thought they were supposed to be right behind me. I wave back, wishing she would wave me back, hoping that Angie has changed her mind about wanting me to go after this guy. But it's not happening. I turn and see a break in the traffic; I run across the avenue, across another parking lot and into a greenbelted area, already weary with running, the endless wind of the day chilling me into a husk. I slow down, unable to keep my pace, and make my way towards the lacrosse courts.

Then I see him. Emerging from the dugout type area. He looks about. Sees me. I raise the broomstick and try to look threatening. I guess it works. He bolts. I run after him, quickly rested and re-energized, the chase picking up. His lanky legs cover ground fast. I try to keep pace. He turns towards the trees at the edge of the greenbelt. Uphill again. Thinking he'll lose me in ascension. Maybe thinking I'll peter out and tire. Like I can't handle the rough going. Like I'm not built for it. All these thoughts. I'll show him. I dig down inside me. Find that extra stamina. It burns through me. Up up up. I close the gap. I can see the flap of his oversized coat billowing behind him. I reach out and try to grab it. Try to pull him towards me. Nothing but air. He dodges around a willow bush. Weaving this way and that. Around birches and willows, poplars. Fear is in him. I'm getting frustrated though. So close but can't grab him, can't reach. So I throw the broomstick at him, like a spear. A vibrating thwack against the back of his head, a deft shot to the skull. The shock stumbles him. Tumbles him forward. His legs snag and twist. Down he goes. I lunge onto him. Just as my body collapses onto his I wonder, *What the hell?* What in the hell am I doing? Soon his arms are thrashing, trying to clock me with epileptic fists.

"You stole that cup!" I holler, trying to pin him down, wind whistling through the life-dissipating birches, dead wet leaves blowing down onto us.

"I don't know what you're talking about! My head! Whatch ya do to my head? Get the hell off me!" he screams and simultaneously ramrods me in the side of the head with a panic-stricken, bone-curled fist. I feel myself rock, my thoughts in absentia, my sense of pain taking over. Teetering back onto the earth with the wind coarsing through me, leaves in a swirling plaster about me, the slithering sound of him picking himself up, through the haze of my fogged up eyesight I see him, looking at me . . .—Then: gone. I have a headache. I am cold. It is cloudy. Low clouds, scudding past with haste, in a hurry to get away from this place . . .

"Dean. Oh my God, Dean! Dean, are you alright?" Kate's hands slide down onto my cheeks and I shake my head, shake the muss from my mind. I look up at her downward looking eyes and smile at her as I lift my head. She grabs my coat by the shoulders and pulls me up into a sitting position. She is squatting down beside me, looking at me, looking for assurances that I am alright. "Are you okay? Tell me you're okay."

"I'm okay."

"Tell me that you mean it."

"I mean it," I say, trying to rub away the burn that seems to be corroding away the side of my head.

"Good Lord, we saw it all. We hopped into the car and followed you here. We were just coming up to help you when he decked you."

"I'm okay," I say, nevertheless still feeling wobbly, wondering what exactly it is they would have done to help, even though I know it would have been something.

"I should never have let you do it," Kate says self-critically, full of anxiety about the whole situation. "He could have had a knife or something. He could have slashed you a wide one right in the gut. This was not something for you to be doing alone. That damn absinthe. I wasn't thinking straight," she says admonishing herself.

I shiver at the thought that I might have been stabbed, the whole scene taking on much more sinister permutations now that it is over with. "He said he didn't know what I was talking about. Maybe he didn't take the cup. Maybe it was the wrong guy," I say, my mouth pulsing away to all the thoughts that are cramming into it, eager for expression.

"No, it was him. He took it." Kim's voice, her words definite.

I try and get up. I still feel wobbly. Kate helps me up. Kim is holding the cup. It's broke into two pieces.

"Where was that?" I ask Kim.

"About twenty feet away or so. It must have gotten broken when you jumped him. He must have chucked it. That was quite a performance, Dean."

"Were you impressed?"

"I wasn't unimpressed," she says. "I was cheering for you." I feel myself smile, feeling not too bad anymore.

"Feeling better?" Kate says, putting an arm around me and then turning into me for a hug. "I was so worried. This whole thing was insane. What were we thinking?"

"What was *Angie* thinking?" Kim says. "She should have known better than to scoot out after that guy. It was just a cup."

"It cuts into her overhead," I say amusedly, reiterating what the girl told us at the coffee shop. I feel wired and tired at the same time, in a complete dither, excited and perturbed by what has transpired. Kate is holding my hand. She hasn't stopped touching me since she got to me.

Kim picks up the broomstick. "I know I shouldn't have, but I laughed when you hit him with the stick, Dean. It looked funny. It didn't seem real. I guess that's why I laughed," Kim says, almost apologetically it seems to me.

"I wasn't even thinking about anything once I was close to catching him. It just all happened."

"Angie should never have taken off after him. She should have called the police or the security. That place has security guards walking back and forth all day long," Kim says, in evaluation of the situation, not wanting to let Angie off the hook.

"I guess she was just fed up," I say, for some reason not wanting to lay the blame on her doorstep. We walk down the hill towards the car, Kate and Kim beside me. "She has an unfortunately inflated opinion of her ability to handle things," I continue on, still fidgety, ready to expend some of my energy with conversation.

"What do you mean?" Kate asks as we reach the car. "Get in the passenger side. I'll drive," she says, climbing into the driver's side. Kim slides into the back seat and I get into the front. Kate starts up the car. "Do you want to change your clothes before we go to Wendy's mom's for dinner?"

I look at my clothes. They are wet in places but don't seem dirty. Besides, they are dark and the wetness isn't all too noticeable. "No, I'm okay. We're probably already late as it is," I say.

"Are we going to return Angie's broomstick?" Kim asks.

"I suppose," Kate says and I can tell she's impatient to get on with this dinner now, to put all this mess behind us. She sips on her second latte, the first one long gone already. I remove mine from the tray crammed up on the dashboard and begin to sip on it. It is still fairly hot, which makes me think of how brief that whole flurry of activity really was—and yet it will live on in my mind forever.

"What were you saying about Angie, Dean?" Kim asks, taking a drink of her vanilla bean latte.

"Oh," I say, still worked up over the chase and thus, still ready to talk. "Angie once beat up Wendy," I say, tossing the sentence out matter-of-factly. It might as well come out now, for it will sometime along the way anyway.

"What?!" Kate says, completely blindsided by this fact, the front wheels of the car screeching as we jerk into a minor swerve. "I didn't know that. How come you never mentioned it before?" she says, the tone of her voice telling me that she is very bothered by the fact that I haven't.

"I don't know. Because we never had much to do with Wendy, I guess. In fact, we never had *anything* to do with Wendy, until a couple days ago," I say, trying to explain the reasons for my tight-lipped attitude on the subject. "It never seemed important."

"Of course it's not important. But that doesn't mean it wouldn't have been interesting. My goodness, the wealth of secretive knowledge you sit on is remarkable."

"Yes, so tell us, Dean. Tell us the story," Kim chirps. I look at her, feeling that her words and vocal inflections are somehow being used to my detriment, to get me into trouble, but of course there is no way I can prove it. I shoot her a sly glance though, to let her know that I am onto her. She smiles back coyly.

Kate is worked up. "I could have gotten on Angie's bad side if I let it slip that we were going to dine with Wendy tonight, do you know that?" she says, her voice castigating me.

"I was very tense about just such a thing maybe happening."

"*Very tense!*" Kate repeats disgustedly. "I spit on your tensity. Come now, out with the tale," she says impatiently, ready to forgive me so long as I keep talking.

"Yes, tell us the story, Dean," Kim says, her inflections unwavering. I wonder if she is still a little drunk.

"Well, Angie used to live with the guy who co-hosted the movie show on ArtVision with Wendy. He was there way before Wendy ever came on board but, anyway, I guess he and Wendy hit it off right away and slept together."

"Yes, I remember that guy. What was his name? Daniel something. I never liked him," Kim says, shaking her head judgmentally. "His opinions about movies were much too effusive. He went on long after you got the point."

"I saw him around once in awhile. The first year I was in the beauty pageant it was held in the building where they taped that show. He was always clinging about the girls. A real leech. Anyway, go on," Kate says.

I take a sip of my latte and look around. We are already parked outside the coffee shop. Kate is leaning towards me attentively, wanting to fully absorb everything I have to say. And Kim is leaning forward, her chin on the shoulder of the seat in front of her, close to me.

"Well, Wendy told me that he never mentioned he was living with Angie. She said she never would have, to use her words, 'fucked him silly', if she'd known he was involved with another girl. Anyway, she said she had a good time with him and wanted to see him but didn't know where he lived so she got his address from the station, but of course the address was Angie's place, and when she went there she got ambushed by Angie. That's what Wendy says. Or at least said. We stopped talking soon after, right up until we went there the other night."

"We'll get to that mystery later. Ambushed, she said? How?"

"Angie pummeled her with a stick."

"This stick?" Kim asks musingly, holding it before us all. We all gaze at it.

"I don't know. It wouldn't surprise me though," I say. "Angie said she thought Wendy was a burglar. This is what Angie told me. And she said she beat her up good. Knocked her cold and that it felt even better once she found out that Wendy was being, as she put it, 'cock strafed' by Daniel. But Wendy thinks differently. Wendy told me Angie knew all about the liason and cold-bloodedly assaulted her out of jealousy. It gets tangled after that. It's all opinion and emotion," I say, wearing down, my energy levelling out. "Anyway, I think that's why Angie thinks she's tough sometimes. She's living on the memory of walloping Wendy."

"Wow." Kate punches me in the shoulder, hard.

"Ow! That hurt."

"Serves you right. A heck of a thing it was to keep that story from me."

"You know my stand on gossip," I say, trying in vain to once more offer up a valid reason as to why I never mentioned any of this before.

"And you know ours," Kate says. "We don't take kindly to being out of the loop. Any old loop."

"Yes, any old loop," Kim reiterates. "Angie and Wendy. It seems like such a mismatch. I'll bet Angie *did* ambush her. Though with this thing it would certainly be easier to win a fight." Kim holds up the broomstick again and examines it. "Should I return it to her?"

"If you don't mind," I say, not in the mood to hash out the whole scene of my fight with the bandit to Angie.

"What'll I tell her if she asks what happened?"

"Just tell her I got in one good one with the broomstick but that he managed to escape."

"But that we'll get him next time," Kate assures.

"Yes," I say, about to repeat what Kate has said before realizing what it is she has said. I look at her, utterly perplexed, as Kim gets out of the car to return the broomstick to Angie. "What do you mean we'll get him next time?"

"I want my revenge. Nobody hurts you," she says protectively.

"You're biting off everything you can chew lately. And, in case you don't know, it's way too much," I say.

"Is that a reprimand?" she says, leaning over and opening the glove compartment. She takes out a sugar cube and pops it into her mouth. She begins to chew it loudly, appealingly crass.

"I don't know," I say. "I don't know anything when it comes to the subject of you."

"You're one to talk."

"Is that a jibe?"

"I'm not telling," she says in a child's voice, shutting her lips tight in the proverbial clam up, looking girlish and good-natured.

Kim comes back.

"Well? What did Angie say?" I ask, suddenly curious to hear how my exploits have been received.

"She told me to thank you for your effort. And that your next latte is free."

"Hey, that's alright, isn't it?" I say, pleased with myself for earning both Angie's thanks and a free latte.

"And she also said that the siren to war has been sounded."

"She said that?" Kate asks disbelievingly.

"That's what she said. She said it gravely too. Her face looked like granite. It was very peculiar."

"Well then, at least we know we have another ally in this fight."

"What fight?" I ask, as Kate starts up the car and begins to drive.

"You'll have to direct me to where Tuppy lives," Kate says, her thoughts off on new tangents.

"Yeah. What fight?" I repeat.

"Why, the good fight, of course."

Chapter 9

I direct Kate to Tuppy's. "We're almost there now. There, up ahead. That townhouse," I say, pointing.

"Okay, I see it," Kate says, beginning to slow the car down to a crawl. "Which driveway?"

"She lives in the middle house," I say.

Kate slows even more. Suddenly a car springs back, out of Tuppy's driveway and onto the road, in a backward turning lurch, the shocks bouncing it jaggedly as the brakes are stomped on. "That's Wanda! And her driving's as psychotic as she is," Kate exclaims, her foot hitting the gas pedal just as Wanda takes off in a wheel squealing spinout. She's driving an odd, foreign looking car, one that doesn't look like it would go too fast, a fact that Kate leaps all over. "We can catch her. We can get that toaster back," she says excitedly, turning single-minded, ready for the hunt.

"No, not now," I say, everything starting to unfold the way I expected it to, not expecting this exactly, but knowing that something along these lines was destined to take place. "We're already late. We'll get her later," I say, trying to appeal to her common sense. "The last thing we need now is a high speed chase. I've had enough excitement for one day."

Kate looks at me levelly. "I suppose you're right. Besides, I am getting hungry. How about you Kim?" she asks, letting Wanda get away and circling around the block for a return visit to the townhouse.

"I am a little famished," Kim says, applying an oxymoron to the conversation. "I feel a little out of place though," she says, a look of worriment about her, her light absinthe and whiskey-fueled mood in decline. "I don't know any of these people."

"They're alright," Kate says, pulling into the driveway, behind a rugged looking red Jeep.

"How do you know? You never met Tuppy," I say.

"I know Wendy. And she has a very ingratiating way about her. Besides, they invited us over for dinner, didn't they? That's always a good indicator of civilized folk."

I breathe deeply, mildly worried, but not to the degree I thought I'd be. It must be because Wanda's been removed from the equation. I'm groundlessly certain she won't be back tonight.

"What are they like?" Kim asks, trying to get all the information she can, like a student cramming at the last minute for the big test, trying to get as much as she can into her head so she won't be caught off guard.

"Wendy's easy to talk to. You don't even have to talk. She does enough for everyone," Kate says, an accurate opinion of Wendy, one that just about everyone must have after meeting her. "And Tuppy's supposed to be, well, I don't really know. What's she like, Dean?"

I open the car door and get out and then wait for Kim. She hands me the cantaloupe, the little bottle of Wiser's in her hand. She gets out and takes back the cantaloupe from me, cradling it against her stomach. "Tuppy's unpredictable," I say to her as I shut the car door, the only euphemism I can think of.

"It sounds all too mysterious," Kim says. "Makes me wish I had bought some tangerines," she adds ambiguously.

"Do we need to bring the muscatel in?" Kate asks.

"No, save it," I say, suddenly becoming selfish over it. Kate must have too, otherwise she wouldn't have asked if we should bring it in. She would have just grabbed it. "And, oh yeah, she might be nude," I say to Kim.

"What? Goodness. Are you serious?" She looks at me. "I mean, I guess you are but, well, how does one brace for that?"

"It's not easy," I say vaguely, perhaps suggesting to Kim horrifying memories on my part, not saying anything else, not knowing myself what's in store for us.

We walk up the steps and Kate rings the doorbell. We can hear the muffled voice of Neil Young from out here. He is singing "Helpless." "Their taste in music seems just fine, anyway," Kate says encouragingly.

There are plants on the stoop, all of them with withered leaves. "We have to get more plants," Kim says of herself and Sam. "We really do need more houseplants." She sounds emphatic on the subject.

"Us too," Kate agrees and rings the doorbell again. I wish someone would answer. I'm starting to feel cold.

After a brief wait we hear someone call out, "Come in, if you please." A man's voice, deep and booming, but oddly disarming.

Kate and Kim look at me for answers. I have none. I shrug. "I don't know who it is," I say, when they continue to look at me following my shrug. I open the door and the heat from within surrounds us invitingly. We step inside and shut the door behind us. I slip out of my shoes hastily, ready to get on with this, my shoe removal a definite sign to myself that I can no longer back out of this.

A big man comes over to greet us, about six foot five. He is wearing a yachting cap, a big, heavy, grey woolen sweater and sporting a full, greying beard. He looks like Mitch Miller. His face is made up of coarsened skin but his eyes are lively and friendly. I have never seen him before. He comes over and shakes my hand. "Hello, young sir. You must be the Mr. Dean Dorian who Wendy said was graciously coming over to partake of our company and what we hope is a satisfactory offering of victuals."

"Yes," I say, our hands still shaking vigorously. He pats me on the back with his left hand and then grips my shoulder and shakes me, as if to see what sort of mettle I am made of. He then removes me from his clutches and turns his attention to Kate.

"And you, you are Kate Carlo. I have of course heard of you via your much esteemed reputation but I would have recognized you in a crowd regardless, merely from your dignified manner." He extends his hand to her.

"I like the way you talk," Kate says approvingly, looking up at him to meet his gaze, taken by his manner and no doubt also because he is treating her like the beauty queen she once officially was, and (to my way of thinking) unofficially still is. He extends his hand to her in a remarkable change from the boisterousness with which he greeted me. With Kate he shakes her hand gently, almost diffidently.

He is also the same way with Kim, taking the cantaloupe from her so as to gently shake her hand. "And you, how nice of you to grace our humble abode. You of course are a friend of Miss Carlo's. I can tell right away by your pleasant demeanour and great fashion sense. I admire your shoes."

"My shoes? Oh," Kim says, looking down at her feet, one shoe on and the other removed. She slips out of the other one. "They are comfortable, I'll say that much. My name is Kim," she says, looking up at him to greet him eye to eye.

"Ahh Kim," he sighs peacefully, seemingly delighted by the name.

"And what's your name?" Kate asks.

"My name? Ahh yes, how rude of me to fail to introduce myself. I am Jim Chimney. Won't you all come in and sit down?" he says, stepping aside to let us pass.

Kim hands him the little mickey of Wiser's. "We brought this and the cantaloupe. We thought it might be nice to eat some melon slices with dinner."

"How wonderfully thoughtful of you. Your generosity is matched only by your good taste. These will enhance what is sure to be an already sumptuous feast. The Dame Tuppy has outdone herself tonight once again, if I do say so myself. Tuppy, our guests have arrived. Come and say hello!" he calls out resoundingly, even though the kitchen is close and visible to us from where we stand. This is a small housing complex. I wonder how we are all going to fit into the kitchen to eat, it is that small. It occurs to me that I wondered this the last time I was here for dinner too.

Tuppy comes out, her hair dyed shock orange, looking even tinier than I remember, wiping her hands on the full length apron wrapped about her. She's wearing clothes anyway; that's always a good sign. A sense of momentary normalcy begins to descend upon me, even though I am slightly fearful about seeing Tuppy again. After all, the split between Wanda and myself was a sordid debacle full of great animosity. I can only wonder what kind of exaggerations and lies she has told Tuppy in regards to myself. Jim Chimney steps forth as though to greet her and then drops a heavy oaken arm around her severely gaunt frame and pulls her close to him. They are indeed an odd-looking couple, his massive physique threatening to absorb her, save for her crackling, penetrating green eyes. I can feel them on me.

"Hello, Dean," she says, her voice unnervingly dispassionate. I can sense the clicking of her thoughts behind those examining eyes, eyes that take me in with a deeply perceptible severity. She then turns them on Kate. Where's Wendy? I wonder. She's supposed to be the buffer for us. But then, as though psychically sensing my rising worriment, Wendy appears from around the corner, coming out of the bathroom.

"Hello peoples," she says cheerily. "I see you have met the Commander," she says, indicating Jim Chimney.

"Yes," I say, though my eyes are on Tuppy. I haven't seen her in almost two years. "Hello, Tuppy. So, how have you been?"

"Wanda left when she found out you were coming," Tuppy says to me reproachfully and then turns to Wendy with darkening eyes, as if to suggest that we are in some way in cahoots together.

"Ahh, let it go, old woman," Wendy says dismissively. "Wanda's nothing but an old warty stick up the ass anyway."

"I see." Tuppy turns to me. "Is that how you feel too, Dean? Is that how it was?" she says critically, alluding to my marriage.

I find myself hanging my head, trying to look repentant. "We just sorta drifted apart," I say obscurely. I lift my head to see how my comments are received. Tuppy looks unimpressed and gives the same look to Kate. But Kate seems unfazed. Kim, on the other hand, looks about ready to squirm. "This is Kate. And this is Kim," I say, introducing them, getting it out of the way.

"So you're Kate Carlo. The apple of Dean's wandering eye. Is he faithful to you at least?"

Kate looks at me, unable to comprehend the question, but I fail to grasp the meaning of it either and feel adrift because of it.

"Tups, please, this is supposed to be a sociable get together, not some volatile confrontation. Holster your guns, if you will," Jim Chimney says calmly, the voice of reason. I see him remove a pipe from his trousers, a lighter appearing from within his sweater cuff, as though magically. He begins to apply a flame to the bowl of the pipe. I can hear him sucking on the stem, his breath bellowing the contents of the bowl into smoke, the aromatic incense of pipe tobacco filling the air. I look at Kate, who is breathing it in deeply, almost hypnotically.

"Dean has never given me a single moment to doubt him," she then says, defending me, quickly over her tobacco want.

Tuppy nods rigidly, acceptant of Kate's statement, if not quite believing it. She completely ignores Kim, who is not immune to such snubs and looks momentarily forlorn. In an attempt at compensation I reach around behind Kate (who is standing between us) and tug at Kim's arm. We step back so as to have a full view of each other. I begin to talk to her.

"There's something I want to ask you," I say. "How come the vanity plate on your car says 'Basil'?"

"It's really quite simple. I am an enormous fan of *Fawlty Towers*."

"Ahh," I say, and that brings to an end all I can think of saying to keep our conversation going.

"Supper will be ready in a bit," Tuppy says, her mood turning into one of diluted soured acceptance.

"Here she is, your lady," Wendy says to Jim Chimney. Wendy is sitting on the couch and watching tv. Joni Mitchell is on and is singing "Coyote."

"Miss Joni, yes," Jim Chimney says serenely, oddly capable of fading into the background considering his size, leaning against the mantel of the flaming gas fireplace, the smoking bowl of his pipe cradled philosophically between his index finger and thumb, the stem pointing at the tv.

I sit down beside Wendy, who slaps me hard on the knee. "So, Dean, how the hell are you?!"

"I'm fine," I say exhaustedly, my conversational powers having escaped me. Kate sits down on the love seat and Kim sits down beside her. They watch tv, intrigued by what has transpired thus far, but playing it cool until they get a better grasp of the situation.

"Good. Glad to hear it. You should've seen the tantrum that pinchcunt of a sister of mine threw when she found out that I invited you all over here for some good times and happy chatting. It was a real blast."

"Miss Wanda can be a tad emotional," Jim Chimney says euphemistically, plumes of smoke billowing from his pipe.

"Yes," I say.

"Look. Neil Diamond," Wendy says excitedly, pointing at the tv. "This is *The Last Waltz*. The greatest concert film of all time. Another feather in the already fully plumaged cap of Mr. Martin Scorsese. I put this film on every time I have—or am invited to—a dinner. What a mood it puts one in. Listen to Neil sing, Dean. Just listen. Are you listening?"

"I'm listening!"

"Good. And good gad! Where are our manners? Would any of you like a cocktail?"

"Yes!" all three of us say in unexpected but authoritative unison.

"Well, Commander, what do you say? Would you mind doing the honours?" Wendy says, looking at Jim Chimney

"Not at all, not at all," he says, sucking blissfully on his pipe. "What can I get you all?" he asks, standing before us, his shadow looming but completely unthreatening.

"Some Wiser's in a glass for me," Kim says, easy to please.

"What are you drinking?" Kate asks Wendy, looking at the glass on the coffee table that she has taken a sip or two from.

"A rusty nail."

"It's Sunday, isn't it?" Kate says, thinking about work tomorrow and whether or not it's a good idea to imbibe in such potentially lethal drinkery. "Aw heck, I'll have one of the same, Jim Chimney," she says, surrendering to her desires.

"Sounds good to me too," I say.

"Three rusty nails it is," he says, Kim about to raise a finger in the air to protest but, when realizing that a reiteration of her drink order would simply fall on as deaf a pair of ears as her original request, she refrains. I look at her and shrug. She shrugs back in a manner that denotes it's no big deal to her. She just wants a drink. We all need to loosen our moods in this place.

Soon Jim Chimney emerges from the kitchen, his rough mammoth hands creatively managing the oversized tumblers gleaming with booze and keeping them from cascading to the floor. He sets them down on the coffee table and we all simultaneously grab at the tumblers. We each take a sip and I can sense the collective sigh of relief that the alcohol has given us. We are watching tv intently, waiting for the booze to kick in and restore our voices.

Tuppy comes out. Clothed still. Kim looks at me, thinking the same thing, and I half—laugh, trying to gulp it down and contain it but unable to. I find myself coughing. Wendy pelts my back with slaps as I sit hunched over, trying to regain control of my pipes.

"Are you alright, Dino?" she asks concernedly.

"Fine," I say chokingly, sitting back up. I look at Tuppy, who is standing beside Jim Chimney and drinking a glass of red wine. One hand holds the glass and the other is holding the bottle. Every time she takes a sip or two she pours more into her glass, continually topping it off. I feel I should talk to her, to at least try and igratiate myself into her good books before supper is served. I get up and take a slow casual stroll about, looking at the books on the shelves, the pictures on the wall. "The old place still looks the same," I say, trying to appeal to her nostalgic virtues, to the brief but essentially amicable relationship that existed between us those few times I came here.

Kate senses my attempt at appeasement, gets up and comes over to where I am, looking at some pictures on the wall. Kim sits where she is, a slight wash of uneasiness still vibrating through her. She introduces herself to Wendy and Kate and I are instantly full of apologies for failing with the formal introductions between them. Wendy immediately begins to talk about her show, asking if Kim has seen it (she has once or twice) and asking for feedback, even though she doesn't stop talking long enough to receive any.

Kate clasps my hand, putting our solidarity on display. I glance at Tuppy and see her upper lip contort into a sinister curl. There is a little ring stuck through her upper lip that I hadn't noticed when we came in. I never knew her to be into piercing but, then again, I didn't ever really know her at all. The ring glistens in the golden light of the room and accentuates her sneer.

"I like this picture," Kate says, inspecting the painting on the wall.

"Yes yes, it's one of the Dame Tuppy's," Jim Chimney says proudly, pointing to it with his pipe stem.

"I didn't know you painted," I say.

"Yes, well, I'm not surprised," Tuppy says, as though wounded by this fact. It is a picture of a horse scuffing its right hoof into the dirt, a little cloud of dust arising into the air as a result. A man stands on the left edge of the frame, looking at the horse, his head tilted slightly upwards, as though in the midst of a favourable nod. The colours are faded, purposefully it would seem, as though to suggest a transitory nature, or of a time long since passed.

"Tell the children the story of the painting," Jim Chimney affably says, his pipe stem pointing at us now.

Tuppy comes over and looks at the picture. She looks at us. I almost expect her to spit on me. She pours some wine into her glass. I look at Kim, who is being bombarded by Wendy's tales of work stresses. Kate's clasp around my hand tightens, our fingers interlacing, as though to notify me that everything will remain fine.

"This painting is entitled "Clever Hans." Clever Hans was one of the Elberfeld horses and this is my vision of him."

"I see," Kate says.

"Elberfeld is in Germany," Tuppy continues. "Clever Hans was of course owned by von Osten, who trained him. Clever Hans was trained to tap his feet every time von Osten nodded his head. Later horses were trained by Krall. They were believed capable of coming up with the answers to long-winded arithmetical problems but that, of course, is a fallacy."

"Of course," Kate says in agreement, looking as though she's deeply informed on the subject. She turns to Tuppy. "But what is it about the Elberfeld horses that made you so taken with them that you had to paint one of them?"

Tuppy has an answer for her immediately, even though she seems surprised by the question. "The myth that we are willing to believe animals, such as horses, to be capable of much more than they actually are."

"We overestimate them."

"Yes. But I like our naive willingness to perpetuate such beliefs nonetheless."

"By extension, do we believe humans capable of being much more than they actually are?" Kate is in an inquisitive mood, and has always felt that any question asked can shed light onto a person. And she wants to know all about Tuppy. It's a way for her to bore into my past.

"No. I think we *under*estimate ourselves. We—us, humans—are capable of anything." Tuppy's words have a diabolical ring to me. I think of the murders and expect Kate must be thinking of them too. But she doesn't bring up the topic, even though she has the perfect opening to. Instead, she merely takes a sip of her drink, digesting all that Tuppy has said.

"There is also something sad and unsettling about a horse. Their eyes always suggest isolation and fear. It is easy to relate to a horse," Tuppy glumly adds.

I feel bummed out and take a sip of my drink. I go and sit back down. Wendy is still going on. Tuppy seems to have changed. She is full of despair. I look straight ahead at the front window, at the thick rivulets of rain running down it. It is pouring again. Kate sits back down beside Kim. Jim Chimney and Tuppy remain standing by the fireplace, soaking up the heat being sent out by the gaseous flames.

"So, how did you two meet?" I ask, looking at Jim Chimney.

"Groan," Wendy says, after quickly flaming up a cigarette. "Groan groan groan. My gad, Dean, is that the best you have to offer us in the way of conversation? And me telling Jim Chimney that you were a conversational lion, wildly interesting and full of rock salt."

I feel strained and tight, on my heels. "Sorry," I say, my apology dripping with a solemnity that Wendy's own lighthearted jibes are completely devoid of.

"Now now, Miss Wendy. Don't be hard on the lad," Jim Chimney says and takes a long meditative puff on his pipe.

"I must attend to the elk steaks," Tuppy says and leaves the room.

"Elk steaks?" Kim says, looking disoriented and anxious. "Did she say elk steaks?"

"Yes," Wendy says, watching the conical stream of smoke she exhales from her mouth as though it's the most beautiful thing she has ever seen. "I know a hunter by the name of Silas McPhee. He lives in the deep woods near the Headless Valley, that place where they found all those decapitated bodies, back in the day. He shot an elk a few weeks back and on one of his rare excursions up this way he dropped by and laid a sack of meat on my table and said I was welcome to it. So I took it. I'm not one to refuse meat." Wendy laughs aloud at her double entendre. "So if you're worrying that the steaks might be freezer burnt, don't. They're fresh."

"Oh, okay," Kim says hesitantly.

"The story of how I met the Dame Tuppy is an interesting one," Jim Chimney says, from out of the blue. I turn my attention to him, surprised.

"No, it's not," Wendy retorts. "Not interesting at all. Here, I'll tell it. You drag it out in such a way that one forgets what the hell it is you started to talk about by the time you're finished telling it."

"Now now." Jim Chimney looks down at me in confidence. "Miss Wendy has a way of exaggerating. She hasn't yet learned the art of relaxed conversation."

"I have a talk show, that's why. And I have no time for shilly-shallying on it. It has to flow. Flow, I say." Wendy turns to Kim. "Tuppy used to live at a nudist commune in the coastal range this side of the Indian Nation. This was the late sixties. Need I say more? Jim Chimney was a forest ranger and he met her one day when she was picking berries. She was naked as a jaybird, as I'm sure you will see for yourself before the night is up—"

"Goodness!" Kim interjects, deeply worried about Wendy's hint of foreshadowing.

"Yes, and they started talking about . . . What in the hell was it you two started blabbing about? I can never remember this boring part of the saga," Wendy says, looking to Jim Chimney for clarification.

"Welllllllllll . . ." Jim Chimney says, the word he utters one distended note of reflection as he looks at us serenely and scratches his beard. "I had lost my hat . . ."

"Oh yes, of course. That damn hat. He had been booting it through the backwoods in his Jeep—"

"That very Jeep sitting out in the driveway," Jim Chimney interjects, proud of his Jeep.

"That damn Jeep," Wendy says, an entirely different thought seeming to momentarily corral her. "Anyway, his hat blew off and landed in a huckleberry patch by the side of the road. And then Tuppy picked it up when she and some of her nude-nik cronies came there to pick berries."

"And I was at the Ranger Station when I realized that I had misplaced my chapeau," Jim Chimney says, taking over from Wendy, who looks irritable because of it. "So of course I had to retrace my steps, so to speak, in the hopes that I would find it, because I didn't want the cost of a replacement hat to come out of my pay, which it surely would have, and, as well, it doesn't become an officer of the woods to look shabby, which I of course did without my headgear. So I got back in the Jeep, the very Jeep that is sitting out in the driveway, and I began to drive the trails. And it was a half hour later that I first laid eyes on the exquisite vision that we all know as the Dame Tuppy. She was crouched over, picking berries, and she was wearing a hat, a pink scarf around her chin and up around the hat and knotted on top. She looked divine."

Tuppy tromps in. "Dinner is served."

We stand up and begin to file in. I look behind me and see Kate, the last one to enter the kitchen. She has been quiet, listening. She arches her eyebrows at me playfully when our eyes meet. As I enter the kitchen all I can think is that what happened in the living room has in no way prepared us for what will happen in here.

Chapter 10

On each side of the table there is about a foot between it and the counters and cupboards along the walls. Not much room at all. A real cramped area conducive to great familial volatility. Just like old times.

"Where would you like us to sit?" I ask.

"Any old place. What do I care?" Tuppy says, not even bothering to look at me.

"I'll take the far end," Wendy says. She squeezes between the backs of the chairs, on tiptoe, her rump sliding along the countertop edge, drink glass in hand, her breasts casting shadows onto the plates on the table. She makes it to her chair, plunks down in a state of fatigue and lights up a cigarette. I go next, moving into the seat next to Wendy and Kim takes the other side, so as to sit across from me and Kate follows behind Kim. Kim is protected on all sides from Tuppy and Jim Chimney, who takes a seat beside me. Tuppy gets the end, sits down and glowers at Wendy, who glowers back.

"So you can imagine that I was in deep wonderment, Dean. Could that hat on the head of this angelic creature be mine, the one I had lost?"

"What?" I ask, looking at Jim Chimney, mystified.

"The story," Kate says, looking at me and nodding, trying to pry my mind into a clearer state with her active stare. "Jim Chimney is telling you about how he met Tuppy."

"Oh, oh. Right. I'm sorry," I say, turning to meet his gaze, ready to listen.

"Why do you insist on reliving all those dusty old times?" Tuppy says scornfully to Jim Chimney.

"Now now Tups, the children have a genuine interest in how our paths came to intertwine."

"Bah. I never would have taken the hat if I'd known it was yours. You tried to hoodwink me."

"How'd he do that?" Kate asks, having, to my mind, gauged the social situation for what it is and now ready to insert herself into it more fully.

"Never you mind, little miss. Eat now. I didn't waste another day of my life just to see this slop go cold before anyone eats it."

I reach out for the plate of elk steaks and take one. I pass them around. Wendy takes one and passes the plate on to Kim, who also takes one, looking at the steak as though it is full of great unforseeable intrigue, perhaps even danger. I watch Wendy cutting her steak, working her knife while cradling a cigarette in the same hand, the smoke corkscrewing my way. I cut off a piece of my steak and take a bite.

"How is it?" Tuppy says, her voice completely changed, now one of eagerness and worried expectation as to how her food will be received.

"It's good," I say, smoke stabbing into my eye and causing me to blink rapidly.

"You're just saying that," she says, dismissing me with an irked wave of her hand.

I shrug and eat more steak. The fact that I keep eating it seems to convince Tuppy that I took a bite of it out of more than mere politeness.

"It's a bland meat," she says to me, suddenly relaxed to my presence. "There's something about its texture, a certain density, almost waxiness, that makes it resistant to spice. You really have to work with it," she says, imparting to me a little of her culinary wisdom.

"Well, it doesn't taste bland to me," I say, my way of complimenting her, even though it is kind of bland at that.

"Nice," she says and begins to cut up her own steak.

All talk momentarily ceases as we fill up our plates. Tuppy has made pasta turtle shells, and she has stuffed the shells with mozarella and ricotta cheese, spinach, egg whites and shredded carrots. The shells are coated in tomato sauce and Parmesan cheese. She has also made a Waldorf salad and garden herb Focaccia bread, which tastes of onion, garlic and oregano and seems to have found a fan in Kim, who looks delighted to be eating it. There is also a plate with sliced tomatoes, olives, pickles and, of course, cantaloupe. We find ourselves eating a bit of everything, though I refrain from the cantaloupe, hoping to annoy Kim, though she seems oblivious to my melon prejudices at the moment.

Kate breaks the silence. "We think we're on the verge of breaking the case wide open," she says to Wendy. "We have a major clue."

"Case? What case?" Tuppy interrupts nosily, as though she has a right to know.

Kate cuts up a turtle shell and deposits a generous portion of it into her mouth. I watch her eat. I watch her chew. I watch her swallow. "The murder case. Those four murders that have us all on edge," she finally says to Tuppy.

"Murders? Oh, those. You want my opinion? He has an overactive endocrine gland and a penchant for porno, you can take that to the bank. You have too many hormones and access to the almighty beaver shot and sure as shootin' you'll run amuck, that's the way it's always been. But of course they'll blame the mother. Always do, believe you me. When they catch him he'll have a knife in one hand, a strangling cord in the other, a bulbed out cock—and it'll still be the mother's fault. Load of rubbish. Absolute rubbish," Tuppy says, in a rising lather of coarse ill will.

"Oh, cork it," Wendy says. "You're not the one on trial."

"Not yet," Tuppy says, standing up and stabbing a fork through the air, in Wendy's direction. There is a piece of elk meat jammed in the tines, dripping butter onto the flower-patterned table cloth. She sits back down, in a barely controlled seethe. "But I expect to be anytime though. That damn whiny show of yours, it's only a matter of time before you decide to take the low road and play the blame game with me. A matter of time."

"A matter of time indeed," Jim Chimney says, his comments seeming to support Tuppy, though his contemplative demeanour suggests him to be on another level of thought altogether. Which turns out to be the case, for he says, "So I went up to this vessel of pure womanhood and inquired as to where she came across the hat she happened to be wearing—"

"Would you for once in your life cease with that damn paranoia of yours," Wendy says, her irate words stopping Jim Chimney in mid-sentence.

"Paranoia?! How dare you—"

"Tut! Quiet. I'm in no mood for you. Kate has something to say. What clue have you found, Kate?"

Kate allows time for Tuppy to speak, but she doesn't. So Kate begins. "We have come to believe that the glasses found on those dead girls were safety glasses from a dentist's office."

"Glasses, yes. I was wearing glasses when I first encountered the Dame Tuppy. I had to remove them and wipe the lenses on my shirt before restoring them to my eyes. I was sure I had been deceived, that I had not seen the beauty before me, that it was a mere apparition—"

"A pox on you and the low down way you talk to your mother. Paranoid?! Not bloody likely, you insolent pup!" Tuppy explodes in a paroxysm of fury.

"Go on Kate. Just ignore her. Ignore the ranting cunt!"

"You think you're so damn big with that show of yours. You use it as a threat, that's what you do. Always, always with the inferences that you're going use our past as therapy for the entertainment of your google-eyed audience—"

"And to back up our assertion is the fact that the last girl was missing two of her teeth," Kate interjects, deciding to be more aggressive in her conversing.

"Yes yes, the missing teeth. Of course!" Wendy quickly agrees.

Kim eats more bread. I sip on my drink, wanting to gulp it but it's almost gone and I feel I need to ration it as I'm not sure when I'll be offered another. I'm on complete edge. I decide to venture into a topic less hot button. "So, Kim, they showed that *Degrassi High* movie again the other night. Did you see it?" I ask, us two being the only two outcloseted fans of the show I know.

"It's so lamentable. The way they're all swearing, and then Joey has to go and lose audience identification with us," Kim says disconsolately, taking solace by nibbling on a piece of cantaloupe.

"Identification, yes. The Dame Tuppy asked to see mine and I showed it to her. Content that I was the forest ranger I said I was, she removed the scarf, untying it with great delicacy. And then she handed the hat back to me with her uniquely apposite grace. And that's when I determined to fuck her."

"You what? Good Lord!" I say, Jim Chimney's vapid discursiveness turning upsettingly blunt but also garnering immediate interest on my part.

"Goodness," Kim says, reaching for more cantaloupe to temper her startled state.

"Shut yer yap, old man. Why do you have to spill your guts about everything? I suppose you're also going to tell them about how you were foiled, about how it was my fertile time and I didn't want to risk a knock-up."

"It was indeed a sad time to learn of such devastating knowledge," Jim Chimney says, his pipe appearing from out of nowhere, along with a pouch of tobacco. He begins filling the pipe, after reaching back and knocking the burnt contents of it out into the sink behind him.

"And so I was thinking, because you happened to mention that you are good friends with Fluff Chang and that since the first girl who was murdered was an acquaintance of Fluff's, well, I thought that maybe you could perhaps find out who that murdered girl's dentist was from Fluff. I'll bet you the house that whoever he is is also the dentist of those other three murdered girls," Kate says.

"What do you mean that Joey lost audience identification? In what way?" I ask Kim.

"Well, he was always the coolest one on that show."

"Because of his hat, right?"

"That's one reason."

"I like where you're going with this. You've got a beaded sight on this case, no doubt about it. I'm sure Fluff will know. She knows everything that goes on at The Lily Pad, they all do. Nudity makes you more candid about your life, it really does. They tell each other everything down at that place," Wendy says.

"Candid, yes. And that is why I felt I could speak to the Dame Tuppy with great open sincerity. Because of her candid nudity. I told her I wanted her and that I wanted to have her right then and there. That I wanted her to gorge on my privates down by the stream. But alas, it was not meant to be," Jim Chimney says ruefully, lighting up his pipe.

"I told you, I didn't want to risk a pregnancy and plus, I was already married at the time. Though I don't know why I should have let that stop me from going off with you, considering who I was married to. The worst mistake I ever made was the day I let that good for nothing Mel Michigan enter my life. Buddhist guru, my ass."

"Look, how many times do I have to tell you to stop putting Daddy down? Speak ill of him again and I'll swat your withered hide."

"I mean, why did they have to have Joey cheat on Caitlin by having him sleep with Kathleen? He was full of mischief but he wasn't a cheater. There's no way Joey Jeremiah would do that. There's just no way."

"She's always putting Daddy down, Kate. I don't know what to do about her. I've been trying to get her to see my analyst, to try and calm her down."

"You see an analyst?"

"Oh yes. Let's see . . . Hmm. I guess I've being seeing Dr. Ribb for going on eleven years now."

"He's a fool if ever I saw one. A dirty quack."

"You've never even met him."

"Wait a minute. Joey wasn't sleeping with Kathleen. He was sleeping with Tessa," I correct.

"I don't have to meet him. All he does is lay blame at my feet, they all do. Bunch of mother haters, the whole misery breeding lot of them." Tuppy pours more wine into her glass and gulps it back until the glass is empty. She immediately pours more into her glass and drinks that down too, her face in a ferocious scowl.

"I used to think I had an Electra Complex. But Dr. Ribb made me see clearly that I don't."

"How you ever thought you could've is beyond me," Tuppy says, shaking her head.

"Was it Tessa? Yes, I guess it was, though it really is irrelevant. They shouldn't have had him cheat on Caitlin, period. They just shouldn't have. It wasn't right," Kim says passionately.

"That's true. Daddy is a bit of a crank. I guess I just always wanted him to like me. Waste of time though. Look around, do you see him? Bastard. I don't know why I'm so instinctively protective of him. You're right, Tuppy, he is bad news."

"Bad news, yes. Like when the Dame Tuppy informed me she was married to this Melvin character and my dreams of us uniting for a juicy coital foray in the grasses down by the river faded into a puff of smoke. My heart was crushed. But life has a way of rectifying the wrong, yes it does. One just has to be patient. Patient indeed."

"And you're nothing if not patient, I'll give you that much, Commander. Tell me, I'll bet you felt like you'd been zapped by a lightning bolt when you saw Tuppy again after all those years," Wendy says, suddenly attentive to Jim Chimney's ramblings.

"Zapped, yes. That's a fine way of putting it, Miss Wendy, a fine way indeed," Jim Chimney says, as reflective as ever.

"Listen to you," Tuppy says compliantly, reaching out and putting her hand on Jim Chimney's. The entire mood of the room seems to loosen from its powderkegging constriction with this simple action. That fast. But it shouldn't surprise me. It was always like this when I was a part of this family. Their emotions run the gamut but always come back to settle down into some tangent of odd agreeability. For a few minutes or so at least.

Tuppy continues. "I just thank my lucky stars I stopped in at the taxidermist's that day last summer. I wasn't going to, you know. It was a complete afterthought."

"It was fate, my Tups. Fate brought us together. And our love, that is what will keep us together," Jim Chimney says, derivatively and declaratively, his teeth visibly clamped down on the chewed stem of his pipe.

"Anyway, time for dessert. Who would like some apple cobbler?" Tuppy asks sprightly, standing up and looking at us, from one to the other and back again.

We all agree to it, afraid to say no.

"Would it be too rude to ask for another drink?" Kate says mercifully.

"Not at all. Not at all," Jim Chimney says, reaching behind him and grabbing the drambuie and scotch from the counter, beside the sink. He sets them on the table before him, pushing aside his plate. We pass him our glasses and he makes us each another drink. "Sorry about letting you all run dry like that. It is not our usual policy. Not our usual policy at all. Now if you'll just pass your glasses to Wendy, she can reach back and fill your drinks with ice. Our refrigerator has an ice maker," he says proudly.

"Sweet deal," Kate says, her voice a mixture of hyperbole and sincerity.

"How much ice?" Wendy asks concentratedly.

"Pack it full," Kate says, grabbing at a slice of cantaloupe. "It's good, isn't it?" she says to Kim.

"Is it ever. It's so juicy," Kim says, eating another slice.

Wendy hands us back our drinks one by one, Jim Chimney dropping a wedge of lemon into each one, having cut up the remainder of the one that was sitting on the counter.

Tuppy dishes out the cobbler. She stands at the head of the table, watching us, and the rapidity with which we eat a dessert of her making makes her smile with joy. And then she takes off her top.

Chapter 11

Tuppy pulls her top off over her head with one expert yank of the hand. I look at it dangling in her hand, inside out and lifeless. Her removal of it reminds me of the way I pull off my socks.

I look at Kate, sitting upright and slanted backwards, as though she expects to get some sort of spatter onto her: at Kim, her cobbler-filled mouth agape: at Jim Chimney, who is looking upwards at the light fixture, smoke from his pipe swirling about the orange glowing orbs, which makes me for the first time realize just how cozily dim it is in here: at Wendy, who reaches over and pulls open a utility drawer. Her hand rattles through it and comes out clutching a pair of sunglasses. She snaps them on and breaks the shock of the moment with a sickened sounding, "Agghh!"

I shake my head unsteadily and look at my cobbler. One mouthful left. I shovel it into my mouth and swallow it without chewing. At least the eating's done with and not a moment too soon, for my appetite is gone.

"Dammit, I told you not to do that. A blinding sight if I ever saw one," Wendy says. "Like a welding flash, that's what it is to be witness to those tits."

"Tits, yes," Jim Chimney says, turning to gaze at Tuppy. "How I remember us leaving the taxidermy for a ride in my Jeep, going off to the park for a delightful walk which culminated in you allowing me to massage your tits and dry hump you against an oak tree."

I look at Kate, who smiles and tries in no way to smother it. She is calmly amused by all of this.

I look at Kim, who looks emotionally askew for a brief moment but then chins up and faces Tuppy head on for a few seconds. After getting a good look at all Tuppy has to offer, the shock is over and Kim relaxes somewhat.

Tuppy sits back down, seemingly oblivious to the controversy she has engendered. But Wendy doesn't let it slide. I suspect she never has.

"Why must you always be such a goddamn exhibitionist?"

"It's hot in here. And besides, when I am in a fine mood I see no reason on earth why I should let clothes try and put a harness on my mood. For that is what they do. Clothes are inhibitory. I know this and so does your father. Miss Tallulah Bankhead knew it and—"

"Oh, I know it too. But for you—*you!*—to put yourself on public display like this is disgusting."

"Oh, but when someone like this little girl here"—Tuppy points an open hand at Kate—"puts herself on display that's just fine and dandy, is it?" She turns to Kate before awaiting an answer from Wendy, who looks in no hurry to supply one. Wendy simply sneers and lights up a cigarette.

"I just thank God these shades of mine dim the scene. What's the scene like, Kim?" Wendy asks, overtly curious it seems, despite her protestations of revulsion.

"Goodness. It's . . . it's . . ." Kim takes a drink of her rusty nail, hoping to find her voice. "It's full of surprises," she says, as diplomatically and as ambiguously as possible.

"That's what happens when you join a commune. Off come the clothes and away goes the mind. And you can never get it back. Your sanity is gone forever," she says to Kim, nodding deeply.

"I'll bet," Tuppy says to Kate, "that you felt more on display when you were a beauty queen then I feel right now. I feel free and easy, without a qualm or worry in the world. And yet I'm the one being crucified, and you, you were the one being honoured. Where's the sense of it all?"

I look at Tuppy's breasts. They look horrifyingly skeletal. Deathly white, cold and cadaverous. Her left breast is punctured by a nipple ring and it jiggles every time she says a word. It has a way of magnetizing my focus. I can't look away, even though I can hear Kate talking, even though I know she is looking at me from time to time as she does so.

"If you are implying that I in any way felt trapped, then you are wrong. Of course, one is on display when one enters a beauty pageant, there is no avoiding it, that's the nature of the entire activity. But I've always felt confident about how I looked. I don't mean that to imply that I think I am the most beautiful girl out there. Not at all, because I know I am not. But I still felt myself worthy enough to enter. The first time was out of curiosity, to see if others would give me the validity that I've always given myself. And happily enough, and unexpectedly enough too I might add, I won. I was proud to win, though if I had lost I expect you would see the same girl you see before you right now."

"Wow, you sure can talk," Tuppy says combatively, feigning a wearied expression, unimpressed with all that Kate has said. She sits back and removes the ring in her upper lip and attaches it to her left nostril.

I turn my attention to Kate.

"You *never* felt trapped?" I ask her and she looks at me as though it is a loaded question, as though I am fishing about for a reason as to why she won't marry me. But then she relaxes when she sees that I am in no way trying to be deceptive. She says I have a sign, one of those things, a tick or involuntary or unconscious movement, that signals to her when I am attempting to engage in trickery. Of course, she will never tell me what it is. But I guess it is absent from my question to her now.

"All of us are somewhat vain in some way, aren't we?" she says, turning indirect and allusive.

"Vain, yes," Jim Chimney says, from out of nowhere again. I had almost forgotten he was here. "I would agree with what you have said, Miss Kate, with the singular exception of the Dame Tuppy. She is completely without vanity. That is what makes her whole."

"Oh quiet," Tuppy says, but in a voice suggesting that she doesn't really care for him to stop.

"How I remember our first night together, in this very home in which we are exchanging pleasantries right now, and how void of self-consciousness or vanity it was. In fact, if I am not mistaken, this is the very same table on which we finally consummated our long awaited appointment with destiny. Our loins burned with fiery completion that night—"

"Oh yes indeed. It was splendid," Tuppy says, now delighted, pouring herself a glass of wine and then, after a quick gulp, hopping up and disappearing out of the room. I see a freshly coloured tattoo of a frog, with a cane and wearing a top hat, on her right shoulderblade. The one from those Bugs Bunny cartoons.

Kim is aghast, looking at the table, the very table on which Tuppy and Jim Chimney . . . I cannot complete the thought. Kim drops the slice of cantaloupe she has been eating onto her plate. She is done with food for the night. She takes a drink.

Wendy picks up the line of conversation I had meant to engage Kate in before Jim Chimney jumped aboard with his unpleasant memories down carnal lane. "Being a celebrity myself, I can understand all that you were going through as a beauty queen. The recognition is just wonderful, isn't it? It *does* make you feel special, I don't care what anyone says."

"Yes, it does," Kate replies quietly, her gaze one of reminiscence. "Of course, my recognition factor was a lot less than yours—"

"Don't sell yourself short."

"Oh, I'm not. But it is true. And I'm glad I'm no longer part of the pageant. Even though all I did was mostly cut ribbons at the opening of a new supermarket or some such thing, it still got to be tiring, a drain on my time. And yes, I guess, to answer your question, Dean, I did feel a bit trapped after awhile. It started to define me in a singular sense, at least by those who knew me by name or face only. Though when I lost the last one I was still crushed, I really was. I don't think I took it for granted that I would win, even after winning three times in a row, but I still wasn't prepared to lose. I guess it was because I had won the first time out."

"You should have won. It was the dress," Kim says self-reproachfully, a greatly dispirited look gathering about her eyes. She made Kate's dress for the last pageant, the one she lost.

"That wasn't the reason I lost," Kate says softly, just as Tuppy re-enters the kitchen, swivelling her hips, tossing her head to and fro and snapping her fingers, her motions full of gentle grooviness, a blare of music following her in. Carly Simon's "It Was So Easy" is playing.

"Music," Wendy says, seeming to give great thought as to Tuppy's decision to put some on. "Yes, that's what we need," she then says approvingly. "It will help dilute the bad taste of your omnipresent nudity, even if it is easy listening."

"It was *one* of the reasons you lost, I'm convinced of it," Kim says, not letting herself off the hook with what she feels is a dark mark against her. "What was I thinking? I shouldn't have made a crocheted neckline for that dress." She covers her face with her hands, full of welling regret. "I thought it was trendy and yet old-fashioned at the same time. I'm sorry."

"Kim, get a hold of yourself," I say, reaching out and putting a hand to the limp wrists that now lay on the table before her, defeated.

"Yes, it wasn't that at all. It was my stupid decision to play the flute in the talent competition. I should have stuck to my gut feeling and sang a song."

Jim Chimney starts clapping his hands, oblivious to Kim's tortured state and starts singing along to the voice of Carly Simon, watching Tuppy dance. Encouraged by Jim Chimney's mood, she steps onto her chair and keeps dancing, looking like a demented, emaciated go-go dancer from *Laugh-In*.

Jim Chimney leans close to my ear and begins to talk to me. "The Dame Tuppy is a wild creature. And innocent. Only the truly innocent could do what you see before you. She has been unsullied by society. She is a mystery. She is an experience. She is whole and pure and true. I am in love." He sucks blissfully on his pipe.

"Why didn't you sing a song?" Wendy asks of Kate.

"I thought it time to mix it up. I thought that I couldn't just keep singing a song every year. So I learned to play the flute. My one constant mistake was putting too much pressure on the flute, which distorted the natural shape of my lips. I constantly had to be aware of that. And then I played a tune of my own creation too, another big mistake. I set out to play an Irish ballad and ended up playing something that sounded like the soundtrack to a spaghetti western."

"A Sergio Corbucci film, I'll bet. I would have loved to have heard you play the flute," Wendy says, exhaling an impressive amount of smoke. I can see Tuppy's twisting body reflecting off the dark lenses of her sunglasses.

"Yes, well, in this case it was a big mistake. I should have sung a song like I had originally intended, before I did all that second guessing. I had one all picked out too. And I had it down pat."

"Which one?"

"It was "What's Up" by 4 Non Blondes. I loved that song then and I love it now. I was was quite taken with my version of it too."

"It's true. You did a really bang up job," Kim says, her sad mood receding.

"But the song was being so overplayed at the time that I thought I would risk a backlash on behalf of the judges," Kate says. "Still, it would've been better than that darn—what did you say?—Sergio Corbucci music? It would've been far more appropriate than that."

"Tough break," Wendy says in consoling tones.

"I remember that song by 4 Non Blondes so well," I say, my mind retreating to the early 90's. "I danced a pretty close and meaningful dance with a girl to that song," I say, Kate knowing all about this story and me deciding to bring it up because it takes me back to my great early adult youth more than anything else.

"Was it Wanda? Or did you cheat on her with more than one girl?" Tuppy says perniciously, unforseen belligerence turning my way. Her feet deliberately slip off each edge of the chair and her rump comes thudding down onto the chair, her eyes on me with mutinous judgment the whole time.

"That was before I met Wanda. Way before. I never laid eyes on Wanda until I met her that night at the Alice Cooper concert," I say, defensive and even wrathful.

"Yes, that's when it was," Wendy says, suddenly enlightened, knowing it to be true because she was there too. "It was when Alice sat off at the edge of the stage and did a wondrous rendition of "Only Women Bleed." And a big crowd was milling about, trying to get as close to him as possible. And then Wanda fell because of all the pushing. And you saw it happen and pushed your way over to her and helped her up. She said you were gallant."

"I was," I say, proud to be referred to as such, just as "You're So Vain" begins to play, which Kate forces me to realize by lip synching it at me. "She gave me her number that night," I say, momentarily unable to keep quiet about the past.

"And you took it from there," Wendy says.

"Yes," I say.

"What went wrong, Dean? Wanda gets ballistic whenever I try to talk about it. She needs to talk about it, she really does. It would do her a world of good to purge herself. Settle her down and keep her from stealing other people's toasters."

"Yes, toast," Jim Chimney says musingly.

"She deserves that toaster," Tuppy says, venomous saliva foaming along the corner of the left side of her lips. "And everything else she can get. A terrible deal. Why'd you do it, Dean? Why'd you turn on her for a roll in the hay with this tart?" Tuppy says derisively, jerking a thumb Kate's way.

"Hey! I resent that. Treat your guests with the respect they deserve or you'll have guests no more."

"That's telling her, Kate. You'd think it was Tuppy here who was scorned and not Wanda. Yes sirree, there's not much worse out there to encounter than a woman scorned," Wendy says.

"What are you all talking about?" I say to Tuppy, having about had it with all these accusations. "I never cheated on Wanda. I didn't take up with Kate until after the divorce was final. I met her right after it was final but it was still final."

"Really?" Wendy says, genuinely surprised.

"I don't believe it," Tuppy counters.

"It's true," I say, sputtering to control my temper. "And look what she did!" I say feverishly, tearing the band-aid from my forehead to reveal a little bruised cut. "She hit me in the head with an ashtray!"

"Good for her!" Tuppy snarls.

"Heavens! If what you say is true, Dean, and I've no doubt that it is, I wonder what it is Wanda is trying to hide then," Wendy muses, suspicions about her sister beginning to arise. "That sneak. I'll bet it's something dirty too. I'll just bet. The divorce is actually her fault, isn't it, Dean? What is it? What?" She looks at me, expectant for a revelation.

"Nothing," I say, retreating, hoping to put an end to this line of conversation, noting Kate's flagging patience as I do so. "We just fell out of love."

"*Fell out of love*? Oh come on now, Dean, you can do better than that," Wendy says, pushing for answers.

"That was all," I say, wondering why I am so reluctant to spill the truth, especially since it is so utterly ordinary and commonplace.

Wendy sits back. "Okay, you don't want to talk about it. I understand. But it's going to come to light very soon nonetheless. I am on the case."

"And we, we should leave," Kate says, standing up and ready to go. "After all, we do have to work tomorrow."

"Yes," Kim says quickly, standing up and ready to go as well. "Sam will have called already to check up on me. He'll be worried that there's no answer."

I stand up too. We all thank Tuppy for the meal, telling her how good it was.

"Fine. Leave then. Do what you want," she says, sounding bitter and utterly abandoned.

We thank Jim Chimney as well.

He nods and stands up, putting a hand to the bill of his yachting cap and graciously tipping it to Kate and Kim. He then shakes my hand. "We must do this again soon, Master Dorian. We most surely must."

I nod. "Yes," I say and say no more. I breathe a sigh of relief. This night has come to an end. But when I look at Kate—full of thought and strange determination—I soon change my tune. The night may have come to an end but a whole lot of other things have barely just begun.

Chapter 12

It's been a slow day, which allows for even more daydreaming about Kate. I stare at the picture of us on my desk and wonder if she somehow knows that I am thinking about her right now. I like to believe that she does because then that means that our relationship has forged a mental link that can only strengthen the bonds we already have between us. Or something. It would just be neat, I guess is what it basically boils down to, when I really think about it.

I look at the clock on the wall. It's almost time to leave. There is no lineup at the front counter, a most definite contrast to this morning, when a loud, noisy one snaked all the way down the hall and around the corner, everyone panicking because it is the last day of Add/Drop, the last day for them to get any kind of refund for dropping a class, and avoid being locked into having to stick it out in whatever hated class it is they want out of. All that sort of stuff.

The minute hand reaches that desirable twelve and it is now four o'clock. Time to leave. I grab my stuff, say goodbye to the few who haven't bolted out ahead of me and leave, sick to death of all the administrative strife I deal with. Kate says I should teach since I'm qualified for it after all. I'm beginning to think she's right. We've talked about teaching abroad for a year or two, in Japan or somewhere. We might yet.

I zip up my jacket at the doors and step out into the frenzied winds. Kate is waiting in the pickup area. The sight of her causes any other thoughts I may have to fall away. I hurry over and hop into the car, her presence enveloping me immediately. She has the heater on and the stereo is playing.

"I just bought a Carly Simon cd. That one that Tuppy was playing last night."

"As though we needed another reminder of that night," I say, cringing slightly.

"Oh come on. It was fun," she says, skipping through a few songs on the cd to get to "It Was So Easy." She begins to drive. I pick up the cd case and look at it. It is titled *No Secrets*. There seems to be irony and meaning behind this purchase. But I don't say anything.

"So, how was your day?" I ask. "Did your headache go away?"

"Yes, not long after I got to school. I think it was the absinthe."

102

"I don't doubt it."

"That was a failed experiment. We'll never lace sugar cubes again, at least not with stuff that harsh. Though of course drinking it straight might have had something to do with contributing to the condition I was in this morning too."

"Yes," I agree. "I was thinking about you all day today," I say, changing the subject.

"You tell me that at least twice a week."

"Do I?"

"And you always act surprised to find out that you do. Why do you tell me that you think of me? I know that you do."

"How do you know?"

"Because of the way your eyes look me over when you get into the car. You look gratified. Why do you always talk like this when you get off work?"

"Because it's the end of the longest gap of separation that exists between us. I feel thankful to see you at the end of those eight hours is all, I guess."

"You make me feel wanted when you say things like that."

"Isn't that the point of me saying things like that?"

"I guess it is."

"Will you marry me?"

"Aha! There's the real point. To weaken me with sweet talk."

"No. I don't want to sully all I've just said by making you feel that way. I take it back. But will you?"

"No."

"How come?"

The cd skips around on random play and settles on "We Have No Secrets." Kate looks down at the player and then at me.

"I hate this disc," I say.

"It's beautiful."

"Yeah," I concede. I slump down and gaze out the rain-stained window, in the throes of a momentary sulk.

"I called Wendy at lunch," Kate says, changing the subject. "She says that between writing her screenplay and preparing for this week's episodes of her show that she has no time to see Fluff Chang."

"She's writing a screenplay?" I say, sitting up.

"Yes, and she went off on an excited tangent about it for about five minutes. She said, now let me see if I can remember her exact words . . ." I look at Kate as we sit in traffic at an intersection, waiting for the light to change. She is biting her lower lip, her eyes rolled upwards, in deep recollection. "It was something like, 'It's a thriller movie with supernatural overtones that will have everything in it, from a graphic hatchet murder to Bernard Herrmann type music to the welcome resurgence of Betty Buckley.' Who is Betty Buckley? I tried to ask but it's hard to get a word in edgewise with her."

"Betty Buckley? She's . . . hmm—Oh! She was Abby, the stepmom in *Eight is Enough*."

"Her? That's strange. I mean, I would never think of putting her in a movie if I was making one, not that I have anything against her. How obscure."

"I know she was in that show because she was also the gym teacher in *Carrie*. I remember watching that movie and thinking 'Hey, that's the stepmom from *Eight is Enough*.'"

"Oh, maybe that explains it. We really should rent *Carrie* again, now that I think about it. Anyway, Wendy said she would call Fluff and set up a meeting between the three of us tomorrow at The Lily Pad."

"What? Why? Why doesn't she just ask her the questions over the phone? Or you could even call her for that matter. Why not do it that way?"

"I don't know. Fluff is suspicious of phones or some such thing."

"What does that mean?"

"I don't know. Look, we have to play it Fluff's way. It won't be that bad. And look on the bright side, you'll get to see some strippers."

"Me? You mean I have to go too?"

"Of course. Didn't I just say that Wendy was going to set up a meeting between the three of us tomorrow?"

"I thought you meant you, Wendy and Fluff."

"No. Aren't you listening? Wendy's busy all week."

"Alright. Can Uncle Hav come? I could kill two birds with one stone that way."

"No, you better not invite him. We don't want to spook Fluff."

"Spook Fluff? What is she, selling government secrets? We're just asking about some dead stripper's dentist is all."

"This is a delicate situation. Murder is in the air." Kate pulls into our parking space and puts the Galaxie into park. But she doesn't move. She is thinking.

"What?" I ask.

"We should have done a few things before coming back here."

"Like what?"

"Well, I wanted to buy a plant. Kim gave me the itch. Are you into it?"

"Buy a plant? Now?"

"Just one. Or maybe two. Yes, two. It won't take long. I was thinking about it during recess today. I think a nice philodendron and a dracaena would help spruce up the apartment. What do you think?"

"I guess," I say.

"Good." She puts the car in reverse, backs up and takes off again. We go directly to a plant store where she gets exactly what she said she was thinking of getting: a philodendron and a dracaena. "This is what they call the Warnecki variety," she says of the plant that I am now holding in my lap, the philodendron being in the backseat. "You've got to keep the soil moist at all times and every now and again you're going to have to air layer it."

"*Me*? What is air layering?"

"Silly. Now, how about getting those movies?"

"What movies?"

"Well, I was thinking about this at lunch today. I would like to know if your aunt really does look like Nova Pilbeam. So we'll get that Alfred Hitchcock movie."

"They won't have it any place here. They only have new releases."

"I was thinking about that too. But we'll check it out anyway. Besides, I forgot to tape Christine Cushing, so we'll have nothing to watch tonight if we don't get a movie." So we go to a number of video stores, where Kate also inquires about *Red Line 7000,* but to no avail. I don't even go in with her at the last video store we come to. I just sit in the car and delicately finger the leaves of the dracaena and listen to Carly Simon.

Kate comes back, gets into the car and slams the door in disgust. "I asked that dumb whelp in there if they had any Alfred Hitchcock movies and he said to me, he said, get this: 'Who's Alfred Hitchcock?' It put me into an immediate fume."

"You look like you're fuming alright."

"I can't believe it. It's one thing for a person not to know who Betty Buckley is, but Alfred Hitchcock? Come on! Don't you think so?"

"Oh, I think so too. I'm just not as surprised by it as you."

"How discouraging. Why must the world provoke me so?" she says, turning to exaggeration and jokey self-martyring to alleviate her frustration. She laughs. "Oh well. They did have a copy of *Carrie* though. I was going to get it too, until he showed his ignorance. That ignorance cost him a rental."

"That's showing him."

"It sure is."

"I guess we'll just have to wait and see if we can catch the other shows on PBS."

"Not likely. All they ever show is *Casablanca.*" She reaches over and takes two sugar cubes from the glove compartment. She pops them into her mouth and begins to suck on them. "Now let's go home," she says and we proceed directly home.

When we get home our first priority is to find a place for the plants. Kate settles on the top of a speaker for the philodendron.

"What about this?" I ask, still holding the dracaena.

"I'm thinking. We should maybe put it in the bedroom. How about on top of your dresser?"

"There's too much junk on it."

"Well, couldn't you move some of it?" she says, going into our bedroom.

I follow her in. We stand before my dresser and look at the top of it. It's full of all sorts of stuff: papers, loose change, a book, a clock, underarm deodorant, cologne—which Kate keys in on, picking it up.

"We could put this and the deodorant in the bathroom. Say, what is this? Canoe? I didn't know they still made this stuff."

"Just leave it. This is my shrine to me."

"What about that?" she asks, pointing at the ashtray, the one Wanda made for me (and hit me in the head with).

"Can't we just put the plant somewhere else?" I say, tired of all this.

"I really want one in here."

"Then put it on your dresser," I say, a little miffed, and hand her the plant.

She takes it and gives me a dirty look. She's miffed too. She goes over to her dresser and pushes aside a few things with a gentle sweep of her arm and sets the plant down on the edge of her dresser.

"It looks just fine there," I say. She says nothing and leaves the room. "What'd I do?" I ask, suddenly feeling the need to appease her. I follow her out. She's in the living room, searching through some cds. "What are you looking for?"

"I'll know when I find it," she says. I plunk down on the couch and watch her. "I should have brought that Carly Simon cd in."

"Want me to go get it?" I ask, thinking such an act a sure way to get back in her good books.

"No, never mind. Dinner last night brought 4 Non Blondes back to the forefront. I'll play them." She puts on a cd of them and stands up. She goes over to the bookcase and looks at it. She removes one, straightens up and puts the book on her head. She begins to walk back and forth before me. "Is the book moving? Or wobbling at all?" she asks.

"No. It's motionless."

"I still have poise," she says, now mollified and quietly satisfied with herself. "I always placed a lot of importance on it when I was in the contests. Listen, here it is," she says, indicating the song that is beginning to play, "What's Up." She begins to sing along with it. "How is my voice? Do I sound cracked?"

"Not at all."

"I think I didn't sing this song partly because I was smoking a lot at the time. I was afraid my voice would sound like a smoker's croak. So that's also partly to blame for the flute debacle that ensued: my fear of singing that year."

"Well, I'm sure your worry was all for naught. Of course your interpretation of the song is different."

"How?" she asks, pivoting on her left heel, turning and walking in the direction from which she's just come, her back arched, her arms straight, her chest outthrust.

"Well, it's quieter, more reflective almost."

"That's my age infecting it." She stops, tilts her head and catches the book as it drops from her head. She sets it down on the coffee table and sits down beside me. She breathes deeply. "Do you think I still have it?"

"You never lost it."

"You sound so flip."

"I don't mean to."

"I wonder if winning made me vainer than I would otherwise be. I think about my looks far too often lately."

"I don't know how to ease your concerns other than to say that to me you're better now than at any time previous. And I've known you just about longer than anyone."

"That's true. Thank you. Compliments mean alot, they really do. Anyway, put something else on. Are you hungry? Want me to make you something? I was thinking at lunch that I was in the mood for chicken. I was thinking about chicken in champagne sauce, but then I remembered that we still haven't found our Vincent Price cookbook, have we?"

"I think you lent it to Kim."

"Maybe I did. I keep forgetting to ask her if she has it."

I put on *Bringing It All Back Home*, a Bob Dylan cd.

"Oh, this is a good choice."

"I think so too. Don't worry about supper. We'll just make sandwiches or something."

"I have the urge for flan. It's making a comeback, you know."

"No, I didn't know that."

"How come you're not checking the messages?" she asks and I divert my attention to the answering machine by the phone. It's blinking.

"It's Uncle Hav, that's why."

"Yes, I suppose it is. You know, I feel like a bath."

"Then have one."

"I should do some marking first."

"Have a bath."

"You just like to watch me take off my clothes."

"I won't even try to deny that. I'll help you mark though."

"Okay, we haven't done that in awhile."

She gets up and stands before me. "Are you ready for an eyeful then?" she asks, full of playful seduction, her hips in a enticing swivel. She removes her cardigan and then begins to unbutton her cotton shirt. "Is it getting to you?"

"Is it ever," I say, arousal surging through me.

She takes off her cotton shirt and then reaches back and removes her bra. She tosses it at me. I catch it and set it aside. "Oops. I should have removed my pants first, shouldn't I have? I'm a terrible stripper."

"It looks to me like you have it down pat."

"Mmm, is that so?" she says, unbuttoning her twill pants. Soon she is out of them. And then her panties too. She tosses them at my head. I catch them. She watches me.

I set them down on the couch, on top of the bra. "What?" I say, feeling oddly shameful.

"I thought you might sniff them."

"Surely you didn't. Anyway, I don't have to. I have you."

"True. Anyway, I'm glad you didn't. Sniff them, I mean. That would be, what? Gauche?"

"Something along those lines." I look at her, smooth and curvy, lithe and pinkish, full of health, limber and graceful.

"Don't stare too long. I'm starting to feel self-conscious."

"I can't help it," I say. "It's always a miraculous scene. I'm always amazed that you're here. And that I'm here with you."

She smiles. "I'm going to draw a bath and whip up some suds. Grab the notebooks," she says and then disappears from the room, into the bathroom. I stand up, dizzied with desire for her. I go into the bedroom where the plastic milk crate is. She brought it in along with one of the plants when we came home. The crate is filled with notebooks. I grab a half dozen or so of them and a red pen too. I see her bowler sitting beside the dracaena. I grab that too and proceed into the bathroom. She's in the tub already, foamy soap suds in a burgeoning growth via the heady rush of the tap water. I close the toilet seat and sit down upon it. I set the notebooks on the edge of the sink. I put the bowler on her head.

"Why'd you do that?"

"Because I like it."

"I knew there was a reason," she says, sinking down into the hot water, her lively breasts submerged by water and soap, tantalizingly elusive from view. The hat is tilted low on her head. I can't see her eyes. Her head rests against the back edge of the tub. "Well, read me a story," she says liltingly, her voice indicative of just how soothing she finds the bath.

"Right," I say, first reaching over and turning off the tap.

"Thanks," she says. "I was just wondering how I was going to find the strength to shut it off myself."

"Okay, are you ready?" I ask, opening a notebook to the section that isn't marked.

"Fire away," she says, appearing lost, though I know her focus will be entirely on what I have to read. I begin:

"'The theme of "Wanted, a Goldfish" is that you shouldn't jump to conclusions and should explore all the possibilities because what you first see and hear may not actually be what it is like. Perhaps it seems different but if you find out more about the situation it may then seem perfectly logical. This also shows that there's more a situation than what meets the eye.'"

"*. . . more a situation . . . ?*"

"Yeah. A small omission."

"Okay. Add 'to' with the marker."

I do and continue on:

"'Another part of the theme is that using sense and shrewdness pays off because the professor got out of going to the looney bin by using his shrewdness and wits, and on top of that he cleverly managed to make it look the policeman was a fool.'"

"*. . . look the policeman . . . ?*"

"Yeah. I'll add 'like' to it."

"Good. Is that all?"

"Yes."

"Who wrote that?"

"Danielle Sanders."

"That's an A, awfully good for someone in Grade 6. Don't you think?"

"I don't know. I never read the story."

"Oh. No, I suppose you wouldn't have. Anyway, if her interpretation of irony is on par with her interpretation of theme it's an A. Read on."

I do. When it's all said and done Kate gives her an A.

"There are no spelling mistakes at all?"

"Nope."

"Good. Good." I read from a few more notebooks and correct and grade them on Kate's orders. "Okay. Lift the hat," she then says. I remove the hat from her head and set it on the edge of the sink, as she slides down the tub, her head going underwater, one hand pinching her nose shut to keep out the water. She sits up and shakes her head, engaged in the same ritual she has performed—she has often told me—since she was four or five. She squeezes water away from her closed eyes, water shimmering down her sharp features. She then grabs some shampoo sitting on the tub ledge and squeezes some onto her hand. She then rubs it through her hair and begins to lather it. I just sit where I am, placidly still, watching her act just as she would were I not here. The freeness of her bathing makes me realize how comfortable she is with me, it always does. I always feel this way when I watch her. I have her trust and she gives me her private moments because of it. When she is done lathering she lays back down in the tub and slides her head back underwater, her hand pinching her nose shut again. She shakes her head and the shampoo dissipates. She sits back up and wipes her face with her hands. She looks at me, her brown eyes bright and wide from the rejuvenation of the bath. "Boy, I feel good," she says, her voice full of vigour.

"There's nothing like a good bath," I say.

"I now have the energy to finish the marking."

"How long will that take?"

"An hour or two. Same as always."

"I guess I'll just read then or something until you're done."

"Good idea. You can start reading that book we bought the other day."

"I was just thinking that," I say, standing up. Kate pulls the plug on the water and then stands up herself. I hand her a towel and leave her alone to dry herself off. I go into the living room, grab the book off the coffee table and sit down on the couch, feeling perfect.

Chapter 13

It was an abnormally long day at work. Nothing went right there and nothing is going right now. I can't seem to find the right key for the lock.

"Hurry up," Kate says impatiently. "The phone is ringing."

"I hear it," I say, fumbling my way through the key ring and finally getting the right key into the lock. I open the door. Kate rushes in, over to the phone. I shut the door behind me and take off my shoes and coat. I lay my coat over the chair beside the door. Kate comes over to where I am, phone in her hand.

"It's Hav," she says.

"Was there ever any doubt?" I say wearily, taking the phone, sensing Uncle Hav's irritation before I even say a word to him.

"Where were you last night?" he grumbles. "How come you didn't return my message?"

"I forgot to check the messages," I say, wandering over to the computer and sitting down before it. I check my e-mails. Nothing but junk.

"Oh come off it. You can't spend a whole night in the living room without seeing the red blink of an answering machine. There's no damn way."

"Who said I spent the whole night in the living room?"

"Well then, where in the hell—You lucky bastard. How was she? I'll bet Kate's just as frisky now as she was the first time you did it."

"You know I don't like to talk about that kind of stuff."

"Then you shouldn't have brought it up. Besides, I let you in on the stories of all my pleasurings."

"I never ask you to."

"You're so damn Victorian, do you know that? A real prude. You're a lot like my mom in that respect. I think that's part of my problem, being related to people like you. I feel guilty about having fun. It scares the women I like away. This damn mental gout."

"Look, what do you want?"

"Are we going to The Lily Pad or what? After all, you promised."

"Just a sec," I say, covering a hand over the mouthpiece and turning to Kate, who's sitting on the couch, changing the channels on the tv with the remote. "He's asking about The Lily Pad. Can't we bring him along?"

"No. He's always on the make. He might scare Fluff into not confiding in us," she says, her thoughts on the matter definitive.

I sigh and return to talking to Uncle Hav. "No can do. It's a funny thing though. Later on tonight we're actually meeting with one of the strippers who works there."

"What did you tell him that for?" Kate says, sitting upright, her eyes rebuking me.

I don't actually know why I am telling him this.

"What?! With who?" His voice rings sternly in my ear.

"Um, Fluff Chang."

"That Asian import? She's a skank. You mean to tell me you'd rather break bread with some cum crusted whore than with your own uncle?"

"It's strictly business."

"Bah, what kind of line is that?"

"It has to do with the murders."

"What murders?"

"The ones that have been going on all year."

"Those? Some virgin with a malfunctioning prick is behind those, everyone knows that. Come on, really, what are you trying to hide?"

"Nothing. Kate feels she can solve the mystery and thinks that Fluff might have some info. Wendy arranged it."

"Wendy? Well well. Aren't you the socialite. Why must you constantly throw all your good pussy fortune in my face?"

"That's it, I'm hanging up."

"No, wait! I'm sorry. I certainly wasn't including Kate in that company, if that's what you're thinking. Where are you meeting Fluff?"

"Well . . ." I know he'll go to The Lily Pad on his own and jump us if I tell him that that's where the meeting is. I shouldn't have gotten into this line of conversation with him. "We're not sure yet."

"Can I come? I've always had a kind of a thing for Fluff. I have a fetish for Asian strippers, did you know that?"

"No, I didn't."

"Yeah, they're big into rubbing oils. They like slippery genitalia."

"That sounds rather dubious, if you ask me. I've never heard that before."

"I don't doubt it. One becomes completely removed from reality when they take up residence in an ivory tower for so long."

"You're giving me a headache."

"Well, that's more than you ever give me. When are we going to The Lily Pad? Tell me."

"I can't say. It's pretty hectic around here. Maybe later in the week."

"Maybe maybe maybe. You never commit, do you know that?"

"I'm sorry."

"You should be. Fuck. What am I going to do tonight? I need a night on the town, and soon. I'm a nervous wreck, you know. I'm on Wendy's show in three days and I don't have a clean pair of jeans in the house."

"Well then maybe you should do a wash."

"Ahh, who has the time? You know what else? I ran out of wine."

"So go buy some."

"It's a bitch not having a woman to take care of these things for me. Do you know if Fluff is attached to anyone?"

"Tell you what. I'll ask her tonight. I'll tell her all about you. Build you up good."

"Would you really do that?"

"For my uncle, anything."

"Quit calling me your uncle. You know how damn old that makes me feel."

"I'll try."

"I should hope so. Alright. Call me when you get home. I want to know how it went."

"Okay. So what are you going to do?"

"Damned if I know. An old friend came by the other day. I bought some more fish. Maybe I'll can them."

"Sounds like a full night."

"Don't mock me, you prick. Alright, I'm going now. Call me later."

"Okay."

He hangs up.

I breathe out deeply, exhausted.

"Why'd you tell him what we were up to?" Kate asks, annoyed.

"I don't know. I guess I get some sort of perverse pleasure out of torturing him. He thinks I'm so connected."

"I think you like him to think that you're so connected."

"Maybe I do."

"Anyway, hand me the phone. I want to call Kim before we do anything else. I want to see if she has that Vincent Price cookbook."

I hand Kate the phone and she calls up Kim. "Hi, Sam, is Kim there?" she says. Soon she's talking away to Kim, mostly about work. I go onto the internet and check out the news of the day. Ten minutes later Kate is off the phone.

"Well, does she have it?"

"No, she never even knew we had a Vincent Price cookbook. I think they're quite rare."

"Maybe," I say, never having given the matter much thought. "How come Sam is home? I thought he wasn't coming home until Wednesday."

"He was worried about Kim, so he came home early."

"Isn't that sweet?" I say sarcastically.

"Yes, he's a sweetheart," Kate says sincerely, ignoring my tone of voice.

"Can he come along? Sam, I mean. I'll feel really weird about being in a strip club alone with you, I just will."

"Sam? He can come, I guess. He can be a bit raunchy after a beer or two but so can you. At least he won't be hovering over Fluff like Hav. Call him if you want. I'm just going to change into jeans and a sweatshirt. Best to dress low key for this outing, I think." She gets up and disappears into the bedroom.

I click off the internet and pick up the phone. I call up Sam. Kim answers. "Hi, Kim. Is Sam there?"

"Goodness. No, he's not. He just stepped out. We're out of figs, one of our breakfast staples. If Sam doesn't get his morning fig he gets quite fidgety."

"Really? I didn't know that. How'd his dental visit go?"

"Good."

"Well, we're going to The Lily Pad in a bit. I just wanted to know if you two wanted to come. Or if Sam does anyway."

"Goodness. I don't know. We still haven't eaten."

"Well, if you do decide to come, meet us there."

"I'll tell him."

"Okay. See you."

"Bye."

We click off. Kate comes out of the bedroom. "Well?"

"He wasn't home. He went out to buy figs."

"Oh. Well then, now what?"

"I guess I'll have to suffer through it without him," I say, standing up. We go over to the entrance and slip on our shoes and put on our coats.

"You know, I was thinking. When you were having trouble opening the door it occurred to me that Wanda somehow got past our locked door. Does she have a key?" Kate looks at me with a face of interrogation.

"No," I say.

"Then how'd she get in?"

"Did you ever meet her first husband?" I ask, as we step outside and lock our apartment door.

"Once. We encountered him in the express line at the supermarket. What's his name? Dick?"

"Yeah, Dick Jemima."

"You say his name so bitterly. I know there's a past between you two. But you never tell me what it is."

"We were both married to Wanda. That's our past," I say, feeling the need for more evasion coming on. "Anyway, he's an ex-con. A burglar. He taught Wanda how to pick a lock with a hairpin. I'll bet that's how she got in. I musn't have attached the chain lock, or used the deadbolt. I often forget. Talk about sloppy. I was like that when I was married to Wanda too. She must have been counting on me doing it again when she came by the other night."

"You're way too lax in this age of uneasiness when it comes to security."

"You're probably right. Anyway, it's quite easy to pick a lock with a hairpin, you know. Wanda taught me how to do it too. I don't know how many times I locked myself out of our apartment and had to use a hairpin. I used to keep one in my wallet. I don't know why I just didn't get an extra key."

"Strange indeed," Kate says. We leave the apartment and make our way to the Galaxie. Kate says it's my turn to drive. I take a slow roundabout way to The Lily Pad but we still get there far too soon. I park the car and we hustle inside, the rain beginning to hurl down in gusting sheets.

I look at Kate as we step into the seedy ambience that defines The Lily Pad. She looks fascinated and not at all appalled, which I find strange. Though this place does have an allure, I have to say.

"Well, what do you think?" I ask.

"It's like the 70's exploded in here," she says, her wide eyes soaking up the grimy decay, the old red velvet curtains stuck to the smoky wood-panelled walls, the worn and sticky red rug, the shiny hardwood stage: a semi-circle jutting out from the far end, around which are numerous tables, all of them full of characters of varying stages of ill-repute. The dj booth is behind the stage. Strobe lights give intermittent visions of a chopping, jolting surreality. "Where should we sit?" she asks.

"Let's sit at a back table. After all, we didn't come here for the floor show, did we?"

"Well, *I* didn't anyway."

"Hey, you're the one who dragged me here."

"You're right. I shouldn't have said that."

We take a seat at the back.

"I'm the only woman in here, if you don't count the waitresses and strippers," she says, oddly enthralled with such a fact.

A waitress comes over to serve us. I order a beer. Kate orders a Singapore Sling.

"Why'd you order that?" I ask.

"An strange locale requires a like such drink."

Soon our drinks come. As the waitress is setting them down before us Kate asks about Fluff Chang. "She's expecting us. My name is Kate Carlo and this is Dean Dorian," she says, introducing us in a very businesslike tone.

The waitress, boisterously breasted and strangely perky considering the grind this place must be if one has to work it on a daily basis, is open and amenable to conversation.

"Oh, you just missed it. It was terrible. Fluff should be out soon but she had a bit of an accident."

"Accident?" I say.

"Yes, it happened in her last act. She used too much force in her dildo act. Too much anal upthrust. She started to bleed."

"Goodness!" Kate exclaims, borrowing one of Kim's catchphrases.

"Yes, it was a horrifying sight, it always is. She rushed off the stage and I immediately hurried into her dressing room with a box of tampons. She should have things just about under control by now though. The blood should be just about all soaked up. Want me to tell her you're here?"

"If she's up to it," Kate says concernedly.

"Oh, she'll be fine. She always is," the waitress says, rather frivolously it seems to me, and goes to the far end of the club and disappears behind a shadowy door.

"I would never have expected *that* to happen," Kate says, putting the straw to her lips and sipping from her drink. "So this is what goes on in these places," she says, taking an evaluative gaze of the place, her head in a slow pan. "Look at how spellbound everyone is. They'll be having some pleasurable dreams tonight I'll bet."

"Yeah," I say, both of us looking at the stripper on the stage. She swings erotically around a pole.

"Wow. I could never do that. You know, there's a real art to this, isn't there? It makes my strip show for you last night seem all the more pallid."

"Don't sell yourself short," I say, turning to her.

"Still, I'm not on par with them."

"I'm sure you could be if you set your mind to it."

"I suppose. If you were here with Hav and Sam right now instead of me what would be happening?"

"Well, we would probably be sitting up close, if we could find a table. Uncle Hav would watch every second of every show and Sam and I would lose interest after about five minutes."

"Really?"

"Yeah, our attentions are only ever really grabbed at the beginning of each set, when they come out, and at the end, when they take it all off. It becomes bland after awhile, at least to me. Maybe if I didn't have you it would be different, though I doubt it."

"That's interesting," she says, sipping on her drink.

The waitress comes back with whom I assume to be Fluff Chang. Fluff has a donut shaped air cushion tucked under her arm. She is wearing a kimono and her hair is wet and stringy. She has just come from showering it would appear.

"Here's Fluff, back from the brink," the waitress giggles.

"Cut it, Sheba, you don't know what real pain is like."

"I'm sorry," Sheba says, not sounding sorry at all as she turns to leave.

"Get me a beer," Fluff calls out to her. Fluff sets the cushion on her chair and sits down, grimacing as she does so. She has a hairbrush in her hand. She begins to comb her hair, which has a lustrous black sheen to it. "So, you two are Wendy's friends," she says, barely looking at us, her face clamped with a kind of withering scowl, her voice completely devoid of Asian inflections, instead wearily anglicized.

"Yes, hi," Kate says, somewhat tentatively it seems to me. "We were sorry to hear about your accident."

"I shouldn't have lubed up the damn thing. It sucks up slick when I do that. But that's what the chorus wants to see though, isn't it?"

Sheba comes back with more drinks, handing Fluff a beer and Kate and myself another of what we've been drinking. "I figured you two could use a refill."

"Thanks," I say, finishing off the remnants of what I've been drinking.

"Are you done with that?" Fluff asks, pointing at the empty in my hand.

"Yeah."

She reaches out for it and I hand it to her. "I need an ashtray," she says, taking a lighter and a pack of cigarettes from a pocket in her kimono. She lights one up.

"You're not supposed to smoke in here, Fluff," Sheba chastises, her tone childlike.

"So go tell on me. I've had a terrible night and no one's going to tell me what to do."

Sheba frowns, sticks her tongue out at Fluff and leaves us. Kate and I slowly drink our drinks.

Fluff exhales deeply and flicks some ash down the neck of the beer bottle. Kate watches her intently. "What? I suppose you disapprove of this too," she says, holding the cigarette up to Kate's face with a defiant, clenched fist.

"Quite the contrary," Kate says calmly and says no more on the matter. "Anyway, we don't want to take up too much of your time. All we want to know is if you know who your friend's dentist was, the one who was, well, the one who is no longer with us."

"Her name was Trini. Trini Albacore."

"Trini," Kate says. "Right. I'm sorry to be so insensitive as to treat her as just another statistic."

"You're no worse than any of the others, in fact you might be better. Wendy says that you and her are trying to get a handle on this thing."

"Yes, we are."

"I had to go downtown and identify her you know. It was terrible." Fluff looks around furtively, suddenly on edge. "I think it's someone who comes down here, someone Trini knew. Someone I might even know. And I think he's afraid that I know something, because Trini and I were so close."

"I didn't know that. Wendy said you knew her but not that you were friends. Again, we're sorry for you."

"Just because you have sex with someone it doesn't mean that they tell you all their secrets."

"Still, Wendy felt that everyone here was close enough to each other that you might know—"

"And just yesterday I was put on even higher alarm. My brick of hash is gone. I keep it in the lettuce crisper. Someone knew that. The phones here are bugged. I can just sense it," she says, her pouty lips closing around her cigarette. I feel cramped. "How else would they know to check the crisper. Someone's playing games with me.

"Her mouth was all contorted, from rigor mortis. She looked hideous, not at all the Trini I knew. Lady Death, you are a bitch. Damn," she says, adjusting her position on her cushion. "I have to stop with the dildos. I'm not up to it anymore. When I was younger I made some art films in Taiwan. I gave it my all and my ass went mush as a result. That's why I relocated here. It's a calmer environment. At least it was. Still, I'm a fast healer. I'll feel better tomorrow." She drops the butt of her cigarette into the beer bottle. She looks at me. "Have you ever seen my act?"

"I don't recall."

"Then you musn't have. You wouldn't forget if you had. I've got very animated tits."

"How serendipitous," I say.

"I don't know what to do. I'm thinking of buying a piece. For protection. That asshole Grundy is no help. Worst bouncer ever."

"What about the police?" Kate asks.

"Don't get me started on them. They don't even listen. Like Trini had a gold eyetooth for instance. It was gone. That's why her lips were so contorted. They were all cut up from the pliers or knife or whatever it was that was used to pull it out. A real amateur job. But the cops didn't even seem to think that was important. It's that lead detective. She's a real twat."

"So Trini was missing a tooth too? The last victim was missing some teeth too. We don't know about the other two yet. Who was Trini's dentist, do you know?"

"You think it's the King?" Fluff says astoundedly.

"The King?"

"King Cloke. He's her dentist."

Kate unzips her little purse and pulls out her notepad and pencil. She flips it open to an empty page. "How do you spell his last name?"

"C-l-o-k-e."

She writes down his name. "Have you ever met him?" she asks.

"He was here once. He's a stud."

"What do you mean?"

"I mean he's a stud. He gets more tail than Scott Baio."

"Did he get Trini?"

"Once."

"And then?"

"There wasn't enough time for an 'and then'. Trini was killed a few days after spending the night with him."

"I see. How very interesting. And you've never considered him a suspect yourself?"

"I consider everyone a suspect. I shouldn't even be talking to you and I wouldn't be either if Wendy hadn't vouched for the two of you. But I can trust Wendy and if she says you're both on the up and up then you are."

"Thanks," I say, mostly in order to keep my contributions to this conversation from being completely nil.

"Look, I have to go. I feel vulnerable right now, what with my spurting rectum and all."

"We understand. Thank you very much," Kate says, extending her hand.

Fluff shakes it, stands up and looks at Kate, as though for the very first time. "Wendy said you were a beauty queen. You do seem nice. Well, I've got to go. Don't worry about the drinks, they're on me."

"Thank you," Kate says.

"Just make sure you get the killer, whoever he is. I think I need a valium," Fluff says and then briskly walks away.

Kate looks at me. "King Cloke," she says.

"Yeah," I say, starting to feel a little uneasy in here, as though we might be in danger of being targeted ourselves.

"K.C."

"What?"

"His initials are K.C."

"So?"

"My initials are K.C. too. It's so evidently symbolic."

"Of what?"

"Everyone has an arch enemy and we have just been introduced to mine." Kate stands up. "And so now it's time to set the trap and reel him in."

Chapter 14

I was holding out hope that we wouldn't have to go to Wendy's show because, now that we are, I have the gnawing suspicion that we are going to be singled out by Uncle Hav. I suppose I should have returned at least one of his calls since our visit with Fluff. But I didn't and now he's really going to be ready to let fly. I hate embarrassing situations and this is sure to be one. As well, taking time off at noon will give Kate more free time to try and formulate some sort of plan to nab King Cloke. She's been poring over newspaper clippings relating to the case all week but is still stymied for a plan. The whole idea seems ridiculous in the extreme to me but all my naysaying comments on the subject have fallen on deaf ears.

"Obviously we have to infiltrate his ranks. Somehow gain his confidence. Too bad Sam already went to the dentist. We could use him," she says as she pulls into the parking lot of the television studio.

"He wouldn't go anyway. And neither would I," I say.

She parks the car and shuts off the ignition. "What's the matter with you?"

"*Me*? What's the matter with you? We're dealing with a killer. Do you think he'll have any qualms about offing us if he suspects we're on to him?"

"Nonsense. It will never come to that. At the appropriate time we'll turn over all our information to Trish Mindy. She can put the nab on him."

"Why are you doing this, really?"

"It needs to be done. And I guess it just makes me sad."

"It makes me sad too, but . . ."

"But what?"

"I don't know. Everything about this seems above our heads. The idea of us doing it seems totally improbable."

"It's not improbable. We can do anything we set our minds to. You'll see. Now," she says, turning contemplative again. "Maybe I should go and see King Cloke myself. Tell him I heard about him from Jen Mallard."

"Who's Jen Mallard?"

"The last victim."

"Oh. That's a nice name," I say quietly.

"Yes. Once one knows their names the whole case seems more personal, more melancholy," she says, reading my mood perfectly. "Mentioning her name to King Cloke is a gamble though. He *might* admit to being her dentist or he might clam up about it altogether. I don't know. But we have to chance it."

"There's another possibility, you know. That she might not have been his patient at all. What if he says that? Are you going to believe him?"

"I'll be able to tell."

"How will you be able to tell?"

"Well, I can always tell when *you're* lying," she says, as though that scientifically settles it. "Now, come on. Wendy wants us to drop by backstage and wish her luck."

We get out of the car but I still don't want to let the issue drop. "Don't you think the police have probably looked into this angle? At what the victims all had in common? I mean, if they all had the same dentist that is surely a red flag that must've already jumped out at them."

"Wendy says Trish is putting great importance in the blacked out lenses. She thinks it's the m.o. of a career creep. She's so way off," Kate says and doesn't elaborate.

We enter the studio and encounter a girl just inside the entrance with a headset and clipboard.

"Hi, I'm Kate Carlo and this is Dean Dorian. Wendy said we were her VIP's for today's show. She wanted us to go backstage and wish her luck before the show."

"You're cutting it close. We're on in ten. At least we're supposed to be. Come this way," the girl says, full of efficient terseness. We follow her down a maze of hallways. We can hear Wendy's voice, getting louder and louder. She's irate, I notice, as the girl with the headset steps aside and allows us through an open door, upon which time we see Wendy. She's in a makeup chair, a bunch of people milling about her, getting last minute details down pat.

"My hoops, my hoops. Where in the hell are my hoops?" she says, full of ill-humour. But when she sees us her tone turns brighter. "Kate. Dean. I was beginning to think you weren't going to show."

"We wouldn't miss it," Kate says supportively. "We came to wish you luck."

"Nice," Wendy says as she turns to a harried looking individual, a tall blonde guy with a flabby waistline that seems out of place on the rest of him. "Linus. Where in the hell are my hoops?"

"I don't know."

"I don't like that answer. Chop chop! Get a move on and find them. I'm not going on without them."

Linus mutters something unintelligible under his breath and hurries out the door.

"I heard that!" Wendy hollers out after him. "Alright alright. That's enough blush, Janice. Christ, what am I, a vagabond hooker? Go away. All of you, leave."

Janice disappears and so does the rest of the entourage, leaving just Wendy, Kate and myself.

"Hoops?" Kate inquires.

"Yes. I wear hoop earrings when I do this show. Every show I wear them. It's kind of my signature look. Sally Jessy had red-rimmed glasses, Oprah uses the name 'Harpo' on the credits and Donahue wore a dress. You need a signature. A stand out feature. And once you've got it you can keep them hooked with your personality. If you have a good personality, that is. And, strike me down if I'm bragging, but I've got a great personality for this type of crap. And I'm not too hard on the eyes too, I think. Which my audience will bear out. Have you seen them?"

"No, we were led back here right away."

"Good show. I'll have to give Sarnia a pat on the back for that kind of efficiency. But my audience, a real coffee diner crowd. Nosey old men who get off on my sassiness, my brassiness and my toss of the head, replete with eye roll. And of course there's all the gossipy old hags too. The rest are younger, like you two. I'm beginning to develop a cult. Same faces here as at The Hob-and-Nob. Anyway, how's the case?" Wendy asks, standing up and looking at herself in the mirror, tearing away the napkins that are tucked into the collar of her argyle-front sweater to prevent makeup from being accidently marked on it. She then slips on a blazer.

"Pretty much the same as when we talked last night. I'm still trying to come up with a plan."

"Yes, it's a perplexing issue. I talked to Trish after I did you. She is aware of King Cloke and said that angle is dead."

"Why?"

"She wouldn't say. She was uncharacteristically tight-lipped about it, the old cunt. Which made me think that maybe we're on the right trail after all, and that she's just trying to discourage us, for some reason. She wants all the credit herself, probably."

"Exactly," Kate says, as though she's known this all along. I can sense a rift suddenly developing between her and this Trish Mindy, even though she's never met her. Which means that we are likely *not* going to cooperate with Trish Mindy now. Which means . . . I don't know what it means.

"Where the hell are my pills?" Wendy says, picking up empty pill bottles on her dressing table and then dropping them. "Oh my," she says, standing up straight and breathing out deeply. "I think I'm beginning to hyperventilate. It's like this everytime. Before each show and before I get fucked. Where are my cigs?" She returns to the table and finds a lone cigarette lying on the table. She lights it up. "Whew! *That* is the stuff." She takes three quick drags but then becomes alarmed again. "Where the hell is that fucking Linus? The prick's been riding on my gravy train for far too long. When you finally want some hustle out of him he can't do it. Did you see his gut? He used to be a rail when working for T. Dooley. Linus! My hoops!" she hollers. "Excuse me, I really must find him," she says, stepping out the door. "Your seats are reserved for you. Front row centre. See you out there." And then she hurries off, in search of Linus and her hoops.

We look at each other and leave the dressing room. We pass an open door while searching for the way that will lead us into the studio. We spot Uncle Hav, sitting in a recliner and smoking a cigarette.

"Hey!" he calls out. We stop and look in. A bowl of complimentary fruit sits on the coffee table before him.

"Do you mind if I have a banana?" Kate asks, stepping into the room.

"Oh sure. When you two want something then you're on speaking terms with me."

"I'll take that as a yes."

"Why won't you return my calls?"

"It's that crazy time of year," I say.

"You talk in riddles, you know that?" Uncle Hav says, as disgruntled as ever.

Kate peels the skin off a banana and begins to eat it. "Are you nervous?" she asks Uncle Hav.

"I'm damn near ready to throw up. My stomach's in a twist."

"You'll be fine. We'll be in the front row, for moral support."

"Yeah?" he says, somewhat comforted by this. "Say," he says, turning to me. "What about Fluff? Does she want to go out with me or not?"

"I don't know."

"What do you mean you don't know? Dammit anyway, Dean. Quit dragging your feet."

"She was in no mood to hear about you, so I didn't bring you up. She had just suffered rectal damage when we saw her."

"Yeah?" he says, seedily aroused but feigning disgust. "She's a volatile whore," he says sulkily. "They all are, you know."

"Oh," I say, at a loss for words. "Look. We have to get to our seats."

"Go on then. Leave. Who needs you?"

Kate finishes her banana and Uncle Hav watches her as she does so. "I know what you're thinking," she says to him in a rather merry tone of voice. "You have a dirty mind."

"Bah! No one understands. Go!" he orders, an embarrassed flush to his cheeks.

We leave. We find our way into the studio. The audience is full, full of the types Wendy had spoken of, and we make our way to our seats, under the direction of Sarnia.

We sit down. I cross my legs and then uncross them, nervous.

"What's with you?" Kate asks, putting a hand on my knee gently. "You're not the one who's going on."

"I feel like I am."

"Just relax, honey."

I look at her and smile. "I like it when you call me that."

"Things will go fine," she says soothingly, giving me a gentle poke on the end of the nose.

The show soon begins. But things do not go fine. Not at all.

Chapter 15

After about five minutes of waiting Linus comes out onto the stage and the crowd goes into a hush, patently aware of the routine involved in the show. He has a microphone in his hand and stands before us. When the crowd reduces itself to the occasional inaudible buzz he looks at a cameraman, awaiting the signal. The cameraman points at him. Linus begins to speak, introducing Wendy.

"Thank you all for being here. And now, the woman you all came to see: Wendy Michigan!" he hollers, his introduction disappointingly banal to me, despite the fact that his voice is splitting with an excitement I would have thought impossible backstage when he stomped off huffily in search of Wendy's hoops—which he must have found, for I see them dangling from her ears as she emerges onto the stage, a German language version of "The Happy Wanderer" being piped through overhead speakers in seemingly inappropriate accompaniment to her appearance. Everyone rises and applauds deafeningly, greatly excited.

"Wow. I didn't realize she was as popular as all this," Kate says.

"Neither did I. They're fanatical about her," I say, the two of us also clapping vigorously, caught up in the swell of the rest of the audience.

"Thank you, thank you," Wendy says with appreciative, gesturing arms before sitting down in a cushiony chair. The crowd sits down right after she does, their applause over, their eyes all on her. She reaches over to the nearby coffee table and picks up a mug full of something. She takes a sip and sets the mug back down. She looks at the audience directly. "Now, before we begin, let me say a little about the music you just heard being played when I entered; it is a little dose of the kind of mirth you will encounter at The Hob-and-Nob the next number of days, as we are going all out to celebrate Oktoberfest. It's going to be a blast. I would love to see each and every one of you there. And I hope I do. But enough with the self-serving plugs and onto new business: today's show, to be precise.

"Now . . ." She pauses and puts her hands together before her chin, prayerfully, meditatively. "Today's guest is a troubled soul," she says in a voice of deeply concerned austerity. "Oh, I don't mean that his problems are overwhelming and unmanageable. But they are lingering, the kind that are incurred in childhood and fester and fester until their continual growth renders one ineffectual and dysfunctionally incapable of forging relationships of lasting value, problems that inhibit one from making progressive strides in society." Her hands are chest level now, greatly visible, clasped tightly in a gesture of pained empathy. "My guest, in short, suffers from a condition known as the mental gout. And I would like you to meet him, to listen to him and to allow him to share his story with us. For from his pain I feel that we can all learn, not only about him, but also a little something about ourselves: about what makes us who we are, who we are not, and who we would like to be. Ladies and gentlemen," she says, standing up, "allow me to introduce to you . . . Havilah Pilbeam." The audience begins to wildly applaud, endorsing Uncle Hav right from the get go.

"She's good," Kate whispers to me. "I misjudged her. When I watched her before she must have been having an off day. But the way she paused for effect before saying Hav's name—she knows what she's doing. I'm starting to feel a little emotional myself already."

"It's infectious. I'm feeling it too," I whisper back, no less impressed with Wendy's gift of turning ludicrous hyperbole into emotional reality.

Uncle Hav comes out, looking as dishevelled as ever, despite the makeup on his face. His hair must have been combed but you would never know it. It's unkempt and spiky. He walks tentatively, overtly aware of being on display. He comes over to Wendy, who embraces him and kisses him on the cheek. She removes herself from the hug and looks at him, with moist eyes of concern. "Havilah," she says tenderly, welcomely. "We're so glad you decided to share your story with us. Please, do sit down," she says, sitting back down in her own chair. Uncle Hav sits down in an opposite chair (there are three guest chairs— an ominous sign) and faces her.

"Hello, Wendy," Uncle Hav says hoarsely. I wonder how many cigarettes he's smoked today.

"Hello, Havilah. Ladies and gentlemen, give him another round of applause." The crowd readily complies. "It must have taken such courage for you to come here today," she says after the heavy spate of clapping reduces itself to a sputter.

"Yes, yes it did, Wendy."

"Now, Havilah," Wendy says, leaning forward earnestly, her legs crossed, "do not be afraid to jump in and tell me if at any point if I am touching on a nerve simply too raw for you to expose and I will refrain from that line of questioning. Just reach over, touch my arm and say, 'Wendy, please.' And I will put a halt to what I have brought up. Okay?" she says, her voice soothingly maternal.

Uncle Hav nods appreciatively. He casts a timid look at the audience but then quickly turns his eyes back to Wendy.

"Now, just for audience awareness, I would like you to tell us in your own words what exactly the mental gout is?"

"Well, Wendy," Uncle Hav says, his voice shuddering, "I am thirty-one years old and have two failed marriages behind me."

"Did you say *two?*" Wendy asks, in an astonished voice that must have taken great practice to perfect.

"I did."

I look around as a buzz arises throughout the audience. People are nodding and looking heavily disquieted, as though something of the utmost gravity has just been revealed.

"Please continue," Wendy says, her voice conveying intrigue and compassion.

"And, well, I have had several other failed relationships with women."

"I see. Have you ever considered the possibility that you are a homosexual?"

"Have I . . . What? No, not at all."

"I see. Please continue."

"And, well, I . . . uh, it's so hard to explain."

"Take your time. Healing is not something that usually occurs in a minute or so. It sometimes takes the whole hour."

"Thank you, Wendy. It's just that, well, I had a very ideal childhood. As good as you could possibly imagine. I have not one bad memory of my childhood."

"I see. Well . . . Wait a minute. That doesn't sound quite right. I thought you told me, from the notes I made in preparation for this show, that you consider your mother to be at fault for your present condition."

"I do, Wendy. I most sincerely do. Her and all my relatives. All of them are salts of the earth, and therein lies my problem. It's ironic, I know," Uncle Hav says, sounding much more comfortable than he did when he first came out, perhaps because he has now spotted me and Kate in the audience.

"I'm afraid I'm lost. We seem to be getting off topic. What is the mental gout? That is what we wanted to know."

"I'm getting to that, Wendy. My mother gave me such a fond childhood that I never wanted it to end. I think of life in naive terms; everything fails to live up to the beauty I experienced as a child. I was always satisfied as a child and I try to live my life in such a way that that satisfaction remains. But women see this as an attempt by me to be selfish and it alienates them. My childhood memories are inflaming my mind. I can't think straight and see a situation for what it is. I instead see it for what I want it to be. I can't see things clearly. That is my mental gout, Wendy."

Wendy sits back and crosses her arms, studying Uncle Hav, turning over his convoluted explanation in her mind. "I have to say, Havilah, that I feel you have somewhat betrayed me."

"I . . . What? How?"

"You told me that your mother's hold on your life was preventing you from progress and that she was stultifying your chances at positive growth."

"But she is . . . in a way. I mean, it's not her fault. Even though it *is* her fault. Oh damn. This is such a conundrum."

"Indeed it is. Still, Wendy Michigan is not here to pass judgment. I am here to help. Tell me, Havilah, what failed measures, prior to contacting me, did you undertake to try and clear your mind of all the wondrous childhood memories that ail you?"

"Well, Wendy, I thought if I changed my appearance that maybe I would see myself in a new light, that I would no longer see the happy child I once was and that I would then be free of that particular burden. So I've let my hair grow. I tried to grow a beard too but I just didn't have the stamina for it. Also, I've allowed myself to gain some weight. And I even bought a pubic wig."

"I see. Now why on earth would you do that?"

I feel myself groan. "Has he no shame?" I whisper to Kate.

"Shh. I want to hear this," Kate whispers back, leaning forward in her seat, transfixed.

"Because," Uncle Hav continues. "I thought that a thick rug would enhance my organs, or rather in some way redefine them, and make me less hesitant with the ladies. My pubes are rather pallid coloured," he adds.

"And why are you hesitant with the ladies?" Wendy asks, mercifully ignoring the comment about the colour of his pubes.

"Because my childhood dictates that I stay innocent."

"I see. Well, to get to the root of this vexing problem I thought it best to contact one of the people of your past, one of those who know you best." Wendy stands up. "Ladies and gentlemen, let's have a nice round of applause for Havilah's second wife, Belinda Fem."

"Oh oh," I say, starting to sink in my seat, as Belinda saunters out, a cup of coffee in her hand. She's a voluptuous redhead about six feet tall, really striking but also severely tempestuous. Her hair is cut short, which makes her look more threatening for some reason. There's no hair to hide her hard expressions, I guess.

Uncle Hav stands up in shock. "What in God's good name are you doing here?" he asks as Belinda sets her cup on the coffee table and goes over to hug Wendy. She then sits down in the chair beside Uncle Hav, who remains standing. "I *said*, what are you doing here?"

"I'm here to set the record straight," Belinda says, her voice cutting and confident, her legs crossed, the top one bouncing mischievously.

The audience lets out a collective "Oooohh!"

"What the hell is she doing here?" Uncle Hav says to Wendy, looking disoriented, his voice grating.

"Havilah, please sit down. It is often therapeutic to get the insights of another. It will lead to a greater understanding of the self."

"Malarkey! It's all malarkey! She's certifiable. She doesn't know what she's talking about. And not only that, she's a communist!"

"Havilah! Do sit down," Wendy orders, pointing to his seat. He complies, grumbling away, full of hot misery.

"Now, Belinda. What can you tell us about Havilah that will shed some light onto his current condition?"

"He calls himself innocent, hah! What crap! And if there's one thing he's not, it's hesitant with the ladies. He's a hound dog, pure and simple. His problem is that he likes to fuck around and expects us all to be okay with that. Oops! Can I say 'fuck' on this show?"

"There is some precedent for such language," Wendy says. "But don't worry, we have a five second delay, which allows us to beep out words, should the conversations get too unruly."

"In that case, fuck you Belinda! Lies lies lies!" Uncle Hav shrieks, pulling on his hair, looking ready to lose it entirely.

"Havilah! I will not tolerate such outbursts on my show. So contain yourself. You will have ample time for rebuttal."

Uncle Hav slumps in his seat, his eyes burning with frustration.

"Anyway, Belinda, do go on," Wendy says calmly.

Belinda goes on. "He had the freedom that a great childhood entails and he wants that now too. He just doesn't want to commit and he views this character trait of his as something that is beyond his control, when in fact he's just too lazy too work at commitment. By the way, his mother is a lovely woman and will most likely be horrified by these shenanigans."

"She will never know of them. Neither she nor any of her friends watch this show," Uncle Hav delusionally pipes up.

"Stupid. You can't keep something of this kind of public magnitude from her," Belinda says.

"That's true," I say noddingly to Kate. "I said as much to him."

"Oh yeah? And just how is she going to find out?" Uncle Hav asks contemptuously.

"She already knows. Despite our divorce she and I talk quite often. I told her I was coming on this show. She's probably watching as we speak."

"How dare you!" Uncle Hav screeches, hopping up out of his chair, deeply offended. "Come on, stand up, you brazen harridan, you! We're going to finish it right now," he says threateningly.

"What the hell are you talking about?" Belinda says quizzically, strikingly unfazed by Uncle Hav's insane ballistics, her leg still bouncing away.

"I said get up!"

"No, I'm comfortable sitting down, thank you very much."

Wendy stands up instead. "Havilah! This is not helping the healing process at all. Sit down!"

"Never! I will not be humiliated on this show by this woman. By this, this, this hideous milk tit! I will not!"

Wendy puts a hand on his shoulder and tries to guide him back into his seat but he shakes free of her grip. Wendy looks offstage, raising her hand and swirling her index finger in the air, an obvious signal. Linus comes out for support.

"You! Sit down. You're disrupting this show. Wendy is only trying to help you," Linus says, getting between her and Uncle Hav.

"Some help! By bringing out this, this slattern of an ex-wife of mine. She has thwarted all my attempts at self-improvement, and at every turn."

"Sit down!" Linus says, grabbing Uncle Hav by the arms. They begin to tussle back and forth, Uncle Hav trying to free himself from Linus's grip.

"Dean! Dean, help me!" Uncle Hav screams, his face dodging around Linus's frame, his gaze reaching out to me for help.

"What should I do?" I ask Kate, nervously wringing my hands.

"Nothing," Kate says hypnotically, her eyes glued to the sight unfolding before us all.

"Dean! For God's sake! And you," he says, his eyes coming back to Belinda, who sits calmly in her chair, "you're next. And quit bouncing that goddamn leg! That smirking foot! Go to hell!"

"Come now. Let's all of us settle down!" Wendy says authoritatively, trying to dampen the fanning flames.

The audience grows tense. Expectation in the air.

"Never!" Uncle Hav screams. He shakes his right arm free from Linus's grip and hauls back, ready to punch him.

"*Now* we should do something," Kate says, leaping from her seat. I am a half second behind her. But we are too late.

Uncle Hav cocks his arm. His fist flies forward. Right at Linus. Linus ducks. Uncle Hav hits Wendy. Square in the face. Wendy staggers. Falls back into her chair. Which tips over backwards. I jump on Uncle Hav. He and I and Linus collide into a chair. Kate rushes over to check on Wendy. Belinda sips on a cup of coffee. The crowd goes nuts.

Chapter 16

There is a piece of bloody gauze stuck to Wendy's lower lip. She is sitting in the recliner in her dressing room. Two of the makeup girls and someone in a business suit are leaving just as I enter.

"Dean, how are you?" Kate asks, rushing over to me and giving me a hug.

"Someone hit me in the head with a roll of duct tape."

"Really? How queer," Wendy says, as Kate runs her fingers through my hair feeling for a lump and, upon finding it, gently rubbing it.

"Anyway, I got Uncle Hav calmed down and told him to go home. The audience is still wild over this. I've never seen anything like it."

"You mean Linus hasn't dimissed the crowd? Surely everyone must know that the show is over," Wendy says alertly, sitting up. "I can't go on like this. I won't. I am battered and wounded."

"Yeah, they're leaving now, but slowly. They can't stop talking about it though. As for Linus, he was knocked out."

"He was? The useless bastard. I knew he was lying when he told me he took tae kwon do."

"Uncle Hav kneed him in the head when we were flailing about. He's deeply worried about you," I say to Wendy. "He honestly didn't mean to punch you in the head."

"Your uncle's a jughead. And I would sue his pants off if I hadn't deliberately set out to ambush him by bringing on that ex-wife of his and if this wasn't also the best thing to happen to this show since it's been on."

"What do you mean?" I ask.

"This'll be picked up by every news outlet on the planet. They're all bloodthirsty for this kind of thing. My face'll probably even be splashed on *Entertainment Tonight*. My people are already getting both the tape and the word of this whole debacle out there. It's probably already on the internet, at least it better be. Otherwise it's goodbye Sue. Anyway, I'm a lock for syndication now, not that there was ever any real doubt. Ow!"

"What is it?" Kate asks, going over to Wendy.

"My tooth has been chipped and I think I cut my tongue on it."

"Chipped your tooth?" Kate looks at me, the smile of good fortune splashed across her face. "Let me see," she says, bending over and examining Wendy's mouth. "I never noticed it until now but the top tooth, right by the left eyetooth, is indeed broken."

"And my lip's no damn better. If only I could find my pills. Dean, find me a cigarette, would you? And put on some Suzi Quatro. I need some music. I'm sorry if I'm bossy but Linus is supposed to do all this for me. He was knocked out, you say?"

"Yes," I say, searching the various cluttered tables for a cigarette. I find a pack and a lighter and bring it to her. Wendy takes them and lights a cigarette up immediately.

"Thanks," she says. "Where is he?"

"I don't know. Sarnia was helping him. He was unconscious when I hustled Uncle Hav out the back exit, but he was coming around when I came back," I say, finding the Suzi Quatro cd amongst a mountainous pile precariously stacked by the cd player. I put it on.

"Ahh, that's better," Wendy says, leaning back in her chair, soothed by the music. She removes the strip of bloody gauze from her bottom lip and tosses it to the floor. "That demented cocksucker can sure throw a punch, I'll give him that," she says, as Kate applies a fresh strip to her lip.

"It's just about stopped bleeding," Kate says, medically astute.

"I don't know what I'd have done without you today, Kate. The way you helped me up and whisked me in here before the vultures could circle and do any more damage was an almighty act of cool efficiency. You were like a secret service agent rising to the occasion to save the President from some Jodie Foster-loving-lunatic. Or some such thing. How would you like to work for me?"

"No thanks, I'm fine where I am. Now listen. About your tooth—"

"Listen to this song: "Devil Gate Drive" it's called. Winnie bought me this cd for my birthday last year. It was the first birthday present she ever bought me. It signals a new stage in our relationship."

"Who's Winnie?"

"My younger sister."

Kate turns to me, a fleeting scowl brushing over her face. "You never told me she had a younger sister."

I shrug. "Nobody talks much about her. She was an outcast when I was part of the family. I only ever met her once."

"She's changed now though," Wendy says to me. "Prison was the best thing that ever happened to her, even though it was a frame-up from the outset. Extortion is such an ugly word. They convicted her because of that word. Consanguinity is the word that will save her now though. Con-san-guinity. Wendy Michigan's name means something to people and now, by extension, so will Winnie Michigan's. I'm doing everything I can to help her. I got Fluff to arrange an interview for her at The Lily Pad. Winnie's always been sinewy. She's been blessed in that respect."

"Yes, well—" Kate stops in mid-sentence, seemingly bewildered by Wendy's talk. She shakes her head, as though it's full of cobwebs, and continues. "Now, about your tooth."

"Yes, my tooth. I can't keep my tongue off of it. My oh my, but I must look the hillbilly. I must go and see Dr. Ribb right now."

"I thought he was your psychiatrist," Kate says.

"Dr. Ribb looks after all my mental and physical maladies. He's a wise man and, now that the malpractice suit has been settled out of court, he will be able to build his business up again and not have to exclusively depend upon me and his import trade to make ends meet."

"Yes, well—" Kate turns to me, disbelief in her eyes, and wipes sweat from her brow with her hand. "My, it's hot in here," she says, turning back to Wendy.

"Yes. Linus didn't turn down the thermostat. He's lucky he got knocked out, otherwise I'd show him the meaning of wrath. Incompetency—that's the main ill plaguing the world today. I think I need a blast of Scotch and some fried peas. I must go straight home after seeing Dr. Ribb," she says garrulously, sitting up. "I think I'll watch a Yul Brynner movie tonight."

Kate stops Wendy from getting up by putting her hands to Wendy's cheeks. She faces her squarely, intently. "Listen, Wendy. Your tooth is just the ticket. It has given you the perfect excuse to go and pay a visit to King Cloke."

"King Cloke?"

"Yes, you could tell him that he was recommended to you by Jen Mallard, the last victim. Mention of her name may stir him up and get him talking. Especially since your visit to him will be so glaringly legitimate and smack of no ulterior motive whatsoever."

"What a plan! My God, yes. It's perfect," Wendy says, eyes alight.

"Except that he might not know of Jen Mallard," I interject.

"Nonsense," Kate says. "The King is the key. He's behind it all."

"What do you hope to find out though?" I ask.

Kate stands up straight and looks at me. She begins to pace, her left hand massaging her chin, in profuse thought. "Yes, that's a good question. We have to have a definite plan. Just getting him to admit that he knows Jen Mallard will not be enough. And if he was her dentist, and there would be undeniable intrigue in such a fact, it still does not go beyond that at this point. The fact that he was maybe Jen and Trini Albacore's dentist, well, it can merely be argued as coincidental, no more than that."

"You know, I think it's better not to go in with a prearranged agenda," Wendy says. "Spontaneity is better. It's more real. I'll just try to get him talking. Once you get a killer talking he can't shut up. They're all egotists. They want to brag, to tell people how smart they are."

"Good idea. King Cloke is undoubtedly too smart to confess but he might beat close enough around the bush so as to give us a break, some major and heretofore undetected clue."

"This is all so half-baked," I say, aware of sounding like the voice of negativity yet again, and though not liking it, unable to position myself into a different state of mind regarding this situation.

"That's because we're only halfway there," Kate says, her words inexplicably ringing with legitimacy.

"Right," Wendy agrees, standing up. "Let's go. Say, where in the hell are my people? None of them are even coming in to see how I am."

"That's because you told the makeup girls to spread the word that you didn't want to be disturbed under any circumstances," Kate says.

"Did I? My, but I must learn to curb my cuntly outbursts. No one likes a bitch. Well, let's go," Wendy says sprightly, leaving her dressing room. We follow her out. The studio is eerily ghostly now, in complete contrast to how it was a mere half an hour ago.

"You know," I repeat to Kate as we follow behind Wendy, "I'm sure the police already know who each of the victims had for a dentist."

"Perhaps. But since Trish is not being forthcoming about it we have to find out for ourselves. We have to be more resourceful in obtaining information since we don't have a badge to flash about and bully people with. And it is this resourcefulness of ours that will lead to the big break."

I don't say anything; Kate's conviction on the matter is too unwavering for me to overcome. We follow Wendy out the back exit, into the parking lot. We follow her over to a small, odd looking car. She pulls out her keys.

"What an odd looking car," Kate comments, her thoughts running parallel to mine.

"It's a Citroen. I thought about going retro and getting a Maserati but that seemed predictable and trite. So I decided to go counter-retro and get this baby."

"Wasn't this the car Wanda was driving away in when we came over for dinner the other night?" I ask.

"Indeed it was. She stole it, the unmanageable hag. But I knew she was going to Dick's. She always goes there after a hissy fit. So I stole it back. Two can play the thief game."

"Dick's? Dick Jemima?" Kate asks.

"Yes. That relationship is as on again/off again as a lightswitch. I get fatigued just thinking about it. I think she took up with him again right after your split, Dean."

"Yes," I say, my thoughts turning sullen.

"Anyway, so you two will follow me to King Cloke's?"

"We're right behind you," Kate says.

"What? We're going too?"

"Of course. We can't expect Wendy to allow herself to be thrown to that wolf in King's clothing without some backup. We'll be in the waiting room to make sure."

"To make sure of what?"

"Don't be so deliberately obtuse. To make sure that no funny stuff goes down, what else?"

"I hardly think he'll kill her in his office."

"Not if we're there he won't." Kate turns to Wendy. "He works at the Stem Building. Fifth floor, Room 507. I looked him up in the phone book last night."

"Gotcha. See you in ten," Wendy says, getting into her car and starting it up.

Kate turns and begins a brisk walk across the puddle-drenched parking lot to the Galaxie. I have to hustle to keep up with her. She hands me the keys when we reach the car. I unlock the doors and we get in. Soon we are on our way to the Stem Building. We pull into the parking lot and spot Wendy walking towards the building. I quickly find a spot and park the car. We hop out and rush to catch up with Wendy. But there was no need. She stops by the entrance and lights up a cigarette. We wait around with her as she smokes it. Several other individuals are gathered around under the entrance overhang too, out of the rain, smoking alone and silently.

"It feels weird smoking with a puffed lip."

"I'll bet," Kate says.

"I think I'm a little nervous. That's why I lit up," Wendy says, a shade of vulnerability momentarily creeping into her speech.

"Do you want to back out?" Kate asks concernedly.

"Heavens no. Wendy Michigan cowers in the presence of no man. Not even you, Dean," she laughs, shoring up her appearance of invincibility. We all laugh. She butts out her half-smoked cigarette. "Let's roll," she says and we all enter the building, on our way to see the King.

Chapter 17

There is no one in the waiting room. I don't know what to make of it, though the superstitious side of me is taking it as a bad omen. There isn't even anyone at the desk. Kate puts her hand down on the bell on the front counter and taps it repeatedly. A fifty-ish, matronly looking woman with a tight-bunned hairdo comes out from one of the back rooms.

"Yes? . . . *You?*" she says to Kate, examining her with recollecting eyes. Her expression then changes, from deep concern to odd relief.

"Yes, it's me," Kate announces nonchalantly, "and this is my much more famous friend, Wendy Michigan." She motions to Wendy with her hand. "You may know her from tv. She is in need of emergency dental attention and insisted on seeing Dr. Cloke." Kate is really taking charge now. I'm sitting in a chair beside Wendy, taking no charge at all.

"I'm awfully worn out, Dean," Wendy says to me wearily, seemingly indifferent to our surroundings. "I'm thinking of going on sabbatical. I've always wanted to see the vineyards of the old country. It would be a good place for me to try and reconnect with my astral plane."

"I suppose it would," I say, preoccupied with Kate.

"Well, I'm sorry, but the doctor is busy," the matronly woman says curtly.

"Tell him it's an emergency. Wendy only sees the best and she's heard that Dr. Cloke is the best."

"Where did she hear that?"

"A friend."

"I see," the matronly woman says, looking at Kate with stealthy, narrowing eyes. "And who are you?" she says, her voice now reeking condescension.

"I am Kate Carlo," Kate says, revealing her name with an always available readiness, like she's James Bond or something. "But you already knew that," she adds with impatient annoyance.

"I most certainly—" The matronly woman is cut off by the emergence of a man from one of the back rooms.

"What is all this racket?" he asks. He is about five foot nine, with precise granite features, a cleft chin, black hair and smokily intense blue eyes. He has a rather mod hairstyle. He is wearing jeans, a wine check sports shirt with the two top buttons open (revealing a gold chain swinging from his neck), and a buckskin fringed vest. He is about forty-five, I surmise. "Penny?" he says, looking at the matronly woman inquiringly.

"I'm sorry for the disruption, Dr. Cloke. But this lady—"

"My name is Kate Carlo. And surely you know Wendy Michigan," Kate says, eliminating Penny from the conversation and directing her comments to King Cloke.

King Cloke looks at Kate strangely and then, after a brief moment, past her and at Wendy. "Yes, I am familiar with Miss Michigan's work," he says, after a brief pause.

"Thank you," Wendy says from her seat. "It's always nice, as a professional, to be appreciated by another professional."

"What seems to be the problem?"

"I chipped a tooth during a talk show accident. Can you perhaps spare a moment to look at it?"

"Well," King Cloke says, his voice deep and resonant. He looks at Penny, who scowls and shakes her head disapprovingly. "I have to," he says, taking her aside. Kate makes no attempt to be anything other than a blatant eavesdropper. "We must go on as before," he says.

"But her? She's the very type—"

"Enough," King Cloke says with quiet authority. "Our bookings have been sparse as of late." He turns to Wendy. "If you please, Miss Michigan, follow me and we'll see what we can do for you."

Wendy gets up and looks at us with puffy pursed lips of giddy satisfaction. "Well, here goes," she says, passing by Kate, who remains standing where she is. King Cloke and Wendy disappear from sight. Penny sits down in her chair behind the front desk, a rigid dissonance in her manner.

"You might as well sit down and wait," she says to Kate.

"Yes, in a minute. Can I ask you something?"

"Are you from the press? Look, I don't have to answer anything you ask. I told everything I'm going to tell to the police."

"So they've been here?"

"Of course. When two of one's patients are murdered, the police are of course looking for a connection. But if they knew Dr. Cloke they would realize that someone as gentle as him could never be involved."

"I see. And he of course has an alibi?"

"He was out of town when all the murders took place, all four of them. They're trying to pin the other two on him too. He was at a dental convention each time," Penny says, saying a lot for someone who seemed so bent on not saying anything at all.

"And what about you?"

"I of course went with him. Dr. Cloke and I—ahem! Just never you mind. Now go and sit down. I have work to do and am tired of talking to you," Penny says rancorously, shooing Kate away with a pencil. Kate turns and comes over to me. She sits down beside me.

"May I just ask you your name?" Kate calls out.

"Penny."

"Yes, that much I gathered. Penny what?"

"Penny Odette. Now quiet."

Kate looks at me. "There's something going on here," she whispers to me.

There is a framed watercolour of a sailboat on the wall to the right of me. I examine it sleepily. It's been such a long day already. I turn to Kate. "What do you propose to do now?" I whisper back in belated response.

"I don't know. They've caught me off guard by being so forthcoming. They're good. Real good."

"What are we doing for supper tonight?"

"I don't know. I kind of have a yearning for Chinese food."

"I like that yearning of yours," I say, my thoughts starting to revolve around dry garlic ribs and deep-fried prawns.

"Good. At least that's settled. Now, we have to figure out our next move here. What should it be?"

"You're asking *me*?" I say. Kate looks at me with imploring eyes. She really wants my help. I try to think about our so-called next move. "Well, if he has an alibi . . ." I say falteringly, so easily stymied, unable to come up with a finish to my half-thought.

"We'll wait and see what Wendy has to report. I guess that's all we can do for now. We have to be patient; even though some future life may be on the line we have no other option."

"I guess not," I say.

"What are you two going on about?" Penny asks distrustfully, her head popping up from behind the front counter.

"Just go on with your work," Kate says.

"How can I when you two won't be quiet?"

"What is this, a library? Or perhaps it's a mausoleum."

"What kind of an insidious crack is that?!" Penny says harshly, catapulting out of her chair and standing behind the counter with great looming irritability, her clenched stares a vain attempt to browbeat Kate, who remains coolly composed.

"What in tarnation is going on out here?" King Cloke says, rushing out, a paper bib fluttering around his neck, thin white rubber gloves covering his hands. "I will not tolerate shouting in my office, not even from you, Penny." He stands before us, as though expectant of something ready to break out and more than assured that he will be the one to put a stop to it.

"But they are making inferences. Inferences, I say. I suspect grave duplicity."

King Cloke looks at us, his eyebrows arched questioningly. "Is this true?" he asks us.

"We were just talking. Is it against the law to talk in here? Or is this office some sort of little island of fascism?"

"I will not even dignify that with an answer," King Cloke says disgustedly. He turns to Penny. "Let them be," he says to her with quiet authority.

"But—"

"No buts about it, Penny. Go about your business or else the doggie gets no bone," he says, his voice off-puttingly suggestive.

Penny's lips threaten to pout but she steadies herself and sits back down, throwing us a steely gaze as she does so.

King Cloke looks at us. "It will be a little while before I'm finished with Wendy. I've discovered three other problematic areas in my cursory examination of her mouth. You might want to leave and then come back."

"I see. Can I talk to her for a moment?" Kate asks, standing up and already walking towards King Cloke.

"Be my guest," he says and Kate disappears into one of the back rooms with him. She comes back in about a minute.

I stand up. "Well?"

"Wendy told us to go. She's fine." Kate walks out of the office and I follow her. We stop at an elevator and wait. "We're witnesses to the whole scene so they won't try anything. She said she's going to call me tonight."

"Oh," I say. "They do seem touchy. The cops must really be harassing them."

"It's a regular aquarium in there. Completely fishy," Kate says.

A woman about our age suddenly rushes up to us and taps Kate on the shoulder. Kate turns swiftly to face her. "Yes?"

"Hi! . . . Oh. Oh, I'm sorry. I thought you were someone else."

"That's quite alright."

"I just thought you were a friend who I haven't seen in awhile. I'm sorry."

"That's okay," Kate says and the girl leaves. The elevator doors open and we get in. "What are you thinking?" she asks me as the elevator takes us down to the main floor. "You look pensive."

"I was just wondering if today has been productive and fortuitous. Or if it has been a dead end."

"Oh, it's just the tip of the iceberg, believe me. It's leading to something big. Really big."

Really big? I don't like the sound of that. I think of Chinese food instead.

Chapter 18

I lay the blanket out on the floor and then set two plates and some cutlery on it. Then I take the bag of Chinese food from the table and sit down on the blanket. I begin to unpack the food. Kate comes out of the bedroom, wearing one of my sportshirts over her t-shirt.

"It smells good," she says, coming over and sitting down on the blanket cross-legged, across from me, the food between us. "I think you made the right choice with beef and tomato lo mein."

"I think so too," I say, strangely beaming over this unimportant fact. I pop a few dry garlic spareribs into my mouth.

Kate picks up a prawn and takes a bite. She stands up. "What are you in the mood to drink?"

"Beer," I say.

"Another perfect choice," she says, looking at me. "The cut on your forehead is hardly noticeable anymore. You're a fast healer," she says, a statement that fills me with warmth for some reason. She goes into the kitchen and comes out with two open bottles of Heineken. A cool swirl emanates from the bottle she hands me. I take an immediate drink. She dims the lights so that a warm and comfortable glow permeates the apartment. Then she goes over to the stereo and puts on a Bobby Darin cd. "I was going to put on some of our grad-era music but I figured you were probably listening to this when you were eighteen anyway. This *is* your grad-era music."

"That's true enough. I never liked most eighties music until the other day."

"That recently?" she asks, sitting down cross-legged again. She takes a drink of her Heineken.

"Well, give or take a few years."

"I really must remember to bring in that Bangles cd."

"Is that what you were thinking of putting on?" I say, my plate now heaped with Chinese food. I dig my fork into some mushroom chop suey.

"No, I was actually thinking about *Rattle and Hum*." She takes the container of lemon chicken and spoons some onto her plate. Soon her plate is full too.

"Oh? I always liked that one. It's one of the few from those years that I discovered right off and not belatedly, as has usually been the case."

"Those were heady times," she says reflectively, generally.

"For you, maybe."

"Was your life really so stultifying back then?"

"No, I suppose not. But it wasn't particularly wild either."

"I'm sure you had your moments."

"We all did. And do."

"I must confess that when I thought about you during the years we were apart that I always hoped you weren't doing much and that you were still in town. Such a thought comforted me."

"At least there would always be one constant in your life, is that what you mean?"

"I suppose. I suppose it was a selfish way of thinking. But I'm glad it turned out to be somewhat true. Otherwise I wouldn't be here right now."

"You've given all my years of static procrastination meaning and purpose."

"Any way I can help," she says laughingly and takes a drink of her beer.

"It was all part of the grand plan. Or so it would appear. I remember when I saw you again that day, after all those years. It was like a thundercrack going off in my head. I felt tingly and giddy and afraid—the way I always felt when I used to see you and talk to you. It was an astonishing moment. But I knew it would evaporate fast and that I had to act."

"I didn't even see you, yet we couldn't have been more than ten feet from one another. I had just moved back and I guess I was suffering from too much inward thinking and concerns about how I was going to furnish my new apartment. I was too immersed in the set of cookware I was looking at."

"I'm usually never even in that part of a store but my divorce had just come through and all the cookware had been Wanda's. Talk about a coincidence."

"Life is predicated on coincidence, don't you know that yet? When I heard the words 'Hello, Kate,' I knew it was you. I just knew it, even though I hadn't heard your voice for so many years. I think I even said 'Hello, Dean,' before I raised my head to confirm that it actually was you. It was a weird moment. It was like it was scripted out for us. It was destined."

"What would you have done if I hadn't asked you out right then and there?"

"I don't know. I never did anything when you never asked me to dance at school dances or when you failed to ask me out on a date when we were in school, so . . . I don't know. It was always hard to gauge your interest. It still is sometimes—and I know you better than anyone now. You have a way of withholding yourself that is hard to read."

"I just had to ask you out. I felt a pounding immediacy about me. A complete fear that you were just going to walk away. That I was going to let you walk away and not even take a shot. And my life was in such a shambles then, what with . . . with Wanda."

"Yes."

"Because of that there's always a small part of me that wonders if you doubted my intentions at first."

"What do you mean?"

"I mean, did you think that I asked you out on the rebound?"

"The thought crossed my mind after I found out about Wanda. But I never gave it much credence."

"Good. Because I would've left whoever I was with to be with you. No matter how happy I might have been I know that I would be happier with you."

"My. That could've caused some major disruptions and resentments."

"I don't care."

"Tell me about you and Wanda."

"You already know."

"I think I do. But I want you to tell me. Really tell me. Once and for all."

I pause and feel about to stutter. But then I brace my thoughts and begin. "I was supposed to be out of town one weekend on a camping trip. We were tenting. But it rained so much that we decided to pack it in a day early. I came home and found that I didn't have my house key. My buddy had driven and so I had left all my keys at home. Wanda wasn't supposed to be home either. She had made plans to spend the weekend with Tuppy, in my absence. Or so she said. But I remembered that I had a hairpin in my wallet and took it out, deciding to try and get into the house. And lo and behold I got in. But I could hear noises and knew that Wanda was home. I went to the bedroom, looked in, and there she was, in bed with her first husband."

"Dick Jemima," Kate says in hushed and cautious tones.

"Yes. And by the sounds they were making I knew they were having a good time. They never even knew I was there because I just turned and left. I honestly didn't know what else to do. I went to a motel and spent the rest of the weekend there. When I came back home Wanda acted as though things were normal. But they weren't. I just couldn't be with her anymore from that point on. But I never told her I saw her and Dick. I don't know why. I just did this song and dance in which I told her that I felt we were drifting apart and that maybe it would be better if we separated. She was—surprisingly or not surprisingly, I'm not sure which when it comes to Wanda—readily agreeable to my suggestion. I guess she wanted to go back to Dick at the time. I can't help but wonder if it has ever occurred to her that I know what she was up to with him."

"Obviously not. Otherwise she wouldn't be playing the part of 'a woman scorned', as Wendy put it. She thinks you dumped her for me. I get it all now. She thinks you were fooling around on her with me but kept it under wraps so that she would be more easily cowed into an amenable divorce settlement but then as soon as everything was final you brought us out in the open. Remember we saw her a day or so after our first date? That must be what she concluded; that's why she thinks you wanted a divorce, because you were having me on the side. And now she feels you put one over on her."

"I suppose. I never really thought about it like that because she's so unpredictable—delusional even, but at dinner the other night when Tuppy said that I was unfaithful to her it all began to make some sort of sense to me."

"Well you have to tell her the truth, that you saw her and Dick that night. That's the only way to get her off our backs."

"I was thinking about that too."

"I figured all along that you had caught her with another man."

"I know. Why didn't you make me tell you about it sooner though? I mean, you had every right to force the issue."

"I knew it was a sore point with you. I knew you were still hurting. But I'll admit that I have been growing very impatient with you about this."

"I always thought that divorced people were merely inherently dysfunctional. I was always so sure that when I got married it would last forever. Not just a couple of years. But when it happened to me it made me realize that I was just like everybody else. It knocks you down off your high horse, that kind of knowledge. Plus, I can still see and hear them in my mind sometimes. It makes me just feel somehow small and inadequate. It all just lingers. It's hard to get over."

"That low and silly woman. We should call her up. We have to get this all straightened away, the sooner the better. And plus, we have to get our toaster back. We simply *must*." Kate reaches over for my empty plate and stacks it on top of hers. She then sets the cutlery on the top plate. She gets up with the dinnerware in her hands and goes into the kitchen. I re-pack what's left of the Chinese food and follow her into the kitchen. She's putting the dishes in the dishwasher, her mind churning away with thoughts. I put the Chinese food in the fridge. The phone rings.

I sigh. "I'll get it," I say, going into the living room and picking up the phone. It's Uncle Hav.

I try to say hello but he cuts me off halfway through the word. "How's Wendy? Am I in trouble?"

"No, she's letting you off the hook."

"Good. That whore. I should sue her, that's what I should do. Do you know how much emotional damage she's caused me?"

"I'm sure you'll tell me."

"How come you always sound so disinterested in my plight?"

"Because I am."

"Oh go to hell, you sassy prick! Did you know that my mom just called? I just got off the phone with her. She watched the show!"

"I told you she would."

"That damn Belinda. What a whore. My mom said she was deeply hurt that I chose to lay blame for my situation at her feet. When it's her fault, no less! You should have heard her, a regular martyr's voice. I'll be hearing the crushed hurt of that voice in my nightmares for years to come. Another thing to pin me down and inhibit me. How did this happen?"

"I knew that show was a bad idea."

"A fine time to tell me, isn't it? Half a day after the fact. Just what the fuck are you good for?"

"Hey, fuck you. You made your own insane bed, now lie in it and face the consequences. Pubic wig. Man. What were you thinking?"

"Ahhh, you're right. It's my own fault. I apologize. It's this damn mental gout. I never did get a chance to fully explain the nature of it. They could have maybe named it after me. Called it Havilah Syndrome or something."

"I like the sound of that."

"At least it would have given me a little cachet, wouldn't it have?"

"More than a little, I'd say."

"Yeah? Oh, if only—if *only*—it had all worked out. Anyway, what should I do about my mom?"

"Buy her some flowers and apologize to her, profusely and effusively. Tell her you've been under a lot of stress."

"There's no denying that. Sometimes I wonder why I even bother to get up in the morning. I bought too much fish, did I mention that? It's like a production line over here. I'm canning salmon day and night."

"We'll have to come over and take a few jars off your hands."

"I'll believe that when I see you over here. Did you talk to Fluff yet?"

"No, not yet."

"What in the hell is wrong with you? Hurry the hell up. It's only a matter of time before some seedy miscreant snaps her up. They always go for real lowlifes. I'll never understand women. What's Kate up to?"

"We just finished eating. She's cleaning up."

"Ohhh, to have a woman like her. What'd you have to eat?"

"Chinese food."

"Chinese food? You *know* I love Chinese food! I haven't had Chinese food in years. Why couldn't you have invited me over? What am I to you anyway, some kind of plague? Don't answer that, you'll just bruise me with some kind of smart remark."

"You're touchier than usual, do you know that?"

"It's just that life is so unjust. It's hard to deal with. And I'm out of cigarettes again too. What am I going to do?"

"It's tough, I know."

"No, you don't know. You have Kate, you lucky stiff. You don't know what it's like to suffer like me, not at all. Christ! Do you think it's too late for me and Wendy to get together? I really liked her for the first few minutes of the show today. I thought I detected sparks between us and I think we could recapture that magic if she'd just give me another chance."

"I'll ask her."

"Right. Like the way you asked Fluff? Please. Don't fill me with false optimism. Anyway, I just heard the door. I've got to go. I called in an escort for tonight. I need some soothing. I hope she brought some creams."

"That's it. I've heard enough. Bye," I say, hanging up.

Kate's sitting on the couch, having done her kitchen chores. "He sounds in a typical mood," she says.

"Yeah, he is," I say, coming over and sitting down beside her.

She puts her head on my shoulder. "I'm quite tired," she says.

"It's been a long day." I put my arm around her and sigh. "I'm glad I finally told you about Wanda. I'm sorry I dragged my feet so long. It was very unfair of me. It's just that the whole thing, in my mind, makes me seem pathetic and stupid."

"It's not your fault. You're the victim in all this."

"Yes, well, victims are often pathetic and stupid."

"Pathetic and stupid are cute on you though."

"I'm glad to hear it. Still, it made me feel like there was something wrong with me; why else would she go to him?"

"She's a promiscuous nut. You can expect no less."

"I suppose. I just still think about it. I don't know why I let it bother me still. After all, things have worked out far better than I could have ever imagined. That night after I discovered them my thoughts were running pretty low. I never imagined being where I am these days."

"I'll bet. When a relationship is over it's a hard thing. That's why I moved back here. I had to start all over again too. Contrary to what they say, you can come home again."

"Yeah. I'm sure glad about it too." I squeeze her close. "Are you going to call Wendy?"

"It can wait. This is much too nice to put an end to. I was thinking about working on my story tonight too but I think I'll let it pass. I'd much rather do this," she says, snuggling up against me.

"Did you get a jolt of inspiration in regards to the story?" I ask.

"I think so. I have to explain why he combs his hair with a fork. So after the first line, which I've remembered by heart—Do you remember it?"

"'Jean-Paul always combed his hair with a fork.'"

"Wow, that's right. Anyway, after that it will go something like: 'He preferred forks to combs because the tines were spaced farther apart on forks than the teeth were on a comb. Spacing was very important to him, as it pertained to hair grooming implements.' How does that sound?"

"Good. You should write it down before you forget it."

"Oh, I won't forget. Those sentences have been rolling over in my mind with great regularity," she says. "Besides, I'm not moving off this couch."

"Nice," I say. We don't say anymore. We drift off.

When I next awaken Kate is on the phone. "Look, just get her. It's an emergency," she says.

I wipe my eyes with fisted hands and look at my watch. It's after two in the morning. "Who are you calling? What's going on?"

"I'm calling Wanda. I started thinking about her again and she's really starting to irritate me beyond all acceptable bounds. So I decided to bushwack her with a late night call. Quick. Get on the fax phone and listen in."

"I hop up, dizzy with startled weariness, and stumble over to the phone. I hear Wanda's voice.

"Who is it? What's the emergency?"

"This is Kate Carlo. I'm calling on behalf of Dean."

"*You?* YOU!! What kind of tomfoolery is this? You better have one hell of an explanation for getting me out of the sack at this time of the night."

"We want our toaster back."

"Well you can't have it. I've found that I can't do without my morning toast."

"You are bringing it back or else."

"Or else what?"

"We will either go a litigious route or come over, rough you up and take the toaster back. I haven't decided which as of yet."

"I'm hanging up and going back to bed. Talking to you is causing the mudpack on my face to crack."

"Who's in bed with you? Dick?"

"Dick? A likely tale."

"Well, it's his number I called," Kate says, looking down at the open phone book before her.

"You understand nothing about the nature of the social co-op. Besides, I blew that ditch monkey off last week. Washed my hands of him completely. Not that it's any of your business."

"I know about you two."

"What are you talking about?"

"I know you were engaged in carnal experiences with him that weekend Dean was out camping with his buddy. In your own house no less. In yours and Dean's bed no less! Have you no shame? You overwrought tart."

"What are you talking about?"

"I think you heard me."

"Who told you this? Dick? LIAR!!! I will not tolerate such besmirchment. It was Dean who was cheating. That cad, finagling his weiner into another. Into you! Don't deny it."

"Oh but I do deny it. Because it never happened. You—you are the cheater. You agreed to divorce him because you wanted to be with Dick again, plain and simple. Now bring the toaster over."

"Get real—Wait! Does Dean know about these accusations?"

"I don't believe that to be pertinent to the matter. So, since we've established that you took the toaster for reasons now conclusively proven groundless you can bring it back. You have no reason to be mired in hatred for him."

"Wait. Shut up and let me think." There's dead air on the line for about thirty seconds. "It's all lies you know. All lies."

"My source is irrefutable."

"Pure innuendo. I'll bet Paco told you all this. Was it Paco? Does Dean know?"

"Is that so important to you?"

"He musn't know these things. He's naive enough to believe such lies. And then he'll think I was a terrible wife."

"You were a terrible wife."

"I was a grand wife. Simply grand. Dean married me because I'm spiritually pristine. And he still thinks of me in that way. And your presence will never take that away."

"He *what?* You're mad."

"That's it! I've had it with you and your conjecturing. I'm coming over!" I hear the phone slam down, a loud crack that causes me to jolt the receiver away from my ear.

Kate gently hangs up. "Did you hear her? She still loves you, in a twisted kind of way."

"I never heard her say that," I say, hanging up.

"Of course she did. She doesn't want you to have a low opinion of her."

"How could she possibly think I feel the same way I once did?"

"She's a lunatic."

"Yes. And now she's coming over."

"Yes. But this time we'll be ready."

Chapter 19

I keep staring at the clock, watching the seconds tick mercilessly away.

"Are you still uptight about her? She's obviously not coming. She hoodwinked us," Kate says from the kitchen table, marking one of the many notebooks spread out before her. "It's been fifteen hours."

"And eleven minutes and counting," I say. I grab a glass from the cupboard, go to the sink and fill it with water. I take an agitated drink. "Maybe we should call her."

"Again? I've already called her three times. She's wise to us now. God only knows what deviousness she's up to. She really steams me. Tell me again what you saw in her."

"We're seeing the worst of her now. It's her inherent restlessness. But when we were together at first she was, well, I don't know, she was kind of funky."

"*Funky?*"

"Yeah. And I could make her laugh. I liked that. She was fun and exciting. Wendy said it wouldn't last though because of Wanda's promiscuity. That's what started the feud."

"Oh right. I keep meaning to bring that up. *That* started the feud?"

"Well, she said it right to our faces, in front of everyone, at our gift opening no less. It *was* kind of tactless. And then one thing led to another and all sorts of ugly things were said, from both sides. But in the end Wendy turned out to be right."

"Wendy: she is blunt, that's for sure. But in a likeable way. At least that's how I find her. I like her energy. Hmm. I should call her up again," Kate says, setting her red pen down and standing up. She stretches. "Do you think we should be worried that we haven't been able to reach her all day?"

"No. She's a busy girl. She's probably at The Hob-and-Nob or at the tv studio or something."

"I suppose you're right. Still, I'm curious to know what went on with King Cloke yesterday." At that she picks up the phone and tries to get hold of Wendy. After a brief wait she sets the phone down.

"No luck?"

"None. Remember at her show yesterday she mentioned that The Hob-and-Nob is celebrating Oktoberfest this week?"

"Yeah. You want to go?"

"I think we still have the *Elbsegler* hats. In fact, I'm sure we do. I should go check the storage room," she says and then whisks away into the spare room, which she calls our storage room because it's cluttered with all the stuff we can't find room for in the rest of the apartment. Meanwhile, I open the fridge door for the hundredth time today and look through it. "I found them!" she exclaims excitedly, coming out of the room and into the kitchen. She pulls the flat cap down onto my head. She is already wearing hers. "How do I look?" she asks, in a pirouetting spin.

"Precocious yet innocent."

"That's exactly the look I was going for. What are you doing? Looking through the fridge again? Maybe we should go grocery shopping."

"How much longer until you're done marking?"

"Oh, I'm just about done already. I can finish it up tomorrow. So, the rest of the day is ours. What do you want to do?"

"I don't know. Want to order a pizza instead of shopping? We could go shopping tomorrow."

"I suppose we could. Alright."

The intercom buzzes.

"I wonder who that could be?" Kate says, going over to it. She presses the button and talks into it. "Yes?"

"Is this Kate Carlo?" I hear a shady voice say as I move up close beside Kate to listen.

"Yes."

"We met yesterday, under rather strained circumstances. It's me, King."

"King Cloke? What do you want?" Kate asks, annoyed yet also oddly unsurprised that he is here.

"Can I come up?"

"What for?"

"Look, I can't talk to you like this. May we speak face to face?"

"Alright." Kate buzzes open the entrance door.

"What did you do that for?"

"We have to get to the bottom of this," she says.

"Of what?"

"Of whatever this is. I want to know why he's here."

We wait for what seems like a long time. I sit down at the kitchen table. Another looming confrontation to put me on edge. I begin to tap the tabletop nervously. The doorbell rings. Kate opens the door a crack. "What do you want?"

"May I come in?" King Cloke asks. I can't see him from where I'm sitting but his voice is brimming with clarity.

"What do you want?" Kate says unshakably.

"I couldn't help noticing you yesterday. You have a nice smile. That should mean something to you—coming from someone like me. As a dentist I've seen just about every kind of mouth there is and I can spot every sort of flaw you can imagine. But *your* teeth, they're very fine indeed."

"Is that what you came here for? If so, then you have wasted a trip. For I am immune to your repugnant come-ons."

"Don't be like that, sugar."

"Call me that again and I'll poke you in the eye."

I decide that my presence is now necessary so I get up and approach them. Kate's left hand is holding the door ajar, preventing King Cloke from entering. I move in behind her, put my hand over hers, replacing it as she pulls hers away. I swing the door fully open, ready for action if need be. "What do you want?" I say, announcing myself.

"Oh . . . Ahh. I see. My. This is somewhat awkward. My name is King."

"I know. I'm Dean."

"Aren't you Wendy's assistant?"

"No."

"That's funny . . . Hmm. It seems I was misled. Penny's playing games with me again. She probably sees this as a necessary trick, to try and set me right."

"Set you right how?" Kate asks.

"Well, let me say right off that this visit was meant to be a social one."

"Obviously. But, as you can see, I am taken," Kate says, moving in close beside me. "And, as such, I am not in the need of social visits from playboy dentists."

"No, it would appear not. How indelicate this situation has become. My. I feel fraught."

"Where's Wendy?"

"I wouldn't know. We are not to see each other until tonight."

"Tonight? What for?"

"She thinks it's to get information from me but as far as I'm concerned it's a date. But let's not talk about her. Tell me, have you heard of me in any circles, other than the unsavory one pertaining to these unfortunate deaths?"

"Murders, you mean."

"Please. I hate the abruptness of that word."

"You killed them."

"Kate!" I say censoriously.

"I most assuredly did not." He puts his right finger to his temple and begins to rub it. "I get migraines when accused. Please answer my question. Did you ever hear of me outside of connection with these murders?"

"No."

"Ahh. Well that answers that, then. And here I thought my reputation preceded me. You are not far off in calling me a playboy, not far off at all. I take such a moniker as a compliment of the highest order. I believe in swinging."

"Yes, well—"

"Please, let me finish. Before you concretely form such an odious opinion of me let me say that I was indeed acquainted with all of the deceased girls and that two of them were my patients. It's no secret. Many people know all about this already and I am not about to hide such an unfortunate fact. But I was out of town each time one of those murders occurred. And so was Penny, my helpful assistant. And thus, no case can be made against either of us."

"You can't make us go away with such admissions. We're not like the police. We're much more dogged and we're going to get you. So don't come over and try to bowl us over with your forthrightness, because we know it's all just an insidious act."

"But I assure you it most certainly is not. It's just that you are a very special looking girl and the only way I know of to get to know a very special looking girl is to pursue her. And that is why I am here. I had only hoped that you would be of a mind to get down with King Cloke. But since, alas, you have never heard of my reputation and have given yourself to another, I shall make my way home. Penny will be most happy at my failure. Anyway, goodbye my sugar—Ow! What in tarnation?"

Kate has just poked him in the eye. "I told you not to call me that, you smarmy sex renegade. Now go on your way. We will undoubtedly meet again but it will be on our terms and not yours." She puts a hand to his chest and pushes him back, out into the hall. She takes the door from my hand and shuts it. And then locks it. She looks at me. "Talk about your cretins."

"You showed him though."

"That's how it is with people like him. You have to assert yourself. Otherwise they run roughshod over you with their despicable ways. Anyway, what were we talking about before being interrupted by him?"

"Not too much. I was considering ordering a pizza."

"Oh, right. Do you think that's a good idea? After all, if we have a pizza we won't be in the mood for sauerkraut and smokies at The Hob-and-Nob."

"Are they serving such food there?"

"Of course. Wendy wouldn't do anything half-assed. Which reminds me, I should try and reach her again." She goes over to the phone and tries to get hold of Wendy. There's no answer. She looks concerned.

"I'm sure she's just out doing whatever it is she does. Which is quite a lot, from what I've been able to gather over the years. Give me the phone," I say. "I'm going to call Sam."

She hands me the phone and disappears from sight. I can tell that she's worried.

The phone rings. Kim answers. "Hi, Kim. Is Sam there?"

"Goodness. No. He just stepped out for some rice cakes. It seems we're always out of something."

"Oh. I was just wondering if you two wanted to come with us to The Hob-and-Nob tonight."

"That sounds inviting. We *are* hungry. But we've already made plans, I'm afraid. We're going to a Vietnamese restaurant. We've been dying for some hot and sour tofu soup all week now."

"Oh. Say, did you mention to Sam that I was wondering if he wanted to go to The Lily Pad?"

"Yes. He said he's into it. If ever he has a spare moment I'll get him to call you. We're awfully busy lately, for some reason."

"It's the shorter days," I say, looking out the window at the darkening sky.

"I suppose it is. I knew it was something."

"Or maybe you've just outgrown me."

"Not that I'm aware of."

"I'm glad to hear it. Anyway, I'll let you go. Goodbye."

"Bye. We'll do something soon though."

We hang up. I go over to the fridge and look at the list of phone numbers that is stuck to it by way of a plastic rainbow magnet. I call up the pizza place and order a large pepperoni and cheese and a litre of coke. I put the phone down and set about looking for Kate. She's in the spare bedroom.

"What are you doing?"

"I came across all my softball equipment. How come I don't play anymore?"

"I don't know."

"I'll have to join a team next summer and get back in the groove."

I nod, thinking it a good idea. I should get back into sports too. I miss floor hockey, now that I think about it.

"Did you talk to Sam?"

"No, he wasn't home, as usual. So I went ahead and ordered a pizza."

"I figured you would," she says, hunched over, her attention buried in the cluttered closet. She stands and straightens, facing me. "Do you think I should wear my *dirndl* dress tonight?"

"Well, it does have that low neck I like."

"Yes, it does fan the flames of your breast fetish, doesn't it?"

"Do I really have a breast fetish?"

"Let's just say that you have an acute awareness of them."

"I like yours best of all though."

"That is a lame response. And yet I still choose to embrace it," she laughs. "Look what else I found," she says, holding up a pair of black 'Rio' dress pumps with three-inch heels. She sits down on the end of the bed and slips into them.

She stands up. "Now I'm very nearly as tall as you. I'm six feet tall with these on. Intimidated?"

"A little," I say.

She steps up to me and gives me a gentle poke in the nose. We put our arms around each other, our gazes even and interlocking. I kiss her. And then she kisses me. She grabs the brim of my hat and pushes it down over my eyes. I lift my head so as to see her from beneath the brim. We laugh. I shake my head and then adjust the hat so that I can see better. She sits back down on the bed. She rubs her legs together, looking at me seductively. "I'm feeling very frisky all of a sudden."

"There's always time," I say, my blood running hot and feverish.

"Yes. But I feel it would be better to let it build all night. Let it swell."

"A fine choice of words."

"Just about everything's a *double entendre* if you think about it hard enough. See? I just sort of said another one."

The phone rings. "It's not just in the movies that it rings at the most inopportune times," I say, discouraged.

"Better get it."

"It's Uncle Hav."

"It might not be. Come on, we'll save it. It'll be grand."

I choke down some saliva in a hard swallow and back out of the room, watching her. "Alright," I say acceptantly and then dash over to the phone. It's Wendy.

"Hi," I say. "Kate's been trying to get hold of you all day. We were starting to get worried."

"No need for that. I'm coach of a ringette team and we had a big game today. I know you're probably thinking that it's too early in the season to be a big game but they're all big, Dean. They really are."

"I suppose they are."

"Oh yes. And I also got into an almighty heated argument with the opposing coach today. The dumb slut. The four-inch hole on that rubber ring has got nothing on her cratered twat, I'll bet you the house on that. You just can't carry the ring over the blue lines, Dean. It's unheard of. You have to pass it or shoot it in, everyone knows that. Sam Jacks is turning over in his grave, he must be, knowing the game he invented has gone to hell in a handbasket. But you know these newcomers, they bastardize everything. Not a purist in the lot. Even the ref was reluctant to step in and set things right. The fuckin' twit. They don't want to make it too intense for six years olds he told me. Well, have 'em stay home and play cards with the cat if they don't want to nurture a competitive spirit. It tires me out, Dean, having to deal with these hammerheads all day long, it really does. Fortunately for me though, Fluff had my meds for me when I showed up at The Lily Pad after the game."

"Did she ever find her brick of hash?" I ask, the question for some reason popping into my head.

"No. Grundy swiped that, I'm sure of it. I know how his type operates. But who can prove it? It's a tough scene."

"Do you want to talk to Kate?"

"No time. I just wanted to touch base. I have to rush to The Hob-and-Nob now. I've got to help the new band set up."

"*New band?* What about the other band? What about Rennie?"

"Him? A joker, that's what he turned out to be. His damn cell phone was always going off in the middle of a song and it would be his mom and he would stop singing to take the call. Take the call, Dean! They'd argue about when he was coming home and if he was going to pick up butter and milk, shit like that. It got to be like performance art and, like all performance art, excruciating. I had to sack him. But I've got a new crew I'm tailoring to my liking. They're called Malignant Pussy. I know I know. I'm working on a name change right now. I've got to come up with one before they start their first set tonight. The German crowd that's showing up there tonight will be horrified if a band with that kind of name is introduced. But they do have a mean accordian player and that'll go a long way in appeasing all those old krauts. Anyway, gotta go."

"Wait! What happened with King Cloke?"

"He fixed my teeth up good as new. When he wasn't ogling my tits, that is. The fiend. He seems harmless enough though. I'm seeing him tonight, actually— if I can find the time that is—to try and iron out a few facts. But being in that chair while he was working on my mouth, well, it was actually a very sensual experience. Have you ever had tooth sex, Dean?"

"No, I don't think so."

"It's Biblical. But Thomas Pynchon wrote all about it in *V.*, so there's nothing more I can add to the discussion. Oh, and the King has an alibi for all the murders too, did you know that? Anyway, he doesn't look good for the perp at all. I think we're on the wrong train track. Back to square one, I guess. See you," she says, clicking off.

I set the phone down and go over to the fridge yet again. I open it and pull out a glass container of grape juice. I take a drink straight from the container.

The buzzer rings. I go over to it. "Yes?"

"Did you order a pizza and a coke?" a female voice says through the intercom.

"Yes," I say and ring her in. I turn and go into the spare room. Kate's still sitting on the end of the bed, immersed in looking at an old picture album, wearing a softball glove and tossing a softball into it.

"Who was on the phone?" she asks.

"Wendy. She was talking like she was on speed or something."

"Or something. Well, at least she's safe. Didn't she want to talk to me?"

"Too busy, she said. She'll be at The Hob-and-Nob though. We can maybe talk to her there."

Kate sets the photo album aside and stands up, stretching, continuing to toss the ball into her glove. "Where was she all day?"

"She coaches ringette."

"Really?"

"That's what she said."

"Hmm. That only reinforces my own determination to get back into sports." She tosses the ball softly into the glove, stretching and smiling. I can tell she's more relaxed now, relieved that Wendy's fine.

The doorbell rings.

"Our pizza," I say hungrily, leaving the spare room. I take another drink of grape juice.

I go over to the door and take some money from my pocket. I open the door. I see a rather tall, somewhat attractive girl standing before me. She is wearing a baseball cap, a windbreaker and jeans. The pizza box is balanced over her right hand. Her left hand is down by her hip, holding the bag with the coke.

"Smells good. How much?" I say, holding out the money.

"Kiss the floor," she says grittily, flinging the pizza box at me. It flies into my face. I bat it away, stunned, staggering back. The paper bag is ripped away to reveal a pistol in her hand, the plastic coke bottle empty and taped to the end of the muzzle. My eyes go wide and tense. And then she starts blasting.

Chapter 20

Two things save me: my weaving backstaggers of surprise and the pizza girl's crummy aim at a moving target. The plastic bottle taped to the muzzle might have something to do with her wild shooting and—whatever help it is to me in preventing me from being hit—it is worthless to her as a silencer. The gunshots are loud and reverberatory. Kate comes rushing out of the spare bedroom, just as one of the bullets explodes through the grape juice bottle in my hand.

She rushes out into the hall. "What's going on?! Dean! The juice!" she says, grape splatter all over the walls and floor in a messy gush. Another bullet flings past my head and into the wall and another zings past me and down the end of the hallway, into the open bathroom, smashing into a water glass, shards of glass tinkling down into the sink.

"Get down!" I yell to Kate, off balance and sputtering to get my bearings and make sense of it all.

Kate hits the floor. She still has the softball in her hand. She hurls it at the front door just as she takes her nosedive. Kate has never been much of a pitcher. Fielding is her game, as she can run like a track star. But her bad aim does prove fortuitous this time. The softball hits the doorframe and ricochets right into the pizza girl's face.

Kate sits up and takes quick stock of this sudden turn of events. "Take that!" she says declaratively, pointing menacingly at the pizza girl, who has stumbled against the doorframe for support, stunned into momentary, shaky submission by the unexpected blow to her nose, which is now spillng blood. With this break in the gunfire I see a chance and rush towards the door. I slam it against her gunhand.

She yowls, profanity spewing from her mouth in demonic snarls of pain. "Stinking fucker! Feckless cock ring! Bastard lackwit!"

I lean into the door, pinning it against her wrist. Spit flings venomously through the crack of the opening, just missing my face. I wrestle with her hand, trying to get the pistol free from her grip. But the gun is welded to her hand. I

156

cannot separate them. Another shot blisters out of the pistol, into the ceiling. The barrel smokes. The smell of gunpowder clouds the air.

Kate watches in frozen, horrified fascination. But then snaps together and disappears into the spare room. She comes out with an aluminum bat. She races over to where the battle rages. Choking the bat on the top end of the grip she brings it down with a swift heavy rap, the aluminum clanging gun and bone. The hand unclenches in shocked, limp torment and the gun clatters to the floor. I kick it away down the hall. I remove pressure from the door. The hand zips back and disappears from sight. I slam the door shut.

I look at Kate. She looks at me, the *Elbsegler* hat scrunched low over her head, making her look childish and vulnerable. She hands me the bat. "There's another one in the bedroom," she says, beginning to turn single-minded. She rushes into the bedroom, her high-heeled feet splashing through the grape juice puddle in the middle of the floor. She comes out with another bat, gripping it firmly, taking practice swings, the bat swishing through the air. "Let's go get her," she says, excited, scared and angry, lockjawed with determination.

I slip on my shoes and fling open the door. No one to be seen. I breathe deep, my heart pounding.

"You take the stairs. I'll take the elevator," she says. I nod. She rushes down the hall, holding the bat back over her shoulder, ready to strike.

When I get to the door leading to the stairwell, I stop. I breathe deeply and then yank open the door and run down the stairs. I make it down one flight when I encounter a thick group of people, elderly folks, our next door neighbours and some of their friends. They are out of breath.

"Damn elevator is out again, Dean," Joe Sodium, our neighbour, says.

"Did a girl pass by you?" I ask.

"Nope. Haven't seen a soul," Joe Sodium says, he, his wife Fran and everyone else looking at me curiously.

But there's no time to explain. "Thanks," I say, turn and run up the stairs. Kate and I live on the top floor, the tenth. The only place the pizza girl could be if she didn't take off down the hall is on the roof. The door to it is supposed to be locked but it never is. I recklessly hurry up to it and fling it open with brazen thoughtlessness. I run out into the dark and stormy night. Freezing rain pulverizes my face, in a windy whip of contemptuous disregard for my presence. I can see very little. There is a light above the door and it is bright, but it is not the beaconing floodlight I would like. Malicious shadows emerge with every move I make. I turn cautious and step forward carefully. On the lookout for her. For anything suspicious. Then I feel it. The mere shock is enough to almost cause me to have a heart attack. The deep heavy impact. She smashes into my side. Her arms form a vice around my waist, pushing me with all her sinewy might, with all the force of her propelling body. My feet slide along the slick, rained-over surface of the roof. I try and hit her with the bat. But hit air instead. I contort. Trying to turn. Trying to nullify the effect of her surprise attack by grabbing at her. But she just keeps pushing me. I don't realize the danger involved in what she is up to until—

My vision cartwheels, my body in a flip. Right over the railing. Head thunking against the top rung, goose-egging semi-consciousness threatening to overrun my waking abilities. My hands fly about in a flailing refrain of last chance survivalist motion. My right hand clasps around the bottom rung of the railing in a wet smacking smear of skin against iron. My head snaps back. Then hangs. I see my feet dangling down, disappearing into dead blackness, touching nothing, the parking lot below me. Far, far below. A world away but easy to meet. I feel my grip slipping. I shut my eyes. My arm burns, already worn out, tired. The rain pulses against me, weighing me down, everything working to free my hand from the bottom rung of the railing. I swing up my left hand, trying to get it around the rung. Momentary success. I pull myself up, see Kate and the pizza girl fighting by the entrance door, the light above in a luminescent downward arc, framing them. The pizza girl running at Kate, kicking and swinging. Kate dodging aside, belting her in the forearm with a swack! of the aluminum bat. My left hand slips. I swing pendulously, precariously. My kidneys feel knotted, expectant, burning to let loose. I reach up again and grab the rung with my left hand. I again try to pull myself up. See Kate and the pizza girl continuing to barrage each other with swings, Kate getting in most of the blows, the pizza girl kicking and karate chopping at Kate, my vision of them altered by the sheeted white downpour before me. They look as though rotoscoped by water. Unreal. This whole thing is unreal. It cannot be. The iron rung is like grease. My left hand slides off again in a wet rubbery smear, the rung showing me no mercy, now tickling the fingers of my right hand with icy numbness. I look down. The parking lot seems unavoidable. I shut my eyes. Feeling heavy and weak, surrendering to disbelief. My little finger slip slip slipping off the rung, the ring finger next, and then—

My hand feels iron no more. It's stretched out taut, upwards at nothing, grasping for the rung. A cinching clasp around my wrist. I look up. Kate has me. Her left hand cuffed around my wrist. "Hang on," she says, the veins in her forehead strained and pulsing. She is hanging over the bottom rung, trying to pull me up. I can hear guttural sounds coming from her mouth as she struggles to pull me up. "You're heavy," she says, fighting against defeat. I look up at the slender thread saving me: her hand bound to my wrist. And then—and what a time for this to happen—I remember.

I have to let her know. I swing my left hand up to her own left and grab it right above her wrist, which my right hand is now ossified around. "Good," she says, her right hand quickly clenching over my left in an encouraging reinforcement of safety. "Don't let go. Whatever you do, don't let go. I'll get you up, Dean," she says, her voice worried but also firm. "I just need leverage," she says, trying to reposition her lower body, trying to pull it back, so that she isn't so precariously balanced atop the bottom rung. "If I can just get my feet flat against the brick lip of the building, if I can just . . ." She doesn't finish her sentence, she is too caught up in the struggle of getting her body positioned right without letting me go. I can feel the heaviness of my body on her arm, feel the agonizing pull I am subjecting her to.

"Kate," I say, having no other words to offer. I look down into the abyss. I look back up at her. "Kate," I say again, desperation really beginning to well up in me.

"Hold on," she says and suddenly I can feel myself lifted up by about a foot. With her feet wedged against the brick lip of the building she is using the weight of her body and the force of her legs to her advantage. Pushing herself back and, in the process, pulling me up. I feel my forearms against the bottom rung. I let go of her grip with my right hand and grab the rung. I grip it tight and swing my right leg over. I roll over the rung and plunk onto the rooftop, beside Kate, who is lying in a skim of dirty water on the pebble-spackled roof. She is panting heavily, looking up at the dark roiling sky, exhausted, her eyes weary and slightly lost.

"Kate," I say, sitting up, beside her. I grab her by the hands and pull her up. I hug her. She hugs me back.

"Oh, Dean," she says, her voice in a panicky sob. "I thought I was going to let you go. I thought . . . I thought you were going to die! I didn't think I could do it. Oh God," she says, spent.

I hold her close and tight. I grab the brim of the hat that is squashed down to her ears and remove it. I readjust it on her head. "Don't cry, Kate. You saved me. And I knew you would too. I just knew."

She pulls back to look me in the eyes, the light above the outside door reaching out and dimly sketching our features in the otherwise pitch dark rain. Water and tears are running down her face. She smiles, full of relief and pride in herself. "I did do it, didn't I?"

"Yes. I'd be dead if not for you."

"Oh, Dean," she says, hugging me again. "I'm so glad."

"Kate," I say. "I remember now."

"What?"

"When I first met you that day in kindergarten. When I passed by you wearing my gym clothes and you were hugging your mom's leg I reached out and touched your wrist. I touched your little wrist. The one that just saved me."

She looks at me and beams, a smile of relief and thankfulness and endearment. It's her turn to adjust my hat, the hat that has, amazingly, stayed on my head during this whole unbelievable ordeal. "Yes," she says quietly, almost bashful. "That's what happened. That's the way it was. It made me feel so safe. That's the only way I can explain it. Because that's the only explanation there is."

We help each other up and make our way to the door. Kate retrieves her bat from a puddle. "Where's yours?" she asks.

"I don't know. I think it went over the building along with me."

"Maybe *she* has it. Who is she, Dean?"

"I have no idea."

"Here," she says, giving me the bat. "I'm too shaky. She might be waiting for us, ready to try and finish the job."

I take the bat and we enter the stairwell, shutting the door behind us. We find ourselves hurrying down the top flight of stairs with a surprising lack of caution, all our adrenaline not yet spent and now funneling its way into a growing determination to get whoever it was who attacked us. We run down another flight. And then another, the bat in my hand, gripped securely, ready for bone-smacking action. Down another flight. Right around the corner. Ready for quick descent down another. But then—

Face to face with Wanda, toaster in her hand. Her eyes blow wide open, sheared with instantaneous panic. "Acch! Don't hit, don't hit!" She tosses the toaster and a book at us, pivots awkwardly as though in fear of her life, turns and stumbles down a few stairs before finding her coordination and disappearing from sight, her booming voice echoing throughout the stairwell. "Killers! Mercenaries! Ambushers!" she yells, on and on, her voice elevating in strength and thunder with each step she takes away from us. "Dirty pool! Filthy nerve!"

"Wanda, wait—" I say belatedly, long after she has disappeared from view.

Kate picks up the toaster that broke apart upon hitting the wall beside us and now lies in a wrecked heap by our feet. "Well, this is no darn good anymore," she says disappointedly. And then she picks up the book and examines it. She looks down the empty stairwell, as though at the aura of Wanda, at her vapour trail—something. Anything of Wanda to berate and scowl at. "That awful witch," she says, turning to me. "She's the one who had our Vincent Price cookbook."

Chapter 21

Kate calls 9-1-1 as soon as we get back to our apartment. I look at the grape juice mess on the walls and floor. Kate comes over and joins me as soon as she is off the phone.

"They're sending someone right over," she says.

"Should we clean this up? Or is it crime scene evidence?" I say.

"I don't know," she says, disoriented and concerned. I look at her. She's soaking wet. We both are.

"I think we need a quick drink," I say, heading towards the cupboard in which we keep the liquor.

Kate follows me. "I think that's a good idea," she says and I pour us each a couple of large shots. She takes her tumbler and gulps down a good portion of whiskey. She looks at me. "I just keep seeing you going over the edge. It's a nightmare image. I thought right then and there that you were gone."

"I didn't know that you saw that."

"The elevator was out of order and when I was coming back to catch up with you I ran into Joe Sodium and he said you went up to the roof. I'd just reached the door when she pushed you over. I cried out, thinking that that was it for you. But then I saw your hand gripping the rail. She was just going to step on it when I called out to her and then she just turned and attacked. Just attacked. Without a moment's hesitation. She was like a rampaging bull. She was nuts." Kate finishes her drink and I pour her another, the bottle not leaving my hand. I suck back mine and pour myself another as well.

"I tried to pull myself up, a couple of times, and each time I saw you two fighting in the rain, by the glow of the light. The whole thing seemed so delirious."

"I kept hitting her with the bat but she wouldn't go down. All over her legs and arms and then finally I was able to connect a good one and I cracked her across the back of the head. It was a sharp little blow and she staggered and clutched at her skull and she was hunched over like some kind of rabid beast, snorting and yowling all these things I couldn't understand and she shot me a murderous glare with cracked red eyes and then she bolted through the door and down the stairwell. And that's when I came to see if you were still there. I wanted to go slow because I was so afraid that what I was fearing would turn out to be true, but I knew I had to act fast. But there you were. And I just grabbed at you. I don't know how I got you up. I really don't."

"I'm safe now but I can still feel the closeness of it. The sense of it. The danger of the predicament, I'm still awash with it. Look at me."

"You're shaking."

"I know." I pour some more whiskey into our glasses. "Where'd you learn to fight like that, anyway?"

"It's all about poise. People shouldn't scoff at beauty contests. You learn things in them that help you your whole life." She does a pirouette to try and lighten her mood. I look at her feet. She is wearing only her socks, which are soaking wet.

"What happened to your shoes?" I ask, only now noticing their absence.

I broke a heel on one shoe when I tried to pull you up. I managed to kick them both off. It was easier to get leverage in my stockinged feet."

"When we first split up out in the hallway you went running to the elevator. And then you were fighting. Running and fighting in those high heels," I say, amazed at her abilities. "You must be the only girl alive that can do that in those kind of shoes."

"Well, I don't know if I'm the only one . . ." she says, her voice fading away thoughtfully, liking the idea of my statement. "That girl in *Remington Steele*, she could really run in high heels."

"Her? Yeah, I guess she could. Well, you're in a select group at the very least."

"I wondered whatever happened to her. You never see her in any shows anymore."

"Maybe she retired. She probably made a lot of money from that show."

"Maybe," she says, still thinking about it. "I always liked that show."

The buzzer alerts us. I go over to it. "Yes."

"Are you Dean Dorian?"

"Yes."

"Police. Let us up."

I ring them in, not liking them already. Their voices sound belligerent and unheeding. I wait at the door. Soon the bell rings. I look through the peephole and see two uniformed cops. I open the door and let them in.

They're both short and stocky with fleshy bulldog necks. One of them has a pad and pencil in his hand. "You Dorian?" he says.

"Yes," I say.

"We had a very hysterical call about a disturbance."

"It was hardly hysterical," Kate says, coming over to the door.

The cop with the pad and pencil eyes us up and down, his attention particularly taken with the drinks in our hands. The other cop stands in the open doorwell, his thumbs looped between his holster belt and pants. He watches us with severe haughtiness.

"One at a time," the cop with the pad and pencil says. "I want to talk to you first and foremost," he says, pointing to me. "What happened?"

"Well, as you can see," I say, pointing to the grape juice mess on the floor and then down the hall at the hole in the tiled wall right above the sink, "we were shot at tonight. She fired four shots in all, I believe."

"I see. Who shot at you?"

"I don't know."

"What do you mean you don't know?"

"I mean I don't know."

"Sure you don't," the cop standing in the doorwell says, his voice dripping with sarcasm.

"We ordered a pizza and I let a girl into the building who said she was the delivery person and when I opened the door she was holding the pizza but she threw it at me and then started shooting."

"That's probably how Wanda gets into buildings. By pretending she's delivering something," Kate muses to herself, her thoughts momentarily off-topic. "The gun's right over there," she then says, again alert to the situation, pointing to the spot where I kicked it to.

"I've had just about enough of you," the cop with the notepad says snappishly to Kate.

"My taxes pay your wage. Don't get short with me," Kate says, her words stinging the cop with the notepad with multiple meanings.

"What kind of a crack is that?" the cop with the notepad says, puffing out his chest and short-hopping onto his tiptoes to try and meet me eye to eye before coming back down to stand in a stationary position, frustrated and wearied at his attempts to be taller.

"May we have your names?" Kate says.

"I am Officer Root and this is my partner, Officer Relish. But enough of these asides. Why did she shoot at you?"

"I don't know," I say.

"What did you do to have someone want to shoot at you?" Root persists.

"Nothing."

"I'll ask you again. What did you do?"

"Nothing. Look, shouldn't you pick up the gun or something? Isn't it evidence?"

"Don't tell us what to do. We'll do what we do when we get to the bottom of what you did. What did you do? Why did she shoot at you? To protect herself?"

"To protect herself? From what?"

"You tell us."

"I don't know."

"This is all nonsense. Are you two even cops?" Kate says.

"You, hush up. And you—" Root says, pointing the sharp end of his pencil at me, "you are in deep trouble, buddy boy. Deep trouble. Threatening a woman and attempting to assault her is no joke. You make me sick," he declares and furiously begins to scribble away on his notepad.

"What?! You're out of your tree. She shot at us. *Us!* Haven't you heard a single thing I've said to you?"

"Numbskulls," Kate says.

"You called her over and then you tried to attack her with a bat and then after she got away you concocted this pathetic frame job so as to make yourselves look like the victims. That's how it went down, didn't it? Didn't it?!! Say it!! Say it!!" he screams obstreperously, momentarily flipping out, his face turning into a wad of beet red flesh. "Miss Michigan is very distraught about your near lethal bat attack. And buddy, we're going to make sure that your kind is prevented from trying to harm someone as innocent as her ever again." He pokes me in the chest with the eraser end of his pencil.

"Wait a holy rolling minute," Kate says, stepping forth. "What kind of tune are you trying to whistle? I am the one who called 9-1-1. *We* were attacked by a gun blasting lunatic. *We* were using bats to protect ourselves from her. *We* chased after her after wrestling the gun away from her. And then, after a number of things that I won't bother to detail since your thought-challenged minds would fail to grasp them, *we* ran into Dean's ex-wife, Wanda. And she freaked out and now is apparently trying to frame us. Trying to pin some dastardly goods on us. But that bag of goods is full of hot air. And the frame will not hang because there is no picture in it. It's just another shameful display by some pantie-less maroon who will do anything to try and disable the relationship between Dean and myself. Now, when is someone going to respond to our real trial, our real dilemma, our real danger? Dean, would you pour me some more whiskey? All this oratory is making me dry," she says, wiping her brow with the back of her hand and holding out her glass. I pour some whiskey into her glass and watch her toss back a mouthful, mesmerized by her.

Root removes his hat and scratches his head, looking perplexed and at a loss as to how to proceed next. "There would seem to be two stories of great variance. I think maybe you two better come down to the station so that we can straighten things out."

"That won't be necessary, Officer Root," a female voice interjects, coming from the hallway. A woman steps forth. She is tall, well over six feet, and is wearing a tan-coloured trenchcoat that comes down to her knees. Her hands are in her coat pockets. She is wearing a fedora that sits perched atop a mountainous perm of red hair that flows down past her shoulders.

Root turns at the sound of the voice, surprised. "Oh. Yes, yes of course. We just came here because of a report of a domestic disturbance." Relish removes his hat deferentially and allows her to pass by him and into our apartment. Root also steps aside. The woman approaches Kate and myself, followed by two plainclothes men.

"I'll be taking over this investigation now," she says to Root without even looking at him.

"Sure," Root says, nodding timidly. He and Relish step out the door. "Would you like my notes?" he asks.

"That won't be necessary," the woman says. She watches the officers leave and then removes a hand from her pocket and snaps her fingers. One of the plainclothes men hurries over and shuts the door. She turns to us. "Tell me what happened."

"Who are you?" I ask, scrutinizing her.

"I am Trish Mindy. I am this town's lead homicide detective and this case is now mine."

Chapter 22

I tell our tale to Trish Mindy. When I'm done she just looks at me with distaste. She evaluates me with a domineering stare, averting her eyes every now and again to look at Kate. Her two companions are standing over the grape juice stain. One of them is taking pictures of it with an archaic old Polaroid and putting the pictures in his pocket without even waiting for them to develop fully.

"So you're Trish Mindy," Kate says, after it is apparent that Trish herself is in no hurry to speak.

"I am," Trish says, and then says no more for about half a minute. She then points to her companions. "And these are my associates, detectives Dude Bagley and Hard Larson."

Kate glances at them momentarily but then turns her eyes back to Trish. "Why aren't you out after King Cloke? He's obviously the one behind this. He was here this past afternoon, no doubt getting a feeling for the place so that he could lay it all out for his minion before she came over to put us on ice."

"King Cloke is innocent of any wrongdoing. He was out of town when each of the murders occurred."

"Don't you think that in itself is suspicious?" Kate says.

"Yes, I've thought about that," Trish says reflectively. She looks at her two companions, still milling about over the grape juice stain. "Dude. Hard," she says to the two of them and they look at her attentively. "Make a note of the bullet holes. And mark the gun down as evidence, though the serial number has no doubt been filed off."

"How do you know that?" Kate asks contrarily, not taking to Trish at all.

"I am an officer of the law. I know. Now, tell me, what did the girl who attacked the two of you look like?"

"Well," I begin, "she was about Kate's height I guess. Same type of build and hair colour and—"

"She looked like Miss Carlo then, is that what you're saying?"

"Well, no. No one looks like Kate. But I guess in a general sense, maybe. I mean, she was sort of attractive but she was harder edged. Her face was more gaunt, meaner looking."

"I see. It's definitely her, then. Dude, have you processed the gun?" Trish asks impatiently.

"I have," Bagley says, holding the gun before him in a plastic bag. "There is a serial number on it too," he says, his tight wiry little frame seeming to vibrate with excitement over this fact.

"No matter. The gun will be stolen."

"You're sure of that?" Kate asks dubiously, even though she would likely agree with this new assumption of Trish's if I were to ask her.

"I am. Now, you two are friends of Wendy's, are you not?"

"Yes," I say. "She used to be my sister-in-law."

"I see. I should have all of you arrested."

"On what charge?" Kate says challengingly.

"Obstructing a police investigation."

"That's ridiculous. We're just trying to find the killer. We're good samaritans if we're anything."

"You both almost got killed tonight. I must insist that you both lay off this investigation or I will have to take action against you."

"You just don't like the idea of us stealing your thunder."

"Listen. We have strong reason to believe that your attacker is linked to the murders of the young women that have occurred in this city. The description you gave of her near to clinches it. We have had her under surveillance for some time but we lost her in this vicinity earlier tonight. So lay off, not only for your own safety but also because I am beginning to find your snippiness intolerable, Miss Carlo. You beauty queens, you're all the same."

"And just what is that supposed to mean?"

"Stay out of my way," Trish threatens. She removes a hand from her pocket and snaps her fingers. Bagley and Larson come over to where she stands and look at us menacingly. "I have means and resources you cannot begin to comprehend. Stay out of my way, I'm warning you. Hard, pick up that pizza box. My stomach is astir."

Larson picks up the pizza box and opens it. He holds it before Trish and she removes a slice of cold goopy pizza. They all do.

"Help yourself," I say antagonistically, put off by their nerve.

They begin to eat their slices. Larson goes into the kitchen and sets the box on the counter, by the sink.

"Are you going after King Cloke or not?" Kate questions, ready to prod Trish for some information.

"I will not say any more on the matter," Trish says between mouthfuls, stepping forward, beginning to peruse our apartment. "Nice pad," she says anachronistically.

"It suits our purposes," Kate says, following Trish. Trish goes over to the table where Kate's students' notebooks are. She flips the pages of one and examines it cursorily. "A teacher, are you?"

"I am," Kate says. "Don't touch those notebooks. Your fingers are greasy."

"They most certainly are not."

"Answer me this: who was it who attacked us?"

"We have a notion," Trish says obliquely, finishing her slice of pizza with a shark-like chomp.

"What are you going to do about what happened to us tonight?"

"What would you like us to do?"

Kate looks at Trish seriously. "Tell us the whole scoop. That way we'll know where we stand and how best to handle the situation."

"That would be compromising the investigation."

"You're talking smoke. I don't think you know any more than we do."

"Don't push me. I know. I am an officer of the law."

Kate sighs, wearied with Trish, who seems to now be evaluating her in great detail.

"So you actually saved your boyfriend from falling to his death?" Trish asks, still not quite believing my version of events as I told it to her.

"I guess I did," Kate says quietly, humility and sobriety in her voice. It is still something that she can barely comprehend and something that she is unable to be flippant about. The effect my near death has on her fills me with thankfulness and a somewhat selfish joy. To know that my death would fill her with such sadness adds lustre to my sense of who I am and what I mean.

"You don't look that strong."

"She's the strongest person I know," I interject protectively (though somewhat sillily it strikes me), seeing Kate momentarily lost, shuddering again over our close call.

"Yes. Hmm," Trish says, looking at me, her tone of voice suggesting less than favourable thoughts about me and my manhood. "Well, in any event, your attacker won't be back."

"And just how do you know that?" Kate asks.

"She will be moving on to less suspecting victims. As well, you're too hot for her now. And besides, I am an officer of the law. I know. I have nineteen years experience. I am the lead investigator."

"So you've said. And then said again," Kate says, a snarky twang to her voice. "So we're to be left to the wolves then? And all because you don't want to impart any information to us."

"You already know too much. That silly little Wendy. I have half a mind to strafe her ass with a garden rake. I have always understood our conversations to be confidential, but apparently she is not to be trusted either. Say, she didn't mention anything to either of you about a Dr. Ribb, did she?"

"What?" I say.

"Never mind," Trish says hastily, seeming to regret her last outburst. "Just heed my warnings and listen to what I am about to say. We're about to tear this case a new asshole and when we do everything will make sense. So until then, do as I say, and lay off. We do not need any outside interference from the cast of amateur hour. It will only hinder our broadening dragnet. Do you understand?" Trish looks severely at Kate, who looks back at her acerbicly. Trish then looks at me, awaiting a response from one of us. I half-heartedly shrug, which seems to satisfy Trish that we have acquiesced to her orders.

A sudden squawking burst of static erupts. Larson—who is even more wiry looking than Bagley, if possible—is on the receiving end of a torrent of words coming from his oversized walkie talkie. When it's finished he says, "Ten-four." He looks at Trish. "There's been a car theft reported over at the old movie theatre."

"Sounds like her m.o.," Trish says, seemingly baselessly. "Let's roll." She steps past us and over to the door. She swings it opens and pulls the fedora down tightly over her head. She swivels her head suddenly and looks at us. "Remember," she says with castigating eyes. "Pursue this matter and you're asking for the big nosedive." She turns away and leaves, Bagley and Larson following closely behind her, a couple of salivating sycophants. They slam the door on their way out.

I look at Kate, mystified. "What the hell was that all about?"

She grabs the bridge of her nose with the thumb and index finger of her right hand. She shuts her eyes, full of thought. "I don't know. I doubt that they even know. They're just running around like headless chickens, hoping to fall into a break."

"I guess the Wanda stuff is over with anyway," I say, relieved, not at all open to the idea of having to go to the police station to straighten out a domestic dispute.

"Not as it pertains to us. We have to get back at her somehow. Make her realize once and for all that the reality of you and me as a couple is not going to go away." She goes over to the fridge and takes out two Heinekens. She opens them and hands me one.

I set down the bottle of whiskey that has been glued to my hand and take a drink of beer. It seems to refresh me. I go over to the stereo and search through our cds.

"Make it a nice soothing one," she says.

I put on Eddie Cochran's "Three Steps to Heaven."

She smiles serenely. "You never take a misstep when it comes to putting on music," she says.

"Thanks," I say. "What about the grape juice? Should we clean it up now?"

"We've waited too long already. It's sticky. So we'll just leave it till morning."

Kate takes off her hat and tosses it on the table. She runs her right hand through her wet, matted hair. She takes a drink of beer. "Look at me," she says, her eyes directing me to her hand, the one holding the beer. "I'm still shaking."

"We both are. You need to get out of those wet clothes."

"Yes. I'm still full of energy though too."

"It was an adrenalized night."

"It's not over yet. Dean?"

"Yes?"

She sets her beer on the table and grabs me by the hand. "Let's go to the bedroom. I wanna get thumped."

Chapter 23

If ever Kate is to display complete vulnerability it is during the sexual aftermath of our intimacy. She curls her body up against mine, snuggling tight, full of quiet lassitude and thought. I always think of her as trying to absorb me; she has just shown me everything of herself—and given everything of herself— and in some ways I think this act momentarily reduces her. By giving herself over to me as she has she has left herself open to the possibility of a hurt that only she understands. I know her last relationship ended badly. She told me all about it, with a forthrightness that I myself can never find the courage to adopt. Even so, her words—no matter how articulate—still fail (I think) to make me fully understand the nature of what she went through. Sometimes you just can't put into words how you feel. But I do know she was hurt by the relationship and I think the fact that she was surprised her. And then frightened her. I think she always thought she was tough, and though she is, she is not as tough as she thought. That's why she clings to me sometimes. A mixture of fear and memory overwhelm her at times like this. No one wants to find themselves alone after giving everything they have to another, as she just has with me. For Kate is not a docile lover. She lacerates me with a sexuality that demands equal reciprocation. I just try to keep up.

I feel her body's breaths swell against mine. I am lucky and very much aware of it.

I fall asleep. When I am next conscious, Kate is gone, restored to her usual self. I can hear her outside the bedroom, milling around. I know what she is doing even before I get up. She is cleaning up the grape juice stain. I slip on my clothes and exit the bedroom. She is mopping up the floor, just finishing. There is no evidence of the grape juice stain anymore.

"Did it clean up fairly easily?" I ask, going over to the remainder of the pizza and picking up a slice.

"Look at the notebook on the table," she says, other things on her mind. "The one Trish was flipping through last night. She flipped it back to what you read to me the other night when I was in the tub. I happened to look at it again this morning and it blew my mind wide open. I just took one perusal of it and said 'A-ha!' It's quite meaningful, wouldn't you say?"

"In what way?" I say, looking at the writing in the notebook.

"Read."

I begin to read.

"Read it aloud. The part about about the theme."

"Okay. 'The theme of "Wanted a Goldfish" is that you shouldn't jump to conclusions and should explore all the possibilities because what you first see and hear may not actually be what it is like. Perhaps it seems different but if you find out more about a situation it may then seem perfectly logical. This also shows that there's more a situation—more *to* a situation than what meets the eye.' Is that the part you mean?"

She puts the mop in a utility closet and comes over to where I am. "Yes. Do you see how it applies to this case?"

"I assume you've come to the conclusion that we're looking at it from the wrong angle."

"Yes. King Cloke's involved. But only peripherally. He may not be my arch enemy after all. Anyway, he's not responsible for the murders but he's the reason they're being committed. A self-proclaimed swinger like him has undoubtedly broken a heart or two in his time. And that brings me around to something Wendy said when we were at Tuppy's for dinner, something she's actually said a few times, in regards to Wanda: that there's nothing much worse than a woman scorned. That girl from last night, she was scorned by King Cloke, in some fashion, but, instead of taking out her wrath upon him, she is instead out to kill some of his other conquests, or those who have garnered his attention. It's all so clear. Don't you see it?"

"It sounds possible," I admit. "But why is she killing them? To frame him, or out of pure jealousy?"

"Definitely not to frame him. Jealousy, I would think. She can't have him but doesn't want anyone else to have him either. That's why she kills them when he's out of town. She loves him and doesn't want him to be charged with the murders and hopes that if she knocks off enough of these girls he will come back to her because she will be the only one left. Or something like that. It's hard to know exactly what these nuts are thinking right down to the threaded bolts."

"So . . . Then she came here to kill you because she saw you as competition," I say, starting to get the hang of all this speculation.

"Yes. She watches him and follows him—followed him here—and knew where we lived because of that. She probably came across the pizza delivery person in a fortuitous moment, paid him off and took his place. She's no dope. And she used a gun instead of trying to strangle me because she knew you'd be here too. She knew she couldn't strangle *us*, not when we're both together."

"I'm not so sure she couldn't have strangled at least me. She almost took care of me as it was. She's pretty tough."

"Oh please. I'm sure you would have clocked her from here to Friday. But, in any event, that's all irrelevent. What do you think? It all figures out."

"What about the glasses on the victims?"

"Something symbolic, I guess. I don't know. Maybe Wendy'll have an opinion on the matter. I think I'll call her. She might have more inside info from Trish."

"So we're not in any way going to abide by Trish's orders to lay off?"

"Don't be ridiculous. We're too close to back down now, can't you see? That Trish Mindy, what a disappointment she turned out to be. She's no help to us at all."

"Yes, but it's all getting rather dangerous, don't you think?"

"We'll take the appropriate measures," she says, confident and ambiguous, and goes over to the phone. "No one comes into our home—our sacred home— and does what she did. Now, pick up the fax phone and listen in. That way all your questions will be answered."

I comply. She punches in Wendy's number on the phone.

"Hello?"

"Hi, Wendy. It's me, Kate. Did you go out with King Cloke last night?"

"I did. But I was too busy with that damn band to spend much time with him. I told them that they had to change their name, that Malignant Pussy just wouldn't fly. And they became all outraged! As though they were artists or something. The redneck crackers. But I let fly and told them a thing or two about reality. So then they offered up KnuckleCock as an alternative, but that's just as bad. Finally, I got them to tone it down to Wet Tissue. Amazing, the hicks one has to deal with. By the time they finally agreed to go on it was so late they only got one set in. Bastards. I should can their white trash hides."

"Oh," Kate says, momentarily at a loss. I failed to bring her up to speed on Wendy's band problems.

"But that King Cloke—you know, the way he looks with that hair and those far out clothes, he could pass for one of the Bay City Rollers. Do you remember the Bay City Rollers?"

"Yes."

"Who's your favorite Bay City Roller?"

"That band begins and ends with Stuart Wood."

"Yes! I've always been of a similar opinion, I must say. We do think alike, don't we?"

"So it appears. Anyway, did you find out anything else from King Cloke?"

"The cops are tailing him, or so he suspects. The bastard grabbed my tit during our one and only dance, a mighty grope fest it was too, the tentacled pig. I've had my share of him. Say, what happened with you two last night? God, I must sound so self-absorbed, rambling on about my bruised tit when here you two are having just survived both a gun battle and a run-in with that dingbat sister of mine."

"You know about that?"

"Yes, Trish contacted me late last night. She came over to pick up some ointment that Dr. Ribb left with me to give to her. And then she told me what went down. Sweet Tarzan, that must've been one dastardly scene."

"It was *very* dastardly. Not to mention dire. What else did Trish say?"

"Oh, just the usual mumbo jumbo about us keeping our big beaks out of it. She's afraid we'll spook off the main suspect."

"You mean that girl who shot at us?"

"No, Trish is on another line of thinking. It has to do with the felt-penned glasses."

"Now there's a coincidence. Dean and I were just talking about that and thought you might know a thing or two more about it since we last talked. What does Trish think? She wouldn't tell us a thing."

"That doesn't surprise me. Ever since she got that sore she's been Bitch Central, more so than usual. She's been very secretive about it all. But I did get her to confide in me after I gave her that cream. She felt soothed and more talkative. She gave me hell for being such a drippy mouth and told me not to tell anyone what she was about to say—so don't tell anyone what I'm about to say. Trish swore me to a new level of confidentiality and I don't take such oaths lightly. Anyway, she's after an ex-con, a rapist who used to tie up his victims and then, after getting his jack off, lipstick their eyes before leaving. He was known as Lipstick Jones. And he was released earlier this year from Stiffrod Asylum and moved back here a few weeks before the first murder occurred. He was put under surveillance after the third murder—why they waited that long is beyond me but you know how cops operate—and was seen in the presence of the girl who is believed to have attacked you last night. But he apparently got wise to being tailed and has since disappeared from the radar. He's apparently changed his name and gone underground. Trish thinks he's the one, that he's turned things up a notch and has graduated from rapist to murderer. She thinks the felt-penned glasses are the link to his m.o. from the old days."

"Interesting. And how does the girl who attacked us fit into the situation?"

"Her? Trish doesn't know but thinks she's somehow bait. That she befriends the girls and then leads them into the web of the Big Fate. Why she tried to off you two is anyone's guess."

"And what about King Cloke?"

"No one knows that connection yet."

"We think we have an angle on it, on why we were just about iced and a lot of other things."

"Oh wow. I'd just love to hear you out but I can't talk just now because I have to go to The Lily Pad. I'm counselling Fluff on some relationship matters. It appears she's got a new stalker. Say, why don't you two come over tonight for some dinner. I'm frying a chicken. We'll eat, have a few drinks, talk about all these new developments and maybe watch a Peter Sellers movie. What do you say?"

"We'll be there at six."

"That's what I like to hear. Well, gotta go. Hugs to you and kisses to Dean. See you." Wendy hangs up.

Kate sets down the phone and looks at me. "Well, this is all turning out to be plenty interesting. I can't help but think that both our theories are right. Strange, isn't it?" She bites down on her thumb, beginning to think. She goes and picks up her flute and begins to play a tune of her own creation. "Am I getting any better? she asks wonderingly.

"It's soothing," I say, going over to the couch. I sit down and pick up a book from the coffee table, the one we bought the other day, *A Confederacy of Dunces.*

"How is that book anyway?" she asks, watching me, pausing in her fluting.

"I've just read a little of it so far. But it's good," I say, opening the book to where I left off, feeling the need for a nice bit of relaxation on the couch today as my muscles are stiff and sore from all that transpired last night. But then the phone rings. Kate sets her flute down and answers it. After a bit of inconsequential conversation she hands it over to me. "It's Hav."

I sigh and set the book down. "I might have known," I say, taking the phone from her. Kate takes her sweatshirt off and tosses it at me. "I haven't showered yet," she says, turns and skips out of the room.

"Hello?" I say, my mind not finished watching Kate in all her glorious half-nudity, even though my eyes can no longer see her.

"Dean, what's going on over there? How come it took you so long to answer the phone? Did I catch you and Kate in the act?"

"No. The phone only rang twice anyway."

"Fine. Be that way. Where the hell were you two last night? I called and you didn't answer. So sure as fuck, I thought to myself, I bet they all went to The Lily Pad. I called over there and tried to page you but they wouldn't page you. They don't do that, they said. Can you believe that? What kind of establishment are they running over there? Unbelievable."

"We weren't there anyway. We had quite a night last night. Someone tried to kill us."

"So anyway, I ended up calling Finestra."

"Did you hear what I said?"

"Why do you always interrupt me? I'm trying to tell you about Finestra."

"Who's Finestra?"

"That girl I called. The escort. The one with the oils. And not only does she have oils but she also has salves and a wide array of lotions, some of them from the Orient and made out of goat udders and powdered deer antlers. You know, I think there's something going around because she said I wouldn't believe the demand. It's that sick time of year, I guess. Anyway, I had her over Friday and again last night. Dean, I think she's the one. She's going to carve a Halloween pumpkin for me and put it out on the stoop. She loves the stoop my house has."

"Yeah, it is a nice stoop. What kind of name is Finestra though? It sounds like a last name, or something made up."

"This is typical. Just typical. You always have to be the raincloud to dampen my sunshine. I find your cynicism tiresome."

"Look, what do you want? I'm trying to read."

"Read? Why are you doing that?"

"I like reading."

"Typical. Here you are reading about life when I'm trying to tell you about it, about what it's really like, the stuff you don't can't find in books. I *know*, you know? I've been here and I've been there."

"Yes, well . . . Say, what happened with your mom?"

"I apologized, of course, and sent her some flowers. Cost me a pretty penny too. It's so unfair having to be so misunderstood. But Finestra, she understands me. She was so agreeable to all my pleasuring."

"How much did she cost you?"

"This isn't about money. How can you be so crass?"

"Look, what do you want? Really?"

"I was just going to tell you to maybe hold off on telling Fluff about me."

"No problem there. Besides, she has her own problems to deal with right now. Apparently someone is stalking her."

"I'm not surprised, a whore like that. If she doesn't like the attention she shouldn't wear all that 'come fuck me' apparel. It's disgusting."

"Anyway, is that all you wanted to say?"

"I guess. Are you coming over for your fish today or what?"

"I don't know. We have to go to Wendy's later for a chicken dinner and some drinks so—"

"Well that's just typical."

"Would you quit saying 'typical'?"

"I'm just fed up with being ignored by my own family. It's not right."

"Look, we'll go to The Lily Pad one day this week. I absolutely promise."

"With Sam?"

"I don't know. He's hard to get a hold of lately."

"That doesn't surprise me. Not at all. The doodling bastard."

"What does that mean?"

"Look, would you cut it with the third degree. It's getting old. Besides, I have to go. I have to find a bank machine. My credit card was declined last night when I went out to get some smokes. Can you believe it? This is another example of the systematic persecution of the individual. When things like this happen I can understand why people think about things, you know, about sounding off. Society has no right to treat the individual this way, no right at all."

"I have to go."

"Fine. Bye." Uncle Hav hangs up.

I set the phone down and rub my temples. Kate comes out in a bathrobe, drying her soft hair with a towel, already done with her shower. "By your look of weariness I assume that he wanted nothing more than to vent about his poor poor life."

"I think we need to change our number. Get an unlisted one."

"This'll pass," she says, sitting down on the couch beside me and putting a hand on my knee.

"I hope so. Anyway, what are we going to do until we have to go over to Wendy's?"

"I was just wondering how much I remember from the macrame course I took at the college last year. I was thinking about making a plant hanger."

"You think we need more plants?"

"I was thinking about getting more, yes. What do you think?"

"I guess so. I mean, I like that look, you know? The plants go well with the wood floor. It makes it all so warm and cozy, which is what it's all about. It's like being in the seventies. Plants were big in the seventies, weren't they?"

"I don't know, maybe, now that I think about it. Why do you say that though?"

"I just think of all the movies I saw as a kid and I seem to remember all these plants in the houses. Like in *The Long Goodbye* and *Blume in Love,* those kinds of movies. I could be wrong though, of course."

"The seventies were a mellow time. Everyone was suffering from sixties burnout and plants helped them relax better. *Blume in Love*? We watched that. I remember you insisted on it. Isn't that the one with Kris Kristofferson?"

"Yes."

"That's the one where he sings "Chester the Goat" and drinks Yuban coffee, isn't it?"

"That's the one."

"I always wondered why you adopted that preference yourself. What's so great about Yuban coffee?"

"I just find it amusing, I guess. A little in-joke with myself."

"Well, it *is* kind of amusing. Did you and Wendy ever talk much about movies? You seem to know almost as much about them as she does, even though you seem to like to pretend that you don't."

"Well, I no longer see a need in referring to movies that most people have never heard of. It would make me seem like a know-it-all, wouldn't it?"

"Not necessarily, though I do see your point."

"And no, Wendy and I never really talked about movies. We hang out with her more now than I ever did at any time while married to Wanda."

"Wanda. Yeesh. Her very name steams me. Just when you think she can't top her malicious streak she does. Accusing us of assault. What gall."

"It does tend to grate one to the soul, doesn't it?"

"To the very soul. Anyway, what's on the agenda for the rest of the day?"

"I don't know. Do you think it's possible that I'll ever be able to get hold of Sam? We really do have to go to The Lily Pad. That might get Uncle Hav off my back for a day or two."

"Why do you need Sam?"

"Because Uncle Hav's too negative. I don't need that anymore. I went through enough of it myself before I met you."

"It stems from being lonely."

"Oh, I know that. Too much loneliness makes you bitter. But now that I've escaped it I don't want to live through it again, even if it is only vicarious and intermittent."

"But it might make you appreciate all you have now and I don't mean to sound full of myself when I say that. I know I'm not your saviour."

"Of course you are. You really are. If I hadn't come across you I don't know where I'd be. Bitter and lonely, I guess. In some empty room, alone, drunk and suicidal."

"You don't mean that. I know you don't. Don't even joke about such things. It's bad karma. Besides, I can't ever imagine you being bitter. Even when you found out about Wanda's extracurricular activities I can't imagine it."

"Why?"

"You never speak too ill of her. I get the impression that you're just sad about everything."

"Well, I guess I do let a lot of things slide with her. She was my second love you know."

"Do I have to ask about the first?"

"I'm looking at her. When you're in kindergarten and you touch a girl's hand it means something."

"Yes, but you forgot all about it until last night."

"When my whole life flashed before my eyes."

"How come you never remembered it before last night?"

"I don't know. There's no excuse for it, is there?"

"I wouldn't go that far. I guess it just took you longer to realize what it meant. Men are slower that way."

"Are you looking for some kind of argument?"

"It seems that way, doesn't it? I shouldn't have said it. Tell me something about us that only you remember."

"Is there anything?"

"Don't cop out. There's something. There must be. At our age the steel trap minds we have are starting to rust. I can't remember everything."

"We're not old."

"No, but we're not outrunning it by such a longshot anymore."

"Okay, I'll tell you something, just to stop you from this depressive age jag you're on."

"It comes from being a beauty queen. I'm sensitive to it. I was over the hill at twenty-three in that world."

"Crazy."

"Tell me that *something*, before you forget it."

"We were in grade five and I sat behind you—"

"That was grade six."

"Well, whenever it was. You were wearing a bra already."

"Maybe it was kindergarten," she laughs.

"A woman from day one," I say, laughing along with her. "I had this compass that I was playing with, and your forearm was leaning on my desk. You were turned and were talking to the girl who sat beside me."

"What was her name? Deena?"

"I think so. And you and I had a kind of pestering relationship at that point and I decided I was going to gently poke you in the forearm with the point of my compass and I was just about to and the teacher happened to see what I was going to do and she yelled at me and when she yelled out my name I jerked back in surprise and I thought the compass had slipped and run along your arm. But it had missed and scratched along the desk. I often think about how close I came to bloodying and scarring up your tender little girl arm. I could have hurt you badly and that realization near to kills me. Still."

"I don't remember that."

"I didn't think you would."

"It doesn't seem like an overly sweet story but that's how it plays."

"It's all in the way I tell it."

She leans over and kisses me. Then she puts her hands on my cheeks and looks into my eyes. "It still scares me to think about last night. It'll always scare me to think about last night."

"That's why we're going on with this insanity though, isn't it?"

"No one does that to us. Not here. Not ever."

"You can turn tough on a dime, you know that?"

"We have to see it through. We can't quit."

"I know."

Kate's hands slide off my cheeks and she stands up. She goes into the bedroom and gets dressed. I lay back on the couch and do some reading. She comes out and decides to call Kim and let her in on all that happened last night.

Kim is understandably shocked. After they're done talking Kate and I lounge away the day in the minutaie of domestic bliss. At about five-thirty she goes to the closet and gets our coats. I sit up and set down the book. I take my coat as she hands it to me.

"How's the book?" she asks.

"It's great. It's really funny."

"So Kim picked out a winner."

"Yes. But I don't know how I'm going to tell her that."

"Straight out."

"I guess. What's the weather like out there?"

"It's snowing. Blustery."

"Great."

"You drive," she says, tossing me the keys.

"I'll do my best," I say.

Soon we are in the car and on our way to Wendy's, the music of the Bangles playing away on the cd player. We get to Wendy's and I park behind her Citroen. We get out of the car.

Kate snaps her fingers all of a sudden. "Fudge. We should have brought some wine or something."

"That muscatel is still under the seat," I say, already unlocking the door and digging for it. I pull it out and hand it to her.

"Perfect," she says. "Is it any good? I don't remember ever drinking any muscatel before."

We make our way up the steps of Wendy's house.

"It's sweet, baby, sweet. Just like you, my little chickie," I say, in sudden Rat Pack mode.

She smiles and rings the doorbell.

The door swings open.

Suddenly we're face to face with the Coffee Cop Bandit.

"You!" Kate yells, in a moment of immediate, seething recognition. I respond to her mood by jumping on him in a frenzied rush. We fly back and clatter to the floor, rolling about. I get on top of him and start strangling him. I hear Wendy's excited voice:

"Woo hoo! A good old-fashioned donnybrook. Sweet gizzard, it's been awhile."

Chapter 24

"What do you mean it's been awhile? You were just involved in one on your show the other day," Kate says. "Now, what's going on? Who is this?" And then, so as to give me incentive in the fierce battle I am waging on the floor, at her feet, she becomes my cheering section: "Get 'em Dean! Oh yes, revenge is sweet!"

"Let me go!" the bandit says, flailing away under my weight, grabbing at my wrists. "You're crushing my windpipe. Get off my chest. I can't breathe," he hoarsely utters.

"You're a thief, you low down dirty bugger! You stole Angie's cups," I say righteously, feeling the law on my side.

"You're a tough one, Dean. I respect that," Wendy says. "But I guess Kate is right. It hasn't been all that long since the last donnybrook. Best save your energy for when the next one is really called for." She bends down and tugs at my jacket, signalling me to call an end to all this.

I release my grip and stand up, looking down at the bandit with all the threat my face can muster, my hand in a fist, cocked, ready to go. I feel tough.

"Just like Ali," Wendy says approvingly, her voice full of merriment.

The bandit stands up and begins brushing his grubby clothes with his scabby hands as though they were immaculate up until the point I jumped him.

"What's going on?" I ask Wendy.

"That's what I'd like to know," the bandit says. "And you! You're the savage who broomsticked me in the head," he says accusatorily and then fingers me. "Dirty fuck," he says. "I had migraines all the next day. I had to buy some Tylenol. That stuff's not cheap you know."

"Hush," Wendy says. "I'm not paying you to talk."

"You're paying this seedy earwig?" Kate asks.

"Yes. I pay him fifty bucks a month to steal coffee cups from Angie's. I have a rather tempestuous history with that little bitch. It doesn't cut into her overhead the way she'd like you believe though, especially since this nimrod is so inept a criminal and can barely swipe the minimum five a month I demand he take—"

"Hey!—"

"I told you to hush. Now zip it or I'll kick you in the nuts. Cretin." Wendy turns her attention back to us. "So Dean, you're the one who broomsticked Manny?"

"Manny?"

"Oh my, yes. Let the introductions proceed. Dean, this is Manny Hobo. Manny, this is Dean and his special someone, Kate."

I give him a surly, suspicious nod. Kate refuses to give him even that.

"Well? Were you? Wendy asks.

"What?" I say, all confused now.

"Did you broomstick him? And if so, I'd like you to lay out for me your connection to that awful little Angie."

"Yeah, I did broomstick him. I couldn't let Angie go after him."

"Why the hell not? She's psychotic. She probably could have killed this wastrel. I'd love to see her up on a murder charge," Wendy says, chuckling maliciously to herself.

"I can *hear* you," Manny says, taking offense.

"Good. Then at least I know that one of your crack-addled senses is working."

"Hey!—"

"Shut the fuck up, Manny. I've just about had it with your egregious ineptitude."

"What do you want from me? I told you how aggravated she was this morning when I took the two large sized mugs—"

"Yes, yes, so you did say. I like to hear that," Wendy says, her face starting to beam. "I would love to have seen her expression. Ha! My, but that's rich." She turns to Kate. "Angie's so cheap. It eats her up to lose a cup, eats her up from twat to tonsils."

"Oh," Kate says impartially, not taking sides.

"Yes. She once busted my cuticle with that broomstick. It's made out of hickory you know, and it damn well fucking hurt, let me tell you. She knocked me out with it too. And then, minutes later, when consciousness permeated me again, she said—she had the goddamn nerve—nerve!, to say that—and I'll never forget this and I'll never forgive it, that I had fake tits. Fake tits! Me! My wonderful plaything of a body is as natural as the dew on a birch leaf on a frosty morn. I look after myself and all and I don't dig falsity. I've never condoned going under the knife. We must respect what God gives us. I am pure and my tits are tight and true and reflect that purity. It galls me, the disrespect that little pigmy demonstrated towards me. I may have had an afternoon squish or two with her boyfriend at the time but that was his fault. He never told me of her, the witchy wetcock. He said, or at the very least implied, that he was unattached. The damn dirty liar. Liar! All men are like that though, save for the good ones. And you Dean, you're one of the good ones, at least you will be if you can tell me your connection to Angie in a way that is to my liking. Well, what is it? Tell me

Dean," Wendy says, running out of breath. She lights up a cigarette and exhales orgasmically. I see Kate's neck crane forward to take in a breath of the secondary smoke filling the air. She spots me noticing her and pulls her head back.

"Well, I know her from the coffee shop. She makes good coffee, so me and Kate always go there. And me and Angie also went to high school together. We just sort of have a mutual history."

"Ahh yes. Mutual histories cannot be taken lightly. They are the lifeline to shared memories. And without shared memories there are only individual memories and what the hell are those good for because all they show is that you are alone. And alone we must not be," Wendy says, now philosophical and tranquil, seeming to have lost the angrier strains of her original conversational intent. "Oh my. Who wants to listen to Burl Ives?" She hops away and goes over to her stereo. Pretty soon we are listening to "Little Bitty Tear."

I stare at Manny Hobo, trying to look tough, though the music Wendy has put on is starting to take all my attempted edge away.

He shrugs in response to my stare. "The fortunes of war," he says enigmatically, seemingly acceptant of all that has happened.

"Are you staying here for dinner too?" Kate asks him, her voice telling us all how cold she is to such a prospect.

"Oh God no," Wendy says, returning. "But he is maybe going to do a job for us. Dean, what kind of gun were you and Kate attacked with?"

"A .38."

"Are you sure?"

"Dean knows a thing or two about guns," Kate says. "He taught me how to shoot."

"You don't say. So, do you fancy yourself a redneck or connoisseur? Ahh, who are we kidding? You're a connoisseur, much like myself. I despise the term 'gun nut'. It has such ugly connotations for people such as you and I. I collect Saturday Night Specials you know."

"No, I didn't know that. I just don't like going into the deep woods without protection," I say. "I used to camp out quite a bit."

"We should do some of that next summer," Kate says, always full of ideas as to future activities. "I got a kick out of shooting cans. So did Kim. She'd never shot before that day, did you know that?"

"Amazing," Wendy says, even though Kate was talking to me. "But back to business. You're sure it was a .38?"

"It was."

"I knew it! Didn't I say so, Manny? I told you it was going to turn out to be a .45 or a .38 or a .32 or a .22. I just knew it! So now you know what to do. Off you go!" Wendy claps her hands delightedly and then kicks Manny in the ass.

"I'll be back at ten to midnight," he says, putting an index finger to the side of his nose.

"The hell you will. And don't go quoting Charles Bronson movie titles at me, you're out of your league. You'll be back at eleven. Now off to the Chief with you."

Manny disappears out the door.

"Where's he off to?" Kate asks.

"I sent him to see an acquaintance of mine in the Indian Nation, Running Goat Redpea. He's a steam tent mystic but there's not much money in that so he runs guns on the side. .38's and .45's are his specialty. I'll bet anything that he sold our twisted sister that gun. After all, Trish did say that the gun was hot. Plus, Manny's got an old personal connection of his own who often sends business the way of the Chief, so he'll probably contact her too. At least he better. We're sure to nab her, don't worry." Wendy claps her hands again, full of glee. "The case is heating up. We're near to solving it. I can feel it in my clit. Anyway, the chicken's ready. The swelling has gone down in my lip so I'm back on the solids. Let's eat."

We proceed into the kitchen and the table's already set. We see a bottle of vodka on the cupboard and a nearly empty glass beside it.

"Oh, we brought you a little something, Wendy," Kate says, unbagging the bottle of muscatel and setting it on the table.

Wendy picks up the bottle, looking at it. "You two really didn't have to do this. How polite," she says, overly touched by our gesture. She takes out some wine glasses and pours us each a glass. She takes a big swig of hers. "Sweet. I love it. Thanks ever so much." She drinks the rest and pours herself another glass.

Kate takes a sip from her glass. "Oh, that is good."

And I take a taste of mine, just as Wendy goes over to a large paper bag sitting on the counter. She removes from it a bucket of chicken and some fries. She sets the food on the table. "Forgive the fast food nature of my feast. I had the most honourable culinary intentions when I woke up this morning. I was going to cook the two of you a lovely meal but I had numerous errands to run and then Fluff was in desperate need of a shoulder to cry on."

"How is she?" Kate asks.

"Very worried about her future well-being. So much so that she gave me shit for not having solved this case yet. Talk about nerve, the indignant twerp. She feels she's being stalked. She's always being stalked by this one fellow, but all he does is send her flowers and suggest she return to making Tiawanese erotica. But she's had it with that scene. Art films are fine and dandy but they don't pay the bills. But there's this other fellow that she's more concerned about. C.P. she calls him. She says that's the only name anyone knows him by. He's been keeping an eye on her ever since Trini got fitted for a toe tag. She's worried that he's the killer. She's afraid that this fellow thinks Trini leaked some kind of info to her and that she's about to implicate him. But her and Trini were never that close. They had a one-nighter but that was all. Fluff was just doing her a favour, as Fluff has always swung more towards the big purple than to the pink bush.

Anyway, there's nothing she can do because all this guy does is hang out and watch the shows. He has in no way crossed any lines of the law. Maybe she's just paranoid. She doesn't know herself and has admitted as much. That's what's driving her batty. Dean, want some gravy with those fries?"

"I'm fine, thanks," I say, energetically gnawing on a wing.

"Do you think there's any validity to her concerns?" Kate asks.

"Oh probably. Fluff's always had an aura about her. She's exotic and most guys with stiffies go for that. I tried to soothe her, told her to hang tight and all, that we were very close to solving it all. But she won't be able to truly relax until she gets another brick of hash. But her Vancouver connection has just been indicted. Everything's so unfair. Anyway, what's new on your front?"

"We have a theory. We think that the girl who tried to kill us has a jealous obsession with King Cloke. She's killing off his lady friends in a fit of rage and in the hopes that he will eventually, by process of elimination, have no alternative but to make his way back to her."

"Wow. Sounds intense. All I really know though is that right or wrong—whatever your theory turns out to be—she sounds like a wackjob. What's she look like anyway?"

"Well, similar in height and build to me I guess and . . ." Kate's voice fades off into a swirl of interior thoughts.

I take a break from my fries and look at her. "What's wrong, Kate?" I ask.

"Hmmm? Oh, nothing. Except that we have to visit King Cloke tomorrow."

"Him? What for?" I groan, hating all this running around.

"I just want to follow up on a sudden thought. It might be nothing . . . But it might be something too."

"Sounds mysterious. Anyway, are you into watching that Peter Sellers movie or not?"

"Which one?" Kate asks, still looking preoccupied, even restless.

"*The Bobo.* And underrated classic. He plays the Singing Blue Matador in this one. Far out and groovy it is."

"I'm always up for some grooviness," Kate says, shifting her mood and taking another drink. "Have you heard any more from Wanda?" she then asks, changing the topic.

"God, yes. She called not moments before the two of you arrived. She's spreading the word to everyone out there that she's had to go into hiding because you two are out to knock her block off. She's just trying to make it sound good for the court case she hopes to embroil you in. But I know it won't go anywhere because Trish said it was d.o.a. It's your word against hers and that's two against one and she ain't no Bruce Lee. Which means that your sturdy two beats her flimsy one. Her goose is cooked. I told her as much too. I expect her to resurface by tomorrow at the latest. Wanda's too nosy to stay away from the action for very long. And besides, tomorrow's Winnie's first night at The Lily Pad. She has to show up for that. At least she better. Families have to support each other and if she's not there for Winnie I'll rupture her asshole with one of my stilettos."

"Do you ever see an end in sight with her?" Kate asks. "At least in regards to her bothering us?"

"Maybe if she gets back together with Dick Jemima, or someone of an equally pathetic nature. Wanda needs a man, someone to sound off on on a regular basis. And if she doesn't have one she looks to the old familiars and you, Dean, are the number one old familiar."

"Why not harass Dick? She was married to him too," I say, feeling victimized.

"Yes, but she doesn't much care for him when she's not with him. She loved you way more than she ever loved him, you know. Annoying you means more to her."

"Yeah?" I say, feeling myself savour this deranged fact.

"Plus, she knows that she will never be able to get you back. She's hurt by that and wants to hurt you for it too."

"Is that right?" Kate says. "Well, as long as she knows she'll never have him back."

"Yeah," I say, smiling.

"You like this, don't you? Women fighting over you," Kate says, punching me lightly on the shoulder.

"It's not that," I say, even though that might partly be the case. "It's just that, well, if I mean something to her then it means that our marriage wasn't a total washout."

"How can any marriage that lasts two years be a washout? Good Lord, talk about a prison term," Wendy says, lighting up another cigarette. "Anyway, how about another round of drinks," she says, standing, her eyes looking momentarily glassy. "I think I'm going to switch to vodka and cranberry juice. How about you two?"

Sounds good," I say.

Wendy mixes us each a vodka and cranberry juice. Soon we all have one in our hands. "Anyway, let us adjourn to the living room. Peter Sellers awaits," she says.

We go into the living room. I see a bookcase with the top shelf full of coffee cups. Wendy turns off the Burl Ives cd that was on its fourth go-round, goes over to the tv and puts on her VHS copy of *The Bobo*. We begin to watch. Britt Ekland is in it too. Soon we notice that Wendy is passed out in her recliner.

"Maybe we should go," I say.

"No. I'm starting to like this movie," Kate says, sipping on her drink and slipping down into a comfortable position on the couch, her body melting against mine.

"Do you think Wendy's finished with my book yet?" I ask, suddenly remembering that she has it.

"Shh. And no, I don't. I can't see how she could possibly have found the time to do any reading with all that she does."

"Do you think Sam's home?" I ask, full of questions and wonderings.

"What's with you? Watch the movie."

"I've seen it."

"Watch it again."

"I'd like to but I can't. I feel restless. There's too much unfinished business."

"Then go call Sam."

"I think I will." I slip out from under Kate and search around for Wendy's phone. I find it and punch in Sam's number.

Kim answers. "Hello?" she says, sounding oddly tentative and slow, the word a strange muted sound on her lips.

"Hi, Kim. Is Sam there?"

"Yes! Yes he is. What do you say to that, buster?!" she says, her voice turning humourously turbulent. I can almost feel her pointing at me with a sharp stabbing finger.

"I'm positively shocked," I say. "Put him on."

"Perhaps," she says coquettishly.

"What are you drinking?" I ask.

"Wiser's straight. What else?"

"What else are you doing?"

"I'm drawing a picture."

"Of what?"

"Of this conversation. Because I'm afraid you won't understand it without one."

I laugh. "I like it when you cop an attitude."

"I know you do. You're a strange, silly boy. And so it's best you talk to another of your kind. Here he is, the one, the only—Sam Dart."

Sam answers the phone, saying hello in the voice of a high-pitched old woman. And then he starts cracking up. "Dean Dorian! Wooo!" he screams, jolting my eardrums. "We've been thinking about you all night."

"Favourably, I hope."

"Every now and again," he says, feigning a musing tone.

"You're a hard man to get hold of."

"It's the price of fame," he says. "You know how it is. No, wait. I guess you don't." He starts laughing again, really cackling away at his old jokes. "Anyway, what can I do for you?"

"A big favour," I say.

"For you, anything."

"Uncle Hav has been bugging me endlessly about going to The Lily Pad. I want you to go with us because I need you there, man. I don't think I could stand it if it was just me and him."

"That's the favour? Asking me to go to a strip club. Well . . . I suppose. For you I will go, yes. I will reluctantly go to a strip club with you."

"What a sacrifice," I hear Kim sardonically call out. "Can I come too?"

"Did you hear that?" Sam asks.

"Kim wants to come?"

"It would appear. What a drunk."

"And with apparent lesbian tendencies, no less."

"I love open-minded women!"

"Kate's gotta come too!" I hear Kim call out.

I call out to Kate. "We're going to The Lily Pad. And Kim's going. Are you in?"

"Kim's going? Then of course I'm in," Kate says, her eyes glued to the movie. "When are we going?"

"When do you want to go?" I ask Sam.

"The sooner the better. Tomorrow night. It's time to put some fresh tracks on the snow of our memory banks."

"What an odd metaphor."

"And here I thought it was personification. Crazy. Simply crazy," he says and then goes silent.

"Alright. What time do we go tomorrow?"

"Get hold of us anytime after work. How does that sound?"

"Perfect."

"I knew it would!" he yells excitedly.

"Alright. Tomorrow then," I say.

"You know it."

"Good. See you, then."

"So long."

We hang up. I go over to the couch and sit down beside Kate. "It's all set. We're going tomorrow."

"Tomorrow? Isn't that when Wendy's sister performs for the first time?"

"Oh geez. I forgot. Now's a fine time to tell me." I think about calling Sam back and postponing things but before I can come to a decision about it one way or another the doorbell rings.

Chapter 25

"What the hell?" Wendy says out of the blue, lurching up suddenly into a sitting position. "What's going on?" she says, startled.

I stop in my tracks. I had gotten up and was about to go and answer the door. "Someone's here," I say, sitting back down.

Wendy stands up and puts a hand to her forehead. "My, but I'm somewhat dizzy. Too many mood shifters in my system. Or perhaps not enough. I need a pill."

The doorbell rings again.

"Shut up! I'm coming. It's that damn Manny, I know it is. I knew he wasn't going to see Running Goat Redpea, I just knew it. 'It costs too much to drive all the way to the Indian Nation.' You wait and see, that's what he'll say." Wendy is halfway to the door when she stops and looks back at us crossly. "Aren't you coming? Don't you want to hear what this shitwit has to say?"

Fortunately the movie is just ending. Otherwise who knows what Kate would have said. She doesn't like to be disturbed when she's watching a movie. We get up and follow Wendy to the door. The bell is ringing incessantly.

Wendy flings open the door. "What is your problem?! I told you I was coming."

"Big news, big news," Manny says feverishly, stepping past Wendy and into the house, waving his hands animatedly, as though swatting at flies. Body stooped, he begins pacing about, back and forth.

Wendy shuts the door. "Well? Tell us."

"I didn't go and see Running Goat Redpea."

"Ha! I knew it. I just knew you wouldn't. You cheap shit."

"There was no need. I called him on his cellphone."

"Steam tent mystics have cellphones?" I say, always amazed at the proliferation of cellphones in the world, especially considering that Kate and I have never had one.

"Hey, they need to be reached too," Manny says, taking offense for some reason. "Now shut up and let me tell it."

"So spill it," Wendy says, lighting up a cigarette. "Where's my drink? Never mind, we need Coronas. Everyone, into the kitchen," she says, herding us into it with fanning, expansive waves of her arms. We all go into the kitchen and sit down at the table. Wendy goes to the fridge and gets us each a Corona. She sets a lime on the table and stabs a steak knife into it. "Cut your own limes. I've quit that scene," she says, sounding put out and ornery, but then proceeds to cut us each a wedge of lime anyway, which we all shove into our bottles. Manny lights up a cigarette too and begins to sip on his beer, looking furtive, his eyes darting this way and that. "Well?" Wendy says impatiently.

"It's like this: I went and saw Sparkle first."

"Who's Sparkle?" Kate asks.

"Would you shut up and let me tell the story!" he erupts.

"Don't ever talk to her like that," I threaten, feeling my voice ring with ultimatum.

"You're right you're right. I'm sorry," he says, his words coming out in a torrent of speed, his hands rubbing together at an equally manic pace. "I'm just full of the scaries is all."

"It's alright," Kate says, putting her hand on mine, appreciating my defense of her. "Just calm down," she says to him.

Kate's voice seems to do the trick. He seems to relax somewhat. "Sparkle is an acquaintance of mine. Actually, she used to be my old lady. She lives in the Jackpole Projects. You ever live in that part of town?"

"No," Kate says.

"You're lucky. It's cutthroat down there. Anyway, I went and saw Sparkle but she didn't want to give anything up, even though I could tell by the look on her face that she knew something. She was a little unnerved. I think she had been told to keep quiet or else. I had to give her all my peyote before she would give me any info. All of it! I'll be back to nutmeg for the next month. Bad scene. The two capacities will be waging battle in my head tonight. The deep war," he says, going off onto a different, abstruse tangent altogether.

Wendy nudges him, yawning, her irritability stemming from having been woken up, I decide. "Come on. Out with it. What did you find out?"

"Oh. Right. Well, someone did come to her and ask about purchasing a gun, preferably a .38, he said. And she turned him on to our man in the Indian Nation, which I later confirmed via a phone call. By the way, Wendy, in return for the info he gave me, he expects—"

"I know what he expects. Go on."

"Anyway, the man's name is Penrod Cooley."

"Penrod Cooley?" Kate says, drawing a blank. "I've never heard of him. What's his story?"

"That's just it. He doesn't have one. He's the walking Satan. He just appeared out of nowhere, to walk the earth and scorch hell upon it."

"Ahh, that's silly," I say, starting to nevertheless feel unnerved. I take a deep drink of my Corona, my hands in a vibratory shake.

"But there's talk."

"Of what?" Wendy says, lighting up another cigarette with the butt of the one she was just smoking.

"That he looks like someone who used to be dead. He's a living dead man. Back to settle the score."

"Oh stop it," Wendy says, beginning to find Manny's dark ramblings insufferable.

"Yes, stop it," I say, beginning to freak out.

"What score?" Kate asks.

"Only *he* knows that. That's what makes him so dangerous."

"How much did you smoke before you came back here?" Wendy asks.

"Well, Sparkle did fire up the pipe for old times sake . . . But that has nothing to do with it."

"Bah," Wendy says derisively, getting up. She goes over to the phone at the edge of the kitchen counter and grabs the phone book sitting beside it. She comes back and sits down at the table. She begins to flip through the phone book.

"He won't be in there," Manny says.

"You're right. He's not."

"Wait a minute," Kate says. "Penrod Cooley. P.C. Wendy, didn't you say that Fluff was worried she was being stalked by someone known as C.P.?"

"By George, that's right," Wendy says, her mood lightening. "That seems like more than a coincidence, if you ask me." Wendy turns to Manny. "Are you sure his name is Penrod Cooley?"

"That's the name Sparkle wrote down."

"She wrote it down?" I ask.

"Yes. She's a mute. She can't speak. I told you it was cutthroat in the Jackpole Projects. God. People don't listen." He gives me a disgusted look and then starts puffing away on his cigarette neurotically.

"And you're an idiot. His name is Cooley Penrod," Wendy says.

"Nuh-uh. It's Penrod Cooley. I think I should know. I'm the one who read the name."

"Yes, but you're dyslexic."

"Oh. Dammit. I forgot about that. Maybe I did forget to take that into account. It might be Cooley Penrod then."

Wendy looks through the phone book again. But there is no such name in it. "Well, I'm stumped for the moment. Time to break out the guitar. Everyone into the living room." She stands up and now begins to herd us into the living room.

We once more step down into the sunken living room and Kate and I sit in the same place we sat when watching the movie. Manny takes a seat opposite and Wendy plunks down in her recliner, an acoustic guitar in her hand. She begins to play "Nowhere Man."

Kate and I sip leisurely on our Coronas and Manny begins to slap his knee to the beat of Wendy's guitar.

"You're a good guitar player," Kate says.

"Thanks," Wendy says. "Tuppy may have taught me nothing about life but at least she taught me how to play the strings."

"How do you suppose this Cooley Penrod figures into the equation?" Kate asks, to no one in particular, speculating on the answer herself.

"Best not to wrap our noodles around it right now. Let the knowledge settle and give the epiphanies a chance to form."

"Satan!" Manny yells out abruptly and for no seeming reason. I almost jump out of my seat. He begins to vigorously pick his ear.

"Shut up, Manny," Wendy says, completely unmoved by Manny's outburst. "Now you made me lose my place. Oh well, it's time to move on anyway. Let me see." She begins to strum away, rather formlessly it seems to me. But soon her strums pool into a direction and evolve into the song, "One Less Set of Footsteps."

"Jim Croce," Kate says. "I haven't listened to him forever. Why is that?" she asks me.

"I don't know. There's no excuse," I say, half-humourously, half seriously. We listen to Wendy sing. She has a nice voice as well.

I look at my watch. "We should get going soon. Unless you want to call in sick tomorrow."

"No. That would be the easy thing to do."

"That's right. You two have to work tomorrow," Wendy says. "I decided that it's re-run week for me, so all I have to attend to is the goings on at The Hob-and-Nob." She reaches over and grabs her Corona from the coffee table and takes a drink.

"One time I was walking alone along the tracks when I felt the presence of the Dark Entity. His breath was hot and full of dead rat stench. He tried to kidnap my molecular luminosity."

"Manny, I think you should leave. This spooky shit act of yours is really starting to annoy me."

"But it's Halloween next week. This is when *his* presence is at its strongest."

"I'm not worried. The world is only 49% bad. Which means that the other 51% is good. Which means that good will always win out. It's never easy but it's always a win in the column of the good guys when the smoke clears."

"You're talking socialism."

"What the hell does that mean? Alright, I've had enough of you and your coke-soaked retardation. Get out!" Wendy says, standing up and pointing her guitar pick at him.

Manny covers his face with his arms, quaking in terror. "Don't touch me with that thing!"

"What?"

"That dirty pick! It's got bad vibrations. It kidnaps spirits, with the guitar string as its power source."

"He's a lunatic," Kate whispers to me as we watch the scene before us with transfixed eyes.

Wendy walks over to where Manny is, the guitar hanging by her side via a strap. She holds the pick directly over her head, threatening Manny with the use of it and looking kind of like a guitar goddess of sorts. I half-expect her to turn invincible, by being struck by lightning, by the hammer of the gods, something. Manny cowers in his seat.

"Get out now!" Wendy says slowly, her words laced with loud threatening implications.

Manny slinks off his seat and crawls away. Then all of a sudden he hops up and runs to the door. "Missed me!" he screams out victoriously.

"If you ever come back here without my expressed written consent I will stab you in the spine with a salad fork!"

"Foo to you!" he says, rushing out the door and slamming it behind him.

"Sorry about that," Wendy says, sitting back down. "But good help is so very hard to find. Anyway, any requests? I worked as a busker one summer on the mean streets of Portland and it was either learn to play or starve for the day. I had a partner once but he abandoned me after a week and got a job at a hotel. He teaches breakdancing now. I knew he'd come back to town. I have half a mind to look him up and see if he still plays. I've been thinking of getting my own band going. That damn house band at The Hob-and-Nob just isn't going to cut it. Ahh, the hell of it all. Life is such a load of red tape. So, requests?"

"Do you know any Waylon Jennings?" I ask.

"That's an interesting request," Wendy says, "but a very impressive one."

"What made you think of him?" Kate asks.

"I don't know. The late night, the good taste of the Corona. It reminds me of when I was a kid and would see all my family doing just this. And Waylon would be playing on the stereo," I say, suddenly deeply nostalgic and feeling the nice warmth of my present situation.

Wendy begins to strum away again and plays "Ladies Love Outlaws." "Another beer?" she asks.

"No, I think we're fine," Kate says serenely. "We should be going soon. We have a big day tomorrow."

A very big day, as it turns out.

Chapter 26

We do a parallel park in front of the Stem Building. Kate puts the Galaxie into park and shuts off the ignition. "I could hardly teach all day. I had the kids read and do group projects, anything not to talk to them. I just couldn't keep my mind on the lessons. I was just so full of energy about this. Do you think I'm crazy?" she asks, reaching into the glove compartment for a sugar cube.

"No. And that's what has me worried. There's probably something to it and that'll lead us to her. And that is not something I'm looking forward to."

"Nonsense. Now that we're prepared for her an ambush is a non-issue."

"I don't know why I choose to believe you all the time but I do."

"It's because I'm so darn cute."

"It probably is," I say, both of us starting to laugh. She taps the end of my nose. "Now let's go and get the job done."

We exit the car and step into the slush, the wind gusting against us. We make our way into the Stem Building and take the elevator to the fifth floor.

We step out into the hall. "Do you remember what she looks like?"

"Not really. About our age. Blonde hair?"

"That's our girl." We begin to walk down the hall, towards King Cloke's office, peering into the waiting room areas of all the other rooms. When we get to Room 505 Kate peers in. "That's her," she says, tugging at my arm. We step in and Kate approaches the counter. "Hello," she says.

"Yes? How may I help you?" the girl, dressed in medical white, says, standing up and approaching us, pausing momentarily when she gets a good look at Kate.

"We were here not long ago and you mistook me for a friend of yours. I don't mean to be nosy but I was wondering if you could tell me who it was that you thought I was."

"Why?" the girl says and I feel myself sink somewhat. Everyone's so suspicious.

"Call it curiosity," Kate says. "I've often been told that I look like a former beauty queen, Miss Golden Leaf of 1989 to 1991, and her name was Kate Carlo. I was just wondering if that was who you mistook me for."

The girl seems to relax after Kate lays out her clever ruse. "No, no it was nothing like that at all. I've never even heard of anyone named Kate Carlo."

"Really? How peculiar. She's quite famous." Kate looks at me and sees my quiet groan. She smiles, having expected to elicit just such a response from me.

"Oh? In any case, I thought you were an old friend of mine, Pepper Jones. She used to work down the hall."

"For King Cloke?"

"Yes. We used to go out Fridays after work for drinks. She quit a few years back but promised to keep in touch. She didn't though and I always wondered what happened to her. She just seems to have disappeared. That's why when I thought you were her I rushed up to you like that."

"So I really look like her?"

"Not really. In a general sense and from a distance, yes. But her features are, well, rougher. She's been through some tough times."

"Oh. I'm sorry to hear that. In any case, I was just curious. Sorry to have bothered you."

"Not at all."

"Goodbye then."

"Bye."

We leave the office. "I had no idea you were so famous," I say sarcastically.

"Please. You must allow me my moments of grandeur and self-delusion."

"It's not asking much, I guess. So, do I have to ask where we're going next?"

"It's time to get to the bottom of the swinging dentist," she says, full of purpose and force. We soon enter King Cloke's office. "Hello, Penny," Kate says, stepping right up to the counter.

"You!" Penny says, hopping up out of her chair to meet Kate face to face. "What do *you* want?"

"To cut to the chase. The other day when we came here with our friend Wendy you thought I was Pepper Jones for the briefest of moments, didn't you?"

"I . . . *what?* No, never. I have no idea what you're talking about," Penny says, taking a step backward, looking defensive and apprehensive, her left eye in an inflamed twitch.

"Don't lie to us, Penny. We know all about it. That little lunatic tried to kill us."

"It's not my fault! Screw you all! . . . I mean, I don't know what you're talking about."

"Another step backward and you'll hit your desk. Why are you backing away from us, Penny?" Kate says, playing the role of the foreboding interrogator with great expertise.

"What's going on?" King Cloke says, appearing from around the corner all of a sudden, a bloody bib around his neck.

He spots Kate. "Well, hello there," he says smoothly, coming over to Kate and propping an elbow on the counter. He leans close, smelling of Old Spice and fluoride.

I groan at his smarmy tactics.

"Who's Pepper Jones?" Kate asks bluntly.

King Cloke stands up stiff and looks at Kate with alarmed eyes. Then he rolls his shoulders and affects a relaxed attitude, attempting to display full composure. "There's no use in lying, I suppose. You asked that girl down the hall?"

"Yes."

"I knew it. I knew she would eventually prove to be a sharp bone up my ass. Thank God the cops are dumber than you two. They completely ignored the other tenants on this floor. Anyway, to answer your question, Pepper used to work here a few years back," he says. "She did what Penny now does."

"I see," Kate says thoughtfully.

"What's that supposed to mean?!" Penny lashes out, taking offense, leaping forward.

"Nothing. Did you fire her?" Kate asks King Cloke.

"Certainly not. She left of her own accord."

"She tried to take the bite out of us with a barrage of bullets the other night."

"I find that hard to believe. This is all simply intolerable. I feel fraught."

"Spill it Cloke. Or else we're going to Trish Mindy with what we know."

"Trish Mindy," he says, spitting the name out in a low growl of contempt. "That woman is inept. But it's police ineptitude that sinks you more than proficiency every time. I don't want her coming back here, not after I bought off her trust with a few well-formed answers to her inane questions. I think she may have hankered me. Oh my." He rubs his eyes, stands up straight and then looks at Penny. "Well, what should I do?"

"Swear them to secrecy," Penny says, putting great stock in oaths it would appear.

"It's not them I'm worried about. But they might point the trail to Pepper, who will sing if she's cornered. Of that I have no doubt."

"Disband the organization until all this blows over. I told you to do it a hundred times."

"Yes, I know. Fine. Thy will be done." King Cloke rubs the back of his neck and looks at Kate, licking his lips. "I was once involved with Pepper but"—and here he looks at me—"you know how the ducks can be. They always want a commitment. But you can't swing to the degree you'd like to if you're committed. Nevertheless, I loved her enough to try and appease her constant yammerings about marriage by involving her in my life—"

"What you were thinking I'll never know," Penny says, looking revolted.

"Please, I've had enough of your third degree. My, but I feel distasteful. The brass. I have brassmouth." He leaves but quickly returns, returns with a hypodermic needle in his hand. "Don't mind me," he says, and jams the needle into his mouth and gives himself a shot of novocaine. "Ahh, that's the ice juice," he says, removing the needle from his mouth and handing it to Penny, who neatly wraps it in a napkin and sets it on her desk. "Now, what were we talking about?"

"I don't exactly know," Kate says. "But please continue."

"If you rat me out to the cops, I'll kill you myself. And if I can say that under the sweet sedation of Mistress Novocaine you can imagine how serious I am. And just how severe I can be when under the influence of nothing but my wrath."

"You won't do a thing to her," I say, trying to sound tough but coming off as more hysterical than anything.

"I have a rather large stable of ladies, a whole network of them, spread out from city to city, like a spider web. Salacious," he says, his choice of words odd but suggestive. He begins to drool out of the frozen side of his mouth. He removes a silk handkerchief from his pocket and wipes his mouth. "And they all love me very much. And are willing to prove it. They work for me." He stretches his arms straight out from his sides. "*Me!!* They insist."

"*Insist.* That's rich," Penny says, laughing bitterly.

"But of course there is always the issue of John Law and Joe Taxman, so I have to keep it all under wraps. All I do is organize things. Should I be crucified for that? Well?!" he says impatiently, expecting an answer.

"You seem to be under a heavy strain," I say.

"Yes! A heavy strain. Never have I heard my dilemma so succinctly put. Penny!" he screams. "Go get that bottle of rubbing alcohol. And you—" he says, snapping his fingers at me "—shut the door and lock it. The King has left the building. So to speak."

I go over and shut the door and then lock it.

Penny comes out with a bottle of rubbing alcohol and hands it to King Cloke.

"I keep gin in here," he says mischievously. "Hee hee hee," he laughs girlishly and then sucks back a plentiful amount of gin.

"But how does Pepper figure in all of this?"

"Why, she's blackmailing me of course. I told her everything in a moment of passionate weakness and now I have to pay her to keep quiet about it. She's got a hot pad at the Pussywillow Apartment Complex and lives a high-falutin' lifestyle, all on my coin. But you didn't hear that from me. Shh shh!" he says, putting a finger to pursed lips, some gin spilling out of his mouth and drizzling onto the counter. "And, once the murders started, Pepper forced me to fudge my employment records to show that Penny has been my only employee for the past ten years. Pepper didn't want the cops a-knocking on her door with questions."

"Why?"

"Because she's afraid the blackmail scam will be revealed if the cops start poking around, or so I assume. And she doesn't want that. What can I do? If she goes down I sink too, so I have to appease her. I refuse to go down to the Bismarck. No way. King Cloke has always been a swimmer. I was a lifeguard during my college years. Those were good days."

"Why didn't she blackmail you into marrying her if she loved you that much?"

"She could've. But she knows I am not a creature of faithful ilk. And to her the institution of marriage is sacrosanct and not to be entered into if both parties aren't completely committed to the idea of monogamy. Go figure." His hands move close together in gnarled opposition. He looks at them, his eyes bulging dementedly. "But I can't help it, you know. I just see a woman's crotch and the idea of arousing it into the wet soak of pulsing desire is just too much for me not to act on. It's a scene—it's *my* scene."

"Do you think she's our killer?"

"Alright, here it is, time to be honest. I suspect yes, if I think about it. But I choose to very rarely think about it. I hate issues of moral conscience. They tend to muddy one's enjoyment of life."

"We're going to bring her down. You've been warned. So disband your organization and do what you have to do. Our fight's not with you."

"That's nice. My, but I feel fatigued. Penny, help me to my chair." Penny comes over and puts her arms around his waist to keep him from falling. He drapes his left arm across her shoulders. His eyes have gone suddenly glassy and he looks about to pass out.

"Now please leave. And don't come back. All your presence here does is aggravate his perforated ulcer."

"Don't be too hard on them, Penny. They're merely upset about being shot at. However, if you want to play it really safe I can set you and your friend Wendy up in a prodigiously successful practice back east. Should you desire. Sort of my own version of the Witness Protection Program," King Cloke says to Kate, his voice hoarse and fading as Penny lugs him into the backroom.

"No thanks," Kate says. She turns me. "What a scurvy wretch of a man."

"Let's go," I say.

"Yes, let's. So, Pepper's our girl."

"What are we going to do about it?"

"Forget about her for the time being. After all, we have to go see Sam and Kim, right? We're going to The Lily Pad, aren't we?" she says, changing her tune in a heartbeat, as I unlock and open the door.

"You seem excited about it."

"It's been a long time since all of us have had a night on the town. It'll be good to take a break from all this nastiness."

"Yes it will," I say, nevertheless unable to shake the knowledge of this Pepper Jones. Her shadow seems to loom over us with a steamrolling, oncoming immediacy. I keep shaking my head, trying to forget her. I think of Kate. I think of Sam and Kim. I think of The Lily Pad. I think of Fluff Chang. But then my heart near to stops, turning to new concerns and worries. I think of . . . Oh no! Winnie.

Chapter 27

"Is she built like her sisters?" Kate asks, ringing the doorbell.

"She has a mighty rack. But I just don't know. For me to watch her up there stripping, well, it just seems somehow incestuous, don't you think?"

"Ask Sam about it. I think you're just a worrier."

"Maybe. It just doesn't seem right."

"You're always so concerned with decorum."

"I guess."

Suddenly the door is winged back, revealing Sam. "Ahh, the couple Dorian," he says pleasantly. Right away I can tell he's had a nip or two.

"Not yet," I say. "Kate still refuses to marry me."

"You haven't asked me in awhile," she says, a statement striking enough to fill me with optimism on the matter.

"I put this song on just for you two," Sam says. "It seems appropriate. At least that's my stance on the issue." We can hear the theme song to *Welcome Back, Kotter* rolling down the stairs.

"Beautiful," I say, all my worries starting to drop away in the presence of Sam.

"Where's Kim?" Kate asks as we remove our shoes.

"Up here, Kate," Kim calls out. "I'm just watering a plant."

"She bought a new plant," Sam says.

"Really?" Kate says interestedly. We follow Sam upstairs and Kim is indeed watering her new plant, which sits on a stool in the corner, by the window.

"It's a Chinese evergreen," Kim says, before Kate can ask.

"I thought so. We were looking at those just the other day. Remember, Dean?"

"Oh I remember."

"You say it with the voice of one who finds it all so tiresome," she chides.

"Hey, I've always been pro-plant," I say, turning defensive but also striving for humour.

Sam laughs. "You seem uptight, buddy. You need a beer," he says mirthfully, disappearing into the kitchen; he soon returns with his hands full of Coronas. Soon we are each drinking one.

Kate takes a drink of hers and then holds the bottle before her, looking at it reflectively. "We were just drinking these last night at Wendy's. They've really tasted good lately, too. I've always thought of them more as a hot weather beer but I'm changing my opinion fast."

"It's always good to have an open mind," Sam says, vague and pointed at the same time. He turns to me. "So, been shot at lately?"

"What? Oh, no, no. But it's aged me, Sam. It's aged me."

"I couldn't believe that story when Kim told it to me. I thought she was junked out on absinthe. But she wasn't. It's an unbelievable story. And yet I believe it. Wow!" he says, not knowing what else to say. There is no easy way to articulate it. And no easy way to respond to it.

"Tell us all about it," Kim says, sitting down on the couch beside Kate. Everyone looks at me expectantly so I lay out the facts as best I can, up to and including our findings of today, the stuff about King Cloke and Pepper Jones.

"Far out. So Kate saved your life," Sam says, blown into amazement after I finish telling the story. "That's what it's all about, teamwork," he says, nodding approvingly, after a moment of contemplative silence had taken over the room.

"What's with you?" Kim asks Sam. "You sound like you're trying to be so philosophical. You've been that way all day. Full of all these strange sayings."

"It just that my dear friends' near scrape with death has put my perspective into perspective."

"I think you're just giddy about going to a seedy strip bar tonight."

"And my woman is going to it with me! The best of both worlds it is," he says, clapping his hands gleefully.

"I shouldn't have agreed to it. It's the Wiser's. It's so seductive."

"Oh, it'll be okay. When I was there the other night with Dean it was kind of fun. Very strange," Kate says.

"Goodness."

"Didn't you get my e-mail mentioning it? I sent it the other day from work during lunch hour."

"Oh, that's right. You did. You were talking to Fluff Chang. My, but you've been an adventurer of late," she says and soon she and Kate are talking about all sorts of things, eventually settling on the topic of work.

I turn to Sam. "I need your wisdom for a moment," I say. "But first get me another Corona. What the hell kind of host are you?" I say, full of exaggerated displeasure.

He takes my bottle. "Kim. Dean thinks we're bad hosts."

"Screw you, Dorian!" she says through gritted teeth, sounding mean but then diffusing all her affected ferocity with laughter. Sam comes back with another beer.

"There you go, young fellow," he says, patting me on the shoulder, sounding aged and wise as he sits down opposite me.

"One of the strippers tonight is going to be my ex-sister-in-law."

"Wendy?" he says, sitting up and looking hopeful.

"No, Winnie. The youngest sister."

"Did I ever meet her?"

"I don't think so."

"I see. Well, what's the problem?"

"I feel like there's a conflict of interest or something. Like it would be wrong for me to see her all nuded out."

"Never fear," he says. And that's all he says. He gets up and puts on a cd. "We'll put our faith in Johnny," he says, putting on a Johnny Cash cd. The song he puts on is "Guess Things Happen That Way." He then comes and sits back down, examining me thoughtfully. "Well, does this song solve your many concerns?"

I scratch my head. My problem is that I'm just not as drunk as Sam. I lack his inebriated clarity. I chug back the rest of my Corona, trying to catch up. But all I really manage to do is make myself dizzy.

"We'd better go before you two are laid out," Kate says, standing up.

I stand up too and then the fast drinking really hits me. I start to feel light and wobbly.

"Shouldn't you call Hav?" Kate asks.

"Why?"

"Because he's the reason you wanted to go to The Lily Pad in the first place."

"Oh, forget about him. He'll just rain on our parade."

"Suit yourself. You're the one who has to deal with him."

"That's right. And deal with him I will," I say firmly, clenching a fist, everything momentarily seeming so simple. "Do you like it when I talk tough?"

"Sometimes."

"What about now?"

"It's not doing anything for me at the moment, no."

Sam laughs. Kim is over by their cd collection, searching through it. She finds what she wants and brings it over to Kate. "I was looking for it and found it last night." She hands it to Kate. We both look at it. It is a 4 Non Blondes cd.

"Excellent," Kate says. "We have this one too." There are a number of sunglasses sitting on the coffee table. She picks up a pair and puts them on. "Where'd you get these?"

"I found them when I was searching for the cd. I used to collect them, sort of."

Kate looks at me, her head in a rhythmic nod. "How do I look?"

"Tres chic," I say. "You look like Julie Christie, maybe Angie Dickinson. Someone like that. You should be smoking a cigarette now. It would give you that classic sixties look."

"Don't think I'm not thinking that very same thing."

"How long have you quit for now?" Kim asks, also putting on a pair of sunglasses, with big dark lenses; she looks like Jackie O. Her action prompts Sam and I to each put a pair on too.

"Over a month now," Kate says.

"Wow. That's pretty good. I knew you could do it."

"Thanks, Kim," Kate says, appreciative of Kim's faith in her.

"I like these shades," I say. "I'm wearing them to The Lily Pad."

"Won't they affect your ability to see the strippers?" Sam asks.

"I'll remove them at appropriate moments."

"I like your style," Sam says. "And that's what it's all about: style."

"Kim's right. You are rather full of sayings tonight," I say.

"Anyway, let's go," Kate says, eager to get things underway.

"It's still early," Sam says. "What are we going to do for food? I don't want to eat at The Lily Pad."

"And I would like to drop off some rolls of film to develop before we go there. Is that alright?"

I sit back down.

"Don't look so hostile, Dean," Kim says amusedly. "You're always in such a hurry."

"I never said a thing," I say, nevertheless a little irritated. It is rather early though. So I come to terms with it all and stand back up. "Alright. Let's rock," I say. "Who's driving?"

"I'll drive," Kim says.

I toss her the keys to the Galaxie.

"Take your car?" she says questioningly, looking at me and then Kate.

"Sure, it'll be fun," Kate says. "We'll put on the 4 Non Blondes," she says, taking another look at the cd.

We all seem to find acceptance in this plan and make our way down the stairs and put our shoes on.

Soon we are in the Galaxie and zipping through town, heading for the nearest photomat. Kate puts in the 4 Non Blondes cd and goes right to "What's Up." She begins to sing along with it. So does Kim. Soon we all do.

Kate rolls down the passenger side window and starts waving at a group of teenagers on the sidewalk who we're passing by. She cranks up the stereo, continuing to sing "What's Up," waving at the kids. They swear at her, finger us and throw a Big Gulp at the Galaxie.

"Stupid kids," Kate says turning the stereo back down to a more ear friendly level. "They just don't appreciate what it's all about."

"We're the last great generation," Sam says.

"I'll agree with you there," I say. "Generation X. The last of a breed."

"You know it. But everyone acts like we all died with the death of Kurt Cobain. And it's just not so. It's just not so," Sam says, turning unexpectedly passionate.

We all seem to become wistful for a moment, saying very little until we reach the photomat.

We all get out and follow Kim into the store. There's a huge lineup too. Kim takes her position at the end of it, Kate standing beside her to keep her company. Kate begins to retie the ribbon of her blue cotton knit top into a bow. Me and Sam wander around the store a little bit but eventually end up standing in line with them too.

"What are the pictures of?" I ask Sam. "Are there any of me?"

"Oh there's always a few of you. We have more pictures of you and Kate than of anyone else."

"Nice," I say, revelling in this small but glorious fact. We wait for what seems like an interminably long time. I get bored and leave the store. It's part of a strip mall so I begin to wander aimlessly. Sam ends up tagging along.

"I'm hungry," he complains. "If I don't get something to eat soon I'm going to throw up."

"I've never understood how someone can throw up on an empty stomach."

"It is rather uncommon, isn't it?" he says as we come to a pizza place. We enter and order a large pepperoni and cheese pizza. Everyone is giving us a second glance because of the sunglasses we're wearing in this darkening, dreary night. We sit down. "What about Kim and Kate?" Sam asks.

"They're rather industrious. I have faith they'll find us."

And they do. They show up about fifteen minutes later and help us finish off the pizza.

"You'll be happy to know," Kim says to me, "that I'm going to pick up the photos tomorrow, so we don't have to wait around to pick them up."

"That's a relief," I say, "though rumours of my impatience are greatly exaggerated."

"I know. I just like to tease you. I find your superficial irascibility an endearing character trait."

"Sounds like you've given me much thought," I say.

"No, not really," Kim says. "It only takes about five minutes to figure you out."

"Everyone picks on me," I whine, working for sympathy and getting none. I change the topic. "Well, should we go?"

"Let's do it," Sam says.

We get up and leave. We get into the Galaxie and Kim drives us to The Lily Pad.

As soon as we enter I hear this voice from the bar call out, "Master Dorian!"

I look in the direction of the voice, full of surprise at hearing the mention of my name, and there at the bar, getting a tray full of drinks, is Jim Chimney. He waves to us and tips his yachting cap in deference to Kate and Kim.

"He's such a nice man," Kim says. "Though a little odd."

"You all find a table," I suggest. "I'll just go and say hi to him," I say.

"We'll do that. It looks pretty crowded in here," Kate says, lifting the glasses from her eyes and sizing up the situation. "There are way more women in here than when I was here with you," she says, sounding somewhat disappointed.

"Times are changing," Sam says, full of high spirits. "Come on. Let's find a table," he says, and the three of them separate from me.

I go over to where Jim Chimney is. The bartender is setting drink upon drink on a tray. Jim Chimney is puffing sedately on his pipe. "I thought it was against the law to smoke in here," I say, spouting out the first thing that comes to mind.

"Fuck the law!" the waitress from the other night, Sheba, utters with great vehemence as she brushes past me to load up her tray with more ordered drinks, her barely concealed breasts heaving angrily. I look at her but she pays me no mind whatsoever.

"I see you've come to support young Winnie in this, the first night of what we all expect to be a long and flourishing career."

"Yes, yes, that's why we're here," I say hastily.

"You must come over and say hello to the Dame Tuppy and Mistress Wendy."

"Wendy? Is she here?"

"Who do you think these tequila shots are for?" Jim Chimney says, pointing to a half-dozen shooters on the tray before him with the stem of his pipe.

"Is Wanda here?"

"We expect her anytime."

I feel my muscles clench. "Oh. Well, yes, I'll come over and say hi at some point."

"You all will. We insist on having a drink with you and your delightful cronies."

"Okay," I say, my nerves sparking with great anxiety.

"But for now I must bid you adieu. The show will be starting shortly and the ladies have whistles in the need of a good wetting."

"Okay, I'll see you later then," I say, already praying that Wanda doesn't show up.

Jim Chimney nods to me as he hands the bartender a number of bills. Then he takes the tray and proceeds back to his table near the front of the stage.

I order a double scotch on the rocks for myself and suck back about an ounce of it right off the bat to try and calm my nerves. I ask Sheba if Kate, Sam and Kim have ordered and point them out to her, at a table in the corner.

"Them? Christ, yes. They've ordered," she says, sounding battered and bitter, not at all like she was the other night.

"Yes," I say indefinitely, not wanting to sound disagreeable. I wave to Kate, who waves me over. I nod, about to go but then I hear the bartender on the phone.

"No! Look, for the last fucking time, we don't page people in this bar. If you want to know who's here you come down here and see for yourself, you meagre shitpick."

I look at the bartender (Grundy I guess his name is), who catches my gaze. "What?" he asks, deeply annoyed, his gaze as severe and daunting as his biceps.

"Is the person you're talking to on the phone named Havilah?"

He glowers at me, put out by all of this, but does indeed ask if the person he's talking to is named Havilah. "Yes," he says and hands me the phone.

"Hello?" I say. "Uncle Hav?"

". . . and you can't talk to me like that, you raped ape, without expecting some sort of tactical retribution. I'm a taxpayer dammit and I know a thing or two about—Say, who is this?"

"Dean."

"Dean? Is that you? I've been trying to get hold of you all day. So that's where you are. At the fucking Lily Pad. That's just typical. I might have known. What the fuck are you doing down there without me? Motherfucking damn fucker . . ." and on and on and on.

Words cannot express the regret I have in taking this call.

Chapter 28

"Can I speak?" I say, cutting him off when it becomes apparent to me that his ranting is nowhere nearing an end.

"Go ahead. Who the hell's stopping you?" he says, full of hot rage.

"Quit being so put out all the time and just listen. I was just about to call you. We just got here ourselves."

"Don't hand me that," he says, nevertheless calming down. "Who's 'we'?"

"Me, Kate, Kim and Sam. There was no room in the Galaxie for you. That's why we didn't come over and pick you up," I say, trying to make my lies sound sincere.

"Yeah, well . . ." He seems at a loss for words. "It still doesn't help me out much. I'm still here all alone."

"What happened to Finestra?"

"She turned out to be a real piece of work. But you know how women are. They expect you to pay for everything. Every damn thing. She's allergic to breadsticks too. At least that's what she said. But I know better."

"Yes . . . Well, why don't you hop in a cab and come over here?"

"I have half a mind to call your bluff."

"It's no bluff."

"We'll see about that."

"Good."

"That's it! I'm coming down!" he roars and I hear the phone slam down onto its hook.

I hand the phone back to Grundy and turn to go over to our table. I am stopped by a tall slinky woman in a bathrobe, who puts an arm out to block my path. "Yes?" I say.

"In-between sets I offer lap dance specials on Monday nights," she says, full of leering promiscuity. "And tonight is Monday night. What do you say? Only sixty bucks."

My extroversion having already been shored up by scotch and Coronas, I begin to feel the fabric of her bathrobe. "Is this satin?" I ask, not quite flirtatiously but rather out of need to satisfy my strange and momentary curiosity.

"It certainly is, sweet thing. I'm Oracle."

"I'm Dean. I have to say no to you though. I already have a girl," I say, proudly pointing out Kate for her, who is watching us, a smile on her face, getting a kick out of this whole scene.

"Hmm. Not bad. Not bad at all. I wouldn't be adverse to giving her one either."

"I don't think she'd go for it."

"Well, just ask. You never know. Throw in an extra fifty and I'll give you both a Cleveland steamer too. But you'll have to wait for my taco dinner to digest. Say in twenty minutes?"

"No, really. Thanks though," I say, stepping aside and hurrying over to where Kate is. I sit down beside her.

"What did she want?" Kate asks.

"She's a lap dancer," I say. "And she's open for business."

"Look. There's that guy," Kim says, pointing out this guy who has just entered.

"Who's that?" Sam asks, taking a drink of his Caesar, just as Sheba arrives with a platter of onion rings and a Chef's salad. She sets them down before Sam. "Thanks," Sam says to her and starts munching away on onion rings.

"I thought you didn't want to eat here," I say.

"Neither did I. It's just one of those things," he says, ravenously scarfing down the food before him.

"That's the guy who was working at the photomat," Kim says belatedly, in answer to Sam's question.

"Kim and I were chatting and happened to mention that we were coming here and he brazenly inserted himself right into our conversation. He said that Fluff Chang was doing a duet tonight. He became very flush and creepy," Kate says to me.

"Maybe he's one of Fluff's stalkers," I say.

"Could be," Sam says, his mouth full of salad. "I wouldn't put anything past anyone. The Swiss cheese in this Chef's salad is terrific!"

"Let me have a bite," Kim says. Sam holds a fork draped in cheesy salad up to her mouth and she takes a bite. "Mmm, that is good." Sheba passes by and Kim stops her, asking about the possibility of ordering some Swiss cheese slices. Sheba says she'll look into it, despite her haughty expression, which indicates a heavy reluctance to.

"I wonder if Cooley Penrod is here," Kate says, beginning to scan the room. "It's really filling up. That's unusual for a Monday night, isn't it?"

"It's hard to say with this place."

"Say, what did Jim Chimney have to say?"

"We're supposed to go over to their table for a drink at some point. Wendy's here. And he said Wanda's supposed to show up too."

"Wendy's here?" Kate searches about the crowd. "Okay. I see her. Off to the side. Should we go over there now?"

"Later," I say, swirling the remnants of Scotch in my tumbler and then downing the rest of it. "I don't like this."

"What are you worried about now?" Kate asks, taking a sip of her drink.

"Is that a Singapore Sling?" I ask.

"Yes, and it's good too."

"I think that's what I'll have next," Kim says, taking a sip of her Wiser's. "It's time to shake things up a little."

"Maybe I need something like that too," I say.

"Yes, maybe it will calm you down. You seem nervous," Kate says.

"Uncle Hav is coming over. He happened to call while I was up at the bar."

"Well, he's easy enough to handle," Kate says. "Look at *that* stripper up there. That's not Winnie, is it?" she asks tentatively. I can tell that she has taken a dislike to the current performer and would hate for her to be Winnie.

"No. Winnie's chestier. And she's also like her sisters, facially. You'll know her when you see her."

"I can't wait. It's all so exciting. What do you think, Kim?"

"I thought we would stand out more. I was as surprised as you to see such a fair amount of girls here too."

"What do you think of the seediness?" I ask Kim.

"It's seedy, but rather comfortably so. I don't like the carpets. They're much too sticky. But this dark lighting is kind of nice. I'm not nearly as apprehensive as I thought I'd be."

Sam finishes up the rest of his meal and wipes his mouth with a napkin. "That was a great salad," he declares.

"That's how they bring in the crowd," I say.

Sheba comes by and asks if we need anything more. We order a round of Singapore Slings. Kim once more inquires about the Swiss cheese slices and Sheba says she's working on it.

"Boy, she sounds snippy," Kim says of Sheba. "But other than her, this place really isn't very forbidding at all," she says, completely relaxed.

"I wonder where Fluff is?" Kate asks, full of intrigue and wonder.

"You seem aroused by all the goings on up on stage," Sam says.

"Nonsense," Kate says. "It's nothing like that." It's not either, I don't think. I think Kate likes it here because it's all so new to her and it makes her feel naive. And she likes the idea of feeling naive. It makes her feel young and innocent.

I continue to look about, preoccupied with the entrance, keeping an eye out for Wanda. And my fears are realized right about the time Sheba returns with our drinks.

Wanda enters The Lily Pad.

Chapter 29

And wouldn't you know it?—I'm the first one she spots. She comes stomping over. My body tightens. "It's going down," I say worriedly, alerting Kate.

"What?" Kate says, initially oblivious to my fear but then seeing Wanda too.

Wanda comes to a stop about a foot away from where we're sitting. Her shadow hovers over the table like some pugnacious vulture of doom.

"Nice clothes," Kate says of Wanda, who's decked out in skin tight leather, looking very much like she did the night of the Alice Cooper concert. "You look like some runaway Harley bimbo who just stumbled out of Oakland."

I look at Kate, surprised by her caustic manner, though I really shouldn't be. Wanda's been a thorn in her side for far too long. Kate's had enough of her and then some.

"What's with the glasses?" Wanda says inquisitively, full of odd and sudden quietude. We had all lifted our sunglasses from our eyes at various points upon entering this place and they are stuck on the tops of our heads.

"Just playin' it cool," Sam says, always up for confrontation when it doesn't involve him.

"Hmmph!" Wanda snorts, her breasts heaving like jello. Her mood changes to full blast irate again. She looks at me, wilting me with her stare. "I've had it with your hijinks. You may have brainwashed the cops to get out of your rightful punishment in a court of law but that doesn't mean the matter's been put to rest. I never forget. Try to crack me with a bat, will you? Evil plotting. The two of you are bad. Very bad."

Kate stands up, ready to counter Wanda's rebuke of us. "It wasn't that way at all and you know it. We've about had it with you."

"Is that a threat?"

"It's a fact. Now leave."

"And after I brought back your toaster. Dean, what kind of treatment is this?" she asks, changing moods again and now beseeching me, her big green eyes filling with vulnerability.

"It's over, Wanda. Can't you just let it go?" I say, trying to be firm but not without compassion.

"Buy me a drink and I'll think about it," she says, pulling up a chair and sitting in-between me and Kim.

"I think Wendy and the others are waiting for you over there," I say, pointing them out for her.

"I've about had it with Wendy and her so-called fame. She's always buzzing around like a drunk mosquito. She's driving me nuts. Where's that drink?"

I motion to Sheba. She comes over and I order Wanda a banana daiquiri. I glance at Kate, who just looks at me trustingly, as though sensing it best to stay out of this and let me try to handle it.

"You remember what I like to drink," Wanda says, pleased, though trying not to show it.

"Can't we just get along?" I say.

"You'd like that, wouldn't you? It would tie your life up into a nice little bow, wouldn't it?"

"Yes," I say, Kate, Kim and Sam saying nothing, just listening.

"What will I do?" she says, sounding lost, seemingly oblivious to the others at the table.

"I'm sure you'll figure something out. I'm sure it'll come to you once you stop with all this running about."

"Do you think so?" she asks hopefully, as Sheba arrives with the daiquiri. Wanda accepts it and takes a calm, meditative sip. "I guess I wasn't a good wife, Dean. But I did like being married."

"It makes one feel safe, I guess," I say.

"Yes. I hate endings," she says.

"Something else'll turn up to take its place," I say, fearful of sounding off with too many dopey platitudes. But Wanda seems to receive them thoughtfully.

She stands up, seemingly only now aware of the others at the table, and looking self-conscious because of it. "I think I'll go. Winnie'll be expecting to see my face front and centre with the others."

"Alright," I say, happy not to have to bring up my trump card of having seen her and Dick Jemima in the act.

"Thank you for the drink, Dean." Wanda leaves, sipping on her drink.

I breathe a sigh of relief and look at Kate. "Do you think it'll take?" I ask her, simultaneously full of hope and doubt.

"Dean, you were masterful," Kim says to me. I absorb her words happily, her compliments always meaningful to me.

"You really were," Kate says. "You played it cool." She looks at me with that serene half-smile of hers that speaks of the great joy between us. I feel her want for me to be at a high-pitch right now and it makes me feel about as good as one can feel.

But that feeling is soon interrupted.

Uncle Hav enters The Lily Pad.

Chapter 30

He looks completely dishevelled and intoxicated. We wave to him, flailing about trying to get his attention, but it takes a long time before he notices us. He finally comes stumbling over and plops down in the chair that Wanda had just been sitting in.

I pat him on the shoulder. "So, how are you doing, Uncle Hav?"

"I told you not to call me your uncle. Dammit, Dean. Why do you always insist on pushing my buttons?"

"I'm sorry. Relax."

"How can I? Life is such a sinkhole of shit," he says, ever the ray of sunshine. "Hey, what's with the plates? I suppose you guys went ahead and ate without waiting for me," he says, examining the table.

"Sam was eating but we've just been drinking," Kate says. "Dean's right. Relax, Hav."

He bores his eyes into Sam. "How come you never call me?" he asks, demanding an answer.

"It's been hectic," Sam says.

"You sound just like this guy," he says, pointing to me with a thumb. "It's all numbskullery if you ask me. Anyway, how have you been?" he asks Sam, momentarily interested in someone other than himself.

"I'm thinking of buying a velcro wallet."

"That's old school," Uncle Hav says, without reproach. Sheba is passing by and he hooks a finger into her apron strings, stopping her. "Hey, baby, how 'bout a drink?"

"What do you want?" Sheba says frigidly, taking an immediate dislike to him.

"Double Rum. Bacardi's only. Two ice cubes and one ounce of coke. Got it? Now on your way, sugar tits," he says and slaps her on the ass.

"Jerk," we can her utter as she hurries away.

"It's all the same with women," he says, sounding defeatist.

"So, what have you been up to, Havilah?" Kim says, taking a polite interest in him.

"I told you! Call me Hav. Christ."

"You never said any such thing to me," Kim says, taking offense with Uncle Hav's attitude and not letting him get away with it.

"Who are you anyway?" he says, in squinting examination of her, his neck craning towards her.

"This is Kim. You've met her many times. You were talking to her at the party we had last month, for pete's sake," Kate says. "Remember?"

"Party? I don't recall any party. The fun I'm excluded from is sad and sickening."

"Oh shut up," I say, tired of him already.

"A fine way to talk to your uncle," he says, in a familiar refrain, fidgeting away. He lights up a cigarette. Sheba comes and slams his drink down before him. Some of it sloshes up and spills down the side. "You see what I have to put up with." He takes a drink and licks the side of the glass on which the drink spilled over. "So, has Fluff been on yet?"

"Not yet. I wish she would come out though. I want to see what all the fuss is about," Kate says, taking off her coat and hanging it on the back of her chair. A warm, congestive feeling is starting to infuse the room.

"You shouldn't talk like that," Uncle Hav says. "People will mistake you for a lesbian."

"Oh please. It's just nice sometimes to see what the competition is packing."

"There is no competition," I say.

"You're so lovey dovey," Uncle Hav says, sounding bitter about it. He then changes topics altogether, talking to Kim. "I hear they have after hours fisting in one of the backrooms. You need one of their VIP Gold Club Cards to get in though."

"That sounds like an urban legend," Kim says skeptically.

"I'm just telling you what I heard," Uncle Hav says, shrugging. "The dj here used to run a blind pig down by the river and he was into that scene big time. Why do you think he was recruited for this place?"

"I don't believe that," Kate says. "I'm going to ask Fluff about it. Even Wendy. She'd know."

"Wendy? *Her*?! Don't mention that name to me. Making me talk about my pubic wig on live tv. The nervy broad."

I'm about to tell him that Wendy's here but I stop myself. He's riled enough as it is.

"Pubic wig," Sam laughs. "I love it. Are you wearing it right now?"

"No. It itches. I think I got ripped off. I don't think it's genuine ox-hair at all. It's probably a dead cat pelt or something. I'm always getting screwed. That's the last time I'll ever order anything from Amsterdam. What the hell kind of music is this anyway?"

"It's "Border Lord"," Sam says. "Kris Kristofferson. The perfect music to play in-between acts."

"I never liked him," Uncle Hav says.

Kim rolls her eyes disgustedly and looks at Kate, who nods in agreement, neither of them willing to laugh about it though, because for them to be in the presence of someone who hates Kris Kristofferson is no laughing matter at all.

"How can you hate him? He wrote "Me and Bobby McGee" and you love that song," I say, giving him a chance to redeem himself in front of them.

"We all get lucky once. Damn, you know what? I'm gonna see if I can get them to play some Kylie Minogue. After all, I'm a paying customer, dammit. They better acquiesce." Uncle Hav gets up and storms off into the milling crowd, looking to get his demands fulfilled.

I shake my head, trying to dimiss him from my mind.

"Lovely relatives you have," Sam says.

"He's the aberration. And yet I see him more than any of my other relatives. Why is that?" I ask.

"I don't know," Kate says, standing up. "But it bears consideration."

"Where are you going?" I ask.

"I have to go to the bathroom," she says and takes her leave.

I catch a glimpse of someone going in behind her, a platinum blonde in a trenchcoat and floppy hat and wearing a pair of sunglasses. "Get a look at her," I say. "And here we thought we were the ones setting the tone for the night by coming in with sunglasses on."

"We *did* set the tone," Kim says re-affirmingly. "She probably saw us wearing them and then went home and grabbed her own."

"We *are* trendsetters, aren't we?" I say, liking the idea and giving my head a jerky nod. The sunglasses drop down onto the bridge of my nose. I feel cool.

"Indubitably," Sam says, ordering a round of crantinis from Sheba.

All of a sudden a certain wave of electricity fills the place.

"What's happening?" Kim asks.

"I think Fluff is coming on. Didn't you say she was doing a duet tonight?" I ask, lifting the glasses from my eyes again.

"No, that's what that strange person at the photomat said."

"I'll bet it's with Winnie," I say, starting to get excited in spite of it all. "Kate's going to be upset if she misses the opening."

"I'll go and tell her to hurry, if she can," Kim says, getting up and disappearing into the bathroom.

Our crantinis come and Sam looks completely delighted to be drinking something ruby red in colour. Then we hear the Emmylou Harris version of "Queen of the Silver Dollar" begin to play.

"How hackneyed and cliched to play this song here," Sam says, slurping down his crantini.

"I love it," I say.

"So do I!" Sam exclaims, in a surprising and immediate change of opinion. Then Fluff and Winnie emerge, each of them sliding down a pole and dressed in matching sequined cowgirl outfits, a pink feather boa wrapped around each of their necks. They begin to engage in choreographed gyrations, their body motions smooth and silky. I find the whole thing quite pleasing. But then suddenly the music stops. I see Fluff looking back, towards the dj booth, surprised and perplexed. But she motions Winnie to keep going. Fluff is a pro.

Then the music comes on again. Only this time it's Kylie Minogue's version of "The Loco-Motion." We hear some voices belt out over the microphone from the dj booth. Some kind of tussle is going on back there.

"Let go! Get the fuck out of here!"

"I'm a taxpayer godammit! And I deserve to hear Kylie Minogue if I want!"

"Let go!"

"My nuts!"

All sorts of crashing and banging ensues.

Fluff stops her act and turns toward the dj booth, stomping her cowgirl boots on the stage in furious protest. "What in the bloody blue blazes is going on back there?! What kind of a garage bar are you running here?! Dirty sonovabitches! A girl can't work in conditions like this!"

She then turns to face the crowd, her expression and demeanour livid. She seems to spot someone of note and steps to the edge of the stage. "You!" she hollers. "I've had enough!" She dives headlong into the crowd as though diving into a swimming pool, her pink feather boa streaming behind her.

My neck cranes toward the melee; I'm in blown away shock by all that's happening. But then other matters divert my attention.

"Sam! Dean!" I hear Kim yell, and we turn to see her emerging from the bathroom with a bloody nose. "Get her! She tried to kill Kate!"

"What?!" Sam and I utter simultaneously, mouths agape, utterly stunned by everything.

We see the girl in the trenchcoat streak past us, without her floppy hat, sunglasses and platinum blonde wig. It's Pepper Jones. And she's on the run.

Chapter 31

Kate lurches out of the bathroom behind Kim, her right arm dripping blood. "Oh my God," I say, weak of breath, feeling myself blanch with panic.

Sam and I rush over to check on them. But Kate and Kim are in no mood for sympathy.

"Forget about us! Get her!" Kate orders, clamping her bloody arm with her left hand, leaning against the wall for support. "I'll explain all this later."

"I boxed her a good one in the ear, Sam," Kim says, adrenalized, waving a tight-gripped fist in the air.

I do a quick pivot, forgetting about all else as per Kate's demands, concerned now only with the chase.

As I bolt towards the entrance I notice Wendy diving into the fray to help Fluff riotously pummel someone she has pinned to the floor. "Bring on the donnybrook!" she wails uproariously. Tuppy is standing over them, swatting the air with her fists, cheering her daughter on. Jim Chimney sits at his table, smoking his pipe, looking majestic as he watches the scene unfold. Other fights are breaking out all over the place. I don't see Wanda anywhere.

I rush out of The Lily Pad, a weather-shifting, chinooking wind sparking my senses into top alertness. Sam pulls up to a stop beside me. We look up and down the avenue and across the parking lot. We don't see Pepper.

"What do we do?" I ask Sam, trying to be calm yet pragmatic.

"I don't even know what's going on," he says, baffled and feverish.

"That was Pepper Jones," I say. "She's the one we have to get." I cross the street, allowing my impulses to carry me. Sam follows. We hurry over to the entranceway of a rundown hotel. Some wastrel is sitting on the stoop smoking crack.

"Did a girl come rushing in here?" I ask him directly.

"She might have been holding her ear," Sam adds. I look at him, his statement seeming odd. He looks at me. "Kim said she threw her a good one," he explains, somewhat proud of Kim's apparent pugilistic abilities.

216

The guy looks up at us, wide-eyed and close to distress. "Yes. She came by alright. She flew, my man. Flew! Put a shoulder into me too. I'm aching bad. Say, could either of you throw me a ten? I'm good for it."

I delve into my pocket and come out with a five. I toss it to him and we rush into the hotel.

"Thanks, man," he says. "Hey wait! This is only five. Chisellers!" he yells back at us as we rush up the stairs, up and up the six flights, to the top floor.

"How do you know she came to the top floor?" Sam asks, both of us panting on the top landing, beside the door that opens into the hallway.

"I don't. They just always do that in the movies. Go right to the top and trap themselves," I say, aware of the illogicality of my logic but not knowing what other strategy to employ.

We open the door, step into the hall and see Pepper's trenchcoat lying in a heap in the middle of the floor at the end of it. We hurry down it, passing by all the doors. The last one we get to, the one nearest the coat, is slightly ajar.

"She must have ditched the coat because it was hindering her," I say, kicking at it as though such an action will hurt her. I then push the door all the way open.

"This is crazy," Sam says, following me in.

A dapper, gray-haired little man in a bowtie meets us in the hall, blocking us from further entrance. "What is going on in here? Who are you and why have you come here? I will not tolerate this harassment anymore. I'm registered and I'm keeping to myself. What more do you want? This is simply intolerable."

"Did a girl come in here?" Sam asks.

"Girl? Good Lord, no. I have nothing to do with girls. However, I was in the bathroom attending to one of those deeply necessary needs when I heard a kafuffle going on. Someone could have *broken* in. What's this all about anyway? You two don't look like police officers."

"Where's your window?" I ask, boldly pushing him aside and running down the hall, into the living room, which is full of assorted sizes of pink, stuffed teddy bears and numerous piles of teen magazines.

We see the window blowing back the gauzy white curtains. We rush over to it and step out onto the fire escape. We look down.

"There!" Sam says, pointing down. We see Pepper, about two stories below, in a downward climb through the ironwork of the fire escape.

"Stop!" I yell uselessly, knowing full well that she won't.

"She won't get him!" Pepper yells back at us, threatening and strange, as we begin the precarious climb down, trying to catch up to her.

The guy who's apartment we'd burst into calls out to us. "No, no, you musn't leave yet. I'm just about to make some hot chocolate. Please come back."

We carefully, but quickly, make it down, seeing Pepper dodge around the corner of the building, back towards The Lily Pad. "She might be going back after Kate or Kim," I say, full of great worry, increasing my running speed, Sam doing likewise.

When we make it back out to the street I see Kate and Kim standing by the entrance of The Lily Pad, an old and cripply beat up wino in a torn mackinaw coat offering them a drink from his box of wine. They refuse and shortly thereafter some guys drag him into the shadows and begin thrashing him.

Kim sees us. "Dean! Sam!" she exclaims, sounding relieved. She and Kate push their way through the pulsing throng of people gathered about close to the entrance.

"She went across the parking lot!" Kate points to where they saw Pepper, her right arm sloppily bandaged up with a white and bloody bar towel.

We take off after her, Kate and Kim now on the hunt with us.

Our pace intensifies with every step taken. But Pepper still eludes our sight. "Where is she?!" I say, feeling a panicky thrill zapping through me.

We stop for a moment to gather our bearings and try to decipher Pepper's likely movements, which seem bizarre, senseless and desperate to me.

"Let's try the red light district," Kate says. "She probably feels it would be easier to lose us in an area where there are lots of people."

We all nod, thinking this theory to have a great deal of validity to it, as the red light district will be totally crowded right about now.

We all immediately break into a run and make our way to the red light district, which is only two blocks away.

When we turn onto it we see the place teeming with hookers and street people of all sorts. The needle exchange is going on and lots of junkies are stumbling about in various states of near seizure. We see a couple of hot dog vendors arguing with each other. We come to a halt and begin to scan up and down the street.

"That reminds me, Kim," I say, watching the hot dog vendors as they bicker over territory and call each other cunts. "I've started reading *A Confederacy of Dunces*. I'm liking it a lot."

"It's funny, isn't it? I knew you'd like it."

"Don't take too much credit for your recommendation. I would have discovered that book eventually on my own."

"Sure. Sure you would've," Kim says tauntingly. "This one's a feather in my cap and you know it," she says, full of exaggerated self-satisfaction.

"I can't deny it," I say. We all begin to walk down the street, slowly, searching for Pepper.

At one of the street corners some skinny little guy is playing guitar, his guitar case open at his feet and full of various amounts of coins, mostly quarters and dimes. Some scarred Indians approach him and grab some handfuls of change from it.

"What are you doing? Please don't. I'm just trying to make a living," he implores dejectedly.

We reach him just as the toughs leave, turning off into a liquor store. "Bad night, huh?" Sam says, as we all take a break, not willing to admit that we may have lost the Pepper trail, though I can sense that each of us is thinking it.

"You know it, my friend. Ever since my breakdancing studio went under I've seen nothing but tough times. I never thought I'd have to turn to street performing again."

"Have you ever tried juggling?" Sam asks, sounding like he's still deep under the influence of his crantini.

"Are you alright, really? What happened to your arm?" I ask Kate, full of deep concern, ready to take a serious look at it. Kate holds out her arm for me and I gently peel away the wrap of the towel, which exposes a bloody deep gash across her forearm, thick with coagulating blood. I am reminded of the time in school when I thought I had scratched her arm with my compass. I feel sick. All I want to do is protect her. I don't want anything to happen to her, ever. I reapply the towel gently. She's shaking. I think I am too.

You're white as a sheet," I say. "Tell me what happened."

"I'm just cold, Dean. I forgot to bring my coat from the club in all the commotion."

I take mine off and wrap it across her shoulders. "Now what happened?" I ask.

"She tried to strangle me," she says, her body conforming to the warmth of my jacket, her voice becoming intense as she begins to relive the scene.

"Juggling's too hard. Besides, I'm an axe man at heart. Want to hear a song? For a dollar I'll play whatever you want," the street musician says to Sam, who hands him a ten.

"God bless you. Thank you so much," he gushes, full of effusive praise and appreciation and immediately pocketing the ten.

"It's all part of the social contract," Sam says, full of general goodwill. "Now play "Heart of Gold" for us."

"Boney M. style or Neil Young?"

"Better stick with Neil," Sam says after a moment of consideration. "What's your name?"

"Roland Lemaire."

"I'm Sam Dart. Please to meet you, Roland." They shake hands. "Now play on, soulful balladeer."

Roland begins to play and Sam's lanky body begins to slowly groove to the music, like a a tall blade of grass in the wind. He then turns his attention back to us. "Let's hear the tale be told," he says to Kate, suddenly ready to listen.

"Well," Kate says, taking a deep breath. She's ready to let it all out, I can tell. She's frightened and full of all sorts of whirling, colliding emotions that she wants to cathartically expel. "I went to the bathroom. I had to go pee. I was in one of the stalls and I'd just finished and I was about to open the stall door when I happened to look down and notice that my shoelace was untied.

"I don't know why I didn't leave the stall and tie it up out where there was more room, but I didn't. I bent over and tied my shoe and as I was doing so my sunglasses popped off my head and fell to the floor. As I picked them up and stood up straight I saw a reflection in them. I saw a blonde in a big floppy hat and sunglasses hanging over the top of the stall wall, her two hands wound with a taut piece of piano wire between them. Obviously, I thought I was drunk, or paranoid or something. I shook my head, but the reflection was still there, and so I looked up and just then I saw the glint of the wire as it came looping down for my throat and I shot my arm up to prevent it from getting around my neck. I think that wire cut my arm to the bone. It hurts, Dean. It hurts so much. She leaned ahead and then back and then pulled and pulled, but she didn't get my throat, Dean. She didn't get it." I put my arm around her and squeeze her close. She continues.

"And then as she was pulling on the wire I bolted forward and she lost her balance and fell down into the stall and we were crashing about and I was trying to punch at her and all. And then her wig and glasses came off and I knew it was Pepper and I struggled to unlock the bathroom door and when I did we spilled out onto the floor and there was Kim." Kate looks at Kim thankfully.

Kim takes over the story now. "And I was understandably astounded. It was the most arresting sight I've ever seen. All I could think was 'Goodness. What is all this?' But I could see all this blood and knew things were bad, even though I didn't know what was happening. I just tried to get them separated. I didn't even see the wire. Finally, I guess Pepper sensed things were not going to go like she'd hoped, so she gave up on Kate and stood up, releasing her grip from the wire. I didn't know what to do. She tried to fly past me but I blocked her from it. I don't know why. It was a spontaneous reaction, I guess, and then she grabbed me and we grappled and she slammed me against the wall by the hand dryer. And she grabbed my throat and then punched me in the nose." Kim points to her nose. It's red with dried blood, along with her lips and her left cheek.

Sam pulls her close. "You look tough," he says, his voice full of levity, trying to alleviate the grim drama of all that has happened.

Kim smiles at him and continues. "But I came up with a windmill. I don't know how, but I did. I drove her a good one in the ear. I even heard a pop," she says, proud of this fact. "And that's when she released me and took off. You guys know the rest."

I look at Kate, who returns my gaze. I now understand what she felt that night she saved me, that night in which she recognized how close I was to being gone. But she saved me. I didn't save her. I feel guilty, even though I logically recognize that I shouldn't. And then I see Pepper.

"There she is!" I point out, stirred up by the sudden renewal of the chase. "She's coming out of the all-night book store!"

Everyone's head pivots, their eyeballs zeroing down my arm as though it's a gun barrel, right to where I'm pointing.

"Let's get her people!" Sam hollers staunchly, his voice a whooping war cry, riled up by the sight of Kim's bloody face and ready to avenge it.

"Wait! Don't you want to hear another song?" Roland passionately queries, just as we're about to take off.

"Play "Mr. Tambourine Man," if you please," Sam says, never failing to be courteous.

"It's about time someone requested some Dylan," Roland says, sounding relieved and bitter at the same time.

We all bolt after Pepper. She suddenly sees us and seems to panic, pivoting this way and that, frozen in her tracks. She then makes a tactical mistake and turns back into the bookstore, into which we run mere moments later.

The bald burly proprietor notices us right off the bat and pulls a big black rubber dildo out from beneath the counter. He swats it down on the hard countertop, using it as a billy club. He points it at us. "If you people came in here to make out in the Wicca section, you've got another thing coming. I've had it with you freaks."

"We've come for Pepper Jones!" Kate declares, laying down the verbal gauntlet.

"Alright. That's it," he says, making his way out from behind the counter, his girth alone demanding respect. "You hopheads are putting a strain on my good nature. You wanna play games? Well, you came to the right place. Papa Topp takes no guff. Let's play."

I catch a glimpse of Pepper, peeking out from behind one of the book stacks.

I'm totally worried she might make a dash for the back door to this place. And I can't let that happen. I have to get her; I have to do this for what she did to Kate. So I dodge past Papa Topp, his dildo swatting me across the back as I pass. I charge towards Pepper, who emerges from the stacks, ready for the final assault. She pulls out a butterfly knife and flips it about with great expertise, letting me know that she's ready to play out the string with a fight.

I leap at her and tackle her, my arms squeezing around her right beneath the armpits. We plough into a rack full of porno books and then veer off into a rack of more legitimate literature, various copies of this and that flying up every which way. I land on top of Pepper and grab at the wrist with the butterfly knife, the right one, which she tries to free, ready to jam me with it.

But I make a mistake. I ignore her left hand. She reaches out and grabs a book. She ends up clocking me in the head with a James Michener. She kicks me off her.

I am stunned by this assault. I see her get to her knees, then stand up before me. She raises the butterfly knife, ready to bring it down into me and end my ripping heartbeat of fear right now.

But then the words: "Freeze! Police!"

Reprieve! I think, briefly full of swelling relief.

But then: no! No reprieve at all. I can see it in her eyes. They crackle with desperate insanity, right on the precipice, with nowhere to go but down. She pauses, her mind in a looping click.

"You won't win. None of you will," she says to me. "I won't allow it. He's mine. I love him and he's mine. All mine. Mine!" she screams.

But then: a gunshot.

But it misses her altogether, instead ripping through a copy of *The Story of O*, which thunks down off a shelf and lands beside my head, a fluttering mess of smoking, gunpowdered paper.

Pepper spins, only now shocked by the presence of cops, but only momentarily. Their lousy aim does little to fill her with much concern. She turns back and bores into me with her hatred, her lips contorting fiery madness. She cackles away, like Satan's rooster. The knife starts to come down in a steel glinting swoosh.

In a last ditch effort I sweep my legs in aerobic fright and knock her off her feet. She trips over my legs and falls in a crash to the warped, undulating floorboards, the butterfly knife flying from her grasp.

She lands right beside me in a snaking twist, wailing torrentially, an insane garble of indecipherable phrases spewing out of her mouth. I get to my knees, reach over and grab her by the hair. I lift her head and then bring it down hard on a nearby Norman Mailer, hoping to pulverize her. Her eyes dim and her mind goes out to lunch. I breathe a deep sigh of relief.

Pepper's reign of terror has come to an end.

Chapter 32

Kate rushes over and hugs me with all the tightness that her wounded arm will allow for. Sam and Kim also close in on me, giving me 'way to go' pats on the shoulder. I see Dude Bagley emerge, one of his uniformed lackeys bending down to put the cuffs on an unconscious Pepper.

"This guy wouldn't let us help you out," Sam says, pointing to Bagley. "He shoved his piece at us and made us stand still."

"We had this situation well under control. No need for amateurs to intervene. You would have just hindered us," he says loftily.

"But you didn't do anything," Kate says accusatorily.

"We take the correct measures when such measures are required. We are the law."

"You couldn't even hit her. You hit a book," Kim says, repulsed by Bagley and taking up Kate's cause.

"Yes, that was unfortunate. But Ricardo's new to the force," Bagley says, as though that settles the matter.

"I tried to blast her in the left blade," Ricardo says enthusiastically, a matchstick clinging from his lips and jerking up and down with great celerity.

"Quiet. I'm in charge, Ricardo," Bagley says. He looks at all of us. "You will all have to make a statement, of course. But it looks as though we have salted away this Pepper," he says, chuckling away. "Another case put to rest," he says to his uniformed subservients in a deeply satisfied voice. There are at least eleven cops in the store, many of them looking through some of the numerous copies of *The Story of O.*

"Who's going to clean up this mess?" Papa Topp says humourlessly, approaching the scatter of books all about the floor.

"Sorry about that," I say.

"Choke on this, you dumb punk," he says menacingly, holding up the jiggling dildo in his hand. He then turns away from us and returns behind the counter and begins to munch on a bowl of pink popcorn.

"So Pepper's the killer?" Kate asks Bagley, trying to put a knot into all the loose ends that this case still has.

"No. Lipstick Jones is the killer. He's her dad. We were trailing him after the third murder but lost him and had a hard time relocating him because he was laying low and had changed his name to—"

"Cooley Penrod," Kate says.

Bagley seems taken aback by Kate's awareness of the name. "Yes. Now would you mind explaining how you came into possession of such information?"

"We're not stupid," Kate says elusively.

"Yes, well," Bagley says, seemingly stumped for a reply. "In any event, he has now been found again. He was involved in an altercation at The Lily Pad in which he was beaten into submission by a Miss Fluff Chang and a Miss Wendy Michigan, the talk show host."

"So that's who it was they were fighting," I say, feeling enlightened and remembering the melee from what seems like a hazy distant memory in the midst of all the excitement that has transpired since.

"Why did Lipstick—Cooley—whatever the heck his name is, kill all those girls?"

"He likes it, for one. Two, he fancies himself a good father. Pepper saw these girls as competition for the favours of a certain King Cloke and she wanted them out of the way. She scoped out the King's movements for I don't know how long and she would decide on the ones she wanted offed. And then she had Lipstick do her bidding—which he readily did, to both satisfy his own demented urges and to please his daughter. And, as you know, they were all wearing protective glasses, the kind you wear at a dentist's office. That was Pepper's idea. We found a whole box of them at her apartment earlier tonight, along with a packet of teeth which she kept under her pillow, as a reminder of the killings and as a keepsake of King Cloke's handiwork. And Lipstick's markering out of the lenses had a twofold purpose: his odd desire to maintain a consistency in m.o. from when he was a mere rapist and liked to lipstick out the eyes of his victims and also because it was Pepper's symbolic way of saying that nobody was to look at King Cloke but her. He was *her* dentist and hers alone. She also made sure that all the murders were committed when the King was out of town. She didn't want him to be sent up the river for them because, if he was, then they very well couldn't get together at some point down the road. At least that's the version we're sticking to until the psychiatrist has a go at her."

"Hmm," Kate says, mulling it all over. "I guess it makes sense. We were pretty much thinking the same thing, sort of."

"Sure you were. Sure you were," Bagley says patronizingly. "Anyway, it was after the third murder that we got an anonymous call that gave us a partial on a license plate to a car that was seen in the vicinity where the last body was dumped, the night before it was discovered. And that, after much deduction, led us to Lipstick, and his connection to Pepper was revealed as a result, as the two of them were spotted together. When we lost sight of Lipstick, we turned our attentions to Pepper and as we didn't want her to get wise to us we kept our investigation of her completely on the q.t. But we've been trailing her ever since."

"Well, you didn't do a very good job. She almost killed us twice," Kate says.

"Don't be testy. We know what we're up to."

Pepper begins to groan. "She's coming to!" one of the uniformed cops screams out in a blurt of panic. All of the cops unholster their guns and point them at Pepper, looking tense and trigger-happy.

"Boys, she's harmless now," Bagley says in an amused and fatherly voice, he and another officer helping Pepper to her feet.

Kim then unexpectedly rushes up to Pepper and begins to kick her in the shins repeatedly. "Take that!" she says hotly, her blue and white shoes welting up Pepper's legs. "And that! This one's for my nose! This one's for Kate's arm! This one's for Sam! This one's for Dean! . . ."

"Look at Kim give her the shinsplints," Sam lovingly exclaims, just as an officer pulls a tenacious Kim away from Pepper, who's hollering in pain and also because she is cuffed.

"Let me go! And what did you say about the teeth? They're mine! Daddy's gift to me! I earned them! *Mine!* King loves me! *Me!* Those fillings should be in my mouth—mine!"

"Makes me glad I stick loyally to my dentist back home," Sam says.

"Come on boys, let's put her in one of the black and whites," Bagley says, handing Pepper off to a couple of officers. They all begin to leave the bookstore. Bagley looks at all of us. "I expect to see all of you at the station within the hour for your statements."

"She tried to kill Kate, you know," I say, not liking the frivolity of Bagley's manner.

"Save it for the statement, son," Bagley says, sounding tiresomely Jack Webbish and incongruously authoritative. He too leaves and soon there is no one in the store except for us, Papa Topp and a couple of green-haired women making out in the Wicca section.

"Well, should we go?" I say, the night seeming to have come to a close.

"We have to go back to The Lily Pad," Kate says. "I have to get my coat."

We nod and leave the bookstore. Papa Topp glowers at us as we pass him. "Do your parents know what you're up to?" he growls, full of volatile crypticism.

Upon exiting the store Sam says, "I feel bad for what we put Papa Topp through." He then motions down the street to Roland and waves him over. Roland closes up his guitar case and picks it up. He hurries over to where we are.

"Yes?" he says hopefully.

Sam gives him another five. "Our friend inside is in a low mood. Stand here and play him a pick-me-up, would you?"

"Any requests?"

Well? Any ideas?" Sam says, looking at us, from one to the other.

"What would you recommend?" I ask Roland.

"Well, if it's a pick-me-up you're wanting to hear, I find that nothing gets the lips humming more than a golden oldie. A song from back in the days when life had hope."

"We leave it to you then, young musical sage," Sam says, sounding wise.

Roland begins to play "Heartaches by the Number," just as Sam goes over to one of the hot dog vendors and buys a chili dog, his slim build in constant need of food for some reason.

We nod approvingly and then say our goodbyes, Roland's voice accompanying us as we make a turn onto another street, away from the red light district and back towards The Lily Pad.

"That's not really a pick-me-up song, if you think about it," I say.

"Yes, but if you sing about your heartaches then the person listening to it feels better because he takes solace in the fact that his suffering is not isolated and singular. And that makes him feel better," Kim says, didactic yet simple. "After all, misery loves company."

"You're so smart," Sam says, still seemingly awash in a crantini buzz, his arm around her and squeezing her tight, his other hand holding his half-eaten chili dog.

We make our way back to The Lily Pad. There are cop cars all over the place. At the entrance we come face to face with Trish Mindy, her hands in the pockets of her trenchcoat, her fedora sitting on her permed hair precariously, looking ready to fall off at any moment. She is talking to Wendy and Fluff. Hard Larson is beside her, diligently taking notes.

"Wendy, Fluff. Are you okay?" Kate asks, rushing up to them. Soon we are all standing about, in a semi-circle.

"Oh heck yes," Wendy says, smoking and upbeat. "Me and Fluff tanned the hide of that yarbo Penrod. I even dislocated one of his nads! Turns out he's the killer too!"

"We know," Kate says.

"You know? How do you know?" Trish Mindy interjects, eyeing us all from head to toe, her face full of grave suspicions.

"We took out Pepper Jones. Dean took her out, actually," Kate says, building me up and me appreciating her even more for it. "Anyway, that's how we know. And Dude Bagley filled us in on the rest," Kate says.

"I'm sure not much of a fighter though. Even though I've been in a good many of them the last number of days," I say, trying to be honest about everything.

"We've heard all about that Pepper too, that awful Pepper Jones," Wendy says, her voice dramatic and concerned. "Trish told us that she's the one who tried to aerate you with lead. Far out."

"She also tried to strangle me in the bathroom earlier tonight," Kate says, holding up her blood-bandaged arm for all to see.

"The hell you say! Out of sight!" Wendy roars.

"Yes, we thought she might try that," Trish says.

"And yet the last time we saw you you said that she wouldn't attack us again."

"I don't recall that. Nevertheless, you should've heeded my warnings. But you didn't. You're a bad girl. Anyway, as I was about to say, we paid another visit to King Cloke earlier this evening. My hunch knee was aching and I knew it was worth a shot on that basis alone. We found him in the midst of shredding several documents, many of them of a pornographic nature. Anyway, we shook his tree, just to see if any apples would fall out, and that's when he broke down and brought up the name of Pepper Jones."

"In exchange for your turning a blind eye in regards to his cross-country prostitution ring."

"Hey! I told you not to mention that. For the last time, a secret's a secret," Trish says to Wendy. She then turns to us. "Anyway, we got a search warrant from Judge Leak right pronto and then went to her place. We did a hard target search of her pad and found a diary of hers detailing the whole sordid affair. She wrote about how she was present at every one of the murders and watched her dad choke those poor girls to death. And we also did a phone dump. Turns out she received a call from King Cloke's secretary, Penny Odette, earlier tonight. Apparently you went and saw King Cloke earlier today?" she says, giving me and Kate the accusatory eye.

"Yes," Kate says.

"Bad decision, as usual. She overheard you and *this guy*"—she points disgustedly at me—"mention that you were coming here tonight just as you were leaving the office. And then she called Pepper. Just like she called her after the first time you came to visit. Penny is suspicious. She'll do anything to protect the King and her own shady interests."

"Goodness. What kind of a svengali is this guy?" Kim queries.

"You," Trish Mindy says, curtly snapping her fingers at Kim. "Keep quiet."

"You want me to keep quiet?" Kim says rambunctiously, puffing up and turning volatile.

"By all means, yes."

"Well tough toenails to you!" Kim declares through gritted teeth, pointing a nasty finger at Trish.

"That's telling her, Kim," Wendy says, lighting up another cigarette. "Don't let the law bully you."

"And where's my cheese?!!" Kim yells venomously, hollering into the bowels of The Lily Pad.

"The things I have to put with," Trish says to herself, sounding forlorn and dissipated.

"*You?!* What about me?" Fluff pipes up in an abandoned voice, her cowgirl outfit ripped and torn, her feather boa missing most of its feathers and wrapped limply around her neck, her straw cowgirl hat crushed sadly atop her head. "Was this Cooley Penrod degenerate trying to kill me or what?"

"Probably. But that was just an aside. He was likely following his own desires in your instance, ones that had nothing to do with Pepper," Trish says.

"That figures," Trish says jadedly, lighting up a cigarette. "I attract nothing but driftwood and dross."

"What about that guy from the photomat?" Wendy asks hopefully.

"He suffers from erectile dysfunction. Besides, even when he does take a hard-on pill he just likes to watch. 'How come I never see you partake in any golden showers?' he's always asking, his thumb running up and down his crotch. He's a total weirdo. No morals at all." Fluff turns her attention back to Trish. "Oh, say, what about my brick of hash? Have you found out who stole that yet or not?"

"It's gone with the wind," Trish says, her hands in a dusting clap. "But just between you and me, it's probably an inside job." She then turns to Wendy, a sudden thought seeming to arise in her. "Did you get that package from Dr. Ribb? He said he was going to leave it with you."

"Yes, I did. I picked it up late last night. It's fresh off the boat."

"Good. Good," Trish says mysteriously, a placated look across her face. She looks at us. "Any other questions?"

"So Pepper's dad bought her the .38 she tried to use on us?" Kate asks.

"What .38?" Trish asks.

"The one Pepper shot up our place with."

"Oh that. It's hard to say. Could be. Any other questions?"

"Did Pepper steal that car the night she attacked us?" I ask curiously, remembering the reason why they left our place in such a hurry.

"What car?" Trish says and then turns away from me.

"Why didn't Pepper get her dad to try and kill us? Why'd she try to take us out herself?" Kate asks.

Trish rolls her eyes at Kate. "I find this explaining all so wearying. But since you insist. Well, I imagine it's because her father is an abject coward who preys only on women. And you being in the constant company of a man, so to speak,—"

"What the hell's that supposed to mean?" I interrupt, taking offense at Trish's denigrations of my character, but she just carries on, failing to acknowledge me at all.

"—was no doubt enough of a deterrent. He likely refused and Pepper had to do it on her own. But this'll all come out in court, so it's rather a waste of time to discuss it all, wouldn't you say? This case is closed. And oh, by the way, I don't know if Dude told you, but you'll all have to come to the station to make a statement. And to lay formal charges, should you so desire."

"Oh, we desire," Kate says firmly. "We'll be there as soon as I get my coat."

"This is all going to make for one hell of show," Wendy declares. "Think of the ratings."

"I hope you'll finally acquiesce and allow me to be on it," Fluff says. "It would be the perfect exclamation mark on my goodbye to this godforsaken life."

"Oh don't worry. You'll get air time."

"What? You're quitting the scene?" Sam asks Fluff, surprised.

"Yes. I'm only going to work here four nights a week from now on. The rest of the time I'm going to devote to being a writer and maybe part-time private investigator. This case has inspired me."

"I knew you were thinking of changing things up. I just knew it!" Wendy says happily. "Things are back on track, my little babies!" she states kinetically, clapping her hands and looking at all of us with warm loving eyes. "I'm having a chocolate fondu next Friday. You're all invited. You too Fluff," she says, turning back to her. "Now that you've decided to become a writer you can help me polish off my screenplay."

"That would be nice. The perfect way to bury the bitter aftertaste of all this ugliness."

"You know it. So, are you all coming over then?" Wendy looks at us eagerly.

"Sure," Kate says. "But now I really must get my coat," she says, taking off mine and handing it back to me. I put it on and realize just how cold I am.

"See you all then," Wendy says buoyantly.

"Bye Wendy. Bye Fluff," Kate says, stepping past everyone and into The Lily Pad. Kim, Sam and I follow her in. The place is packed and a show is going on as though nothing has happened.

I see Jim Chimney applauding to the finale of Oracle's act. Tuppy sees me and motions me over. "I'm just going over to say hi," I say to Kate.

"Okay, I'm just going to get my coat and then we're off."

"How's your arm?"

"It burns."

"We'll take you to the hospital before we go to the station for our statements. You'll probably need stitches."

"I know," she says, sounding worried. She goes off in search of her coat, Sam and Kim sticking with her.

I approach Jim Chimney and Tuppy. "Hi," I say.

"You missed Winnie's act," Tuppy accuses, as splenetic as ever.

"Sorry. It's been quite a night."

"Yes, night. It is indeed night tonight," Jim Chimney says, his eyes lidded over with genial drunkenness. "An old salt like me, go now. Deplore the whistling of the anal fleece. The sea. The sea be gone!" he says, sounding poetic yet confused.

"So how was Winnie?" I ask, turning my attention away from Jim Chimney.

"Like you care," Tuppy says.

"Then why'd you wave me over?" I ask peevishly.

"Winnie was just fine tonight, thank you very much. She didn't need that, that, that Fluff girl at all. She just winged it. Spontaneity has long been an Alabaster trademark."

"I know it," I say.

"Yes. And we don't need you anymore."

"I beg your pardon?"

"Wanda has washed her hands of you. She has found love."

"Really? With who?"

"With me."

I turn and see Uncle Hav and Wanda locked arm in arm, both of them beaming toothy smiles. Kate, Sam and Kim, who've just returned after picking up Kate's coat, notice this new and unforseen development as well.

"I suppose you're jealous as hell and are going to cease contact with me," Uncle Hav says, full of excited anticipation about this possibility for some reason.

"No," I say undramatically, rather calm about this bizarre turn of events.

"No?! Why the hell not?! Why can't you just be happy for me for once?" he says, flying off the handle. "Well, to hell with you then!"

"Hav, calm down, please," Kate says placatingly.

Uncle Hav looks at her sheepishly and then at me. He seems to regain his composure. "Dean, tell Fluff thanks but no thanks. I don't envision us as a couple anymore. She had her chance."

"She'll be crushed," I say flippantly, but he fails to notice. "When did all this come about?" I ask, obviously curious about all this, not exactly sure how I feel about it though, now that it begins to sink in. All this intermingling strikes me as a tad too abnormal.

"She saved me, Dean. Wanda saved me. I was fighting that dink of a dj, grappling with him over the direction of the music he was playing and he ended up sucker punching me. He had me on the floor and would have no doubt fisted me, like he used to do down by the river with all those slumming gay college boys, back when he ran that blind pig, when in comes this sweet leather angel. My sweet Wanda. She saved me."

"I just came in to see what was what, and to also request some Hendrix. All I did was hit him in the head with a chair though. It was nothing really," she blushes. "It was kind of like the way you saved me from getting stomped by the crowd at that Alice Cooper concert, Dean," Wanda says.

"Don't say that. It wasn't anything like that. Goddamn it, don't say that at all! Why must you always compare me with Dean?"

"I'm not comparing him with you."

"Don't backtalk me. It doesn't become you."

"Misogynist!"

"Me?! Why must people label me all the time? You little labeller, that's what you are, a dirty little leather labeller," Uncle Hav moans, looking upwards again for answers. His eyes come down and settle on me. "Where have you been anyway? I could've used your help."

"We helped solve the murders," I say.

"What murders?"

"The ones that have been going on all year."

"Those? Come on. You always think you're so smart," he says dismissively, and turns his attention back to Wanda. They look at each other with loose cannon gazes of restless abandon, their little argument mere moments earlier already on the back burner.

"Let's go," Wanda says.

"I like your style," Uncle Hav says to her. He look at us cheerily. "Goodnight," he says and the two of them turn and leave.

"How long do you give them?" Sam asks me.

"Until the taxi arrives," I say. "Oh well. Maybe it'll keep the two of them out of our hair for awhile," I then say to Kate, who looks at me with enchanting eyes of strange appreciation, almost endorsement. "Hot Child in the City" begins to blare out of the speakers.

"We can hope," she replies to me, the song accentuating itself in our minds. She turns to say hi to Tuppy and Jim Chimney, who return nodding, unadorned hellos and then revert their attentions back to the stage. Another act is about to begin and they seem more interested in it than in us.

"I wonder who's playing the music," Kim asks Sam. "I mean, if the dj was hit in the head with a chair, he must be . . . I mean . . . It's just all so . . . Goodness!"

"You said it," I say, feeling Kim's bemusement. "Let's leave," I say and everyone readily agrees with this suggestion.

We exit The Lily Pad and step out into the fresh air of the unseasonably warm night. The murders are solved and I have the feeling that all is again well. Well, almost. There is still one last matter to attend to.

Chapter 33

Kate looks at her forearm in the mirror. "They did a decent job with the stitches, I guess," she says. "But I'm still going to have a scar no matter what."

"It'll heal up," I say, not knowing what else to say.

"How can you be so sure?"

"Even if I'm wrong it won't be very noticeable."

"No, I suppose not," she says, somewhat assuaged, unrolling her pajama sleeve to cover up her arm. "Would it be unforgivable if I called in sick tomorrow?"

"I hope not, because that's what I'm going to do."

"Well, that's settled then," she says, satisfied. She hops into bed under the covers, watching me as I take my shirt off and drop it to the floor. "Kim sure seemed hyper at times tonight, didn't she?"

"Yeah. It was all the excitement and danger, I guess. I think she was glad to get home though. Sam too. The things they saw—the things we all saw: it was quite a night."

"Yes. Quite a night," she says contemplatively.

I remove my wristwatch and step over to my dresser. I set the watch down on top of it and look at myself in the mirror.

"Well, I guess Trish was right about the killer all along."

"No, I wouldn't say that. Pepper's just as responsible. We were on the right track too. I'd like to think the we were the ones responsible for flushing her out," I say.

"Yes, that's true. And I suppose we would have discovered the entire truth about her and Lipstick Jones eventually anyway."

"I'm just glad it's all over and that things can get back to normal."

"Me too. It's good to know it's done with and that the danger has dissipated." Kate pauses, hesitant to broach the next subject on her mind. "So, how do you feel about this Hav and Wanda thing? Even though I'm sure it won't last," she says, as if to appease me, ever curious to know my thoughts.

"You never know," I say, still looking at myself in the mirror. I notice the ashtray that Wanda made for me. I look at it.

"Does it bother you?"

"Do you think it should?"

"I think I can understand how it might."

"Wanda does what she wants. She always has," I say, my comments seeming peculiarly insightful to me. I run a finger along the smooth circular edge of the ashtray. "It does feel a little uncomfortable though, I'll admit that. I would rather not have anything to do with her at all anymore but—depending on how long her hook-up with Uncle Hav lasts—well, I'm assuming we haven't seen the last of her."

"Like we would have anyway, though she did seem to take to heart all you said to her earlier tonight."

"Yeah, I guess she did." I pick up the ashtray and hold it in my hand, feeling the weight of it. Then I drop it in the wastebasket beside the dresser.

Kate sits up alertly. "Why did you do that?"

"No point in holding onto anything that doesn't have any meaning to me anymore," I say, taking off my pants and socks. "Do you ever look in here?" I say, opening the top drawer of my dresser, the drawer in which I keep various things, papers and keepsakes and the like.

"No, though I often have been sorely tempted to."

"I wouldn't care if you did."

"I know. I think that's why I never have."

"I'm glad you haven't though," I say, removing an item from the drawer and holding it in my fist. "I want this to be the first time that you've seen this."

"What have you got there?"

"Don't you know?"

"Maybe."

I hop onto the bed beside her. We face each other expectantly. "I don't think I can take no for an answer this time," I say, holding open my hand and revealing the engagement ring.

"Are you so convinced that 'no' will be my answer this time?"

"I don't know. Kate?"

"Yes?"

"Will you marry me?"

"Yes, Dean."

I feel an eruption of joy. I am smiling, almost crying, I am so happy. "What changed your mind?" I ask, slipping the ring onto her finger, shaky and excited, trying to keep my composure.

"You, Dean. You changed my mind," she says, full of quiet smiles and giving me a gentle poke in the nose. She looks at the ring, modelling it on her finger, holding her hand outstretched before her. "It's beautiful," she says in hushed, almost reverent, tones.

"How did I do it? How did I change your mind?" I ask, pulling her close and kissing her on the neck, cheeks and lips, my intoxicating love for her throwing me into a heady, passionate swoon.

She looks into my eyes, her own eyes deep and rapturous. "You just did. Just by being yourself. Being with you, well, you make me understand myself better. I was too stupid and unsure to see before. But I'm not anymore. I love you, Dean Dorian. I always have." She kisses me.

"And I love you, Kate Carlo," I say, our breaths hot against each other's faces.

"Uh uh. Better start calling me Kate Dorian."

I look at her bewitching gaze, drunk on her presence. "You'll always be Kate Carlo to me."

I turn out the lights and return to her, holding her tight. I can feel her heart beat winsomely against me as we lay in bed, as I think of the future, of the life about to unfold before us, wondering what new and strange adventures await us.

Printed in the United States
48930LVS00003B/130

9 781413 497670